Brenna Morgan and the Iron Key

Katie Masters

Published by
Fire and Ice
A Young Adult Imprint of Melange Books, LLC
White Bear Lake, MN 55110
www.fireandiceya.com

Brenna Morgan and the Iron Key ~ Copyright © 2017 by Katie Masters

ISBN: 978-1-68046-462-7 Print

Names, characters, and incidents depicted in this book are products of the author's imagination or are used fictitiously. Any resemblance to actual events, locales, organizations, or persons, living or dead, is entirely coincidental and beyond the intent of the author or the publisher. No part of this book may be reproduced or transmitted in any form or by any means, electronic or mechanical, including photocopying, recording, or by any information storage and retrieval system, without permission in writing from the publisher.
Published in the United States of America.

Cover Design by Caroline Andrus

For Isabella & Audrey Otis, who still believe.
Thank you for pulling me out of the fairie ring and sacrificing buttons
to save my life.

And to my mom,
As per the rules of our bet: Hahaha, I win!

Acknowledgments

Writing acknowledgments is sort of like watching the Oscars, only there's no funny commercials or musical numbers in between sentences. Sorry about that. But I'm not sorry for all the people I get to thank! They say it takes a village to raise a child. Let me tell you right here and now that it takes a continent of people to raise an author. Were it not for the multitudes of people helping me over the course of writing this book, you wouldn't be reading these words. So please, as they're announced, be sure to clap extra hard and startle those around you.

Firstly, I would like to thank my parents. My dad for instilling oral storytelling and encouraging my belief in the magical and invisible, and my mom for reading me the *real* fairytales and explaining Victorian words and definitions that she probably shouldn't have been giving a six-year-old. I'm also eternally grateful that when I embarked on my career shift into becoming a writer my mom decided I was worth the gamble and took me into her home again. But I'm a really good cook for her, so I think we're even. Right, mom?

I especially need to thank Caroline Andrus and Fire & Ice for taking a chance on me and my beloved story when I was sure no one would. Thank you for letting my book enter into the hands of readers! This section wouldn't be complete without profuse thanks to Rachel Johnson, my editor. Your love for mythology, your encouragement, and your willingness to keep in so many 'sure's and 'then's to stay true to how the Irish speak…I'm not sure many editors would have been as understanding! Also, for reading my massively long e-mails; lesser men would have run screaming. Readers, if you're reading this section, now is a good time to applaud and startle the person sitting next to you.

If any author has ever told you that the writing experience is a lonely one (I'm looking at you, Hemingway), I'm here to tell you it's just not true. While writing this novel, I had help from all sorts of people in all sorts of ways, and at all different stages! Please clap at the end of each category, and confuse those around you even more.

The Beginning: A huge thank you to my Beta Readers for being both unfailingly honest and equally supportive. Thank you, Betas, for calling me out when I wrote dumb or boring things I thought were genius. (They weren't.) A *massive* thank you to Andrew Meany, who made sure that the Gaelic and Irish slang were used and written correctly. If the slang is off at all, blame the stupid writer, not him.

The Middle: When I was running around looking for agents, I got turned down. A lot. Most of the time they didn't even bother to reply back. The only person to do so was Jenny Bent of The Bent Agency. She turned me down because her list was full, but she told me that I had a good story and not to give up. It was hard to follow her advice after so many rejections, but I did. And now I'm here, published. If you need a tissue to wipe your eyes, ask the worried person to your left.

A huge, massive thank you to Caitlin Jones, Kia Herman, Brittany Lee, Amanda Viliesis, and Jess flint for smacking my face and walking me through my self-doubt and fears at 2:00 a.m. when my defeatist attitude got the best of me, which was (and is) frequently. I also realize that's a lot of girls smacking my face, but it's made my cheeks so charmingly rosy!

And of course, a big, *huge,* **massive** thank you to Philip Gadrow for taking my book trailer idea and making it into something so beautiful. Abbey, John, Audrey, Elys, Tamlin, Noxweiler, Kevin—you brought my characters to life and for that I can never thank you enough. Maddison and Brittany, thank you for donating your amazing makeup and prosthetic talents—my god, you girls deserve awards! And a big thank you to Cheyenne Rain and Emily Lawrence for donating costumes and funds. Those goblins would've looked pretty silly in jeans and tank tops! Seriously, readers, applaud them.

The Sorta-Kinda End: This is it, guys. The end of the beginning, and the beginning of the middle. I know your hands are tired, but you can hold out for a few more people, right? If you're tired, ask the people around you to clap in your stead!

Thank you to Andrew Rowe, Mallory Reeves, Caitlin Jones, Andrew Gaughen, Becca McCarthy, and Emily Hardcastle for your advice, your encouragement, and your infinite patience in answering my really random questions at very random times.

Thanks to Twitter, I've met some of the best, most supportive, most hilarious people on earth. None of what I can accomplish in the future would be possible without them. There are too may too name, and I have to leave a lot of people out because, honestly, this is the Oscars of writing, not a movie's endless rolling credits. Also, the paper doesn't have the bandwidth, okay?

Thank you, Shayla, for being my biggest fan despite not having read the book yet, as well as for the words of encouragement and the letter!

Thank you, Susan Mann, for your constant encouragement, your amazing generosity, and your awesome sense of humor. When I get to Scotland we're drinking and playing with dolls, as promised! Thank you, Kira and Paula, for being my friends, encouraging me, and talking to me even though I'm so horrible at keeping Skype dates. Why are you still my friends, again?

Thank you to all my global contacts who've joined my spy network and are doing fun, totally legal spy things in your towns and cities on behalf of my series. Together, we're going to make the world a magical place!

For all the multitudes of friends I've made on twitter: You're wonderful. I look forward to many more years of your friendship and encouragement of not only me but of one another and other writers. You're the reason I still have faith in human kind's capacity for kindness rather than hate or jealousy in the face of being 'different' or 'other'.

And last, because they deserve their own paragraph, are the friends who have been there since before the beginning. Who have cheered me on over the years, drank tea with me, been on crazy adventures with me, survived moves and tears with me, and never given up on me even when I wanted to give up on myself. Anna Matson, Dana McCallister, Ash Brown, Michael Corr, Trevor Hough—you're the siblings I chose. To paraphrase the knight from *Indiana Jones and The Last Crusade*: I have chosen…wisely.

Also, my cat Soji. Thanks for spending ten years of your life keeping me warm and glaring at me whenever I call you 'fat', when clearly, you're just big-boned. Here's to another fifty years together.

Chapter One

"I don't see a sign, mom. Are you *sure* we're going the right way?"

Brenna narrowed her green eyes and pressed her nose against the window, trying to see past the rivers of water streaming along the glass. All she could really make out was a ditch backed by a low, rock wall that had been with them since they'd left the bustling Irish city of Cork.

"Of course I am! Have I ever gotten us lost before?"

"Well, there was that one time in Peru…" she began.

"Really, that was *one* time *four* years ago." Brenna's mother punched her shoulder lightly, smiling. "C'mon, we're almost there, Bren. And where *is* that sense of humor I gave you at the time of birth?"

"Somewhere between India and the Cork airport."

"I'm sure it'll catch up to you by tomorrow."

The windshield wipers her mother had turned on were almost useless, and the pounding wind and water against the car had her wondering how long it would be until the roof caved in. Brenna wrinkled her nose. If this was what the weather was going to be like all the time, her sneakers were done for.

"Oh look, there it is—Kerry Lane!"

Her mother made a sharp right, and Brenna gripped the side of the car with both hands against the force. In back, several bags tumbled along the seat as her mother laughed. It was times like these that Brenna was sure the woman was a little nuts. Her dad's nickname for her mom was 'Rocket Rachel', and she thought it suited the woman perfectly. The road became bumpy then, and Brenna had to hold onto the doorframe just to keep from hitting her head on the low ceiling of the rental car. The rain continued to pour down around them, and the tires skidded every once and a while on the slick mud.

"Don't the Irish believe in paving their driveways?!" Brenna exclaimed through gritted teeth.

"Now where's the fun in that, Bren? There's the cottage up ahead, and it looks like someone's there. I heard the people in this country are really hospitable. Isn't Ireland wonderful?"

Brenna wasn't sure if "wonderful" was the correct term. Muddy, cold, and miserable seemed a better description. The cottage, however, really did look like something from out of a magazine with its whitewashed walls and thatched roof. Smoke curled out from a chimney to join the mist that snaked its way through the air, and colorful flowers peeked out from boxes nestled against windows sheltered by the roof's sloping eve. A blue door was the only other splash of color in the mist and gloom. Her mother gave a sigh of contentment before she turned off the ignition and leaned back in her seat.

They sat in comfortable silence for a few moments, listening to the rain beat against the car as they took in the view of their new home. The cottage door swung open then, and a thin woman waved at them from the doorway. Together they straightened from their slumped positions.

"Well," said her mother as she reached around and picked up two duffel bags from the floor, "I guess that's the signal to get moving, kiddo!"

"Mom, I'm sixteen, you can't really call me that anymore."

"Oh? I hate to break it to you honey, but since you're not as old as I am, you're going to remain 'kiddo' until you catch up to me."

"Somehow, I don't think the math is working out very well..."

"Less talking, more moving. And," her mother's smile widened as she continued, "since you want to be so grown up, you can carry two duffel bags like the rest of us adults!"

With a small shriek of laughter, Brenna's mother made a mad and very slippery dash to the door where the woman took a bag before going back into the house. Brenna sighed, taking the last two bags as she followed after her. Like her mother, her head barely missed hitting the top of the door frame when she entered, an occurrence she'd had to suffer with for the last few years thanks to a growth spurt and her father's Viking genetics. By the time she got inside both she and the bags were soaking wet.

"Brenna, isn't this place adorable?!"

Dropping the waterlogged duffel bags to the floor, she looked around as her mother disappeared down a short hall directly across from the front door. The cottage was cute but snug. To the left, the living room and kitchen were jumbled together in a mash of faded, mismatched couches, wingback chairs, and a narrow counter that worked as both a stove-top and table to separate the cramped space. Across from the stove rested an ancient, heavy sink under an equally old window while the rest of the narrow kitchen was taken up by a 1950s fridge that barely avoided blocking the entrance.

"Brenna, this is Kathleen Fergus. She lives next door. Kathleen, this is my daughter."

"It's nice to meet you." Brenna stuck out her hand, realizing too late that it was wet and cold. The elderly woman paid no mind, however, and shook her hand. Kathleen's smile was kind and her pale blue eyes were sharp and piercing, reminding Brenna of a gypsy she'd met once who could tell fortunes with unnerving accuracy. A brown, tweed jacket covered her short, slender frame, and a skirt of pink roses seemed at odds with a pair of thick leather boots.

"It's nice to meet you as well, Brenna. My grandson is around here somewhere, probably after some turf. We've got the fire going, as you can see." Kathleen gestured to the large stone fireplace in the living room. "'Tis bad luck to come home to a cold hearth, you know."

Rachel clapped a hand on Brenna's shoulders then quickly pulled it off when she realized how wet her daughter's clothes were.

"We're very grateful for the welcome, Mrs. Fergus. Will you stay for dinner?" She gave a small kick and Brenna echoed the offer, feeling like she was five again. Kathleen laughed.

"Well and sure a warm meal is always something to say yes to. I'm sure Patrick will be glad for the food as well. And please, call me Kate— all my friends do."

"This is so much better than the hut we rented in Columbia, huh Bren?" Her mother laughed. "Your bedroom is the last one down the hall on the left. Why don't you get comfortable and I'll make us all some dinner?

"Sure."

After readjusting the dripping bags on her shoulders, Brenna teetered down the short hallway to the room that would be hers for the next four months. It was small, and the ceiling was slanted with wooden beams that held up the thatched roof. She wondered if the straw was really thick enough to keep out the rain that beat mercilessly upon it. Setting her bags down on the floor with a wet *thud,* she sat down on the bed, wincing when it creaked under her weight. It was a small, wrought iron contraption that sunk in the middle, but the quilts on top were thick and the mattress seemed pretty sturdy.

Standing with a stretch, she quickly changed into jeans and a dry shirt before taking a towel to her wet hair. A small dresser table with a round mirror was opposite her bed, and Brenna eyed her reflection as she combed her long, blonde hair. Her face was pale as usual—save for a smattering of light freckles on her nose and cheeks—and her green eyes were fringed by thick, black lashes that her mother often said just weren't natural *or* fair. She wrinkled her nose at her spare figure, wishing that she weren't quite so thin or tall. At five feet eleven, she often stood out in a crowd and imagined that it was how a scarecrow in a field must feel.

Slipping on a pair of socks and a knitted wool sweater, Brenna headed back to the living room. The smell of cooking pasta made her feel at home and eased the anxiety that the car ride had brought on. Her mother always made spaghetti the first night they stayed anywhere; it was one of the few things that stayed constant in her life. A few feet in front of the counter where her mother stood cooking was a large, overstuffed couch that faced the fireplace and a trunk used in place of a coffee table. The couch was soft and warm when Brenna sank into it, and she peeked over the edge at her mother who was draining the noodles while Mrs. Fergus stirred the sauce.

"Need any help, mom?"

"If you could make sure you're starving, that'd be helpful."

"Ha, ha." Rolling her eyes, Brenna snuggled back into the cushions and looked around. There was no TV or radio, but she was used to that. Tugging on a lock of hair, she looked up. The ceiling above was crisscrossed by heavy beams like the ones in her bedroom, hosting dusty spider webs. She wondered just how many spiders were up there then decided that she didn't want to know.

"Brenna, I have to go to Tralee tomorrow to meet with the publisher there. Do you want to come with me?"

Her mother handed her a bowl of pasta with this announcement and made sure Kathleen had the seat of her choice between the two wingback chairs on opposite sides of the trunk before joining her daughter on the couch. Brenna took a bite of the noodles, mulling the question over. They'd been traveling for three days straight, and she was pretty sure that if she had to go down one more bumpy road she'd throw up.

"I think I'll stay here. I can go exploring or something, if it's not raining."

"It's Ireland, Bren. It always rains." Her mother laughed again and twirled the spaghetti on her fork. The homey atmosphere suddenly changed as the door slammed open, ushering in wind, rain, and a dark figure whose face was hidden in shadow. Kathleen smiled.

"Ah, Patrick, I wondered where you'd gone off to! Come in boy, and meet our new neighbors."

Patrick stepped through the door, pushing a rain cap off with one hand and carrying a bundle of something large and earthy-smelling in the other. As he shut the door, Brenna eyed him covertly over her bowl of pasta, trying not to appear interested. He was tall and broad-shouldered, and his frame—athletic, Brenna assumed—took on some bulk thanks to the thick, wool sweater he was wearing. His hair was damp from the rain and brushed his neck in dark-brown waves. She wasn't sure given the dim lighting, but she thought that his eyes looked green.

For a moment, his eyes caught hers before slowly looking her over from head to toe in a way that made her feel as if he could see every thought she had in her head, much like his grandmother. Brenna felt heat creep up her neck and spread to her cheeks, anger rising at his slow once-over. Neither her mother nor Kathleen appeared to notice the tension, though, and her mother happily offered Patrick a bowl as he set down his load next to the fireplace. He nodded his head in thanks and took his seat in the last wingback chair but remained wordless.

Kathleen smiled at her grandson, pride showing clearly in her eyes.

"Patrick's a bit of a shy one by times. He's about your age I'm thinking, Brenna."

Brenna studied him briefly, not quite sure what to say. He seemed to be older than her, but she didn't want to come across as rude to their new neighbors by pointing out the wrong age. Her mother patted her shoulder, her smile wide.

"Brenna's sixteen."

"She *is* the same age, then! Is Brenna to be going to school?"

"We hadn't really discussed it yet."

Rachel's pleasant demeanor faltered for a moment as she glanced at her daughter, and Brenna hunched her shoulders slightly, gripping her fork a little tighter. School was something her mother almost never put her in. *Why bother?* she'd asked when Brenna had suggested going to a junior high in Hong Kong. *You won't stay long enough to go through the whole process.*

After a few moments of awkward silence, Kathleen spoke up again, her voice cheerful. "Well, if you do go, Brenna, my Patrick here will be more than happy to show you 'round the school. 'Tisn't very big, but it's bigger than some. Here now, Patrick, put the sod on."

He leaned down, took a fat strip of what appeared to be dirt, and threw it onto the fire. Smoke and the unmistakable smell of earth rose, drowning out the scent of pasta.

"Ah," said Kathleen as she held her hands up to the flames, "There's nothing a good peat fire won't cure. It's pleased I am to have you here in this house. It's been a wee bit sad to see it sitting empty. Have you seen any of the Good Folk since your visit, Brenna?"

"Good Folk?" Brenna's curiosity piqued, and it must have shown on her face, for Kathleen smiled and leaned back in what was obviously a story-telling position.

"Fairies. We don't often call them that; t'would be an insult to call them as such. But I'm sure they won't mind this once. They've been known to wander the roads this way quite often."

"That reminds me!" Setting down her bowl, Rachel rummaged through her large bag slumped against the couch before handing Brenna a heavy, slightly damp book.

"I got this for you while we were waiting at the bus stop in

Limerick."

"A fairy-tale book?" Brenna accepted the gift eagerly and Rachel smiled. Like her father, Brenna's love for cultures and stories of the magical variety knew no bounds.

"It's not *just* a fairy-tale book. It's about the different fairies of Ireland. It's folklore. True stories, if you will." Her mother's green eyes glowed warmly in the firelight, and she leaned forward as she often did when she was about to speak passionately about something.

"Did you know that a long time ago houses were built so that the doors all led into each other? They did it so that the fairies could troop through them. If they didn't, the fairies were likely to knock the house down for blocking their path."

"Cool." Brenna flipped through the pages before setting it down, realizing that it was probably rude to read in the middle of a conversation. She smiled shyly at Kathleen.

"I love mythology," she explained, somewhat embarrassed. "But it's probably pretty dumb to believe in things like fairies, huh?"

"You ought to." Kathleen's voice was quiet, but the force behind it was strong. "There are many a strange things as happens in this country, Brenna. Folklore and history have a way of winding 'round each other in Ireland, and its best to believe it all than to be punished for not heeding the words in the first place."

Patrick stared into the fire, but Brenna could tell from the way his body tensed that he was listening intently. She wondered why he didn't speak up or have an opinion; he certainly looked like he wanted to. Brenna started slightly when her mother put an arm around her shoulder.

"Maybe you'll see some fairie—I mean, some Good Folk around here. That'd make for a killer story, huh?"

A strong wind suddenly howled around the house, causing the wooden beams to creak as it blew open a window above the kitchen sink that hadn't been properly latched. The sound of flutes seemed to fill the whole room, and Brenna blinked in surprise, trying to catch which direction the sound was coming from.

"It's the wind," said Kathleen. "When it whistles through the trees behind the house like that, it sounds a bit like flutes, doesn't it?"

Brenna went to close the window, frowning when she realized that all the world had gone quiet and still outside, save for the sound of flutes that continued on like an elusive echo.

"Are you sure? The wind's not blowing now, but—"

"'Tis just the wind, child," Kathleen said a bit sharply, her blue eyes narrowing. "Have you gone into the woods yet?"

Patrick's body jerked slightly, and Brenna paused on her way back to the couch. The musical sound had died away almost as quickly as it had come.

"Are you okay?" she asked.

He nodded his head but didn't quite look her in the eye. She felt the stirrings of unease rise and slowly sat down next to her mother who had just finished her dinner. Picking up her bowl of pasta, Brenna looked to Kathleen.

"No, I haven't. Why?"

"I would warn against it. They aren't always safe around here. There are…animals that aren't always friendly."

"Like snakes?" Brenna gave a small laugh and Kathleen smiled back, but it seemed a bit strained.

"Feral dogs sometimes roam about, hunt the sheep and sometimes people, too. Be sure not to go into the woods."

In the fireplace, a log snapped loudly as it cracked in two, and Brenna gave a small jump at the noise. The tension in the room and Kathleen's intense gaze was almost as unnerving as the wind that had blown through only a minute ago.

Rachel smiled, patting her daughter's leg. "I'm sure Brenna will be having too much fun exploring the town and running down the lanes to go through the woods, anyway."

"Oh, are you going to the village, then?" Kathleen directed this question to Brenna who set her bowl of spaghetti on the trunk, no longer feeling hungry.

"I was thinking of taking a walk to the village tomorrow."

"All that way?" came the incredulous reply along with raised brows. Brenna's smile was large and genuine for what felt like the first time in days.

"It's only three miles, Mrs. Fergus."

"Three miles in mud, moss, and cars driving by at such paces it would turn your head." Kathleen tutted. "The very idea. Here now, you come to my house 'round noon and I'll drive you there meself."

"Really?"

"I wouldn't have offered if I didn't mean it. Come tomorrow at noon, 'tisn't a problem at all." Kathleen stood then, and Patrick followed suit. "Well, it's getting late, and you look ready for sleep, the pair of you. Come on then, Patrick."

With a few last waves and good-byes, Brenna shut the door and sighed. Her mother smiled and ruffled her daughter's hair.

"What a trooper you are, Bren. Here." Handing her a mug of tea, Rachel guided Brenna to the couch.

"I know this place is smaller—and colder—than the places we've gone to before, but it's a new experience, right?"

"Yeah…" Brenna stared down into her cup. "Mom?"

"Yes?"

"Do you think…could I please go to school here? We're staying around here for four months, right? So couldn't I go? Please?"

"Oh, Brenna…" Her mother sighed. "Don't you like being homeschooled? I'm sure you're in your second year of college, book-wise."

"Yeah, but what about life-wise? Mom, I'm sixteen and I've never been to anything remotely normal." Brenna squeezed the warm cup between her hands, tears brimming her eyes.

"Let me think about it, all right?"

"Fine."

As the night wore on, the rain calmed down to a steady pitter-patter, and Brenna trudged her way into her bedroom. Her body longed for rest, but her mind wouldn't slow down. Picking up the book her mother had given her, she thumbed through the pages until the story of a fairie that played a bagpipe caught her attention. Snuggling into the soft but creaky bed, she found herself drawn into the world the words painted and devoured one story after another, heedless of the time going by. Magic and myth—and somewhere in them truth—filled the pages. Eventually, Brenna found herself struggling to keep her eyes open, and she set the book down before turning off the lamp atop a small night stand at the side of her bed.

As sleep descended upon her, she wondered how much longer her family was going to travel. She loved the exotic places they had lived in and the people she'd met, but sometimes she wished that she could actually get to know the people and towns better than a few quick hellos and good-byes. Brenna smiled as the rain tapped against her window and the wind whistled through the cracks in the frames, and she could swear that she heard the sound of bagpipes being played outside. Perhaps Ireland would look better to her in the morning, when the rain was gone.

* * * *

After three days of rain that caused roads to become temporary rivers and forced people to stay to the safety and warmth of their homes, Brenna was ready to scream. She spent her time absorbed in the fairy-tale book her mother had given her, and she read every story at least twice, captivated by the heroes and heroines within. She found herself recalling Kathleen's words of how Irish folklore was often mixed with history and wondered how many of the stories were true. To think that people of the past lived alongside fairies on a daily basis was something nice to imagine as real, and it kept Brenna's mind entertained during the long days spent indoors. By Wednesday, though, she was beginning to realize how her mother must have felt whenever they were forced to stay in one place for too long.

On the fourth morning came a nearly cloud-free sky, and Brenna awoke to sunlight streaming into her room and onto her face. Groaning, she sat up, rubbing the sleep from her eyes before stretching. Half asleep, she stumbled her way into the cottage's one bathroom. It was small and narrow like the rest of the house, and she had to hunch over just to get her head under the showerhead. Muttering under her breath about the injustice of her height, Brenna twisted the knob and screamed as a blast of cold water hit her.

Frantic, she tried to twist the knob to 'hot' only to have it break off in her hand. Grimly, she backed away and considered the ice-cold water streaming from the shower head. Brenna sniffed her clothes and wrinkled her nose. She *had* to take one. As quickly as she could, she washed herself and leapt from the small tub, breathing a sigh of relief when she managed to put the knob on long enough to turn the water off.

Brenna Morgan and the Iron Key

    Throwing on a robe and letting her hair down to air dry, Brenna made her way into the living room. On the counter, a hot pot of coffee waited for her along with a note from her mother telling her she'd gone to Tralee for the day followed by a reminder to go to Kathleen's. She'd also left her some money. Brenna stirred several spoons of sugar and a dash of milk into her mug and took a sip of coffee before going to the window in front of the kitchen sink. A small hill stood before her, and on the ground was grass so green it was hard to believe the color could even exist. Tiny white and yellow flowers that seemed not to have been affected by the rain dappled the hillside, and Brenna felt her feet itching for a run after all of the days spent trapped inside.
    With a smile, she rushed to her room; a quick exploration of the area seemed like a good option for her wandering feet before she headed into town. As quickly as she could, she changed into sweatpants and the white, cabled wool sweater she had taken off sometime during the night and thrown onto the floor. Grabbing her cell phone from the table, she checked the time, wrinkling her nose. She could go for a run as long as it was fast and still make it to Kathleen's in time. She braided her blonde, waist-length hair with a few quick twists and then stepped outside. Her running sneakers sank a little into the damp earth, and she grinned as she saw her breath hang in the air for a moment like a small, crystalline cloud. The sun was on its journey across the sky, and a smattering of white clouds billowed slowly along in the light, cool breeze.
    The grass was springy beneath her shoes as she scrambled up the hill that led to a level field, and Brenna's excitement grew. The crisp air and wind that smelled of sea and earth made her want to fling her arms out and run wild across the vast field like the Celtic Finnian warriors she'd read about in her book. Her feet began to pick up speed, and she gave a shout of laughter as she ran full force across the land. A small, black bird circled above her and seemed to feel her jubilation, for it gave a small trill and darted here and there, sticking close to Brenna. To her far left was the main road bordered by a gray stone wall, and from there a stretch of land only a few hundred feet long leading to a cliff that gave way to the glittering, blue ocean which met and mingled with the sky.
    "Isn't it beautiful?" Brenna asked a sheep grazing nearby. It blinked sleepy, golden eyes at her, its mouth full of grass. Smiling wide, she

waved at it and continued her jog, going around the other sheep that nibbled on the grass and paid her little to no mind.

The wind that had been gentle abruptly picked up speed in a harsh burst, slowing her down. Brenna welcomed the extra weight and was about to lengthen her stride when she heard the sound of flutes again. It was elusive, as if the instruments were being played from far away, and she strained her ears as she stopped to catch hold of the melody. The music disappeared as suddenly as it had started, and she wondered if perhaps she really *was* imagining it. Shading her forehead, Brenna surveyed her surroundings and noticed that the sheep didn't seem to be pricking their ears up to listen to the high notes, and there wasn't a soul for as far as she could see. The story of a changeling fairie that had learned to play bagpipes came to mind and made her laugh.

"C'mon Bren, fairies playing bagpipes. That'll be the day!"

Her musings were cut short when the bird that had been her running companion suddenly gave a small, sharp trill as if it were in pain and swooped down toward her, it's chattering becoming angry. Ducking, Brenna shouted in surprise.

"What gives?!"

She tried to wave the bird away, stopping when she tripped over a rock and landed on the ground. The black bird gave one final cry before it flew off toward the forest that lined the field to her right. Wincing, Brenna stood up and dusted herself off.

"What's that bird's problem?"

As she lowered her hands from her legs to follow the bird's flight, she felt her breath catch. It had gone to join hundreds of other small, black birds darting in and out of the forest like a massive black cloud, screeching and raising such a noise of anger and fear that it made the hair on the back of her neck stand up. Birds never acted like that unless their nests were threatened. *What if*, Brenna thought as she watched the birds begin to cry louder, *an animal has been wounded and they're attacking it?* Biting her lip, she looked back to where the cottage's roof was still visible and wondered if she should just ignore them. The memory of how Kathleen had looked so serious about not going into the woods crossed her mind, but the thought of a wounded animal worried her more. With a nod to herself, she began jogging toward the birds. If there was an injured animal, she could always use her cell phone to call for help, and surely a farmer lived nearby who would be able to aid her if she ran into any major problems.

As she approached the towering trees that bent and waved in the wind, she used her arms and hands to shield her face and head in case the birds tried to attack her, as well. She didn't have to protect herself for very long. They ignored her for the most part, darting and diving around her in an unmistakable sign of panic. Frowning, she plunged deeper into the forest where the birds weren't massing so closely together, hoping that she'd be able to see the wounded animal. The forest smelled of damp, rotting leaves while shafts of light filtered weakly through the tangled branches above. Behind her, Brenna could still hear the screeching birds, but their chattering grew fainter as she jogged farther away from them. She stumbled several times over rocks that had been hidden by the dead foliage, and patches of moss caused her to slip and almost lose her footing more than once. A sense of urgency started to grow in her, and an instinct deep within urged her away from the panicked birds.

Brenna began to run then—almost against her will—and fought her way through trees and small streams until her lungs felt like they were on fire and her feet were lead weights. Her mind yelled for her to stop, that she would get lost, but her legs seemed to have a mind of their own and pushed her on at an even faster pace. It was only when she reached a clearing that they finally gave out, and her ragged, gasping breath was the only noise she could hear aside from her wild heartbeat.

Straightening from her bent position, Brenna looked around and took in deep, steadying breaths. She could no longer hear the birds—or any animal, for that matter. It seemed as if not even a leaf dared move, and when she looked back toward the way she had come, she was surprised to discover that the leaves that should have been ruffled by her mad dash were undisturbed. Fear began to claw at her stomach, but she forced it down. She had to be ready for anything; trouble in an Egyptian alleyway had taught her that lesson all too well two years ago. She shook the dark memory away and concentrated on breathing slowly while she listened for the sounds of any agitated animals, but an eerie silence was all that greeted her ears.

She knew when animals went quiet that meant something big was around. Like a bear. But Ireland didn't have bears. Frowning, she looked up into the canopy of trees. The sunlight seemed different, weaker, and even cold where it fell on her skin. Stillness permeated the air all around her, and she realized with sudden clarity that she had gone somewhere she shouldn't have.

"Maybe this was a bad idea..." Brenna's voice seemed hollow, and she noted with some surprise that there was no echo to it. Without warning, the smell of blood suddenly hit her so strongly that she could almost taste the metallic bitterness of it. Why hadn't she noticed it before? The snapping of twigs behind her had her spinning around, and Brenna felt the world stop. What looked to be an elderly woman lay face down on the ground only a few feet away. She wore a long, green gown, and the hair that fanned out from her head and trailed down to her knees was a brilliant, shining white. The white tresses hid her face, and blood so red it looked black pooled out from beneath the middle of her body and oozed onto the leaves beneath. Were it not for her twitching hands and the slight groan emanating from her lips, Brenna would have thought that she was dead.

Shaking from head to toe, Brenna cautiously inched her way over to the elderly woman, her voice wobbling almost as much as her body as she asked, "A-are you a-all right, ma'am?"

The old woman groaned in reply as she pressed the palms of her hands heavily onto the bloody leaves, trying and failing to rise.

"*An bhféadfá cuidiú a thabhairt dom?*"

"W-what?"

The woman raised her head then, and Brenna blinked hard in surprise. Staring up at her wasn't the wrinkled face of the elderly but the flawless features of a beautiful, young woman in her early twenties or so, with eyes so intensely blue that Brenna thought she might be wearing colored contact lenses. Her voice was soft and melodic, but the words were spoken in a commanding tone, and Brenna was under the impression that she was much older than she appeared.

"Will you help me? Come quickly, we haven't much time."

Brenna did as she was instructed, too shocked and scared to do anything else. The woman's lips were set in a grim line as she struggled to her knees with Brenna's help, and she quickly pressed a hand to a large gash on her stomach from which the blood was flowing heavily. Brenna quickly pulled her sleeve over her hand and pressed it to a part of the wound that wasn't covered, receiving a tight, pained smile as thanks.

"You are a kind one, aren't you?"

"I'm just doing what anyone would do, but my sleeve isn't enough. We need to get you something thicker to slow it down, and you should probably lie down."

The dark-blue eyes studied her intently, and she felt as if the woman could see into her very soul. Brenna offered a small smile, trying not to show her fear, and the woman gave a hoarse laugh, blood trickling down the corner of her lip.

"You have bravery and stubbornness, Brenna Morgan. You will do nicely."

"How did you know my name?"

"How is not important, child. Listen and do as I say."

The woman leaned against her, and Brenna tried not to gag when dark blood fell onto her pants and scented the air even more strongly.

"Take this."

The woman pulled out a slender, black object from a fold in her dress before pressing it into Brenna's free hand, her face twisting in pain as though the object physically hurt her. It landed heavily in her palm, and Brenna held it up. A key made of black iron rested in her hand, and it looked like it was more than a few hundred years old.

"Is this to your house? Should I call a doctor? I…I think that I should." Brenna tried to stand, but the woman grabbed her wrist so hard that she was sure she was going to leave a bruise.

"No, I do not need a doctor. I need your promise."

"'Promise'?"

"Aye." The woman licked her dry lips, and her breath began to grow haggard. "You must promise me you will protect the *leanbh*."

"The what?"

"The *leanbh*. Brenna Morgan, this is a great task I ask of you, but you are the only one I can trust now. You were sent to me for a reason, or you would not be here." The woman gave a shuddering breath that ended with a hiss, and her body doubled over as she coughed. Brenna gripped the key, not sure of what to do.

"What is your name? I...I think you're in shock right now and—"

"I am not in shock. Listen, please." She pressed the key harder into Brenna's hand, and the iron felt abnormally hot to the touch.

"You must promise me you will keep this key safe, that you will find the *leanbh* and protect..." She gasped now, and dark blood trickled rapidly from her lips as she gave Brenna's shoulders a firm shake, her eyes bright and feverish.

"You must promise me. It is the only way I can protect you, child. Promise me now!"

"But—"

A sound pierced the air—a screeching so loud and high-pitched that Brenna had to cover her ears, blood marring her cheeks.

"We do not have enough time." The woman's voice was laced with fear, and she took Brenna's hand, trying to gentle her tone. "Brenna Morgan, you do not understand how important you are right now. There is a strength in you that most mortals can only dream of. You have until *Samha*—"

The screams began to get louder, drowning out the strange woman's sentence, and Brenna only caught the last of her words as the noise grew faint and then finally stopped.

"—take the key and promise me before he comes. *Promise!*"

"I-I-I promise," she stuttered.

"Do you swear it on your mortal soul?" The blue eyes blazed like glowing orbs, and Brenna felt the world around her turn gray in comparison.

"I do."

From the very marrow of her bones, Brenna felt that her answer was the right one. The woman's tense face relaxed into a smile that seemed to say that she saw Brenna's every flaw yet did not care.

"You have promised. Now you must be brave, Brenna Morgan. Very brave. I will protect you as I would my own flesh."

"But...you don't even know me. I-I don't even know your name!"

"My name is Nuala." She brushed a strand of hair from Brenna's face, tucking it behind her ear with a cold, shaking hand. "You remind me much of the great ones that came before you. I could not ask for a better champion."

Nuala's hand slipped from her ear to cup her cheek, filling her with a kindness so warm that tears sprang to the girl's eyes. Abruptly, the motherly smile vanished, her body stiffened, and with a strength Brenna wasn't sure a nearly dead person should have, she stood up. Blood rushed over her fingers and down her dress, a sound that was more animal than human emanating from deep in her throat. Every hair on Brenna's body stood on end as the air was filled with electricity. Nuala stood in front of her, so tall that Brenna actually had to tilt her head back a bit to look up.

"Run, Brenna Morgan."

"But...but what about you? You're bleeding, and—"

"If you do not wish to die, mortal, you will do as I say and *run*."

There was a loud cracking sound then, as if a dozen trees had been struck by lightning, and a blast of wind hit them so hard that Brenna almost dropped to her knees. The black birds that had been swarming the edge of the forest rushed toward them like a dark cloud, swirling in a strange pattern before they started to clump together. Wings, legs, and small bodies melted together in an oddly liquid way, massing and bubbling to form a solid figure. Brenna's mouth fell open as a human shape snapped into focus, and the darkness slipped from the figure as if it were water to reveal a man who looked like he'd stepped straight from the pages of her fairy-tale book. He was the most beautiful thing she had ever seen—and the most terrifying.

His waving, black hair spilled over his shoulders and framed his perfectly sculpted face. Eyes so intensely blue that she almost couldn't look at them glared at her coldly. A green velvet tunic fell impeccably down his tall, slender body, and calf-length leather boots sewn with silver threading in intricate knot work adorned his feet, though somehow no leaves were crushed beneath his boots. A smile that should have been beautiful looked ugly as he stared down at them with contempt. When he spoke, his voice was filled with mockery.

"Did you think you could run so far, Nuala?"

Brenna's companion said something in her strange language— Gaelic, she guessed—and the man growled something back. The hatred that poured from him almost made her flinch, but Nuala stood still and calm. Squaring her shoulders, Brenna edged closer to her, wanting to show the same courage. The man paid her actions no mind, keeping his full attention on the other woman as they exchanged words in a musical-sounding dialogue.

"Give me the key!"

Brenna jumped as his voice roared painfully loud in English, filling the woods but somehow lacking an echo.

"I do not have the key." Nuala said in an almost amused tone.

"You lie! I can smell it." The man narrowed his eyes before looking to Brenna, and the fury she saw there was more than enough to make her take a step back as she quickly hid the key behind her back.

"Mortal!" His words came out as a command, his eyes piercing hers as he drew a bloodied sword. "Come!"

"I-I—" Brenna's mouth seemed to stop working as she watched dark blood drip from the weapon aimed at her.

"Stay away from her, Treasach. She is protected."

"By whom?" He smirked and pointed the sword at the woman. "You, Nuala? That *is* a laugh. Give me the mortal, then, if you will not give me the key. She looks to be a fine addition to our court, and it may ease my temper enough to merely kill you."

Run, and do not look back, Brenna. Nuala's voice filled Brenna's head, and she darted her eyes toward the woman in front of her, trying to understand how she could possibly be talking without moving her lips.

"You will not touch her, Treasach."

"Give me the mortal, you cursed woman!"

The man raised his sword, and the weak sunlight seemed pale in comparison to the light reflected by the blade. Brenna realized he was going to strike Nuala, and she stepped forward, wanting to protect the woman who was so courageously defending her life.

Nuala's voice filled her head once more, and Brenna cried out, jumping back as she felt something hot and searing press against her chest like a hot hand. She looked down and saw that nothing was there, but the pain continued.

Run. I will stall him, but I cannot do so for long. Keep the key safe. Find the leanbh and keep it safe, too. Run to your home and do not come back to the forest. It knows you now and will not protect you. Run,

Brenna—run!

Invisible hands pushed her hard, propelling her forward. She found herself sprinting through the woods at a speed she had never run before. Tears trailed down her face and her breath came out in sobs as the trees blurred together. She had just made it to the edge of the forest when a scream filled her head—it reverberated throughout the entire forest—and she echoed the cry as pain lanced across her stomach. Somehow, she knew that Nuala had died. Brenna tore through the trees, throwing her hands up as branches scratched at her face and neck before she fell through a bush, landing onto the field's soft grass. A few sheep looked her way but continued to amble by unbothered, and Brenna clutched the key to her chest, her body shaking and her scream still echoing in the woods.

With gasping breaths, she scrambled to her feet, her voice so hoarse that when she tried to call for help nothing came out. All thoughts fled her mind, and her body took charge, her hand clasping the iron key against her chest as she stumbled back toward the cottage. She was aware of screeching birds somewhere behind her, but she couldn't bring herself to care. The sight of the cottage's roof snapped Brenna out of her stupor, and with a cry she ran as fast as her flagging body could go. She flew down the steep embankment, going too fast to stop herself from slamming into the door. Her hands still wet and slippery with Nuala's dark blood, it took her several desperate attempts to get a good grip on the knob and fling the door open. Slamming it closed once she was inside, she leaned against the rough wood, clutching the key tightly as she caught her breath. Once her lungs stopped burning, she went to the kitchen, setting the key on the counter before grabbing a glass to fill with water from the faucet

Her hands shook so badly that half of the glass's contents spilled onto the floor, and Brenna's eyes widened when she saw the blood marring the cup's exterior. It wasn't dark-red like she had initially thought, but black. Trying not to wretch, Brenna stuck her hands under the still-running facet. She felt laughter, hysterical and harsh, bubble forth before turning into shallow gasps.

"Okay. Okay, let's not panic. Think." Common sense told her that having blood all over her clothes wasn't helping, and she hurried to the bathroom. Picking up a washcloth and soap, she scrubbed the blood from her face, the fear that had threatened to take over receding with the normalcy of her actions. As she changed into new clothes, Brenna glanced at the clock positioned on a shelf near the mirror and then did a double take. It was noon, and she was supposed to be at Kathleen's.

"No way...I...I left at ten." Brenna took her phone from her pocket, frowning when she saw that it only read ten thirty.

"Maybe the clock's broken."

Brenna hurried to go check the clock in the living room, bewildered to find that it read twelve o'clock, as well. Biting her lip, debated whether or not to go outside. She would have liked to think this was all a horrible dream, that perhaps the cold air and all of the fairy-tales she'd been reading had caused her to hallucinate, but the key on the kitchen counter was a rather physical reminder of reality. For some reason, she couldn't quite fathom or rationalize away, the fairy-tales had become real, and she was pretty sure that she was dealing with...with...

"Fairies." The word seemed silly to say out loud, and she nearly laughed again because it sounded so ridiculous. But she hadn't been asleep, and she was pretty sure that seeing dying fairies wasn't a side effect of too much coffee. Running a hand through her hair, she began to pace the small living room.

"All right Brenna, you're not crazy. That woman was definitely a fairie. That *man*, or whatever he was, was probably one, too. No one has black blood...or a body made out of birds." Feeling a little ill, she took the key from the counter and examined it. It was simple looking with a half-moon for a tooth and an oval at the hilt where a chain could easily go through it. It was heavy and cold but didn't feel unordinary, and it certainly didn't seem like an object to kill someone over.

She wanted to throw the key out the window and never worry about it again, but she couldn't bring herself to do it. Nuala's words played over and over in her head, as did her own promise. Brenna gripped the key harder. She'd promised, and she'd never broken a promise in her life. She sat down hard on the couch. Nuala had wanted her to find a *leanbh*—whatever that was—and protect it. Maybe it was a plant or a tree. The word sounded like it might mean that sort of thing. She could protect a plant. Tucking the key into the pocket of her jean's, Brenna frowned. It felt warmer than it had a moment ago. Before she could pull it out, something slammed against the window. Smothering a scream, she glanced through the glass. Outside, the black birds that had once somehow been Treasach were throwing themselves at the panes like bullets. Brenna dodged behind the couch.

"Go away." Her voice came out small and scared, and she cleared her throat. This was her home for the time being, and here she was afraid of a flock of birds. The memory of Nuala's death fueled her rising anger, and her voice rose as high as it could.

"*Go away!*"

Her words bounced off the wooden beams and, with a trill and a flurrying of wings, the birds departed. Brenna remained kneeled on the floor, holding her breath for several moments. When nothing happened and the only noise that could be heard was the antique clock ticking away on the mantel, she stood up, releasing the breath she'd been holding. Then the knocking started.

Chapter Two

Brenna ducked behind the couch once more, looking around for anything she could use as a weapon. If she was going down, she was going to go down fighting.

"Brenna?"

A voice—male—spoke from the other side of the door. She bit her lip, unsure of whether or not to answer. What if it was that psycho fairie? She didn't know a lot about Irish fairies, but from the stories she'd read tricking people was something at which they excelled.

"Brenna, are you home? It's Patrick Fergus."

"Patrick?"

"Yes. Are you going to open the door, then?"

"Um. Uh…yeah. Just a minute."

Patting the key inside her pocket to make sure it was still there, Brenna cracked the door open. Patrick stared down at her, his eyebrows raised and his expression as unreadable as it was the night she had met him. She opened the door wider and glanced behind him, relieved to see that not a single black bird was in sight.

"Are you ready to go to the village?"

"I thought your grandmother was going to take me." Realizing that she might have sounded rude, she spoke quickly to explain, "I mean, not that I *mind* if you take me. I just thought—"

"Mr. O'Brian down the road is sick. He's an old friend, and she's gone to give him some company." He stared down at Brenna, a quizzical look on his face. "Are you all right? You seem pale, and you've got a fair bit of scratches on you."

"I'm fine. I just…um…wasn't looking where I was going and tripped on a rock when I went for a run. Let me get my coat."

Whether or not he believed her she wasn't sure. He shrugged his shoulders and turned around, heading toward a massive truck parked in the drive. Grabbing a clean sweater, she tugged it over her head before stepping out to where Patrick now sat waiting inside the slightly rusted, green truck that appeared to be older than time itself. With some coaxing followed by a few sickly coughs and sputters, the truck roared to life, and Brenna suddenly wasn't sure if driving was such a good idea. Being attacked by birds was one thing, dying because a truck rolled off a cliff due to a lack of brake pads was another. She picked a flake of the crackling plastic seat cover and raised her brows.

"Are you sure this thing isn't going to break down in the middle of the road?"

"It hasn't done in forty years. I don't think it'll start any time soon."

Patrick smiled then, and Brenna felt her stomach knot. He was handsome, but when he smiled he was downright gorgeous. She could almost forgive him for staring at her the other night. As they bumped down the road, the silence grew and Brenna shifted uncomfortably. She hated such strained quiet; besides, she was going to have to spend the afternoon with him. She cleared her throat and offered her friendliest smile.

"Thank you for taking me to your town."

"'Tisn't a problem, I was going anyway."

"Oh." Brenna waited several seconds and then sighed when no further explanation was given. Refraining from rolling her eyes, she tapped her fingers against the doorframe.

"You're not very talkative, are you?"

"Who, me?" Patrick gave another fleeting smile. "I talk when it suits me, or when I've something to say. If you want, I can talk to you about football." He paused. "Or the weather."

"That's okay." Brenna was about to give up trying to make nice when she saw that his eyes—which looked to be hazel more than green—were filled with amusement, and she found herself smiling back.

"Actually, football would be interesting to hear about. That's soccer, isn't it?"

"Soccer?" Patrick whistled. "The way you Americans play 'soccer' is disgraceful. You're all so polite. In Gaelic football, if you're not bleeding, you're not playing."

While Patrick spoke, Brenna realized that he *did* have a lot to say—mainly about blood and kicking and defense. But he spoke with such a lively and lilting voice that she found herself drawn in even if she didn't always understand him or the numbers he was throwing out at rapid fire.

"And what about you?" he asked after a few moments of now-comfortable silence.

"What about me?"

"You're staying in the cottage in October. Not many people would do that. It's cold here, you know, and once the frost sets in people tend to keep to their homes."

"Oh." Brenna laughed. "My mom wants it that way. She and my dad are writers. They write articles for a travel magazine."

"Is that why your dad isn't with you? I didn't see him when we first met."

"Yeah. He's staying behind to finish writing an article about a village in India."

"Do you always travel on the off-season?"

"There's no such thing 'seasons' for us. Mom says it's about experiencing the world no matter the time of year. We've been traveling around the world since I was ten years old."

Brenna looked out the window, her smile disappearing. The rolling hills that they passed were smattered with white and black sheep and large squares of the land separated not by fences but by thick, green hedges. She could feel Patrick staring at her, but she kept her gaze fixed on the outside world.

"You sound like you're tired of it."

"I was tired of it a year ago." Brenna sighed. "We always travel, and we only stay a few months at the most. Once we got stuck in Brazil for five months because of a war that was going on, and my mom nearly went insane with all the waiting."

Anger laced her words as she spoke, her annoyance mounting. Why couldn't they just stay in one place? Why couldn't she just go to high school and join the cheerleading team? Not that she really wanted to join the team, but she did want the chance to have the option. Instead, she'd been lugged all over the southern hemisphere.

"Sorry. I didn't mean to say all of that. Forget I even said anything."

Silence reigned once more and the fields gave way to houses here and there, announcing that they were approaching civilization.

"Do you not like the places you've gone, then?" Patrick's question caught her off guard, and Brenna had to blink a couple times before she could respond. She was used to making polite conversation with strangers, but most of the time the locals couldn't go beyond pleasantries because of language barriers. Having someone who understood her besides her parents was new and slightly disconcerting.

"I do. It's just…" Frustrated, she lanced a hand through her hair. "It's just that it's hard. I mean, you've gotten to live in one place your whole life, I bet. You have friends and family, a home and a school. I don't have any of those. The friends I did have when I was living in America don't talk to me anymore, and we never stay in one place long enough for me to make really good friends again. Traveling looks glamorous when my mom and dad write about it, but it's really just lonely. I don't belong anywhere."

Brenna could feel tears sting her eyes and she blinked them back, not wanting to cry in front of a boy, least of all one she didn't know. The truck rattled along for a few minutes before Patrick spoke up again.

"You know, you're not such a bad sort when you try."

"Excuse me?" Brenna felt her temper prick as Patrick looked straight ahead, a smile tugging on his lips at her annoyed tone.

"I didn't mean to come off as rude. Earlier, I mean." He cleared his throat. "If you want, I'll be your friend. Our village is full of people who belong too well, I think. We could use a traveler such as yourself in these parts."

"I…" her cheeks burned pink as he shot her a full smile and she looked away, not able to hold his gaze. "I'd like that. Thanks, Patrick."

"Think nothing of it. Here we are, Dugan village. There are about five hundred people in all, but twice as many kids. Most of us run off to another country or a bigger city as soon as we're able, and most don't come back. It's a fishing village mainly, but we've got a nice, old castle and a mound that draws in some tourists. Do you want to see it?"

"Sure."

"Right. Let me swing by the wharf—I have to get my check from Mike. I help ferry the boats into the harbor. It doesn't pay near as much as I'd like, but then, most things don't."

He swung the truck down a rather curvy, narrow street that hadn't been updated since the fifteenth century, and the cobbled path made the truck jostle and bounce so badly that Brenna was sure the bolts holding it together would loosen. After narrowly avoiding hitting several parked cars, Patrick sent the clunking truck into a sharp and screeching right turn that made her question if he'd taken driving lessons from her mother. The vehicle puttered along another narrow road before it skidded to a stop in a parking lot that was littered with driftwood and nearly level with the ocean.

"C'mon then."

He jumped out of the truck and Brenna followed suit, wincing when it groaned from their movements. The air smelled strongly of fish, brine, and the sea. She wanted to hold her sleeve to her nose but decided that doing so would probably be rude. Patrick didn't seem bothered by the stench at all, and she was sure she caught him taking in a big mouthful of the reeking air as he led her to a somewhat rickety dock.

"Wait here; I won't be long. Then we can go to the castle."

"Okay."

Looking around, Brenna quickly forgot about the smell. Below her feet, water lapped against the poles, its color dark even this close to shore. Wooden barrels and crates were stacked together here and there, and fishing lines, netting, and broken buoys had been placed against them. Seagulls cried and zigzagged lazily overhead while a few seals bathed on a rocky jetty on the other side of the crescent-shaped port. As the sunlight dappled on the water's surface and dark clouds billowed in the distance, she could feel all of her anger and fear from the day's events leave her body and join the countless sorrows that filled the Irish sea.

"'Tis a beautiful day is it not, Brenna Morgan?"

Brenna whirled around in surprise, her heart pounding. A short, somewhat elderly man was sitting on an upturned crate, his rough, knobby-knuckled hands working on forming a left shoe. His bright red jacket looked as if it had seen better days, but his brown leather boots and green vest looked new and very expensive. His nose was bulbous and his cheeks were rosy-colored, like he'd been enjoying a little too much Guinness at the local pub. The hair atop his head was a gingery orange, and in between his equally bright bushy beard and mustache was a slender, wooden pipe. Smoke curled and swirled around him without dissipating, twisting its way into strange patterns. His beady, black eyes twinkled with amusement as he continued to work on the shoe. She had never seen someone sew so fast with their hands, much less do it without looking.

"How do you know my name?"

"Sure, and why wouldn't I know it, Brenna Morgan?"

"It's just Brenna."

"Ye've no last name, then?"

"I do. But my first name is Brenna. Not Brenna Morgan."

"That is your name, though."

"It's not—" Taking a deep breath, she quickly counted to ten. "Fine. Yes, it is. How do you know it?"

"Everyone is learning your name, lass. You've gotten yerself into an awful scrape, I've heard, and I only came to offer a little friendly service."

"What service'?" Something about that didn't sound comforting. The man nodded his head and puffed on his pipe, the smoke remaining despite the brisk ocean breeze.

"Aye. As I hear it, Brenna Morgan, you've had a bit o' a run in with the Gentry."

"'Gentry'?"

The man began to sew more quickly, his black eyes never leaving hers. Brenna didn't quite like the feel of him. He felt...off, as if he wasn't supposed to be there.

"Aye. A nice lot all around, but prone to asking help of mortals when they should do a thing themselves. Here now, I've come to give you a bit o' service, seeing as you're such a fair lass."

"Thank you?"

"Think nothing of it. You'll be needing more help than I can give anyway, such as it is."

The smoke seemed to get thicker, and his fingers worked faster, almost to the point that she couldn't distinguish his movements.

"'Tis a fine mess they've tangled you in, and dangerous—very dangerous, lass. Listen to me well and you should come out mostly alive."

"Uh, 'mostly'?" Brenna found herself wanting to laugh at the situation. But the small man's piercing, black eyes weren't laughing back.

"'Tis better than dead, I'm thinking," he said with a shrug, though how he managed to do that and still sew as quickly as he did she had no idea.

"Brenna Morgan, you must go to *Coillearnach* mound in the wee morning. Circle the mound three times, knock thrice, and say the name 'Roibhilin' when you see first light. He'll help you."

"Who is 'Rovalin'? And how do you know what's going on? *I* don't even know what's going on! Do you know Nuala? Do you know what the 'lean bean' is?" Her heart raced, and she could foresee a heart attack in her near future. The man puffed more smoke into the air where it joined the swirling mass.

"I don't answer questions, Brenna Morgan. I can only give you a wee bit o' advice. Do as I say, and Roibhilin can answer any questions ye have. I warn ye now, lass, that if ye go, there'll be no goin' back. But then, ye don't have much of a choice, I'm thinkin'."

Instinctively, Brenna placed her hand on the key in her jean's pocket. It felt almost hot to the touch, and Nuala's face rose up fresh and vibrant in her mind. Her need to know outweighed her fear, and she tried to take a step closer to the strange man only to find that she couldn't move. Overhead, the seagulls had gone silent.

"Sir, can you at least tell me who Nuala was? Or why she picked me?"

Annoyance flashed in his beady eyes, and his hands slowed ever so slightly.

"If Nuala chose you, lass, t'was for her reasons alone. I know not why the *Tuath de Danann* do as they will, nor have I any wish to. Go to the hill, call on Roibhilin, and do what ye must. Here. A present from a luckless soul like meself."

With a flick of his wrist he tossed Brenna the shoe he'd cobbled. It was made of green leather, expertly made, and looked to be just her size.

"Thank yo—"

"Brenna?"

She turned on her heel to see Patrick staring at her, his hazel eyes concerned. Confused, she spun back to where the small man had been and found that he was gone; even the crate he'd been sitting on had vanished. The shoe in her hand was the only reminder that the encounter hadn't been a dream or her imagination.

"Brenna, are you all right? You look as if you've seen a ghost."

"I...I saw a man. He was short and smoked a pipe."

"Oh?" Patrick laughed and stuffed his hands in his pockets as a cold wind blew around them. The dark clouds that had been on the horizon were quickly drawing closer. Far out at sea, lightning streaked across the dark sky.

"Saw a leprechaun, did you? Have you been reading that folklore book by chance?"

"Well, yes but...but that's not the point. I saw one. I saw *him.*"

"It's nice that you like our stories, Brenna, but there's no man here. Or a leprechaun. Just you."

She wanted to stamp her foot in frustration. Instead, she waved the shoe at Patrick, her cheeks pink with embarrassment and anger. "Your stories also say that they can be gone in the blink of an eye. And he made me this. See for yourself."

Patrick's eyes had widened slightly at her vehement tone, and after a moment he took the shoe and studied it carefully. His brows knit together, and he looked up at her.

"I think," he said after some hesitancy, "we should talk to my grandmother."

Thunder rumbled overhead, and Brenna couldn't help but think that the coming storm wasn't the only one approaching.

Chapter Three

The drive back in Patrick's truck—a lorry, he'd said it was called—passed in silence. Brenna had flung her seatbelt on and pulled her knees up to her chest, looking out the window with the leather shoe clutched in her hands. Patrick didn't try to start a conversation, which she was grateful for because she wasn't feeling particularly chatty. As they pulled up to what she assumed was Kathleen's house, the clouds that had been gathering gave a low rumble and began to let loose a few, fat rain drops that fell to the waiting earth. The house resembled Brenna's own rented cottage, though it was a bit more quaint with chickens clucking and scratching at the ground and colorful flowers surrounding the building's exterior. The lace curtains in the windows moved a bit as Patrick parked the truck, and then the door opened to reveal Kathleen.

Her silver hair was braided and wrapped around her head, and her spare form was covered in a floral dress of pink and green. A thick, brown shawl hung about her shoulders, and her smile was warm. "I see you're a bit early. Would you like tea, then? I've just brewed some."

"Tea would be great." Brenna didn't like the hot beverage very much but knew it would be rude to say no.

"I was hoping you would say that. Come in, the pair o' you. The storm'll be upon us at any moment."

Kathleen disappeared back inside the house, and Brenna began to walk more quickly as she felt a rain drop plop onto her nose. She stuffed the shoe into a large pocket in her jacket but paused when she saw Patrick heading away from the cottage.

"Patrick?"

"I'll join you in a moment; the chickens need to be put away."

He veered off to a large coop a bit away from the cottage and motioned for Brenna to keep going. Entering their home, Brenna felt a sense of déjà vu. It was a bit more lived in, but was laid out almost exactly like the cottage she shared with her mom. Large bunches of flowers hung from the rafters rather than spider webs, and instead of a kitchen counter, a large butcher block table stood in its place.

"Have a seat."

Kathleen motioned for her to sit on an old, worn couch covered with several, very ancient-looking quilts. It creaked beneath her weight, and Kathleen smiled warmly as she handed Brenna a large mug before sitting down in a nearby rocking chair.

"Thank you for having me over, Mrs. Fergus."

"'Tisn't a problem. It's sorry I am that you won't get to see the village today. The news said this storm was going to be a fair large one."

"Oh."

The moments were marked by a ticking clock on the mantel, and Brenna took a sip of tea. It was warm and surprisingly creamy.

"And how has this morning fared you, Brenna?"

"It's been, um, interesting." There was no table to set down her mug on, so she held it between her hands, glad for the extra warmth as she took another sip. *Tea* definitely *doesn't taste like this in India*, she thought.

"Ye've been in the woods then, have you?"

Brenna choked on her drink as the older woman smiled into her own cup.

"How did you know?"

"'Tis the truth, that's what everyone says that goes into them." She frowned then. "I thought I warned you against the place. Do you make it a habit not to listen to advice?"

"No, I...um...I...thought I saw something."

"Saw something?" Kathleen's pale blue eyes were sharp, and she lifted her head up from her cup. "What was it that you saw?"

Brenna sat silent, not wanting to lie, but saying out loud to an adult that she was seeing fairies and had been given a shoe from a leprechaun sounded insane. She almost didn't believe it herself. Kathleen tapped her fingers against her cup thoughtfully before leaning back in her chair and letting out a soft exhale.

"Patrick has been in the woods, as well."

"He has?"

"Sure."

The masculine voice from the kitchen startled her, and Brenna almost dropped her cup as Patrick scooted past the butcher block, a mug of tea in his own hands. Frowning, she set her cup onto the floor.

"Why didn't you tell me?"

"It didn't seem the sort of thing to bring up. Gram, Brenna has something she wants to show you."

Brenna glowered at Patrick, not liking being told what to do, but he merely looked pointedly at her jacket. Her cheeks grew red as she removed the leather shoe, holding it out for Kathleen to see. The old woman set her tea down on a small, rickety side table next to her rocker and leaned forward, taking the shoe into her weathered hands. She inspected it carefully, running her fingers along the seams and folds.

Her hands shook slightly, her voice low and almost angry as she turned her attention back to Brenna. "Where did you get this?"

Uncertain, Brenna looked to Patrick who merely nodded his head. Taking a deep breath, she told Kathleen of the leprechaun but not the details of the conversation he'd had with her. Kathleen listened, her fingers absently running along the shoe as she rocked in her chair, her eyes never leaving Brenna's.

"You…you believe me, don't you? I mean, I feel crazy saying it out loud, so I can't imagine what you both must think."

The look Kathleen and Patrick shared was not lost on her, and she tugged on a lock of hair. She didn't know them very well, but she knew that she liked them well enough to not want to be thought of as the crazy American girl.

"Brenna." Kathleen's eyes were filled with understanding. "There are many people in this world who would disbelieve you. But in this home, in this country, it's quite the opposite. And I've a feelin' that you're not telling me everything."

Turning her gaze to her grandson, she smiled. "When Patrick was a wee thing, he got lost in those woods for six days. And just when we had started to give up hope, out he came, walkin' calm as ye please as if nothing were the matter at all!" Kathleen laughed at the memory. "Do you remember what you said Patrick, when we asked where you had gone off to?"

"I said that I was with the Good Folk, that they had played me grand music and danced with me. I had enough wits about me to know not to eat their food or accept their drinks, but the music..." Patrick ran a hand through his hair, shifting in his seat a bit uncomfortably. "I hadn't realized that I'd been gone so long. I thought it was no more than a few hours. When I grew tired, I told them it was home I was after and that I wouldn't take no for an answer. They relented and sent me on my way when they saw my mind was made up. When I came out of the woods, everyone from the village was here."

Brenna listened to his story with wide eyes. If she hadn't already experienced the woods for herself, she would have thought they both needed to be locked up in the loony bin.

"Is that what happened to you, Brenna? Did you hear the music?" Patrick's voice was deceptively light, but the yearning in his eyes was not.

"I...well..." Saying that she'd found a fairie who had died protecting her seemed a little too unbelievable, so she took a gulp of tea instead. "I did. Hear the music, I mean. I was jogging and I heard a flute, and I thought that it was coming from the woods, so I went looking for the person playing it."

"And did you find them?" Kathleen posed this question, her gaze still boring into Brenna's.

"I didn't." She looked away, not quite able to look the older woman in the eyes. "I got a little scared, since I was so deep in the woods, and ran back. I fell through a bush and got a little scratched up, as you can see."

"And did the leprechaun say anything to you, child, when he gave you the shoe?"

Looking from Kathleen to Patrick, Brenna considered telling them what the little man had told her. After all, they had believed her so far, hadn't they? Something made her hold back, however, and she nervously tapped her fingers against the warm cup. She didn't want to lie to them, but she wasn't ready to tell them everything, either. This was *her* problem, and she wanted to involve as few people as possible.

"I'm not really allowed to say, Mrs. Fergus."

"I understand." Kathleen looked out the window, her mind clearly on other things. After a few moments, she spoke up, sounding tired. "Patrick, why don't you take Brenna home? The storm will be too big to drive in safely, I'm thinking."

"Sure, gram." Standing, Patrick slung on his well-worn jacket and left to get the truck while Kathleen stood and took their mugs to the kitchen sink. Not sure what else to do, Brenna trailed after the older woman, ducking her head as she nearly hit a bunch of drying lavender hanging from the rafters.

"Brenna, whatever it is that the Good Folk have planned for you, be sure to keep your wits about you. 'Tis the one thing that will save you above anything else."

"Thank you for believing me, Mrs. Fergus."

"There are many things in this world people ought to believe in that they turn a blind eye to. You're not the first to see things, Brenna—nor that last." Kathleen gave a small smile and handed back the green shoe.

"Mind you don't wear this unless you've a good reason to. The Good Folk don't often give gifts without strings attached. Remember that as well, girl."

"I will. Good-bye, and thanks again."

It was only a five minute drive to her home, but it felt a lot longer thanks to the tension. Patrick's truck creaked and shuddered to a stop close to her house, the rain choosing that very moment to pour down from the heavens in a full assault. Brenna knew that she should make a run for the door, but she found that she didn't want to leave. For what seemed like countless minutes, the two sat in silence as Patrick shifted the vehicle into park and turned off the ignition, the rain blurring the outside world.

"You didn't go into the woods because you heard the music."

The statement was uttered quietly, and she looked over at Patrick who was leaning his arms against the steering wheel and staring out the window. She nodded her head, sure that he could see the motion. He leaned back then, his tall frame slumping heavily against the cracked leather seat.

"I'm not sure what sort of trouble you're in, but if you're wantin', I'll help you with what I can."

Brenna wasn't sure what to say. She'd never met a person who would willingly help an almost complete stranger, except maybe her parents. And, she thought with a slightly ironic smile, herself. She studied the blurry image of the cottage through the passenger window, weighing her options. She supposed that if anyone would understand what was happening, it would be Patrick. Brenna cleared her throat.

"Could you drive me to the mound tomorrow morning, before the sun comes up?"

Patrick did look at her then, his eyes almost golden in the gray light.

"Before dawn, is it?"

"Yeah. I have to be there before the sun rises."

He didn't say anything for a few seconds, his gaze narrowing in obvious displeasure. With a sigh, he reached across her and opened the door, the sound of rain crashing around them ending the strained silence.

"I'll come 'round five. I warn you, though, if it's still raining, there won't be much point in going to the mound. It'd be fair dangerous to try and climb."

"Oh, you're right. How about the first clear morning we have, then?"

"It's as good a plan as any."

Brenna chewed on her lower lip for a moment, hesitating to ask what she needed to. But the word haunting her mind wouldn't leave, and she didn't have an Irish dictionary on hand.

"Can I ask you a question?"

"Sure."

"What does 'lean bean' mean?"

"It means 'child' in Irish. A girl, if you're wanting to be specific. Why?"

"Oh. I heard the word and was just wondering. Thanks. I'll see you soon, okay?"

She jumped out of the truck then paused. Patrick looked as though he wanted to say something, but instead he shook his head and pressed his lips together in a grim line.

"I hope you know what you're doing, Brenna."

"Me, too."

She shut the door a little harder than she probably should have before making the short jog to the house without looking back. As she unlocked the door, she heard the truck's engine roar to life before rattling down the road.

All around her was stillness and quiet, as if the cottage was waiting for something to happen. Or maybe that was just her. Shivering, Brenna flipped on the kitchen light before going into the bathroom to peel off her wet clothes and dry off. Feeling a bit warmer, she padded to her room and slipped into her comfy sweatpants and a sweater. Taking the iron key from out of her damp jeans, she shuffled back to the living room and slouched into the deep, wingback chair, studying the mysterious object. It was still cold to the touch—colder than it should have been.

A little girl. Leanbh.

The word ran in circles around her head, and despite the fact that she was warm in her fresh sweater and pants, Brenna felt a chill run through her body. Setting the key on the trunk, she started a fire in the old hearth then checked her cell phone. It was a little past three, and the display blinked to let her know that she'd received a voicemail. Her mother's cheerful voice informed her that she would be staying in Tralee that night thanks to the gusting winds and torrential rain.

"But I trust you know how to cook without burning the house down," she said with a laugh. "Of course, I'm not sure if you'll poison yourself, but that's a chance you'll have to take. Take care, sweetie, and go to bed at a decent hour, because I have a surprise for you and you'll need all the energy you can get. I love you!"

Brenna sat down in the chair, her mother's words nothing more than background noise as she wondered what on earth she was going to do. The key in her hand was heavy as she held it up, inspecting it once more in the firelight. She wasn't sure if it led to a locked door in a castle or a hut in the woods, but she knew one thing; at least: whatever door it opened, there was a little girl waiting for her on the other side of it.

* * * *

When morning came with the familiar sound of rain, Brenna found herself being woken by the smell of food. Sitting up, she frowned and ran a hand through her hair as she tried to remember if she'd left anything out from the dinner she had made the night before. Throwing back the covers, she ambled down the short hallway and into the living room. Her mother stood at the stove, cooking what appeared to be sausages. She was practically buzzing with energy.

"Mom?"

"Good morning, sleepy head! Did you know that it's almost eleven?"

"Um…"

"And when I came home expecting a big, warm welcome and breakfast after my long absence, do you know what I was greeted with instead?"

"I have a feeling you're about to tell me."

Her mother pointed a greasy spatula at her, red curls bouncing around her shoulders at the movement, green eyes narrowed in mock annoyance.

"Sarcasm without any caffeine in you doesn't count, Bren. But I digress. I came home and found—much to my horror—that *you* were in bed sleeping the day away instead of slaving over this old stove here and cooking me a wonderful breakfast after my treacherous drive back here."

Brenna tried hard to keep from laughing at her mother's antics. Instead, she put her hands on her hips and used her most condescending expression.

"I would like to point out that *you* are supposed to be *my* slave. If I remember correctly, you said that once a person has kids, they become slaves to them and have to clothe, feed, and provide shelter for their progeny. And I'm pretty sure that 'food' means that *you* make *me* breakfast."

With a laugh and a few turns of the sausage links, Rachel stepped out of the narrow kitchen and gave Brenna a large hug, smelling of breakfast and flowers. Brenna hugged her back tightly and felt tears pricking her eyes. She hadn't realized how badly she'd needed a familiar touch since yesterday's events.

"I see that your sense of humor finally caught up with you! And here I was worried I'd have to go to the Cork airport and demand they reimburse me for losing it. Do you want eggs with your sausage, O starving daughter of mine?"

"Sure. And some toast, if you think you can manage it."

"Well, I *am* your slave and live to make you happy." Rachel reached for some bread and popped it into the toaster next to the sink before grabbing a few eggs from the refrigerator.

"Did you do anything exciting yesterday?"

Brenna opened her mouth then closed it with a snap. How could she tell her mother that she'd made a promise to a dying fairie to protect a child, been given a gift by a leprechaun, and found out that their next door neighbor had once danced with fairies without sounding completely crazy? She opted for a minimalistic answer.

"It was okay. I went for a jog, and Patrick gave me a ride to the village."

"Patrick?"

"Mrs. Fergus's grandson."

"Oooh yes, I remember him. Tall, dark, and brooding. Kind of quiet. Had 'poet' written all over him." Rachel slid the scrambled eggs onto a plate along with the sausages and handed it to her daughter.

"Did you get to see anything interesting?"

"Not really. It started raining before we could really go anywhere." She had never had to withhold information from her mother before, and Brenna changed the subject, not wanting to lie outright. "How was Tralee?"

Her mother fixed herself a plate and then sat down next to Brenna on the couch, putting her feet up on the trunk turned coffee table.

"It went well enough. Apparently, your dad won some award for his essay on footwear in Belize. But I did have something I wanted to discuss with you." Her serious tone made Brenna sit up straight.

"What is it?"

"I've been thinking about the conversation we had when we first came here."

"Huh?"

It had only been a week, but it felt as if months had gone by, and Brenna tried to remember whatever conversation it was that they'd had. Her mother smiled and took the plate from Brenna's lap, setting it on the trunk.

"Do you really want to go to school here? You would have to take all of the classes, and I would strongly encourage you to learn Gaelic, as well, even if you aren't required take the class. And you'd need to wear a uniform."

"Mom, are you saying that you would let me go to school?"

"I'm saying," said her mother with a smile as she set her own plate down on the table, "that I hope you like green and blue plaid, because that's what you're going to be wearing for the next four months."

The shout of enthusiasm that escaped Brenna's mouth echoed off of the rafters and caused her mother to wince.

"I take it that was a 'yes'?"

"Omigod mom, thank you! *Thank you!*" Brenna flung her arms around her mother's shoulders, her worry over finding the *leanbh* forgotten for the moment. She jumped up from the couch and tried to keep from bouncing up and down.

"When do I start? Where do I get the uniform? Do I need books? Where *is* the school? Is it an all-girls school? Do nuns run it?"

"If they do, I promise to remind them to only rap your left knuckles so that you can still write."

"Mom!"

"All right, all right. Try and contain yourself for two minutes and I'll give you the details."

Brenna sat down, too excited to finish her breakfast.

"We'll go to town today, pick up your uniform, and take a tour of the school. They agreed to let you attend because they feel your presence would encourage students to appreciate a person with different educational experiences."

"So…you gave them a lot of money?"

"Well, it probably helped." Rachel grinned. "But they understand that you've already received a high level of education and feel that it meets with their standards. I *do* need to ask though, Brenna, are you really committed to this? Because being the new girl is never easy, and high school isn't always a wonderful place."

"I know. But I want the chance to learn for myself." Brenna frowned. "What made you change your mind?"

"Honestly?" Rachel took a bite of sausage, more serious now than she had been before. "I looked back on when we first started traveling. You really enjoyed it the first few years, but as you got older I saw you change, become more withdrawn when you used to be so outgoing, and I couldn't help but think back on my own childhood. I had some good friends when I was your age, girls that I'm still friends with today, and I've taken that opportunity from you. I feel…" she searched for the right words before finishing, "guilty."

Her mother's smile was sad, and Brenna could see from her slumped shoulders just how much strain she had been under. She reached out and held her hand.

"Your dad and I gave up everything to become writers, and we were convinced that it would be a wonderful opportunity for you to really see and understand the world in a way most kids could only dream of. But I sometimes worry that we made you pay too high a price for our decision. There's so much you've had to give up because of us."

"Mom, I like traveling with you and dad, and I love the experiences that I've had. I would never change that, so don't feel bad, okay? I'll make so many friends in school that it'll make up for the years when I didn't have any. And besides, at least this time I can actually understand them!" Brenna gave her mom an encouraging smile, hating to see her look so defeated. Rachel searched her face and gave a small, tentative smile back.

"When did you become so grown-up and wise?"

"I think it was when I drank from the fountain of knowledge in India."

Rachel laughed and stood up, her smile a bit forced now. "I really should keep a better eye on you! Finish your breakfast, and then we'll go into town."

"I don't think I can finish. I'm too excited."

"If you want to leave this house, you will. I got a new rental car, and the agent assured me that it has some of the best tires ever, so rain shouldn't be a problem. I'll just go change into something a bit warmer than a skirt."

Brenna stared at the food on her plate and thought of all the sharp turns her mom was bound to try out. Maybe she could toss the food down the sink while she was changing.

"Don't even think about putting the food down the sink—there isn't a garbage disposal."

"How did you—"

"I can read your mind like a badly written murder mystery, Bren. And don't bother shoving it into a napkin, because I'll check the trash can."

With a sigh of defeat, Brenna shoveled eggs into her mouth. Sometimes she wondered if her mom was psychic. The idea was almost as unsettling as the thought of being in a car with her again.

Chapter Four

"Brenna Morgan, if you don't get out here right now, I'm going to find the most embarrassing picture I have of you and post it all over the village!"

Brenna rolled her eyes as she took one last look of herself in the bathroom mirror. It was full-length and attached to the back of the door, giving her a good view of her new school uniform. The plaid skirt was particularly unflattering, its shape more like a potato sack than the cute, pleated skirt she had hoped for. The white shirt she wore was covered with a dark-blue jacket that bore the school emblem in gold threads. *All in all*, she thought as she wrinkled her nose, *I look more shapeless and stick-like than ever. Guess this is as good as it gets.* Grabbing the iron key that she'd set on the sink counter, Brenna tossed it from one hand to the other, debating whether she should take it or not.

It was probably better to be safe than sorry, she decided and stuffed the key into the pocket of her jacket.

"Brenna, I'm making Xerox copies as I speak!"

"I'm coming, I'm coming!"

With an exasperated sigh, she stomped out of the bathroom and into the living room only to be momentarily blinded as a flash of bright light caught her by surprise.

"Mom!"

"Oh, don't you look adorable! I love what you did with your hair!"

"I only put half of it up." Brenna rubbed at her eyes, purplish spots still lingering in her vision. "What was that?"

"It was the camera. Sorry—I left the flash on."

Rachel took another picture, this time with the flash off, and then spent the next three minutes posing her daughter as she took shot after shot. Brenna glanced at the clock, then at the food on the counter still waiting to be eaten.

"Mom, I thought you said we needed to hurry."

"That was only to get you out of bed so that I could take pictures to commemorate your first day of school! But I suppose we *do* need to get our day started."

After a rushed breakfast, her mother ushered her out the door to face a gray, drizzling world. Brenna paused to look back at the towering trees behind their cottage, the tops of which were hidden by a thick, curling mist. A sense of unease crept over her, and she slipped one hand into her pocket, grasping the key. The iron was ice-cold despite the fact that it was nestled in a warm location, and the unexpected sensation caused her to shiver.

"Brenna, are you coming or should I leave you here? I *could* try to go in your place, but I'm not as young-looking as I used to be and they might suspect something."

"Mom, don't you ever have a *short* reply for anything?"

"I don't think so. Now hustle!"

The new car started with ease and whisked through the rolling, mist-filled hills. The ocean was hidden by gray fog, too, and all that was really visible was the low rock wall and springy, green grass lining the side of the road. It was a lonesome stretch of land, save for sheep and the occasional whitewashed cottage or shrub-like hedges. The windshield wipers swished across the front window, keeping what little views there were visible. Brenna gripped her seatbelt. She wondered why the birds hadn't attacked her again, or why the man who had killed Nuala hadn't bothered to come knocking on her door and run her through with his sword. Was the key not as important as she had been told? The object in question rested heavily in her pocket, reminding her anew of the events that had taken place all of three days ago.

"There it is, Brenna. Are you ready?"

Squinting, Brenna could just make out the tall outline of her new school through the fog. The building became clearer as they drew closer, and the old spires and steeples gave it an almost Gothic feeling. The ancient stones were streaked in white and gray, causing the structure to appear as if it were made of mist. Driving at a slightly dangerous speed down the bumpy road, Rachel skidded to a stop inside the tiny parking lot on the right side of the school. Together, they watched as a slow trickle of students passed their car and made their way through a stone archway leading into the building. The rain had stopped for the moment, and Brenna stepped out of the car. Grabbing the backpack that her mother handed her, she took a deep breath as Rachel rolled down her window.

"You sure you want to go in by yourself, Bren?"

"I think I can manage."

Her mother smiled, her eyes bright with unshed tears, and Brenna leaned forward, placing a quick kiss on her cheek.

"Don't worry, I'm going to be fine. I promise I'll call you if I get lost."

"You better." Starting the car up again, her mother blinked back tears. "Now remember, if you want to come home for lunch I've already signed a waiver and left you things to make a sandwich. I'll pick you up from here at four, all right?"

"It's a date. Bye, mom."

"Bye, sweetie."

Adjusting her backpack, Brenna waited until her mother had driven away before heading down the walkway, pausing in front of the stone arches. Gargoyle heads sat watch on either side, their ugly faces twisted as if they had been frozen mid-snarl. Instinctively, Brenna put a hand inside her pocket where the iron key resided. It now felt warm to the touch, which surprised her.

"They're fair ugly, aren't they?"

Startled, Brenna whirled around. A girl wearing the school uniform stood a few feet away, her skin so white and smooth that Brenna wondered if she was ghost. But her smile was friendly, and her large, dark-brown eyes were warm.

"Yeah, they are. I'm—"

"Brenna Morgan."

"How did you know my name?" Fear shot up her spine caused the hair on the nape of her neck to rise. She remembered the last two 'people' who had said her full name without her telling them who she was. The girl laughed as she stepped closer, and Brenna noted that she was a good head shorter than herself.

"Well sure, everyone does. We don't get international students in this village very often. I'm Deirdre Connelly."

"It's nice to meet you." Brenna felt her body relax, and she offered a small smile.

"And you." Deirdre offered her hand and Brenna took it, surprised at how cold the slender fingers were. The girl laughed when she saw the startled look on her face.

"Sorry, I've poor circulation. Who d'you have for your first class, then?"

"Um…" Brenna dug her schedule out from her backpack, squinting to read the handwriting. "I have English with Mr. Dougart."

"You're in for it! He's got a temper on him, or so says me sister. Says his face can get as red as a lobster. Let me have a look at your paper, there."

Brenna readily handed it over and studied the girl. Her hair fell a little past her shoulders in thick, black waves, some of it tied back with a ribbon made out of the school colors. She was slender, though not frail, and her face was almost elfin.

"Maths class, and PE, as well. They've really done you in for your first day!" Deirdre smiled up at her. "If you're wanting a tour guide, I'd be more than happy to help."

"To be honest, I could use a friend more than a tour."

"Well that's a relief, because I make a horrible guide!" Deirdre looped her arm through Brenna's and began to walk her into the school. "I'm terrible with remembering directions, and I'm always late to class, but I can point you to Mr. Dougart, at least. Have you liked Ireland so far, then?"

Though the outside of the school seemed desolate, the inside was thrumming with hundreds of girls and boys, their voices bouncing off of the ancient stone walls.

Turning her attention back to Deirdre, Brenna responded, "It's nice. Kind of rainy."

"Well sure, what else would it be?"

Brenna paused just inside the doorway then frowned. "Where are all of the lockers?"

"Lockers?"

"For the books we need."

Laughing, Deirdre patted her arm before tugging her forward into the packed hall. "We've only a few classes a day, so there isn't any reason to carry all your books about. Here now, mind yerself!"

Without much thought, the small—and, up until now, friendly—Deirdre gave a hard shove to a group of boys blocking a staircase who, much to Brenna's surprise, merely laughed and parted.

"Eejits, the lot of 'em. Right, so, up you go! Your class will be the third door on the left."

Before she could get a word in edgewise, Brenna was none-too-gently pushed onto a stair step and wasn't given much of a choice to go anywhere else but up as a group of students blocked her and surged upward. Deirdre smiled up after her, waving.

"Meet me in front of the school when lunch comes 'round!"

If making friends was this easy in Ireland, thought Brenna as she dogged into her classroom, *I would have talked to more people at bus stops.*

Class proved to be interesting, if somewhat embarrassing with all the stares and whispers from her classmates. By the time the bell rang for lunch, Brenna was ready to take a break from all of the students.

"Brenna!"

Looking down from the last flight of stairs she'd been descending, she spied Deirdre waving and trying to shove her way against the frenzied, boisterous crowd. Smiling tiredly, Brenna hurried over to the smaller girl, stumbling a bit when Deirdre looped her arm with her own and pulled her along.

"Are you off to lunch?"

"Yeah, I was going to go home and make a sandwich."

"Do you live far from here?"

"About three miles."

"It would take too long to walk that far! Come to my home instead. My da's made a really nice stew, and I'm only 'round the corner. How did you like your classes? Was Mr. Dougart awful?"

Brenna had a hard time keeping up with Deirdre's fast pace even with her long legs, and she was only allowed to slow down once they had made it outside. The sun peeked out every once in a while as clouds scuttled by, and with the mist gone and students wandering around, the Gothic building didn't feel so forlorn.

"The classes were really interesting, especially history. Mr. Dougart's strict, but he's not horrible. What about you?"

"Same awful chemistry class I've had for the past month. Mrs. O'Shea's a right cow. Half the time I can't decide if I want to sleep or jump out a window, she drives me that mad. Oh!"

Deirdre had pulled her to a rapid halt, her attention riveted on a field to their right where a group of boys in their school colors were playing a game. With all the shoving and kicking, it looked to Brenna like a brutal cross between soccer and football.

"There he is."

"Who?"

"Patrick Fergus."

"Patrick?"

Squinting her eyes, Brenna leaned forward slightly to get a better look. The tall, athletic-looking boys were moving so fast that it was hard to try and pinpoint him. It didn't help that they were all dressed the same.

"Are you friends with him?" She glanced down at Deirdre and noticed that her cheeks were tinged pink.

"Not really, no. C'mon then, we don't want to waste any more time."

Not waiting for her agreement, Deirdre marched them onward toward a dirt path leading through a narrow but long grove of trees. Memories of Treasach and his bloodied sword flashed through Brenna's mind, and she quickly tried to think of something else to distract herself.

"What were those boys playing? It looked like soccer, but the ball wasn't round."

"Gaelic football. Have you not heard of it before?" The look Deirdre gave her was one of horror, so Brenna smiled as if she understood.

"Oh yeah, I have."

"Well, that's a relief! Imagine not knowing what GAA is! You almost had me there. You're grand *craic*!"

"I'm *what*?"

Not bothering to explain her words, Deirdre hastily led Brenna up the main road to a home that was more modern in appearance than her own cottage with a red-shingled roof and a very square, two-story design. Walking into the house, Deirdre led her through a rectangular living room to the back kitchen. The scent of stew had Brenna's mouth watering, and she received a knowing smile from her newfound friend.

"Da's a chef. He owns a restaurant down a ways, some of the best stews you'll ever have. Here." Handing Brenna a bowl filled with a thick, brown stew, she motioned for her to sit at the wooden table in the middle of the kitchen. Brenna had tried all sorts of curries and rice dishes while she and her family had traversed India, but this beat out all of them by far.

"So," began Deirdre as she tucked into her soup, "where did you live before you came to Ireland?"

"I don't live anywhere, really. But I was in India before I came here."

"India! Sure, I'd give up three of my brothers, I want to go that bad! What were you doing there?"

"My parents write for a travel magazine and their own books."

Deirdre leaned back in her seat, her eyes wide. "How exciting! Have you been all over the world?"

"They're working on it. Mainly we've been to the countries in South America and parts of the Middle East that were safe to visit."

Brenna shoveled the food down, wishing she'd discovered Irish stew earlier in life. Deirdre watched her and smiled.

"It must be a shock to you, then, with all this rain and cold weather."

"I'm really growing to like it, actually. Rainforests get a lot of rain, but they're humid and muggy and have some of the biggest spiders you'll ever see. I like that its cold here; the bugs are a lot smaller."

The glass doorframe that led out into the garden from the kitchen suddenly rattled, causing Brenna to jump. The wind howled against the glass, setting it to vibrate.

"You're jumpy, aren't you? It's only the wind. It comes on fair strong across the ocean."

"I've had some bad experience with the wind lately."

"Heard the fairie music, have you?"

"*What?*" Looking up from her bowl, Brenna realized that her tone was sharper than she'd intended, and she regretted her snappy voice when Deirdre raised her brows and laughed nervously.

"Come on, now, it's only a saying. When the wind goes through the trees and hedges, it sounds—"

"Like fairie music. I know." Tugging on a lock of her hair, Brenna pushed her bowl away, no longer feeling hungry.

"I'm sorry, Deirdre. I just sort of…had a rough start here."

"'Tisn't a problem. Sure, it's a lot of stress, I'm thinking, trying to settle into a place. You have maths next, right? While we go, you can tell me about India. Are there really elephants just roaming around, wild-like?"

The conversation changed quickly thanks to Deirdre's deft ability to switch subjects, and Brenna helped her wash the dishes before they headed back to school. The sharp winds had settled a little, but the air was colder and smelled of the sea. As they made their way back to the dirt road that led through the trees, a sharp pain lanced Brenna's side and she shouted, shaking her jacket until the key landed on the ground with a dull *thud*.

"Are you all right, Bren?"

"I'm fine…I think."

Brenna tried to snatch it up but dropped it again as the intense heat seared her skin. It felt as though the thing had just come out of a blazing fire.

"Hey there, Brenna, it looks as though you've made a friend! He looks worried himself."

Brenna had just picked up the key with her hand safely wrapped in the sleeve of her jacket when Deirdre's words registered. Raising her gaze, she felt her stomach drop. A small, black bird was perched atop a nearby bush, feathers ruffled and bright eyes glittering as it stared at her, its head tilted at an unnatural side angle. She rose slowly, carefully slipping the key back inside her pocket, afraid to make any sudden movements that might alert to her intentions.

"Are you a fast runner, Deirdre?"

"I'm fair decent. Why?"

"Because we need to run. *Now*."

"Run? We've ten minutes yet till—hey!"

Without waiting for Deirdre to finish her sentence, Brenna grabbed her hand and sprang into a sprint. Behind her, she heard an unearthly cry. She ran harder.

"Brenna, slow down! What's going on?!"

Deirdre's question came out in gasps as she ran, her hand damp and threatening to slip from Brenna's. Brenna slowed but didn't stop while she hunted wildly for a place to hide. She could hear the fluttering of wings followed by a strange cawing sound that seemed to be drawing closer, and she gripped Deirdre's hand tighter. She didn't want to turn around to see what terrifying form the birds had changed into. Ahead, she could see the trees that separated the main road from the school grounds.

"If we go through the trees here, will it still lead to school?"

"Well, sure. But what's happen—"

Deirdre was cut off once more as Brenna made a sharp left into the woods. Using her free hand, she blocked the small twigs and leaves slapping at her face. She could hear Deirdre's labored breathing, but it was hard to distinguish over the din of trees and branches being broken as birds—or whatever it was—flocked after them. The girls broke through the thicket and Brenna's shoes slid as her feet went from mossy, uneven ground to slick, muddy grass. Catching her footing, she lost hold of Deirdre's hand. Glancing back, she saw that her friend had stopped a few feet away from the forest, breathing heavily and her hands on her knees. Beyond her, the leaves and branches were shaking and snapping furiously as if trying to hold back a great storm.

"Deirdre, *run!*"

Brenna felt her body slam into something hard, knocking stars into her eyes. Arms clasped around her in an iron grip, and she screamed for all she was worth as she fell to the ground with her captor, trying to kick and tear herself away.

"Brenna, calm down! It's me!"

She stopped struggling at the sound of the familiar voice and pulled away to see Patrick beneath her, a cut on his lip and a few scratches on his neck from where her nails had embedded themselves. Breathless and shaking from head to toe, Brenna blinked back tears that threatened to fall. She rolled off of him hastily, standing up to pat her jacket pocket and make sure the key was still inside. Behind them, the forest had gone quiet and still, without so much as a single leaf or branch out of place. Standing up, Brenna offered her hand to Patrick, hoping he didn't notice how much it was shaking.

"I'm sorry, Patrick. I'm so sorry. I didn't know it was you."

"It's fine." He grasped her hand and stood up, dusting grass and cakes of mud from his pants as Deirdre ran over to them, her hair nearly as tangled and filled with debris as Brenna's.

"Bejeebus, Brenna! Are you all right?!" Deirdre called as she jogged toward them.

"Yeah. I'm okay." She swiped quickly at her stinging eyes, glancing away when she noticed Patrick studying her before he dusted the last clump of mud from his pants and focused on Deirdre.

"What were you two running from?"

"Sure, like I know! She saw a little bird and took off like the devil was on her! And then there were so *many* birds...Brenna, what happened? Did you have bread in your pockets and clean forget? I did that once."

"No. I didn't. I...I..."

The bell rang then, calling students back into the classrooms. Deirdre slipped an arm around Brenna's waist—her shoulders were a bit too high for her to reach comfortably—and smiled encouragingly.

"Do you want me to take you to the nurse?"

"No, I'm okay. I just need to catch my breath."

With Deirdre's arm still about her, Brenna hurried across the field, glancing back every few seconds to scan the woods, wondering if the birds had really given up or if they were rallying for another attack. Patrick walked a few paces behind them, silent and tall, his face void of any tellable emotions. When they reached the school's entrance, he opened the door for them.

"I'll take her to class, Deirdre."

"Oh, but I really should—"

"I'll take her."

At Patrick's firm voice, Deirdre blushed bright red and nodded her head before patting Brenna on the arm. "Right. See you after school, then."

Patrick released the door he'd been holding and it closed behind them with a heavy *thud* that echoed off of the stone arches and walls. Brenna tugged nervously at a lock of her hair, releasing several leaves as she did so. She wondered just how badly her hair was riddled with nature, but the thought flew from her head when Patrick placed a hand on her shoulder.

"You'll want to use the bathroom, I'm thinking."

He steered her down the hall until they reached a blue door. There he stopped her, leaning in close so that their voices wouldn't carry.

"Brenna, what were you really running from?"

"Birds."

"What sort of birds?"

"The sort that turn into fairies." Her voice was low and Patrick, who had leaned in even closer to hear her, pulled back. He appeared startled, and his brows were raised high.

"You're serious."

"No," said Brenna, egged into sarcasm, "I run away from little black birds because it's fun."

He took a step back, studying her thoughtfully. "You need to go to the mound tomorrow morning."

Wordlessly, Brenna nodded her head, crossing her arms over her chest as she let loose a small shiver. Patrick ran a hand through his dark hair.

"Christ, Brenna, do you have any idea what you're doing?"

"Not really. But I don't want to keep getting chased by birds that want to kill me." She looked up at him warily. "You believe me, don't you?"

He was silent for a long moment before he sighed, looking away as he rubbed his forehead.

"I wish I didn't, but I do. I'll pick you up tomorrow at five thirty. Can you be up by then?"

"Honestly, I don't think I'm going to sleep for a month after what just happened."

The sounds of feet and voices were followed by a few female

students walking down the stairs, and Patrick took a healthy step away. It was then that Brenna realized just how close he'd been standing next to her. He cleared his throat, and she was almost positive that she saw his cheeks color a little as the girls meandering down the stairs eyed the pair of them. His discomfort almost made her smile. Almost.

"Do you want me to walk you to your class, then?"

"I can manage. Thank you for your help. Really. And I'm sorry about hurting you."

"'Tisn't a problem—I've suffered much worse in practice. I'll see you tomorrow."

It took her a few minutes to fix her hair and wipe her face clean and another five to stop shaking enough to look normal for class. Slinking into the classroom wasn't an option given her height, but the teacher simply pointed her to her seat, reminding her dryly that a bell wasn't just to put around a cow's neck but to show up on time. A few of the students snickered, but most shot her sympathetic smiles. The rest of the day ticked by in agonizingly slow minutes, and by the time the last bell rang she was ready to follow Deirdre's lead and jump out a window. Instead, though, she followed the mob of students out of the classroom and found Deirdre waiting for her at the bottom of the stairs.

"Brenna, we need to talk."

Her tone of voice didn't bode well, and the serious look in her large, dark-brown eyes made Brenna wonder how many times she'd have to apologize. She hadn't had a friend in forever, and she wasn't ready to lose the first one she'd made. Together, they walked outside of the school where people were either diving away, being picked up, or milling about. Brenna felt that it was best to get the apologies out of the way.

"I'm sorry, Deirdre."

"For what?"

"Um, for making you run without giving you any explanation."

"Oh, that." She waved a dismissive hand. "I needed some excitement anyway. Did you see how many birds were after us? We must have been too close to their nests. But that's not what I wanted to speak to you about. I wanted to know about Patrick."

"Huh?" If Deirdre had asked her if she could grow wings and fly out of Ireland, Brenna couldn't have been more confused. The smaller girl stopped at the small, gravel lot where Brenna's mother had dropped her off that same morning, then she whirled around.

"How do you know him?"

"I live next door to him, and his grandmother welcomed us to our cottage."

"You met his grandmother?!"

"Is that a bad thing?" The incredulous tone and the saucer-wide stare Deirdre was giving her were starting to worry Brenna.

"Bad? No. Just…you've no idea who his grandmother is, do you? No—of course you don't. Here now, maybe you didn't know this, but Patrick Fergus is the star player on our football team, and all the girls are mad for him."

Brenna was pretty sure that Deirdre was more than a little 'mad' for him herself, but she refrained from saying so.

"I'm just saying that you shouldn't get your hopes up."

"What do you mean?"

"He doesn't go 'round with anyone. He's focused on football, and that's it. D'you see what I'm driving at?"

"Um…not really."

The two girls jumped as the sound of a horn interrupted their conversation. They watched with awe as Brenna's mother skidded her car to a stop, sending gravel flying in a small wave. With the window already down, Rachel poked her head out, red curls bouncing everywhere and green eyes sparkling.

"Making friends already, I see! I told your father that you weren't socially inept, but he wouldn't believe me."

Not wanting to make the situation any more awkward than it already was, Brenna hurried over to her mother with Deirdre in tow.

"Mom, this is Deirdre Connelly. Deirdre, my mom—Rachel Morgan."

"Call me Rachel. Do you need a ride home, Deirdre?"

Shaking her head slightly, Brenna mouthed "no" to Deirdre with just enough fear in her eyes to convince her new friend that she'd surely die if she stepped foot inside the car.

"Thanks Mrs. Mor—I mean Rachel. But I'm only just on the other side of the school. Brenna, I'll see you tomorrow?"

"Yeah."

"Right, then. Bye."

"Bye."

Sliding into the car and fastening her seatbelt extra tight, Brenna and Rachel zoomed down the road, her mother pestering her with more questions than Brenna had ever heard in her life. Frazzled, she wondered if this was how other people around the world felt when her mother interviewed them for her articles. By the time they arrived home, Brenna could barely stay awake long enough to finish her homework and take a shower. While clearing the plates after dinner, her mother—who had for a few moments stopped asking questions—perked up as if she had suddenly remembered something.

"Did you see Patrick today?"

"Why does every one keep asking me about him?!" Brenna asked, exasperated, from the couch.

Taken aback by her daughter's reaction, Rachel's brows raised as she set the dishes in the sink. "Who's 'everyone'?"

"Just…people."

"People, huh?" Her mother's lips parted into a Cheshire Cat grin that Brenna didn't trust at all. "Why the strong reaction, then? Did something happen between you two?"

"No! I barely know him!"

"But you know him well enough that he's driving you to school tomorrow."

Brenna's mouth hung open, and her mother's smile made much more sense now. Not that it made things any better. "How did you know that?"

"I'm psychic?"

"Mom!"

"Oh, all right. He called me earlier this evening when you were in the shower and told me so." Handing her daughter a bowl of ice cream, Rachel sat down next to her on the couch.

"He did? Did he say anything else?"

"Is it important if he did?"

"Would you stop answering my questions with a question?!"

"Touchy, touchy! You really must've had a long day. No, Bren, he didn't say anything else other than 'it was nice to meet you' and 'I hope to marry your daughter by the end of the semester.'"

"*Moooooom!*"

Rachel laughed and shooed Brenna off to bed, seeing that her daughter wasn't in the mood for teasing or banter.

Despite being tired, Brenna found it hard to sleep as worries about what she would face the next morning whirled in her head. With a sigh, she turned on her light and took out the fairy-tale book, searching the appendix for anything labeled 'friendly fairies' or 'mound'. Since the leprechaun wouldn't answer her questions, she hoped that the book might supply some answers. She found the Gaelic term he had used and flipped to the indicated page, reading out loud.

"'The *Tuath de Danann*, considered demigods who once ruled over Ireland, are known for both richly rewarding and cursing people as they see fit. Often it is at the whim of their feelings on any given day.' Huh."

She hoped that whoever Roibhilin was, he was in a good mood tomorrow. Spotting the term 'fairie mound' she flipped to the page and tilted her head at the definition before her. A fairie mound, more commonly known as a rath, the book informed her, was believed to be either the entrance to the fairie realms or the roofs of their underground palaces. Brenna frowned. She was supposed to tromp all over a fairie's roof? That didn't seem like something a person, magical or not, would be too happy about.

"Brenna, lights out!" her mom called as she passed through the hallway.

"Okay."

Switching off her lamp, Brenna stared into the darkness. If Nuala was as kind as Brenna knew, then this fairie 'Rovalin' had to be good, too. Feeling a bit better, she drifted off to sleep, her dreams filled with strange visions and creatures that slipped away almost as quickly as they appeared. Somewhere in the back of her mind she thought she heard a child crying, but like the rest of her dreams it soon faded away into nothingness.

Chapter Five

Five thirty came much sooner than Brenna had anticipated. With groans and half-opened eyes, she dragged herself from the comfort of her warm bed. Outside, the world was still black, and not even a cricket could be bothered to make a noise. Slipping into her school uniform, she added a thick sweater along with a bright-pink beanie for good measure; if the frost she had found on her windowpane earlier was any indication, it was pretty cold outside. Her mother was still asleep and probably wouldn't be awake for several more hours. Closing her door so that she wouldn't wake her, Brenna started the coffee machine as quietly as she could. By the time Patrick arrived, she was finishing a third cup of coffee and munching on her second uncooked Pop-Tart.

She winced when the truck came to a halt with a loud *clunk* that sounded as if the engine had dropped out the bottom. Rushing to the truck to escape the chilly air, she threw her books in the back and hopped inside, surprised by how warm it was.

"You have a heater in this thing?"

"Is that really the first thing you're going to say to me this early in the morning? And me, doing you this grand favor?"

"You're right. Good morning, Patrick." She paused. "You have a heater in this thing?"

Patrick's lips curled up in a smile and he shook his head before backing up the truck. "Are you always this chipper in the morning, then?"

"I have three cups of coffee running through me."

"Ah." His one word held a wealth of understanding, and he shot her an appraising look as he backed onto the main road. "Explains your unnatural enthusiasm for such a dark day."

She laughed, surprised to see such dry humor come from him. She'd sort of suspected he hadn't had a sense of humor, given his affinity for silence. Brenna tugged on her hair. It was strange, feeling so comfortable with someone she hadn't known that long. What had Deirdre meant when she'd said that he wasn't 'going 'round with anyone'? It seemed to Brenna that Patrick went around a lot, as she'd seen him hanging with more than a few groups of friends around school. Maybe Deirdre simply hadn't noticed.

Except for the occasional questions here and there, the rest of the ride to the mound was silent. Brenna slid her hand into her pocket and fiddled with the key, frowning when she noticed how cold it had become despite being nestled inside the warm sweater. The way it kept changing temperatures for no apparent reason was beginning to worry her.

"We're here."

Patrick parked the truck and turned it off. They had stopped in a graveled parking lot that faced a thicket of trees and bushes lining a gently rounded but tall mound rising above them, darker than the sky it stood under. The air seemed charged with electricity and caused Brenna's hair to stand on end despite being swathed in warm wool. As they got out of the car, her breath came out in puffs and her cheeks stung from the cold air.

"The entrance is just there." Patrick pointed to a small clearing in between the trees a few yards away from where they stood. "Do you want me to go with you?"

"No." Gripping the key in her hand, Brenna thought back to Nuala to hold on to the courage that was starting to leave her. "I have to go alone."

"I'll wait by the lorry, then. Give a shout if you need me."

"I will. Thank you, Patrick."

He nodded his head, his expression hard to read. Giving herself a shake and an internal pep talk, Brenna marched up the winding footpath that led through the narrow plot of trees and up the mound. The hill was steeper than it had looked, and she was almost out of breath by the time she got to the top. The lush grass that grew there was covered in a fine, spider-like web of frozen dew, and it crunched under her feet as she walked toward the center. The sky was beginning to lighten, shifting from never-ending blackness to a pale gray, and Brenna looked around to get her bearings. Like soldiers guarding a fort, the trees below the mound formed a circle. Rolling hills on either side created a valley below where mist crept low on the ground, obscuring any animals that might be grazing there. Behind her, Patrick and the parking lot were hidden from view while to her right a partially ruined castle stood on the next hill over, a large thatch of trees obscuring the road leading toward it.

"Okay. You can do this, Brenna. You can do this."

Hesitantly, she began to walk around the top of the mound. By the time she'd made her third loop, she could just see the fiery, bright orange color of the sun peaking over a distant hill. Inhaling slowly, she closed her eyes and squatted down on the ground, knocking on it three times just as she'd been instructed. Rising, she spoke in as commanding a voice as she could muster, not feeling particularly brave.

"Roibhilin."

Releasing her grip from the key, she waited for an answer. When nothing happened and no other voice responded, Brenna frowned and began tapping her foot impatiently. She was still alone on the mound save for some birds flying in the distance as the sky rapidly began to dawn.

"Circle the mound three times, knock thrice, and say the name Roibhilin when you see first light—that's what he said. Maybe I didn't count right."

Again, Brenna marched around the mound, making sure she circled three times before she struck the ground with her fist as hard as she could and yelled the name once more, taking hold of the key in her pocket as she did so. As the seconds flew by, she began to feel more than a little foolish when no one appeared.

"That stupid leprechaun. I never should have listened to him!"

"I could have told you as much."

The musical voice behind her was distinctly male, and Brenna instantly felt the key in her hands begin to burn, forcing her to let go of it. She turned around slowly, eyes wide and heart hammering. With disbelieving eyes, she saw a boy who seemed to be only a little older than herself standing on the other side of the mound. She rubbed her eyes hard and looked again; the figure was still there. His hair was a brilliant shade of gold, and his eyes were the same intense blue of both Nuala and Treasach's. He was tall—taller than Patrick, even—with fine features that she had always imagined a prince must have. His green tunic and the long, cape-like garment encircling his shoulders reminded her of the heroes in the books she'd read. Were it not for the blatant distaste in his eyes and the sneer marring his face she would have thought him the most perfect man she had ever seen. *Why is it*, she thought with some exasperation, *that all male fairies seemed to be constantly disgusted with me?*

"Who are you?" Her voice came out strangled and she tried to clear it. Even from across the mound Brenna could see his lips twitch up in a smile that was more malevolent than amused. Brenna felt the first stirrings of anger rise within her chest. Despite his fine looks, there was something about this boy that she disliked.

"You've been walking on my mound and causing quite a ruckus. Who do you *think* I am?"

"Roibhilin?"

"The very same." He gave a courtly bow, though Brenna felt that it was to mock her. He stood on the other end of the mound a few moments longer, eyeing her from head to toe before strolling leisurely toward her, acting as though a human calling on him was an everyday occurrence. For all she knew, maybe it was. Brenna stuck out her chin in defiance. He stopped abruptly a few feet away, holding a his hand to his nose.

"You've iron on you."

"What?"

"Iron. I can smell it." Roibhilin took a step back, his eyes narrowing. "Human, what want you of me?"

"I—"

"Your voice annoys me." He dropped his hand from his nose then, crossing his arms. "If you've nothing to say to me that is of interest, then depart. I have ruined men's whole fields for less."

Brenna found her voice—and her temper. She put her hands on her hips, the key still clutched in her hand.

"A leprechaun told me that you could help me."

"Now that," he said with true scorn, "is the best reason to avoid your company altogether." He turned to leave, and Brenna started after him, desperation driving her along with her temper.

"Wait!" Grabbing hold of his cape, she stumbled to her knees as he whirled around, his eyes blazing with hatred.

"How *dare* you touch me!"

He drew his hand back to strike her, and he probably would have followed through had she not held up the iron key as she threw her hands in front of her face. Roibhilin's hand stopped a few inches from her head, as if something were preventing him from striking. The fairie tried to push his hand down farther, his entire arm shaking with the effort. After a few more seconds of futile effort, he lowered his arm and stepped back, breathing heavily, his face dark with anger.

"Please," she gasped, "please help me. The leprechaun said you could tell me who Nuala was."

"How do you know that name?" His voice shook with fury, and it took everything within her to stand back up under his intense gaze.

"Because she told me it. She saved my life and she…she asked for my help. Look, she gave me this." Brenna held up the key, and he took another step back, shaking his head in denial.

"She would never ask for the help of a mortal."

"Well, apparently, she would, because she asked *me*. And the leprechaun said that you could answer my questions about who she was."

"I do not help humans, least of all ones who speak lies."

"I'm not lying! She made me promise to help, and…" Tears filled Brenna's eyes as Nuala's kind voice and gentle eyes sprang up in her mind. "She died saving me. You *have* to help m—hey. Hey, are you all right?"

For the first time since she'd spoken to him, Roibhilin looked truly stunned. His face was so pale that it had gone almost translucent, and he put a hand to his chest.

"You lie."

"I do not!"

"*You lie!*" His voice boomed so loudly that Brenna had to cover her ears, and his words gave way to a sudden roar that echoed off of the hills, morphing into a sound similar to that of waves crashing against huge rocks. It shook the ground beneath them, causing birds to fly from bushes and trill in terror while cows and sheep in the valley began to low in panic, adding to the cacophony of noise. The scream seemed to have worn Roibhilin down, though, for he fell to his knees. It was then that Brenna saw sadness and pain so deep in his eyes that it caused pent-up tears to finally fall down her own cheeks. She took a hesitant step toward him but stopped when he pinned her with a hard gaze.

"How did she die?"

"She..." Brenna took a shaky breath. "She was killed."

"By whom?" His voice was strained, fist still clenching the cape gathered at his chest.

"I don't know," she lied, stalling for time.

"Who," he demanded between gritted teeth, "killed my mother?"

"Your *mother*?!"

Brenna took an involuntary step back, her free hand flying to her mouth in shock. Roibhilin was on his feet faster than she could blink, advancing toward her with murder in his eyes.

"Aye, *my* mother." He stepped on her foot with his own, and pain lanced up her leg as his heavy boot pressed her toes into the ground. She tried to pull out from under it, but he refused to budge.

"I-I don't know."

"Then how do you know she is dead?" His words came our harsh, and Brenna gave up trying to escape when he applied more pressure.

"I saw it...sort of. I saw the person who killed her."

"What did they look like?"

"I'll...I'll only tell you if you promise to help me."

She knew that it was cruel, that it was harsh, but she also realized that she'd never get Roibhilin's help if she didn't strike a bargain. She didn't want to hurt him, but she didn't want to die or let Nuala's death be in vain, either.

"A promise?" He seemed stunned and he narrowed his eyes. "You have seen who killed my mother yet you want a *promise*?"

"Yes. If you help me figure out what to do with this key and find what it leads to, then I'll tell you who killed your mother."

They eyed each other for countless moments, Roibhilin's fists tensed at his sides almost as tightly as his jaw.

"Very well—you have my word." He gritted out in a low voice, his scowl deepening.

"You mean your *promise*?"

He opened his mouth and then shut it, crossing his arms against his chest once more as he eyed her suspiciously. "Have you done this before?"

"No."

"Hm." He clearly disbelieved her, but at last he removed his foot from hers. "You've my *promise* that I will do my best to aid you in discovering and finding what that key leads to."

"It's a deal."

Stuffing the key in her pocket, Brenna stood up, holding out her hand. He stared at it in puzzlement.

"What are you doing?"

"We should shake on it."

He curled his upper lip in distaste. "I don't touch humans. You've my promise, and that is enough. Come, then. We must discuss what to do with your precious key."

Whirling on one foot, Roibhilin strode across the mound, and Brenna bit her lip.

"I can't."

"You *can't*?" Turning, the annoyance was clear to see in the fairie's stormy eyes. "Did you not just extract from me a promise to help you? Are you breaking our accord?"

"No. It's just…I have to go to school."

It sounded lame even to her own ears, and he looked at her, nonplused. Heat crept up her cheeks, so she tried another tactic. "I have to go now or else others will start to worry about me, and it'd make it even harder for me to come back here to talk with you."

"Then come when the sun sets, and do not be late, mortal."

"It's Brenna."

"I have no need for your name."

With those cold parting words, he disappeared. Brenna stared at where he once stood, torn between annoyance and relief.

"You'd be the first person who doesn't," she muttered to herself before limping down the hill, her foot still smarting from where

Roibhilin had stomped it into the ground. Patrick was leaning against the truck and immersed in a book when she finally made it down. He looked up, brows raising when he saw her less-than-graceful gait. Straightening, he shut his book before tossing it through the open window of his truck.

"Are you all right, Brenna? What happened to your foot?"

"Oh. Um…a misunderstanding. I'm ready to go now."

He opened her door, trotted around the front to the driver's side, and then got in himself, starting the engine with a hard twist of the key in the ignition.

"Did you find what you were looking for, then?"

"Kind of."

"'Kind of'?"

"It's just a little complicated, that's all."

They rode without speaking for several minutes before Brenna let out a sigh and took off her beanie, running a hand through her flattened hair.

"Patrick, can I ask you a question?"

"Well, sure I'd be surprised if you didn't." He smiled when she rolled her eyes.

"Are fair—I mean, are the Good Folk allergic to iron or something?"

"'Tis true they've a strong distaste for it. Have you never wondered why you have an iron horseshoe hanging above your cottage door?"

She wracked her brain, trying to remember if she'd seen it. "I never noticed."

"It keeps most away. Why?"

"I'll tell you about it later, after I've had time to think some things over."

When they arrived at school, it was still early. Save for a few students trudging down the road, most were still in their homes eating breakfast or otherwise preparing for the day ahead. Patrick drove to the small parking lot, wincing a bit when the truck *banged* loudly before settling down.

"I'd be grateful if you didn't tell people that I drove you to school."

"Why?"

"Well…" He rubbed his neck, glancing around. "It's not

quite…legal-like for me have another person in the car until I'm eighteen. And if the school found out, it would be a right holy show."

"A what?"

"I'd get into a lot of trouble."

"Oh. Well, you've kept my secrets, so it's only fair that I keep yours, right?" She smiled over at him and picked up her beanie from where it had fallen off her lap onto the floor mat, tugging it back on her head before stepping out. After Brenna retrieved her backpack from the front seat, she joined Patrick at the back of the truck.

"Patrick?"

"Aye?"

"Did you hear…any shouting when I was up on the mound?"

"I didn't hear a thing but my own heartbeat. Why?" He looked down at her. "Should I have done?"

"No. Never mind—I was just curious."

"Well sure, and what a fine sight to see so early in the morning!"

Deirdre was making her way quickly toward them, brown eyes wide as she looked between Brenna and Patrick. Her pale cheeks were flushed with color as if she had been running, and her dark hair was braided to one side. Straightening from her slumped position, Brenna smiled and waved.

"Good morning, Deirdre! Patrick and I got to school at the same time. How are you doing?"

"I'd be better if I didn't have to take me three brothers to their school. Bejeebus, they're a handful! Count yourself lucky, Brenna, that you're an only child."

Deirdre set her books down and then smiled, looking up into the sky as if she was watching for something. Apparently satisfied with what she found, Deirdre grinned at Brenna, hands on her hips.

"No more flocks of birds following you 'round this morning, then?"

"Nope. And hopefully they won't be anymore."

Patrick shot her a questioning glance which was not lost on Deirdre. She raised a brow but put the topic behind them and looped her arm through Brenna's, tugging her toward the school while Patrick trailed after them.

"Have you been good to my Brenna, Patrick Fergus?"

"I suppose."

"He's been really helpful, actually. He's going to take me to see the castle after school."

"I am, am I?"

"Yeah, don't you remember? You said you'd take me." Brenna glanced over her shoulder at Patrick who was looking a bit annoyed. She couldn't really blame him. She mouthed the word "please" which caused him to roll his eyes. Deirdre smiled.

"If you don't mind the company, I'd love to come with you. I haven't been there in ages!"

"Oh. Um…" Biting her lip, Brenna thought quickly. She couldn't say no—it might raise suspicion. An idea suddenly dawned on her, and she realized that she could accomplish two things at once. She smiled her brightest smile. "That would be great!"

"Grand! After school, we can take the bus and meet Patrick there. C'mon, I want to introduce you to a few of my friends."

The second day of school wasn't nearly as tedious as the first; the students that whispered and pointed at her the day before now happily approached her and talked her ear off in-between classes. It was easy to make friends and fit in—much more so than Brenna had ever thought possible. By the time school let out, she was sure that she could happily spend five days a week in the building. She was even getting used to being jostled in and out of the school like a canned sardine.

"Brenna, over here!" Standing beside the hideous face of a gargoyle, Deirdre waved her over, looking slightly worried. "I forgot to ask if your mum was going to pick you up again. I hope taking the bus is all right with her."

"Oh, it's fine. I called my mom at lunch and told her about my outing. She asked me to bring back a brochure."

"You're fair lucky! My da only just let me take the buses last year. He's that worried I'll get snatched up."

The sun was out for once with hardly a cloud in the sky. Brenna closed her eyes briefly, enjoying the feel of the sun rays on her face, even if it was a weak warmth. While they climbed onto the bus, Deirdre kept a healthy stream of conversation going that ranged from her favorite movies to the local gossip of who liked who.

"Deirdre, can I ask you a personal question?"

"Sure."

Shifting a little uncomfortably in the bus's cushioned seat, Brenna distractedly wound a strand of her hair around one finger, hoping she wasn't wrong about her hunch.

"I was wondering…I mean, that is to say…you like Patrick, right?"

"Well sure, everyone does."

"No, I mean…" she searched for the right words, "you fancy him, right?"

She could feel heat creep up her neck a little as Deirdre looked at her with wide eyes before laughing half-heartedly.

"Well…I suppose t'isn't a secret at all. I'm that easy to read, then?"

"Only just a little."

Deirdre laughed and then sighed, slumping in her chair as she looked out the window. "I've liked Patrick since we were in primary school."

"Primary school? Is that like junior high or something?"

"No, I think you call it elementary school in the states."

"Oh." Brenna blanched. "*Oh.* That's a really long time!"

"I know. But he's never really given me much notice a'tall."

"I'll make sure he does today."

The look Deirdre gave her was one of serious doubt, and Brenna simply smiled and patted her hand, feeling as if she'd just solved one the world's hardest problems. "Don't worry. I have everything under control. Just leave it to me."

By the time they arrived at the castle's entrance and found Patrick, the building's curator warned them that they only had an hour to look around before the site closed for the day. They walked up several flights of small but deeply set stairs that spiraled up one side of the castle, and small slivers of light filtered in from narrow windows carved into the thick stone walls. By the time they reached the top of the tower they were all a little breathless. Together, the trio began a slow stroll around the top of the building, and though Patrick didn't speak much, the look he gave Brenna when she changed places so that Deirdre was walking next to him told her that she hadn't been as sneaky as she had thought.

"Oh, look—there's *Coillearnach* mound!" Deirdre, leaning

dangerously far over the ledge of a partially intact wall, pointed out a bump in the land only half a mile away.

"Do you know why they built the castle here, Brenna?"

"Because it had a nice view?"

"Well so, that might have been one reason," laughed Deirdre. "But the *real* reason is because the princess of this castle fell in love with the fairie prince living beneath the mound over there. She had her father build the castle so that she could wait for him to appear in the morning. 'Tis said she pined away for him because he never appeared."

The thought of Roibhilin falling in love with a human was so funny that Brenna laughed aloud, receiving questioning looks from both Deirdre and Patrick.

"Sorry. It just seems so silly. I mean…why wait for a fairie prince if all he's going to do is not bother to show up?"

"Oh, Brenna; you don't have a romantic bone in you, do you?! Isn't it grand to think that a fairie prince could whisk you away to an enchanted palace?"

"Personally," muttered Brenna as she stared over at the mound, "I'd rather take my chances on a real guy."

She happened to glance at Patrick but quickly looked away when she realized he'd been staring at her. It was time to set her plan into motion.

"Deirdre, is there a bathroom anywhere?"

"Sure, it's just there by the entrance. Do you want company?"

"No, I'll be quick."

She smiled and darted down the steep steps. Escaping the castle, she looked up to see Deirdre and Patrick move away from the ledge. She felt a little bad but reminded herself that she would only be gone for a few minutes. She needed to explain to Roibhilin that they would have to meet on Friday to have a really lengthy discussion about the key, since there just wasn't time to have one now. If she was lucky, he'd understand her predicament. Roibhilin's angry face flashed through her mind and she rolled her eyes. No, he probably wouldn't.

She ran as fast as she could to the mound—which took only a couple of minutes—and scrambled up the slope. She turned to look back at the castle and, seeing no one staring back at her from the top of the stone keep, she breathed a sigh of relief.

"Is there a reason," said a familiarly annoyed voice behind her, "that you've come early?"

"Don't you think saying 'hello' might be a bit more friendly?"

"And why would I want to do that?"

Brenna turned around. The voice had sounded far away, but Roibhilin was almost right behind her, towering over her with a very displeased expression. She didn't know what it was about him that irked her so—perhaps it was the way he looked down on her as if she were nothing more than a mere pebble on the ground.

"Because it's nice." She paused, putting her hands on her hips. "You know, I've read that the Good Folk and humans used to interact on really friendly terms."

"That was before."

"Before what?"

"If you've come to discuss the key, then get on with it."

The change in topic threw her for a moment, but Brenna realized she wouldn't get any answers out of him is she persisted in her inquiry. Sighing, she ran a hand through her hair, knowing he wasn't going take her news very well.

"That's the thing. I know that I said I could come today, but it was hard to do since I'm in school. I can meet you in three days, at the same time."

Roibhilin narrowed his eyes. "I cannot tell if you're stupid or *very* stupid," he said in a deceptively mild tone. "You call on me, you bring me news of my mother's death, and after making me promise to help you, you wish to delay the offer."

"Look," said Brenna, exasperated, "it's not like I *want* to wait three days, but I have to. I don't have a very good way to get to the mound, and I just found out that the person driving me isn't legally allowed to. I can't come in the morning, and Friday afternoon is the only day this week I can go without my mom being suspicious of where I am after school."

"I am not accustomed to waiting on humans." Though he spoke to her, his eyes were scanning the distance behind her. How he could be distracted and annoyed at the same time she had no idea. Gritting her teeth together, she lifted her hands in a frustrated gesture.

"Brenna. My name is *Brenna*. And I'm afraid you're just going to have to get use—"

She was cut off as Roibhilin suddenly lunged at her with a cry, knocking her onto the ground with such force that she lost her breath and saw stars. Above her, he looked angry, his blue eyes narrowed toward the horizon, body tense. He muttered something under his breath then scowled down at her.

"Did you forget to mention that you were followed?"

"What?"

She was pulled up none too gently as Roibhilin gave a shout and tugged her behind him. A whistling sound filled the air; it reminded her of how a flute must sound if it was played off-key. Her face smashed against the soft fabric of Roibhilin's cape, Brenna's nose was overwhelmed with the scent of earth and some sort of flower that she couldn't place. Before she could pull away, Roibhilin sprang forward, picking his way across the mound and grumbling in agitation. All around them, what looked to be small arrows were imbedded in the hill.

Confused, she trailed after Roibhilin, yanking up one of the delicate arrows lodged in the soft ground. It was made of dark, polished wood, and the tip looked as if it had been dipped in ink. Frowning, she touched it, surprised at how sticky the substance was between her fingers.

"What is this stuff?"

Roibhilin made a strange noise, looking at her as if she had suddenly sprouted horns. He began to advance, eyes fixated on the arrow in her hands. Brenna took a wary step back.

"Hey, if you're trying to freak me out, it's working."

"Be silent."

"But—"

"*Now*." Snatching the arrow from her, he studied the tip before looking back at her, incredulous. "You are not dead."

"Well, I should hope not." She paused. "I mean, you did save me. Thank you."

"No," he said, grabbing her hand and examining the pads of her fingers, "you should be dead. These fairy darts were tipped to poison humans, yet you are alive after touching one. Who are you?"

"I already told you. I'm Brenna Morgan."

He was silent for a long moment, staring off toward the castle, clearly lost in thought. At last he spoke, and the withering look he gave her had her wishing that she'd never gone to the hill and called out his name.

"Come Friday before the last ray of sun is gone."

Roibhilin turned on his heel and strode to the other side of the mound, the arrows disappearing one by one as he passed by them. From deep below her feet, Brenna heard a rumbling sound, like boulders falling in on each other. Without so much as a wave good-bye, Roibhilin disappeared behind the mound, leaving Brenna to stare at where he had once stood. She shook her head, closing her eyes for a moment in the late afternoon sun to try and clear her thoughts. When she opened them once more, the moon was rising high above her head, and bright stars dotted the sky.

"Oh, crap. Not again."

Brenna groaned as she recalled how time had sped up after her encounter with Nuala. Clearly, it'd happened again. Feeling more than a little disoriented, she began the difficult task of heading down the pitch-black mound. Brenna reached for her cell phone in her jacket, coming up empty save for a candy wrapper. She'd left her phone at home. Picking up her pace, she wondered how long it was going to take to get home by foot.

Chapter Six

Brenna was halfway down the mound when she heard her name being shouted. Pausing her somewhat rocky progress, she strained to listen. Again, she heard her name, close enough to recognize the voice.

"I'm over here!"

She heard a few branches snap from the shrubs to her left, and gave a sigh of relief when she saw Patrick making his way out of the trees toward her, a flashlight in hand.

"Patrick! I'm so glad you're he—"

"D'you not know what time it is, Brenna?"

"Huh?"

The grim look on his face told her that she was in more trouble than she had thought. She slowly shook her head and heard him mutter something under his breath before he grabbed her hand and led her to the main path she hadn't been able to find. The flashlight he carried in his other hand danced across the ground in front of them like an oversized firefly, lighting up rows of slender, white trees and thick copses of fern. Nervous, Brenna fiddled with her hair.

"Um, Patrick, just what time is—"

"It's gone on ten. You've been away for nearly five hours now."

"*What?*" Brenna's eyes widened and she dropped her fingers from her hair. "That's impossible! I was only on the mound for ten minutes!"

"You went *back*?" He sounded shocked.

"Well...I made a promise to someone that I would. Actually, I didn't have much choice in the matter."

"And you didn't think to tell me that beforehand?"

Brenna stumbled when he stopped short and turned to face her, the anger in his voice making her wince. In the distance, she could hear several different people calling out her name.

"Brenna, Deirdre thought you'd gone and fallen off something and broken your bloody neck. I understand you want to do whatever it is you're doing on your own, but that isn't how it works when you involve people who care about you. Think about that next time you plan on doing something so *stupid.*" He spoke without once raising his voice, but it was steeped in anger. The guilt Brenna felt melted away into annoyance, and she jerked her hand away from his.

"How was I supposed to know that time would hop like that?!" Brenna shot back, throwing her hands up in exasperation. "Why *did* it happen, Patrick? You seem to know everything. Why don't *you* tell me why I seem to have missed five hours just by blinking my eyes!"

"Brenna!"

Her mother's voice was close, and Patrick took hold of her arm, marching her down the last little stretch of hill.

"I've found her!" he shouted before lowering his voice once more. "Come to my house tomorrow, and we'll finish this discussion."

"Are you sure?" she muttered. "You don't seem like you want me to."

"What I'm wanting," snapped Patrick as they headed into the parking lot, "is for you to trust me enough to tell me things."

"Oh my God, Brenna! Are you all right?"

Rachel ran to her daughter with a crushing hug, tears in her eyes. Brenna was still reeling from Patrick's last comment, but she managed to hug her back. After a few moments, her mother pulled away, studying her from head to toe before placing a hard kiss on her forehead. Brenna's annoyance with Patrick fled, her guilt rising as she saw her mother's fingers shaking when she gripped her upper arms.

"Don't you *ever* scare me like that again! God, Brenna, why didn't you call me?!"

"I'm sorry, mom. I left my phone at home, and I…" She wracked her brain for a good excuse "I got lost in the woods. I'm so sorry."

If her mother saw through her lie, she didn't comment on it. Instead, she hugged Brenna again before slipping off her own jacket and placing it around her daughter's shoulders. An involuntary shiver ran through Brenna at the added warmth. She hadn't realized how cold she was.

"Thank God you're okay!"

Deirdre popped out from the other side of the bushes and, like Brenna's mother, hugged her within an inch of her life. When Brenna saw the tears of relief in the other girl's eyes, she felt even worse for her thoughtlessness. Patrick was right; she should have told someone where she was going.

"I told you she would be safe, Rachel. She's a very smart girl, your Brenna."

This comment came from Kathleen as she stepped out of the forest with Patrick's help. The old woman fixed her with a knowing look, and Brenna wondered just how much Patrick had told her. Kathleen smiled then, leaning heavily on her grandson's arm.

"But sure it's glad I am to see you safe from harm."

"I'm so sorry for worrying you all. Really."

Everyone expressed their relief, reassuring Brenna that she was more than forgiven—Patrick being the only exception. He hung back from the small group surrounding her, his hands stuffed in his pockets as he leaned against his truck, face hidden in shadow. After a few more minutes of hugs and explanations, Brenna was whisked home by her mother, receiving an earful about the importance of technology and how not to lose a cell phone. Though her mother joked around, Brenna could see the strain in her eyes and, when they arrived home, she gave her another hug.

"Mom, I'm sorry I worried you. I really didn't mean to."

"I know, honey. But when I heard you'd gone missing…" Rachel squeezed Brenna's hands. "I just remembered Egypt when you…you…" she choked on her words and then roughly rubbed a hand over her eyes. "Brenna, I would die if you were ever hurt again. Promise me you won't go anywhere without telling someone first or keeping a phone on you."

"I promise I'll never forget my phone again. I'm so sorry, mom."

Rachel smiled, hugging her tightly once more before pulling away, a weak smile on her face. "Why don't you go to bed? You must be tired. I know I am."

"Okay."

Walking toward her room, Brenna peeked over her shoulder to see her mother sink into the couch, pressing a hand to her head and looking as if she was shouldering the weight of the world. Biting her lip, Brenna stole quietly away to her room, promising herself that she would be careful the next time she met with Roibhilin. *Very* careful.

*　*　*　*

School went by excruciatingly slowly the next day, and Brenna was sure it was punishment for her recent escapade. As soon as school ended, Deirdre demanded a full report on what had happened. Brenna explained her made-up story on how she had gotten turned around in the forest between the mound and the castle, that it had gotten dark before she could properly find her way back.

"I thought you'd gone and died. Or run away from boredom!" exclaimed Deirdre as they exited out of the school building and toward the graveled parking lot.

"I would never do that, Deirdre—I promise. By the way," she shot her friend a sly look, seeing a good chance to change the subject, "how did things go with Patrick? I really did mean to only go away for a little bit, to give you guys some alone time."

"You might as well have asked me to spend time with a rock."

"What do you mean?"

Deirdre stopped short to look up at Brenna, a single dark brow raised and a knowing smile on her lips.

"C'mon, Brenna, did you think I wouldn't notice, then?"

"Notice what?"

"Janey Mack, you're a slow one!"

"Who's Janey Mack?"

"It's not a person," laughed Deirdre. "It's an expression. It means 'wow', or something like it. Don't you have a saying like that?"

"Usually we Americans just say 'wow'."

"Brenna."

As one, they turned to see Patrick making his way over to them, his expression as enigmatic as it had been the night before which didn't help settle Brenna's nerves any.

"I'm off for home then, Bren. I'll call you tomorrow." Deirdre patted her shoulder. "Good luck."

"Good luck with what?"

But Deirdre was already retreating to a small group of friends waving her over, pausing to say something to Patrick before slipping away. Brenna watched warily as he approached, a thoughtful look on his face.

"What did she say to you?"

"Nothing. Did you tell your mum to take you to my house, then?"

"Yeah." Brenna sighed, dreading the thought of going to Patrick's.

"Grand. I'll see you soon."

"Yeah. *Grand*."

A beeping horn announced her mother's arrival. With a toss of her books and the click of her seatbelt, Brenna and Rachel were on their way. For a few moments, Brenna thought she might escape the ride unscathed.

"So," her mother began brightly, and Brenna internally groaned; she had spoken to soon. "You seem to be spending a lot of time with Patrick. A *lot* of time."

"We're only friends, mom."

"Are you sure?" Her mother smiled and drummed her fingers on the wheel. "You know, Bren, you're sixteen. When I was your age—"

"I *really* don't want to hear about how many boys you made out with."

"When *I* was your age," her mother started again, "I had lots of boyfriends. *Tons*. And if you're thinking of getting a boyfriend, I think Patrick would be a fantastic catch!"

"Mom," Brenna said slowly, as if talking to a five year old, "it's not like that with Patrick and me. He's just a friend. And anyway, I won't be staying long enough to have a boyfriend."

She knew she must have made a good point, because her mother stopped asking her about Patrick and instead began to recite information from the new article that she was writing. By the time they arrived at Patrick's house, Brenna was more than grateful to get out of the car.

"I'll have dinner ready at six, all right? And no getting lost in the woods again. One heart attack per month is my absolute limit."

"Yes, mom. Bye."

After she had driven off, Brenna waited outside for Patrick. Kathleen was nowhere in sight and, save for the chickens frolicking in the beds of wild flowers, she was all by herself. Resting her hands inside her pockets, she looked past the house where the woods beyond stood watch. It gave her the creeps to be standing out in the open so close to them, knowing that somewhere in those woods an insane fairie with a sword and some poisoned arrows was waiting to kill her. Shivering, she jogged a couple of laps around the broad front yard to ward of the cold October air, stopping when she heard the familiar sound of Patrick's rusty truck coming down the lane. She winced when it came to a stop, white steam curling out from under the hood. Stepping out, he raised his hand.

"Sorry, I got held up by my coach."

"It's all right—I didn't wait long."

Patrick opened the door for her before following after, shutting it firmly behind them. Setting his keys on a nearby rickety table, he motioned for her to sit down on the sunken-in couch. She did so reluctantly. Looking anywhere but at her host, she tugged on her hair nervously.

"Where's your grandmother?"

"Visiting a friend down the road. Do you want anything to drink?"

"Um, water is fine." Brenna's fingers remained tangled at the end of her hair, the tension nearly undoing her as he went about getting a glass. She wasn't sure if he was still mad at her or if he simply wanted to discuss the weather. Giving one last worried tug, she let go of her hair and cleared her throat. If she was going to get yelled at, she'd rather not go through all this politeness.

"Patrick?"

"Yes?"

"I'm really, *really* sorry that I didn't tell you I had to go back to the mound yesterday. I just...I didn't want Deirdre following me. And I *had* to go back."

"You said that last night." Handing her the glass of water, he sat down in Kathleen's chair, leaning forward in a mirror image of his grandmother. "I offered to help you, but I can't do that if you go and lie and hide things from me. Especially when it comes to the Good Folk—

you don't know much about them, I'm thinking, and that's dangerous."

"I know. I mean…I'm starting to get that. They're a lot different from what I read in that folklore book, huh?"

"They are and they aren't."

Sighing, she slumped her back against the couch. "If I tell you everything that happened…do you promise not to run out of the house and call the police? Or the local insane asylum?"

"I do." His lips quirked up into a tentative smile, and Brenna took a large gulp of water before starting her story.

At first, it was hard to talk to Patrick about Nuala, the bird attacks, Roibhilin, and everything else—mainly because she felt crazy for saying it out loud—but the more she told him, the more understanding looking he became. He was, Brenna realized, probably one of the few people in the world who *could* believe her. After all, he'd lived with them once. When she was finished, he remained silent for several minutes, sitting so still that Brenna wondered if he'd turned into a statue. She was about to ask if he was all right when he stirred, his voice low.

"Brenna, did you never wonder why my grams spoke about the Good Folk when you first met?"

"Not really." She offered a teasing smile, trying to ease the mood. "I mean, it's Ireland. Leprechauns are your mascots or something, right?"

Patrick's lips quirked up slightly, but the smile disappeared just as quickly as it came. "The problems you have…they're beyond most of what I know."

"Oh."

"But gram can help you."

"Kathleen?" Brenna tilted her head, confused. "What can she do? I know she believes in the Good Folk and all, but…how can she help?"

Patrick clasped his hands together, looking slightly uncomfortable. "There's not really a good way to get 'round this. Gram is…well, she's a *ban feasa*."

"I'm sorry, a *what*?"

"A fairy doctor." His voice was quiet, no-nonsense.

"Wait, wait." Brenna leaned back, running her hands through her hair. "What's a fairy doctor? Does she treat the Good Folk or something?"

"No. They speak to her when they've a need to. They tell her when a body'll visit, how to get rid of curses if one's been placed on a human by the Gentry, or how to cure a person when they've a mysterious sickness. She's famous for having helped a barrister in England. Most people are half afraid of her, though." Patrick's eyes never left hers, his eyes more gold than green in the dimly lit room. "If you're going to go and get involved with these...beings, at least learn what you're dealing with. If there's any answers you're after, talk to gram instead of listening to things that might kill you."

Numbly, Brenna nodded her head, her thoughts flying miles ahead of her. They sat together in silence save for a clock ticking from somewhere in the living room. Patrick eventually rested back into his chair as Brenna absently took a sip of water, still trying to take in the fact that the frail, pale-eyed old granny held rendezvous with the Good Folk. Did that mean that she already knew what Brenna had been through?

"Now, about last night."

She darted a glance at Patrick over the top of her cup, suddenly guarded. "What about it?"

"I can't answer all of your questions, but I might have an idea of what happened to you on the mound. Did you go there before a between time?"

"A *what* time?"

Patrick rose and began to pace in front of the fire place. "As you may have noticed, time with the Good Folk is a bit...different."

"Only just a little."

The unamused scowl he shot Brenna had her hunching her shoulders in defense, and she averted her eyes back to the rim of her cup as she took another gulp of cold water.

"Time is slower for them—much slower. The only way you can meet with them and stay within our own time frame is to visit them at dawn or dusk, when it is neither day nor night; a between time."

"That must be why Roibhilin wants me to meet him at dusk on Friday."

"Aye. If you meet with them any time other than those, time here speeds up, so to speak." Patrick frowned, halting his walk around the living room. "I don't like that you're going alone to meet him. They're tricky, Brenna, and prone to hindering more than helping, most times."

"I've already made him promise to help." She wrinkled her nose. "I may not like him, but I do trust him enough to believe that he'll keep his word."

With a heavy sigh, Patrick sank down on the couch next to her, wiping his hands over his eyes.

"So, then...Nuala said to use this key to find a child of some sort and protect it. And this man—"

"Roibhilin."

"—is her son, and he's going to help you find this...girl?"

"Right."

"Do you know how to find her, or even *when* you have to find her?"

"No. Nuala started to say, but then that other fairie showed up and I couldn't hear her."

"Try and think back. I'd say it's fair important, if they're killing each other over a *leanbh*."

Closing her eyes, Brenna concentrated, calling back the memories she'd shied away from over the past week. She saw Nuala clearly in her mind, saw the forest and heard the birds screaming as they drew closer. Brenna frowned and opened her eyes.

"I didn't get all of it. But it sounded like 'sow' or 'say', or something like that."

"Samhain."

"'Sow-een'...that *sounds* like it might be it." She blinked at Patrick. "When's Samhain? Is it an Irish word for a month or something?"

"No." Patrick's mouth was set in a grim line. "It's the Irish word for Halloween."

"But that's in two weeks! How am I supposed to go to school, keep this all from my mom, find a kid, and *not* end up dead in two weeks' time?!"

"By acting quickly, I imagine."

"Gee, thanks." Slumping against the couch, Brenna glared at Patrick. "Do you have any ideas that are, you know, *useful*?"

"Sure, I'll think on it." Standing, he took Brenna's cup from her loose grasp. "For now, just read that book your mum gave you and study it as best you can. Maybe there's something in it that'll help. I wouldn't go 'round trying to read any more, though. Information about them has become…muddled. Honestly, it'd be best to just listen to my gram. I'll take you to the mound on Friday."

"Are you sure? Isn't it illegal for you to drive people around? Aren't you worried you'll get caught?"

"It'll be nearing dark, so there shouldn't be any problem." The sound of a car pulling up to the house made Patrick look through the window. "It's gram. I'll take you home now, Brenna." He headed for the door, grabbing his keys.

"Shouldn't we tell her about, well, all of this?"

"No, not now." He glanced out the window again, concerned. "She's looking fair shattered."

Brenna put a hand to her head. She was tired and her brain was stuffed too full of new information to try and understand the strange slang he was speaking. Grabbing her backpack, she slung it on and took a deep breath.

"Patrick?"

"Yeah?"

"Thank you for everything you're doing. Really." Quickly, she threw her arms around him in a tight hug. He hesitantly returned the embrace before pulling away and tugging open the door.

"Right." He cleared his throat. "Let's get on, then."

Brenna waved good-bye to Kathleen as she headed toward the truck, promising the elderly woman that she'd come back for tea in the near future. The ride home was relatively quiet, and Brenna appreciated the extra time to process everything she'd learned. When Patrick pulled up to her home, he put a hand on her shoulder as she opened the passenger door.

"D'you have the key on you?"

"Yeah, why?"

"For all the trouble it's causing, it might be better if you keep it on yourself at all times."

"I will."

After he'd pulled away and disappeared from sight, Brenna went inside to deal with her mother who barraged her with question after question about Patrick. After fending off her gossip-hungry mother with vague answers, she retreated to her room, locking the door in case of another attack. Wearily, Brenna flopped onto her bed, wincing as it groaned and squeaked under her weight. She thought of the science homework waiting for her but shied away from it. She was too tired to try and solve chemistry equations. Roibhilin's annoyed face flashed through her mind's eye, as did Nuala's.

Tears pricked Brenna's eyes as she placed a hand to the cheek Nuala's cold hand had touched. She was going to work with Roibhilin even if it killed her. Nuala had saved her life, had trusted her—had *believed* in her. Brenna blinked back the tears and took a deep breath. She wouldn't let her death be in vain. She was going to find that child, wherever she was, and make sure Treasach paid for what he had done.

"Brenna, dinner!"

Dropping her hand from her cheek, Brenna sat up at the sound of her mom's voice and snuck a glance at her face in the mirror. She didn't think she looked very much like a hero of old like Nuala had said, but then she hadn't believed in fairies until just last week.

"Brenna, if you're not out in ten seconds I'm calling Patrick and telling him you like him!"

"Mom, I'm coming!" Brenna shook her head and laughed. Who'd ever heard of great heroes who feared their own mothers?

* * * *

"'Come Friday before the last ray of sun is gone.' Well, here I am. I'm looking at the last rays of sun, and I don't see you, Roibhilin."

Brenna crossed her arms and scowled at the ground before giving it a few hard stomps with her booted foot. It had rained Thursday, and while it was clear Friday it was still cold and the ground was slick with mud from the previous day's downpour.

"For a guy so bent on punctuality, you sure take your sweet time." She pounded the ground again with her foot. "Are you even there?!"

The sunbeams that flickered over the hills and through the smattering of clouds began to wink out, and Brenna bit her lip. She was *not* going to get her time sped up again. Raising her foot, she decided to try one last time. If this didn't work, Roibhilin could wait until—

"Cease your tromping, human! Have you no sense of time?"

"*Me?*"

Brenna whirled around to see Roibhilin standing on the other end of the mound, glaring daggers at her.

"Aye, *you.*"

"I came exactly when you said to!"

"You came early." With an impatient twitch of his cloak, he gestured for Brenna to come forward. She took her time, knowing that it would annoy him. When she looked past one of his shoulders, she was more than surprised to see that the sun seemed to be stuck in one place.

"What happened to the light?"

"You're in the between. Did I not say that you had come early? I, on the other hand, have perfect timing."

"Well, good for you." Brenna took a deep breath, trying not to get too annoyed. "So, about my key—"

"My *mother's* key," came the defensive reply.

"Your mother's key. Did you know that she had it?"

"No." Roibhilin's gaze shifted away from her, unease in his eyes. "I am not entirely sure that I believe you, either, mortal."

"Again, it's *Brenna*," she ground out, resisting the urge to shout. "Why would I lie to you, anyway? Do you think I *want* to be here with a key and some freaky fai, er, Gentry trying to kill me for it? Or looking for a child that I don't even know *how* to find? Or why I didn't die of poi—"

"You are to find a child?" Roibhilin interrupted her, his own arms crossed. For the first time, he wasn't looking at her as if she were made of sludge. Instead, he appeared almost fascinated. *Well*, thought Brenna, *that's a step up from 'disgusted'*.

"Yes. Nual—your mother told me to take the key to find the *leanbh* and protect her. I thought that she'd meant a plant or something, but Patrick said—"

"Who is this…Patrick?"

"A friend."

"Hm."

Brenna rolled her eyes. Patrick had never interrupted her in all of their combined conversations as much as Roibhilin had done in the past five minutes. How was she supposed to explain everything if he kept chiming in with questions?

"Look," she said, uncrossing her arms, "all I know is that I have to use this key to find a child before Samhain."

Faster than it took to take in a breath, Roibhilin was upon her, gripping her upper arm up in a clasp that was far from gentle. His blue eyes had shifted to a darker shade, reminding Brenna of the dark, foreboding spots she'd seen in the ocean of Bermuda that warned of sudden drops in the sea floor. They were narrowed on her now, mistrust replacing the interest they'd held a moment ago.

"And did my mother tell you this?"

"Yes."

"Then we haven't much time. And you," he squeezed her arm painfully, "will do as I say without question."

"Excuse me, but you can't just tell me to follow you blindly and expect me to do it."

"You..." He released her arm suddenly, taking a step back as he drew himself up. "Never have I met a human who displays such disrespect for me."

"Well," snapped Brenna as she rubbed her arm, "maybe if you showed me a reason to respect you, I would."

Roibhilin's stunned expression and dropped jaw more than made up for her injured arm, and Brenna got the impression that not many people said 'no' to him. Barely able to hold back a grin, she placed her hands on her hips.

"So, how am I supposed to find this girl?"

"*I* will find her."

"But you need the key."

"I do not need a key. If there is a child in hiding, it will be in my mother's...in my forest, where she would be safe. I will send for you when I have need of you."

As if that decided the matter, Roibhilin turned and began to walk away. Brenna marched after him.

"Hey, you can't just decide that on your own! I need to go with you! Your mother's forest is here, isn't it?"

"It is and it isn't." He waved his hand impatiently. "You would only get in my way, human."

"It's *Brenna*!"

Her shout went unanswered, and she growled in frustration as he went around the mound and disappeared. She could feel a faint rumbling beneath her feet, and then all was still. Fists clenched together, Brenna whirled around, furious. Time resumed its normal pace, and the last dying rays of sunlight faded behind the hills. Taking the key from her jean's pocket, she held it up. It was warm, though quickly cooling off. She sighed, bringing it in closer for inspection. It grew hot to the touch every time she was near fairies; perhaps it was letting her know when they were around. Or maybe it worked whenever she was in danger—it was only when she'd been attacked that it really burned.

"Brenna?"

Looking up from the key, she waved as Patrick made his way onto the top of the mound, a flashlight in his hand. Tucking the key back inside her pocket, she made her way over to him.

"Did you meet with Roibhilin, then?"

"Yes. He's so annoying! Finding the girl is *my* job. I promised Nuala. And he…he…" she trailed off.

"He what?" Patrick narrowed his eyes. "Did he hurt you?"

"What? No." She speared her fingers through her soft hair. "Patrick, I read in the folklore book that the Good Folk live below ground. Is that true?"

"Well, some think that. Let's get you home, and I'll explain. It's getting a bit too dark out here."

He led her down the mound and back to the truck, the trip made easier thanks to his flashlight. Once inside and underway, Patrick cleared his throat, clearly a little uneasy with the conversation.

"It's thought that the mounds are the tops of fairie palaces below ground. But, generally speaking, they live amongst us, here."

"Then why can't people see them?"

"Why can't everyone see ghosts?"

"Um…"

Patrick looked sideways at her, smiling. "What, you believe in fairies, but not ghosts?"

"Well, I've *seen* fairies. Show me a ghost and I'll believe in them, too."

He laughed at her disgruntled tone, shaking his head. "Look. The Gentry live on earth, just…invisibly. It's sometimes referred to as the 'Veil'. Their forests, their roads and homes, they're on the same ground as ours, just separated. Do you see what I mean?"

"I'm trying to." She wrinkled her nose. "So, why do some people see them but some don't?"

"Some people stumble upon them, and others are born with the gift to see."

Brenna thought for a moment. "Like your grandmother."

"Yes."

"And you," she guessed more quietly this time.

Patrick's smile faded and he sighed. "Yes."

Brenna stared at him for several moments then smiled and patted his shoulder. "If it makes you feel better, *I* don't think you're crazy."

"And this coming from the girl dragging me off to fairie mounds."

They pulled up to her house, the warm, orange glow of light pouring from the windows invitingly. Brenna hopped out but then paused.

"Patrick, I need to ask you a huge favor. And…you might not like it."

"What is it?"

"I have to do something next weekend and, um…if I don't come home the first night, can you say that I'm staying at your house?"

He eyed her and she held her breath, wishing that he wasn't so difficult to read.

"Where is it that you're going, then?"

"Well…" Brenna shifted from one foot to the other. "I'm going to the woods by the mound. Roibhilin said that if the child was hidden, it would be on his land. I'm going to go there and search for her myself, since he won't let me go with him."

Patrick stared out the window of his lorry, his expression indiscernible. Brenna shifted on her feet again before he at last spoke into the silence, "I've a better idea. I'll go with you."

"But—"

"And that way," he continued on, "if you run into trouble, we can explain it a bit better. Besides, it'll make me feel better knowing you're not going alone."

Tears filled Brenna's eyes and she worked hard to blink them back. "You don't have to, Patrick."

"Sure, I want to. I'll see you 'round, then. Good night, Brenna."

"Night, Patrick."

As he drove off, Brenna wondered how she would ever be able to pay him back.

Chapter Seven

Between homework, making friends, and constantly checking every tree to make sure there weren't any small, black birds waiting to murder her hiding in the branches, the next two days flew by quickly. If Deirdre thought it was strange that Patrick was spending more time with them, she didn't say anything and instead warmly welcomed him into her circle of friends.

"So," said Deirdre on Friday as she caught up to Brenna after school, "what d'you say to a movie at my house tonight with the girls? My brothers have all gone 'round to their friends' places for the night, and da is working late. We could make a night of it with some gossip and drink!"

"Drink?" The way Deirdre said it had Brenna raising her brows. "As in alcohol?"

"Well sure, what else would it be?"

"Aren't we too young to drink?"

"Only if we get caught. C'mon Brenna—it'll be grand *craic*!"

Deirdre looped her arm through Brenna's. She tried to slow her pace when she saw that Deirdre was taking two steps for every one of her own.

"What *does* that word mean?! I've been hearing it all week, and I still can't figure it out. I just keep nodding my head and smiling…and feeling stupid."

"It means 'fun'! So, can you come?"

"I wish I could, but I have to study for my chemistry test. I'm really behind in that class, and my mom said she'd help me." Brenna held her breath, hoping that Deirdre wouldn't detect her lie.

"Well, if you're sure…" The other girl's smile dimmed some. "It won't be as fun without you."

"I'm sorry, Deirdre. But I promise we'll do something fun next weekend. There's my mom. I'll see you Monday."

"Sure. Bye, Brenna."

"Bye. And really, we'll get together next weekend!"

Hopping into her mother's car, she anxiously tapped her fingers against the doorframe as they drove home. She could feel her mom shooting questioning glances, and Brenna kept her gaze directed out the window. If she stayed quiet, maybe her mom would too.

"Any big plans for the weekend?"

So much for that theory. Brenna shook her head, her fingers absently tugging at her hair. "Not really. Well, Patrick is going to take me hiking in the woods tomorrow."

"The one behind the house?"

"No. A different one."

"I see."

They rode in silence, and Brenna began to wonder if mother really *did* see. She'd never lied to Rachel before, especially not in any big way like she was now. She shot a quick side glance at her mother, tapping her fingers against the car once more. The woman was being quiet. *Too* quiet.

"What are you up to this weekend, mom?"

"If you'd been listening to my thoughtful and detailed itinerary this morning on the way to school instead of sleeping, you'd remember that I'm going to be spending the next three days in Dingle chatting up the locals."

"Sorry for not being awake, but *some*one forgot to make coffee."

"Details, details." Her mom laughed, waving a hand dismissively. "Do you want to meet me there after you're done 'hiking' with Patrick?"

"I'd like to, but I really need to study for chemistry." She narrowed her eyes. "Mom, why did it sound like you were implying something else when you said 'hiking'?"

"Oh, did I?" She sounded deceptively innocent. Something was definitely up.

"Mom…"

"All I'm saying—"

"You didn't *say* anything."

"All I'm *saying*," continued Rachel as she made a sharp turn into their driveway, "is that you and Patrick have been spending a lot of time together."

"With Deirdre."

Rachel shot her an annoyed look then turned off the car. Unbuckling her seatbelt, she put her hands on Brenna's shoulders, her smile large and somewhat forced.

"Look, honey, I like Patrick. He's cute, he's a sports player, and he takes care of his grandmother."

"Okay…"

"So I totally understand why you want to go 'hiking' with him."

There was that emphasis again. Brenna frowned, trying to figure out where her mom was going with this. Then it hit her. Her eyes widened, and she put her hands up defensively, her cheeks turning bright red.

"Oh, no. Nononono…"

"Honey, there's no need to be embarrassed. I just want you to be safe—"

"Mom, we are *not* having this conversation. Ever. *Again*. Patrick is taking me hiking, *without* the emphasis."

She made a hasty retreat from the car and headed for cover in her room, her cheeks still burning in humiliation. Taking a few calming breaths, Brenna rubbed her hands on her cheeks, willing the blush to go away. Outside her door, she could hear her mother wheeling around her luggage before she came knocking.

"Brenna, I'm going now—can I come in?"

"Fine."

The door hinges creaked and Rachel popped her head in. "I'm sorry, Bren. I just wanted you to know that…that, well, if you want a boyfriend, you should have one."

"I know. But could you *please* stop trying to push Patrick on me? I only see him as a friend, and he feels the same way."

The look her mother gave her had 'I don't believe you' written all over it, but she smiled and nodded her head anyway.

"Whatever you say, Bren. Well, I'm off for Dingle. I'll see you Monday after school. Remember, Kathleen said that if it was raining she would drive you to school."

"All right."

"And Brenna?"

"Hmm?"

"Call me if you need anything, okay?"

"I will. Love you, mom."

"I love you too, honey."

Brenna sat on her bed for several minutes. Without her mother bustling around or making some type of witty—and loud—comment to herself, the house seemed empty. Lonely.

"Okay, Brenna, time to get ready," she told herself.

Standing up, she opened the dresser drawer where she had stuffed the ankle-high, leather shoe the leprechaun had made. The green material was soft, pliable, and looked expensive. She sank down on her bed, holding the gift between her hands as she went over her plan. Patrick had said that time got weird unless it was dawn or dusk, but what if the shoe acted as sort of barrier? She'd read a story in her folklore book about a person who'd worn a cape, and time hadn't sped up for him. It stood to reason, then, the shoe would do the same thing. She hoped so, anyway.

Setting it aside, Brenna took up her brush from the tiny dresser, staring at her reflection in the mirror above it. Green eyes and a worried, somewhat pale face stared back at her. She dragged the brush through her long, blonde hair, wincing when it hit a knot. She *really* hoped that she was right about the shoe.

* * * *

"Patrick, are you *sure* we're going the right way?"

"What, doubting me already, are you then?"

"No, it's just…" She looked down at the tree stump they'd already passed three times. "I'm pretty sure that we've gone this way before."

Patrick stopped in the small clearing and put his hands on his hips, grimacing as he turned in a slow circle. Brenna took the chance to catch her breath and sat down on the stump. They had started out in a forest only a few miles past the mound and the castle, taking the bus to get there. Patrick had assured her that the woods had a creek that led to a tunnel and that it was said there was an entry way into the fairie world there. It was a little past noon now, and they'd been walking in circles for nearly three hours. Patrick groaned and then sat down next to her, kicking at a stick as he did so.

"I was just here a few weeks ago, with gram. I was sure it was here."

"Maybe you just forgot where it was."

"I didn't." Slapping his hands on his knees, Patrick stood up. "Right, c'mon then. I know the way this time."

With a sigh, Brenna trudged after him. They walked deeper into the woods, and it became cooler and darker as thick, ancient moss-covered branches blocked out most of the light. All around them, small twigs snapped and leaves rustled as birds and squirrels scampered in the canopy above. Patrick stopped short, holding up one hand.

"Do you hear that?"

"Hear what?"

"Water. This way."

Without waiting for her to catch up, he began to pick his way quickly over rocks and ankle-deep piles of dead leaves, pushing branches of ferns out of his way while Brenna jogged to keep up with him. They stopped only when a creek came into view. It was fairly wide and deep, and its dark waters moved swiftly, creating little eddies where rocks jutted out at the sides. They followed alongside its length for a few hundred feet before it went under a naturally formed tunnel of earth. Patrick grinned, wiping sweat from his brow.

"I told you it was here."

"You were right, O fearless leader. I'll never doubt your abilities again."

With a laugh, he slapped a heavy hand on her back, clearly proud at his achievement. *Boys*, Brenna decided, *really must be simple creatures*.

"All right, now it's my turn."

Sitting down, Brenna took off her left sneaker before shrugging out of the backpack she'd been carrying.

Patrick looked puzzled. "What do you mean?"

"You know how you said our time only meets theirs during in between times?"

"Yes…" he said slowly, a note of suspicion in his voice.

"Well, I think I know how to create my own time."

After a few moments of digging, Brenna produced the green shoe. She smiled triumphantly.

"Is that the shoe the leprechaun gave you?"

"Yeah. If I'm right, then I'll be able to see both worlds at the same time. I think." She slipped her foot into the shoe, discomforted by the fact that it fit so perfectly. Standing up, she dusted off her jeans.

Patrick eyed the shoe carefully. "Are you sure it'll work?"

"Not really. But there are a few stories of people who wore objects made by the Good Folk and managed to keep time the same, so I figure there has to be *some* truth to it."

For several minutes, they stood there and waited for something to happen.

"Do you see anything, then, Brenna?"

"No."

Closing her eyes, Brenna put her hand on the key. She had strung it on a chain and looped it around her neck the night before. It was warm, but not searing. That had to mean something.

C'mon…someone…something…show me that you're here.

For a few moments, nothing happened, and then a wind rose, gentle and cold. It brought with it what sounded like voices. She closed her eyes tighter, straining her ears to make sense of the whispers. Voices, light and joyful, came as suddenly as if they had always been there. Over and over they said her name, whispering close to her and then far away. They sounded like crystals clinking together.

"Brenna," a small voice called into her left ear, "Brenna. Welcome home. Welcome home."

The words were copied and repeated by hundreds of other voices in laughing tinkles, so real that Brenna had to open her eyes. There looked to be hundreds of dandelion fluffs flitting around her and the forest. It took her a moment to realize that they were glowing and changing shape. One landed gently on her shoulder, a tiny little being of light and unknown gender. The creature was only a couple of inches high, and it smiled up at her.

"Welcome home, Brenna Morgan of *Coillearnach*."

"Patrick, are you seeing this?"

"Seeing what?"

She looked at him with wide eyes. Small beings were landing on him by the dozens; a few were even sliding down his arms. Brenna laughed.

"I don't know what they are. They're tiny balls of light…sort of."

"Pixies."

"Is that right? I thought pixies were supposed to be like Tinkerbell or something." Brenna giggled as a few flitted around her face. She opened her hands, and several landed on her palms, mimicking her laugh. Patrick smiled.

"Most pixies come from trees and flowers. These must belong to the woods here, I'm thinking. I take it the shoe is working, then?"

"I guess so! But why are they welcoming me home? I've never been here before."

Walking slowly, she began to make her way up the creek where a tree had fallen and created a makeshift bridge. She put her foot on it and then stopped when the pixies swarmed her, pulling at her hair and lightly pinching her cheeks.

"No!" cried the one on her shoulder, and the rest echoed the word in quivering wails. Brenna paused then took her foot off of the log.

"Why? What's on the other side?"

"Something bad. Bad."

Again, the pixies mimicked each other's words, fear in their voices. Out of the corner of her eye, Brenna saw something crawl up the base of a tree trunk next to her. She turned her head, giving a shout of surprise when a small, stick-like creature stuck its face inches from hers. Its large, oblong eyes were completely black, and while human in shape, it was emaciated, brown skin made of bark and hands curled like talons. It opened its mouth and a thin, creaking voice came forth.

"Do not go, Brenna Morgan."

"Why?"

"That is where the goblins are."

Goblins…" The pixie on her shoulder shuddered at the word and left its vantage, joining the other glowing beings as they banded together, shaking in fear as they echoed one another.

"Hurt," they said in one voice. "Goblins hurt…"

The strange, stick-like pixie skittered the rest of the way up the tree, blending into the bark. Brenna licked her lips nervously and examined the other side of the creek. She couldn't distinguish anything save for some trees and another clearing. Goblins or not, she needed to find the child—or at least Roibhilin.

"Brenna, is something wrong?"

"No." She turned to Patrick who stood several feet away. She gave him a bright smile, trying to look braver than she actually felt. "We just have to go across this trunk. Patrick, iron keeps fair—dang it, I mean the Good Folk—from hurting me, right?"

"Generally. Why, is there something over there?"

"Um, not that I can see. But I'm going to find out. I'll be right back."

"Brenna, wai—"

Tucking the key under her shirt, she dashed across the fallen trunk, landing on her knees when she reached the muddy bank on the other side. Scrambling up, she swiped at the mud on her jeans.

"I'm fine! Patrick, are you coming?"

Brenna looked across the dark water and frowned. Patrick was gone, and she could no longer see the pixies hovering in the air. She attempted to scurry up the small, muddy embankment, but her feet slid on the slippery leaves and mud. Grabbing hold of a jutting stone and a sturdy-looking fern, she pulled herself up the incline, taking a moment to inspect the relatively flat patch of land ahead before turning around to scan the other side of the creek.

"Patrick? Ow!"

Brenna hissed in pain as the key burned the skin on her chest, and she pulled it out from under her shirt. It was still the same color, but it felt as if it had just been through a fire. She heard a grunting sound from somewhere behind her, and she ran as quietly as she could to hide behind an ancient oak tree. Pressing her back against its moss-covered bark, she rested her head against the wide trunk, grateful for the low, heavy hanging branches that hid her well.

"Mind where ye swing yer arm, there!"

"Well sure, if *ye* mind where yer walkin'! That was me foot!"

The male voices were rough, as if they were talking with rocks stuffed in their cheeks. Brenna pressed a hand to her mouth to keep herself from breathing too loudly, and her heart beat wildly as every hair on her body stood on end. She closed her eyes briefly, working up the courage to move. Slowly, so as not to make any noise, she inched up the tree trunk to get a better view.

Through the large ferns and trees, two portly, pig-like creatures came tromping into view, walking close together. Their large feet and legs were covered in coarse hair, and their jaws sprouted teeth that poked out of large, fat lips. Their black eyes were beady, and a shag of hair that looked like a horse's mane ran down each of their backs. Brenna started to wish that she hadn't looked.

"I don't see why," complained the taller of the two as it dug into the ground with an oversized hand, "we have ta go 'round diggin' all by ourselves. D'ye suppose the Master meant wot he said? 'Bout giving us humans?"

"He's no reason to lie to us, for we'd gut him first, eh? 'Ere now, mind how you dig! Wot if ye dig too deep and take the *leanbh's* head clean off? She'd be no good to us then, eh?"

"Why don't ye dig yerself, then?!"

They're looking for the child? Brenna's breath caught in her throat. She could only assume that the fairie that had killed Nuala—Treasach—was their master. Personally, if she were them, she wouldn't be so cocky as to think that he could be easily maimed. The two creatures grunted and dug for a while, creating several holes and uprooting small trees while they cursed and heckled one another.

"'Ow many holes have we been diggin', then?"

"Sure, as if I knew, eh! All I know is we're ta find the wee lass alive before Samhain."

"Oooh, Samhain." The tall one made a sound that Brenna presumed was a laugh but sounded much more gruesome. "D'ye remember when we used to go out then? Back when them fleshy mortals used to fear us? All those wee yummy children…"

"If we find this child, we'll have all the children we want. Remember how them mothers used to scream an' beg? This year we'll have our right proper place back, when Treasach sacrifices the wee lass and her blood is on the floor, eh?" Suddenly, the two paused in their work to lift their bulbous noses and sniff the air.

"Ye smell that, eh?" the tall one asked, rising from his slouched position.

"Aye…" agreed the other.

"*Iron*."

Brenna glanced down at the key and quickly stuffed it down under shirt despite the burning sensation. She could hear their giant feet shuffling through the leaves on the forest floor, and she crawled up higher into the tree. The two creatures were perhaps half the height of herself, but she wouldn't want to get caught by them, judging by the trees they had felled and deep holes they'd just created. Slowly, she looked over at the trunk that crossed the creek and nervously pulled at a strand of her hair. If she could find a way to distract them, she could make a run for it. She searched for something to throw then smiled when she saw that a heavy, short branch on the verge of breaking off was within her reach. Carefully, she pulled and twisted it, nearly giddy with relief when it fell into her hands.

She waited until they were close to her tree before throwing the branch as far as she could. It sailed through the air and landed with a spray of leaves a few hundred feet away. The two goblins trundled through the woods in the branch's direction, snorting and grunting like the pigs they resembled. Shimmying down as quickly as she could before jumping the last few feet from the tree, Brenna ran for the fallen trunk, adrenaline lending her an extra burst of speed. Behind her, she could hear the goblins give a unified roar, but they were too far and fat to catch up to her easily. She had gotten one foot onto the trunk when something tugged hard at her hair and she slammed to the forest floor, landing on her back. Dazed and gasping for breath, she blinked several times before her vision came into focus. Above her, Treasach smirked, his wavy, dark hair hanging around his face. His sword was raised above his head, the tip glinting menacingly.

"Foolish mortal," he said in an almost friendly voice. "You really should have run away when you had the chance."

He brought his sword down, and it was only by a few inches that he missed striking Brenna as she rolled away. He cursed and brought his sword back up as she scrambled to her feet.

"You're a fast little thing, aren't you?"

Brenna stuck out her chin stubbornly. How she wished that she'd though to bring some kind of weapon with which to defend herself. She took a step back, and Treasach aimed his sword at her throat, shaking his head.

"Ah, ah—I wouldn't do that if I were you. My friends, you see, are very hungry. Famished enough to eat even you, I think."

A few feet behind her, the two goblins laughed their awful laughs—if the sound could be called that—and the smell of rotting fish emanating from them caused her stomach to churn sickeningly. Tears welled in Brenna's eyes at the stench. How could she escape? She glanced around, searching for anything to defend with.

"Tell me, Brenna Morgan, why I shouldn't just kill you right here?"

"Well, why don't you?"

Treasach laughed, but his eyes were cold and his sword stayed targeted on her. "Because it pleases me to see you afraid. I assume, then, that you have the key?"

She remained silent, balling her fists at her sides. Treasach's smile faded away and he made his way toward her, lowering his sword a bit. She only managed to take a few steps back before she was stopped by one of the goblins. With a grunt, he pushed her forward with one heavy, overly large hand.

"It seems to me, mortal, that we can clear this up quite easily. Give me the key and you can go home unharmed."

"Is that what you promised Nuala?"

He gave a small hiss and leaned in close. "You have an insolent tongue and much stubbornness. I can see why Nuala chose you."

Brenna pursed her lips and jerked her head back. She couldn't fight him outright...but the goblins didn't seem to be the smartest things in the world.

"Did you know," she said, following her instincts to turn and make eye contact with the ugly creatures, "that this man doesn't intend to keep his word? You won't get any children at all. He's going to keep them all for himself."

"Oh, he is now, is he?" The shorter goblin glanced at her doubtfully.

"Yes. He said that you two were too stupid to ever figure it out. That you wouldn't—"

"Enough!" Treasach's voice boomed angrily, and the two goblins looked first at each other then back to Brenna, their beady black eyes glittering with a light that sickened her.

"Ye know…" said the taller one thoughtfully, "I never did get any rewards the likes o' which his kind offered us before."

"Now that ye mention it, I do remember being tricked awhile back ago, eh…"

The two shoved Brenna aside, and Treasach's anger was momentarily replaced by surprise. Without waiting to see what would happen, Brenna made a break for it. She shuddered when she heard a thunderous clap, as if lightning had struck the ground. Pushing her way through the trees, she kept the river in view while she desperately searched for another place to cross. She screamed when the sleeve of her shirt was grabbed roughly and ripped, causing her to tumble to her hands and knees. Before she could stand, another hand yanked her hair, forcing her head to jerk up. The tip of Treasach's blade pressed into the side of her exposed neck, and Brenna's breath came out in ragged gasps. From his position behind her, Treasach made a tsking sound.

"It seems that I underestimated you, Brenna Morgan. I do hate to be wrong. Now, give me the key I smell hanging 'round your neck."

Brenna was too spent to feel afraid, and she struggled to her knees, wincing when the blade nicked her skin and sent a burning pain up her neck.

"No."

"I do *not*," he said between clenched teeth, "have time for your impudence."

Treasach pulled her hair harder, forcing her to stand. Blinking back tears, she tried another tactic.

"If you tell me why you want it, I'll give it to you."

"Do you think me stupid enough to tell you anything?"

"I was counting on it, yeah."

An unnatural growl released itself from his throat, and he jerked her hair to the right, forcing her to turn around and face him. His eyes widened slightly as he stared at her exposed collarbone where her shirt had ripped.

"She has marked you." The tip of his blade nicked her skin once more and she flinched. "Give me the key, and this will all go away."

Brenna thought of Nuala who had given her own life for the key. She couldn't let her sacrifice be in vain. And if this was how he was treating her, what would Treasach do to the little girl? Brenna balled her fists again.

"I will *never* give you the key. And when the time comes, *you're* going to be the one with a sword at his throat."

Treasach laughed and removed the blade from her neck. *He's going to deliver the final blow*, Brenna thought grimly.

"Such bravery from one about to die. Mortals…in all my life I could never understand how they contained so much courage in such weak bodies."

"It's because there isn't any courage in *you*." She put every ounce of defiance she could into her eyes, jutting out her chin stubbornly. "And you never will."

She kicked out, barely grazing his shin as she struggled to pull away. With little effort, Treasach twisted her hair around his fist and yanked hard, causing her to cry out.

"It is a pity, Brenna Morgan, that my master is not here to witness this. Your death would have been much approved of."

Closing her eyes, Brenna waited for the blade to hack into her, but instead she felt the hold on her hair loosen. Opening her eyes, she squinted when she saw what looked like shimmering air a little ways away—much like how it looked on a hot, distant road—and from it emerged a familiar figure.

"Roibhilin?"

He looked angrier than she'd ever seen him, and he was running at them with alarming speed. Her relief and surprise was short-lived as she realized with growing horror that the sword he had drawn was aimed not at Treasach but at her. Brenna's jaw dropped before she snapped it shut again, struggling with renewed effort to get away from Treasach.

"I knew it," she muttered before raising her voice to a shout, "I never should have trusted you!"

Roibhilin ignored her words, and she hissed when Treasach

wrenched her hair again. She saw his face for a brief moment, surprised to see that he seemed just as shocked as she was. Roibhilin was upon them now, his sword raised high above his head before he swung it down, and only then did Brenna shut her eyes, wishing she'd never listened to the leprechaun.

Chapter Eight

Overhead, she heard the clash of steel as she fell sprawling to the floor. Eyes wide, she scrambled up, alive and with her head still attached to her neck.

"You stupid girl!" shouted Roibhilin as he held up his sword to defend a blow from Treasach, "Run!"

Brenna put a shaking hand to her hair. Most of it was gone, scattered around the orange and brown leaves at her feet while what little remained fell about her shoulders in an uneven chop. Tears welled in her eyes. Her hair was *gone*.

"Mortal!" Roibhilin shouted, breaking her out of her daze. "Did I not say to run?!"

With a furious cry, Treasach lunged at her, and Roibhilin barely made it in time to parry the blow.

"I do not have time for this, human—go to the water!"

She sprang into action then, rushing down the embankment toward the creek while Roibhilin followed, blocking blow after blow from Treasach. At least, that's what it sounded like, judging by the ringing metal she could hear echoing behind her. She skidded to a stop when she reached the water's edge, grabbing onto a tree branch to keep from falling in. Frantic, she glanced over her shoulder at Roibhilin—he was close on her heels. Brenna scanned the length of the deep, rushing water but saw no immediate way to cross.

"What do I do?"

"By the moon and stars, human—*swim!*"

Without warning, Roibhilin kicked her in the back, sending Brenna flying into the freezing water. Despite the surprise, she quickly surfaced, her feet skidding over rocks in the swift current. She could see Roibhilin's foot slip as he pushed against the blade bearing down on him, yelling something in his sing-song language. The current was faster than she had anticipated, and she was dragged back down into the depths several times, drawing her attention from the fight to the fact that she couldn't breathe. Her jeans and boots weighed her down as the freezing water began to rapidly numb her body. She struggled to stay afloat, but her arms were tired and every time she came up for breath she found herself choking on more water than air.

Her body was so frozen that she barely felt the hands that grabbed her and dragged her to the muddy bank. Coughing and hacking, Brenna rolled onto her hands and knees, her body shivering as a heavy hand thumped her back.

"Jesus, Brenna, are you all right?"

"P-Patrick? W-where were y-you?"

"Me? Sure, I was standing here waiting for you! You were halfway across the trunk when you disappeared." Patrick quickly shrugged out of his coat and wrapped it around her.

"T-thank you."

Teeth chattering, Brenna sat down to look at her feet, relief pouring through her when she saw that the leprechaun's shoe was still there. Her gaze went back across the creek, and she felt a shudder go down her spine. Not a leaf was misplaced, nor were Roibhilin or Treasach anywhere to be seen. Beneath her shirt, the key was a mellow warmth, and the tiny, light-filled pixies were slowly coming out of hiding from amongst the canopy of trees. Patrick placed a hand on her shoulder, causing her to jump.

"What happened? Your hair—"

Putting a hand to her head, she combed her fingers through the uneven tresses.

"You mean you didn't you see or hear anything?"

"No, nothing."

With Patrick's help, Brenna stood on shaky legs. All around her, the pixies flitted in the air and whispered consoling words. She closed her eyes and shook her head, trying to clear her mind.

"Brenna, what was it that I wasn't seeing?" Patrick frowned. "The way you went flying into the creek—and your hair—"

"I'll tell you when I get home. Oh!" She looked up at Patrick. "What time is it? Was I gone long?"

"No more than an hour. It seems the shoe works to stop time speeding up, then."

"Yeah…it does."

The green shoe on her foot was soaked through and cold but didn't look the worse for wear. Hysterical laughter bubbled forth before it dissolved into tears—at least one thing had gone right that day. Brenna clutched at the jacket while Patrick carefully led her out of the woods, remaining silent. Behind her, the pixies darted about and echoed her cry.

* * * *

"He *kicked* you?"

Brenna winced as Patrick slammed his mug of tea down hard on the table, and she nervously tapped her fingers against her own cup. Fresh from a hot shower and a change of clothes, Brenna now found herself sitting in her cottage living room with Patrick, relating all that had happened. Up until this moment, he had been nothing but attentive and quiet.

"Well," she said, feeling the need to defend Roibhilin's actions, "I wouldn't have lived if he hadn't."

"Sure, he could have broken your back and you're calling it 'saving your life'." He scowled when she laughed. "'Tisn't funny, Brenna."

"I'm sorry." Contrite, she took a sip of tea to cover her smile. "Anyway, what I want to know is why I disappeared."

"You crossed over the Veil, I'm thinking."

"That's what separates our world from theirs, right?"

"Yes." Patrick ran a hand through his hair, clearly frustrated. "I couldn't see it…or the pixies."

"And that worries you?"

"Normally I *do* see them."

"Oh."

Sighing, he stood up. The sky outside was turning gray with the fading sun, and clouds traveled low and dark with the promise of rain.

Brenna put a hand to her hair for the twentieth time, grimacing when she grabbed nothing but air. She'd done a quick job of evening out the locks in the bathroom, and the blonde hair just barely fell onto her shoulders now. It was devastating to know that it was gone, but she supposed that it was better than being decapitated. Returning her palms to her mug and warming them there, she studied Patrick pensively.

"Uh, Patrick?"

"What?" he continued to stare through the glass rather than face her, his stiff posture difficult to decipher.

"There *is* something I didn't mention. I don't know what to make of it, but I think maybe you might."

Turning away from the window, he sat back down in a wingback chair, hazel eyes reflecting the firelight and casting a strange look onto his face. Brenna wished she knew what he was thinking.

"Before he tried to kill me, the…man told me that his master would have liked to see me die. I mean…what kind of Good Folk would want to see someone die? Don't they mostly like people?"

"From what gram has told me, the Gentry both love and hate humans depending on their desires and emotions that day. The same Good Neighbor that gave you gold one day could take offence over something slight and curse you the next. If there's one who would love to see you die…well, I've no idea why. Perhaps you've gone and insulted one on accident."

"Maybe Roibhilin might know."

"No. You'll not go to him again."

Brenna's eyes widened at Patrick's firm tone. Clearly, he wasn't seeing reason. "I have to. He's the only one who can help me. Plus, he saved my life, so he must be more trustworthy than we thought."

"I don't care if he can make gold fall from the sky—you're not to see him again."

"Hey," Brenna set down her cup, frowning. "If you don't like what I'm doing, then you can just stop helping me. But you don't get to tell me what I can or can't do."

They sat in tense silence for several moments, eyes locked, stubbornness etched across both their faces. Finally, Patrick looked away to stare into the fire. Brenna slumped against her chair, feeling a headache coming on. She reached up and tried to rub out the ache in her head, and Patrick glanced her way.

"I'm sorry," he mumbled.

"What? I don't think I heard you all the way over here."

"I'm sorry," he repeated and leaned back, not looking pleased but not looking angry, either. "I *do* want to help you, Brenna. I just don't like the idea of you going to the mound by yourself with all that's happened. When you go back, I'm going with you."

"But—"

"And you're not to go anywhere alone again."

"Patrick—"

"At least not until this is over." The look he gave her was so stern that Brenna meekly nodded her head. Patrick stood up, grabbing his now-dry coat from the back of the couch. "I'll make sure gram picks you up for school on Monday, and I'll check on you tomorrow morning."

Brenna walked him to the door then paused before opening it.

"Hey…"

"What?" The one word was suffused with so much weariness that Brenna felt guilt rise up at the question she was about to ask.

"Um…I do have *one* little favor to ask."

"Does it have anything to do with going into the woods again?"

"No."

"Then what is it?"

"Could you go to town with me tomorrow? I need to find a pair of shoes that will match the one the leprechaun gave me. I don't think I can risk having it off anymore."

"I'll come 'round nine."

"Thank you."

Nodding his head, he made his way to the truck, and Brenna waited until the glowing, red taillights faded from sight before shutting the door. A gentle rain began to fall outside and, with a yawn, she trudged back to the couch to lay down, wishing that her mom was home.

* * * *

"Bajeebus, Brenna! What happened to your hair?!"

The words were the first ones of out Deirdre's mouth Monday

morning, and Brenna smiled, though it was a bit strained. She touched her hair self-consciously.

"What, you don't like it?"

"Well…" Deirdre titled her head, her hands on her hips. "It's just that your hair was so pretty. But sure, you look fair handsome now as well! I just wish you'd let me cut it. Does your mum know about this, then?"

"Not…exactly."

With a low whistle and wide eyes, Deirdre walked up the stairs toward Brenna's class.

"Will she be mad, d'you think?"

"Probably."

"I don't know that I'd want to see your mum angry. Hey, those are odd shoes."

Brenna looked down. She had kept the leprechaun's shoe on and managed to find an almost identical boot at a shop Patrick had taken her to on Sunday. She had dyed the leprechaun's leather shoe black to match the new one, and though it looked a bit odd, it wasn't completely unconventional. They weren't green, at least.

"I found them in a store. They were so comfortable that I forgot I'd put them on this morning."

"Well sure, don't let the teachers see them; you'll get in trouble. I'll see you in PE, then."

With a quick hug and a wave, Deirdre rushed off to her own classroom. Brenna spent the next two hours trying to pay attention to the lectures but found herself staring at her shoes and wondering if it had been such a good idea to wear them after all. On the one hand, she didn't want to get in trouble with the school, but on the other she didn't want to come across a fairie and have time speed up again. She figured that it was better to be safe than sorry.

By the time PE rolled around, Brenna was feeling antsy and welcomed the warm-up jog around the field in back of the school. In the center of the field, several groups of boys were practicing football and the girls had to dodge misfired balls several times, raising catcalls and whistles from the players.

"Boys," huffed Deirdre as they jogged, "are just about the stupidest creatures on earth."

"Well, they must be good for something."

"If I find a good reason," laughed Deirdre, "I'll tell you straight away."

Above them, soft, puffy clouds scuttled by, and bits of blue sky and sunlight peeked through every so often. The weather was as changeable as the sea, and Brenna closed her eyes, enjoying the brief moments of sunlight. Before long, she had far outpaced the other girls as her body found its rhythm, her worries and stress fading away with each step her booted feet took.

The key around her neck suddenly turned hot, breaking her concentration. Slowing down, she glanced to her right where the long stretch of trees she and Deirdre had run through the week before stood. She saw nothing for a few moments, and then a glimmer caught her eye. Brenna wondered if perhaps it was just a piece of trash when she saw another flash appear, then another, each one flitting and dancing around the outskirts of the tiny forest like dust in sunlight. Pixies.

Brenna picked up her pace again, briskly rubbing her arms. She didn't have time to deal with pixies. The key beneath her shirt suddenly flared to life again, hotter than before but not enough to burn her skin. Jerking her head back, she scanned the woods again, nearly tripping over her own feet as she did a double take and came to a halt. Roibhilin stood at the edge of the woods, his green cloak making him almost impossible to see were it not for his bright gold hair. His face was set with displeasure—*when is it not?* Brenna wondered—his arms crossed and legs spread apart as if he were a ship's captain. Several girls ran between them, taking no notice of the cloaked fairie standing only twenty feet away.

"Brenna, are you all right?"

Deirdre came to a stop next to her, her cheeks bright pink and her normally wavy hair frizzing in every direction. Brenna's body seemed rooted to the spot, and for the life of her she wasn't sure if she could move.

"I'm fine."

Roibhilin motioned for her to come and she shook her head, which in turn caused him to narrow his eyes further.

"Sure, you sound as fine as I look!"

"No, really—I'm fine. I just didn't realize how fast I'd been running."

Reluctantly, she broke contact with the fuming fairie and began jogging again, Deirdre at her side. Brenna glanced back at the woods, more than a little surprised to find that Roibhilin hadn't moved so much as an inch. She was sure that he would have lost patience and left by now. She rolled her shoulders uncomfortably and continued running. By the time she was on her second lap, she was well ahead of everyone else once more and Roibhilin continued to eye her with annoyance. With a sigh, Brenna made a sharp right and entered the woods, realizing that he wasn't going to go away just because she was ignoring him. Walking past Roibhilin's unamused form, she made her way through the small forest until she was hidden by trees and could no longer see the field or the people in it.

"I thought," Roibhilin said in his usual put-out tone, "I told you that I am not accustomed to waiting on humans."

"Then I guess you'll just have to keep on being unaccustomed." She spun around, taking a few rapid steps back when she came nose to chest with Roibhilin. She looked up at him and crossed her arms in front of herself protectively, her green eyes mirroring his irritation. "And might I ask what you're doing at my school where anybody could see you?"

"No one can see me, and well you know it."

He looked tense, and there was a tightness about his mouth that Brenna hadn't seen before. He seemed almost…uneasy. Uncrossing her arms, she tilted her head slightly to one side. He clearly didn't like being here anymore than she did, and the sooner she spoke to him the sooner they could both leave. Besides, hadn't she wanted to speak to him about what had happened by the creek?

"Why did you come?"

"I wanted to know what foolish and stupid thing you did to anger Treasach."

"Excuse me?"

"Treasach." He tapped his foot impatiently. "My…mentor, I think is what you mortals would call it. He is normally very patient, and so I can only rightly assume that you did something foolish for him to treat you as he did. Angering him will only make it harder for me to keep my word to you, for when he gets in a foul mood I am the one who must suffer for it. You were very lucky that I was able to calm him down."

The world went still then it spun rapidly and Brenna found herself sitting on the mossy floor, trying to comprehend the enormity of the situation. Roibhilin nudged her with his foot.

"Are you to be sick then, human? Have you finally realized the mistakes you've made?"

"Oh, my God." Brenna dragged shaking fingers through her hair as she looked up at him with wide eyes. "Roibhilin…I…I…" she couldn't finish her sentence. The words were stuck in her throat and she felt hot and cold all at once.

"If you wish to retch, I would recommend you wait until I am gone."

"No, you don't understand. I…I think you're in danger."

Hastily, the fairie took a healthy step back. Brenna slapped her hands against the ground in frustration.

"I'm *not* going to be sick on you!" She narrowed her eyes when he took another step back, clearly not trusting her words. "Look, I know I said I'd tell you who killed your mother if you helped me, but…but things are different now."

"What do you mean by that?"

"I mean," said Brenna, not quite able to meet Roibhilin's gaze, "that Treasach is the one who killed your mother. And I think…I think maybe he might try to kill you, too. Especially now that he knows you're helping me."

For a moment, nothing greeted her announcement but silence, and Brenna hunched her shoulders as she stared down at the mossy floor, knowing what a terrible blow this had to be for him. First his mom, and now his mentor? Brenna couldn't think of a crueler thing to tell him. She couldn't imagine how angry she would be if she'd been told something like that. A pixie floated in front of her, bobbing up and down and mimicking her expression before flitting away when Roibhilin let loose a loud laugh. Brenna looked up at him, bewildered.

"What's so funny?"

"You and your ridiculous lies."

"I'm not lying."

"Am I to believe, then, that Treasach—who has helped raise me as if I was his own son—killed my mother?"

"I have no reason to lie to you, Roibhilin. I just freed you from helping me. Why would I do that if I was lying?"

Slowly, his smile left his face and his eyes changed from bright blue to a near black. Before Brenna could blink, he was upon her, lifting her by her shirt with one hand to dangle her above the ground. She tried to kick at him, but he held her farther away, and for the first time since she'd met Roibhilin, Brenna feared him.

"Please, let me go. I didn't know that Treasach was your mentor. I didn't even know that you *knew* him. Put me down—we can figure this out, okay?"

Whatever he might have said was cut short when he shouted and dropped her, hunching over in pain as he pressed a hand to his cheek. Brenna fell to the floor with a grunt before staggering up and rubbing her bottom.

"I thought I said you weren't to go anywhere alone."

Spinning around Brenna, blanched when she saw Patrick. He was holding several dark, round objects in his hand, looking more than a little angry. Roibhilin straightened, sporting a black mark on his right cheek as if he'd been singed.

"Brenna, get away from him."

"But, Patrick—"

"*Now.*" Patrick never looked at her; his furious gaze remained locked on Roibhilin who had straightened and took a menacing step forward. Brenna jumped between the two, holding her hands up and eyeing them both warily.

"Patrick, this is Roibhilin. I just gave him some…um…bad news. He wasn't trying to hurt me. Were you?" She shot Roibhilin a glare, and he clenched his jaw.

"I did not intend to hurt you, no."

Patrick didn't look like he believed either of them, and Brenna dropped her hands, turning to face him fully.

"What are you doing here, anyway?"

"I saw you go into the woods, and then I saw him."

"Our business is none of your concern, human." Roibhilin drew himself up, his face a mask of disdain. The singe mark on his cheek was already beginning to heal, and Brenna felt a bit ill as she watched the skin move and stretch on its own accord.

"Seeing as you were the one looking ready to hurt Brenna, I would say that it *is* my concern."

Patrick raised his hand to toss another black ball—made of iron, Brenna guessed—and took a step forward. Quickly, she placed her hand around his closed fist, stopping its trajectory before looking to Roibhilin.

"Guys, we *really* don't have time for this. Patrick, I'm fine. Roibhilin, you're free from helping me since I've told you what you wanted to know, so why don't you just go now?"

Turning, she made to leave, giving a shout of surprise when she found herself jerked back. Roibhilin had taken hold of the back of her shirt, a tight muscle twitching in his jaw.

"You will come with me to my home, human. If Treasach has killed my mother, then you will tell me how. Then we will find the child, as my mother wanted."

"She's not going with you." Patrick reached for Brenna, and Roibhilin pulled her farther away, glowering down at him.

"Stay out of this, impudent boy."

"*Boy?*"

Patrick raised his hand, clearly ready to lob another iron ball into Roibhilin's face. Taking a few healthy steps back, the fairie made a strange sound in the back of his throat, dragging Brenna with him as he went. Exasperated, she wondered why boys always relied on violence to solve problems instead of just talking it out.

"Roibhilin, I have to go back to school. I'll get into trouble if I don't. I promise to come to the mound and go to your home later."

"Tonight?"

"Well…" she hedged.

"You *will* come tonight, or I will drag you there myself."

"Brenna? Patrick?"

As one, they all turned to look as shaking leaves and ferns gave way to Deirdre. Brenna stumbled forward as the grip on her shirt was released. She looked back to see that Roibhilin had disappeared. Deirdre glanced between the two of them with narrowed eyes, setting her hands on her hips.

"What are you two doing here? The coach has been looking for you."

"Patrick lost a ball, and I was looking for it."

"Sure, and how would you know he lost it from so far away, then?"

"I...um...I have really good eyesight?"

Deirdre laughed and Brenna joined in, though hers came out a bit more forced. Patrick remained silent, and Brenna could practically see the tension radiating off of him.

"I'm only teasing you! I got worried when I realized you weren't running with the rest of us. You wouldn't believe what just happened on the field! Brian Feeney smacked a ball right into Sarah Shea's face!"

"Who?"

"Who's Sarah Sh—the most popular girl in school! C'mon then, Bren, I want to see if she's gone and murdered him."

Tossing a helpless look over her shoulder at Patrick, Brenna let Deirdre pull her out of the forest and back onto the field. Behind her, the tiny pixies continued to dance and flit around the edge of the forest, reminding her once more that her life was growing more complicated by the minute.

* * * *

"Let me see if I've got this straight. You're going to Patrick's?"

"Uh-huh."

"And Kathleen isn't going to be there?"

"Um...no."

"Bren, if you're trying to convince me that you're *not* dating Patrick, you're doing a really bad job of it."

Rolling her eyes, Brenna peeked up from her backpack to where her mom stood leaning against her doorframe, an incredulous look on her familiar face.

"Deirdre is going to be there, too. We're just studying for history. I promise to call if I plan on staying past ten. I even have my cell phone—see?" She shook the slender device, and her mother sent her green eyes heavenward before straightening from her guard at the door.

"If I had known that having a teenager would be this complicated, I never would have had you."

"I thought you said that I was your little miracle?"

"That was before I realized miracles grow up and start making their own decisions, like chopping off all of their beautiful, golden hair."

Laughing, Brenna slung on her backpack, hugging her mother on impulse.

"Hey now, what's this?" Rachel laughed, her slender but strong arms encircling her daughter, and tears blurred Brenna's vision for a moment. She wished that she could tell her what was happening, that she was about to go into a world she wasn't sure she would come out of. Blinking back the tears, Brenna pulled away and adjusted her bag.

"No reason. I was just thinking how lucky I am to have you for a mom."

"And to think it only took you sixteen years to figure it out."

"Ha, ha."

A knock came at the front door, signaling Patrick's arrival. After one last hug, Brenna left. The ride to the mound was tense and, when they stopped in the graveled parking lot, it was nearly eight. Patrick cleared his throat and flexed his fingers around the steering wheel.

"I should go with you."

Brenna shook her head. "No, I have to go by myself. I don't think Roibhilin likes you much. Throwing iron at fairies does that, you know."

Her teasing was rewarded with a glare, and she sighed before opening the creaking door and stepping out of the truck.

"I promise I'll only be gone a few hours at most. Midnight at the latest." She paused then leaned down ever so slightly.

"Thank you, Patrick."

"Sure."

She smiled and pulled back, closing the door firmly before switching on her flashlight and heading up the mound. All around her was darkness. When she pointed the feeble beam of light upward, the pale trees seemed almost ghost-like, their long branches drifting toward her with skeletal fingers. In between the wavering branches, Brenna could just make out the moon which was less than half full. Shivering, she focused the light back on the narrow path. She tripped on small, loose stones several times before the path gave way to springy grass.

Eventually reaching the top of the mound, Brenna turned off the flashlight to help her eyes adjust to the night. Despite its minimal size, the moon cast just enough light on the world to give it a strange, slightly wild look. It lined the tops of the hills around her in silver, creating shadows that stretched out like a cloak to the valley below. Everything not tipped in silver was washed in shades of black and blue, save for the white trees surrounding the mound like rows of waiting spirits. Turning around, she faced the partially ruined castle that stood a half mile away. Its gray stones were bathed in the moon's cold light, too, the solemn structure looking lonelier than she'd remembered it. She wondered if the princess had really pined away for Roibhilin, wondered why he had never come back for her, if the sad story was true.

"'Tis a beautiful night, is it not, Brenna Morgan?"

Heart in her throat, she spun around. In the center of mound on a rock that hadn't been there just a moment ago sat the same leprechaun from the dock. His red coat stood out in the dark world, and he drew a slender pipe from the inner pocket, his black eyes glittering mischievously. Hand to her chest, Brenna took a wary step back.

"What are *you* doing here?!"

"Sure, I'm here for a bit o' entertainment." The leprechaun clicked his feet together, a wide smile on his face. "I see the shoe has worked for ye."

Brenna glanced down at her feet.

"Yes, it has. Thank you." She narrowed her eyes then, surprise replaced with annoyance. "By the way, if you think you're getting a thank you for your advice to ask Roibhilin for help, you'll be waiting a long time. You knew he hated humans, didn't you? Why would you send me to him?!"

"Well now, he didn't always feel that way. And you went about and fixed that, didn't ye, lass?"

"Not really!" Brenna crossed her arms. "Actually, I probably made him hate humans even more."

He chuckled and put the pipe to his mouth, instantly causing smoke to curl from the opening in thin, white strands. "Just keep at it, lass. He'll come 'round. He's as good and kind a lad as ever you'll meet."

"*Roibhilin?*" Brenna scoffed. "You've got to be kidding me."

"Ye've just got to be sympathetic-like. He's a tender heart, beneath it all."

Wrinkling her nose, Brenna glanced over her shoulder to where the castle peeked out from the forest of trees surrounding the hill it stood on. She couldn't imagine him being so in love with a human that the girl had built a castle to be closer to him.

"So the story *is* true, then?"

"What story?"

Where once the leprechaun and rock had been was Roibhilin, and for once the green cape wasn't draped about his shoulders. Instead, he wore a dark-green vest, gold threads creating delicate, Celtic knot work along the front. His legs were clad in light-green stockings while brown leather boots came up to his knees, his right foot tapping an impatient rhythm. His hair was a brilliant shade of gold even in the dim lighting, and she wondered why it was so easy to see him in the darkness. He eyed her from head to toe as if he wasn't sure she was quite right in the head.

"Who was it you were talking to?"

"I was talking to myself."

He looked less than surprised by her response, and she put her hands on her hips, wishing that he were easier to like. Taking a breath and counting to five, Brenna reminded herself that she needed to try and get along with him. She needed to find common ground.

"Actually…I was wondering if it was true that you loved the princess who lived in that castle."

Something flashed in his bright blue eyes, and before she could blink he was mere inches away from her, his hand wrapped painfully around her upper arm.

"*That* is none of your concern."

Wincing, Brenna realized that despite his angry words his eyes were filled with a pain that reminded her of how he had looked when she'd told him his mother had died. She licked her lips nervously. "I—"

Releasing her arm, he took a few steps back before drawing himself up, looking distant and arrogant once more. Brenna rubbed her arm, scrutinizing him thoughtfully. Perhaps he wasn't as cold and stuck-up as he seemed to be…perhaps he was using his anger to mask his sadness. The thought caused Brenna to blink in surprise. As wrong as his habit of physically lashing out was, at least it made sense. Sort of. She wondered if he used anger to hide other emotions, too.

"Come, we do not have much time to speak. I am to report to Their Majesties soon."

"Huh?"

Rather than clarify, Roibhilin strode across the mound before disappearing down one side, not waiting for her to catch up. With a sigh, she hurried after him, nearly losing sight of him as he rounded the corner. The trek was awkward, as Brenna found herself walking sideways to keep from rolling down the steep mound, giving a small curse when she tripped over a rock that nearly sent her sprawling down the hill. Ahead, Roibhilin ignored her struggles and continued on as easily as if he were taking a stroll on flat land, a fact that only irked her further. When they were halfway around the mound, he came to a sudden stop and raised his hand before casting a vexed look her way.

"Avert your eyes, mortal."

Rather than argue, Brenna simply turned around, wondering once more why the leprechaun had ever pointed her in Roibhilin's direction. She hoped that he was getting some amusement out of it, because she certainly wasn't. Without warning, the ground beneath her began to shake, and she gripped the grass as she stumbled onto her knees. A few feet to her left, the mound caved in, and from the gaping hole a wooden door adorned with intricate knot work and carved figures appeared. Brenna slowly stood and approached the door, touching a hand to a particularly lively-looking deer before stumbling back when it swung open soundlessly of its own accord. A rumbling deep below could still be heard, and Roibhilin swept past her. He paused a few feet inside the entrance before turning around and arching an impatient brow when he realized that she was still standing on the other side of the entrance.

"Are you going to come in or stand there like a dazed goat?"

Roibhilin's mocking tone shook Brenna from her stupor and she glared into the darkness ahead. "I *really* hope that leprechaun is getting a laugh out of this, because I'm going to—"

"What are you chattering on about now?"

"Nothing."

Brenna took stock of the door once more, feeling a little sick to her stomach when the realization that she was actually going through with this sank in. Squaring her shoulders and taking a deep breath, she stepped through, squinting into the darkness. There was a great crashing sound then, and the door shut as quickly as it had opened, enveloping them in utter darkness. Brenna threw her hands out, and as pale as she was she couldn't see them right in front of her face.

"Roibhilin? Where are you?!"

"This way."

"Which way? I can't see anything!"

She heard him make a disgusted sound before her eyes caught sight of a glowing, golf ball-sized light. It expanded rapidly before shooting up, racing along the side of a wall and leaving a row of torches burning brightly in its wake.

"Come."

Brenna returned her gaze toward Roibhilin who was already walking down a flight of stairs she hadn't noticed when she'd first stepped in. She looked down and bit her lip nervously. She couldn't see the end of the spiraling staircase as it descended into complete blackness. Somewhere in the deep she heard the sound of rushing water, which brought little comfort.

"Okay, Brenna, you can do this. If you went into a bat-infested cave in Belize, you can go down a flight of stairs to your doom."

Hesitantly, she followed after him, the echo of their treading feet bouncing off of the surprisingly cavernous ceiling. There was no hand rail, so Brenna put her left hand on the wall to steady herself, pulling it back for a moment when she made contact with compressed dirt in which roots of various thicknesses protruded. The farther down she went, the more the walls changed until dirt turned to rough stone and finally to smooth, marble-like rock. Torches appeared in niches along one wall, casting long, flickering shadows across cold, white steps. For a moment, she forgot her unease and stared up at where she'd come from, surprised to see Gothic-looking arches soaring above them. The next step Brenna landed on was steeper than the last, and she let loose a shout as she pitched forward.

Instead of the long and most likely deadly fall she was expecting, Brenna found herself smashed against Roibhilin's back, and he gave a small grunt. Pulling away, she dusted her hands on her pants, surprised to find that they'd reached the end of the staircase. Roibhilin turned to face her, and she was glad that it was too dim for him see the blush of embarrassment on her cheeks.

"Sorry."

"Are you always this clumsy?"

"I'm not, as a matter of fact!" It wasn't her fault that Ireland's ground seemed to be covered with hidden rocks. Clearing her throat, she looked around. "Where are we, anyway?"

"Home."

They'd arrived at the bottom of the stairs and before them stood arched double doors at least two stories high. They were devoid of any knobs, handles, or locks. The rich wood gleamed brilliantly even in the dim lighting, and strange creatures alongside elegantly dressed people frolicking in a woodland setting had been carved into its surface. Frowning, Brenna leaned forward to get a better look, jerking back when she realized that the figures were moving, gathering together to stare back at her. She took a hasty step back, and Roibhilin smirked.

"Are you scared, human?"

"N-no."

He gave a short laugh, which surprised her. She realized that she'd never heard him laugh before; at least not without a hefty amount of derision. It was a pleasant sound, and she shook her head, wondering where that thought had come from.

"Try to sound a bit more confident when you say that next time, and perhaps I will believe you."

Roibhilin put his hand to the door and murmured something under his breath in a musical language that Brenna suddenly realized wasn't Gaelic, as she had previously thought. The carvings on the door suddenly stilled and, with a little shudder, the double doors swung open, allowing for a warm wind to escape through the opening. It smelled of flowers, fruit, and everything that reminded Brenna of summertime. Roibhilin stepped forward and turned slightly to make room, raising an arm to point into the golden light that poured out from the door.

"Welcome to *Coillearnach*."

Chapter Nine

Brenna had to blink several times before adjusting to the bright light as she stepped through the entrance, and when she was finally able to see, her jaw went slack in awe. The clearing she'd stepped into was surrounded by a forest of ethereal white trees, their leaves a mix of silver and bright green that sounded like wind chimes whenever they brushed against each other. Pixies flew lazily about on warm air currents rather than zipping frantically like she had seen them do in her world. The light-green grass beneath her feet was so plush that it felt like she was standing on pillows. The light was that of a hazy summer day, and several deer on delicate legs pranced about the open field in happy abandon.

"*This* is what's underneath the mound?!"

"Aye." Roibhilin was smirking now, mostly in amusement at her reaction, Brenna bet, and she quickly composed herself. Several pixies had spotted them and whisked themselves into Brenna's shoulder-length hair, their voices tinkling with laughter.

"Welcome home, Brenna of *Coillearnach*."

Their words were copied by the other pixies until they were all repeating the welcome, and Roibhilin frowned.

"Why do they say this to you?"

"I don't know. They said it when I was up in the woods last time, too. Do you know what it means?"

"We haven't time to figure it out. Come—we must go home."

"You mean there's *more*?"

"Did you think I lived in a tree?"

"Well, yeah."

Muttering something under his breath, his face resumed its normal haughty expression. "Come."

Unfolding his arms, Roibhilin began walking, clearly impatient. For once, Brenna was glad of her tall stature, and she easily caught up with his rather lengthy strides. The pixies trailed after them, darting in and out of her blonde tresses.

"Truly, you are the last person I would think my mother would ask for help. I cannot understand what she was thinking when she chose you. This way."

He made a sharp left onto a slim path hidden by tall, golden grass that led into the woods. They entered the shade of the gently chiming trees, and it was only then that Brenna realized the temperature hadn't changed. She looked up at the light filtering through the branches. She couldn't find its source, and wondered how it was generated. *Then again*, she thought with an amused smile, *I* am *walking in an underground world with a fairie*. Finding out how they made sunlight was the least of her problems.

"Roibhilin?"

"Aye?"

"Does all of your world look like this?"

"No."

"Well…is it as pretty as this place?"

"Where the king and queen reside, it is, yes."

"Where do they live?"

Roibhilin waved a hand, dismissing her question as he turned to his right, leaving the trail and entering a thicker part of the woods. Brenna looked down, hating how he could stop a conversation so easily. She wished that she could wave a hand and silence people; it seemed like a useful thing to know how to do.

After walking for several minutes, the tiny pixies floated around them and tucked little flowers and leaves into Brenna's hair, causing her to laugh as she tried to pull them out. But however fast her fingers were, the pixies were faster. Roibhilin looked back at her a few times, but he seemed less annoyed now, and she supposed that it was due to the fact that he was in his own world for once.

"Tell me, human—"

"Brenna."

"*Human*. Why do you not just give the key to me and simply leave us all alone?"

"Why does everyone keep asking me that?" Rolling her eyes, Brenna gently shooed away a pixie that was hovering in front of her face. "Is it really so weird that I would want to help? I promised your mother I would find the *leanbh* and protect her. I don't break my promises. Besides, she saved my life. It's the least I could do."

Roibhilin stopped then, opening his mouth as if to say something before shutting it abruptly. He pressed his lips in a grim line as he eyed her from head to toe. Brenna stared back warily.

"What?"

"It has been a very long time since I have met a human who takes promises so seriously."

"Then you must be hanging out with the wrong sort of people."

"Perhaps." Turning on his heel, he resumed his fast pace, and Brenna trailed after him, smiling to herself as she went. Perhaps the leprechaun was right. Maybe Roibhilin *was* a nice person underneath all of his posturing and arrogance.

"But then," he said in a light voice, "who is to say you're the right sort of human to be around?"

Gritting her teeth, Brenna stomped her feet hard on the ground for a few paces, directing her anger into the dirt. Clearly, the leprechaun had no idea what he was talking about.

"You know, after all the ways I've been helping you, the least you could do is be gratefu—whoa."

A huge mansion loomed imposingly several hundred feet ahead through a clearing in the trees. It was a mishmash of architecture, from turrets and Gothic arches to Roman pillars at the front door and dormers on the roof. Chimneys of varying sizes and lengths peeked out of the tiles several times, and a multitude of windows gleamed brightly in the light. Brenna gawked.

"Is this where the king and queen live?"

"That," said Roibhilin with a smug tone, "is where *I* live."

"So, um, all the land, and the forest…" she trailed off as she caught sight of what appeared to be a tower made entirely of gold.

"Those are mine, as well."

"Oh."

Brenna fingered a few strands of her hair, trying to take in everything around her. The woods swayed gently in the breeze while shafts of hazy light pierced through the branches and lit the green, mossy floor like spotlights, pixies dancing to and fro in the beams of light. She made a slow circle, attempting not to look awed but failing. Roibhilin crossed his arms, a smile of pure pleasure on his face. She was beginning to see why he was so pompous. If she owned all of this beautiful land, she'd probably be a little spoiled herself. *Perhaps*, she thought with a grimace, *I owe him an apology after all that stomping on his mound.*

She cleared her throat. "Roibhilin?"

"Aye?" He was looking more amused by the moment, clearly enjoying her discomfort. Brenna sighed. She felt a bit bad for the way she'd spoken to him, but it didn't give him the right to treat her rudely.

"Never min—ow!"

Hissing in pain, Brenna grabbed the chain from under her shirt and thrust away the key. It was blazing hot against her skin, and she could feel the heat even through the wool jacket she wore. Roibhilin had put his hand to his nose.

"Why does it smell so putrid?"

"It's burning."

"I can see that, human. Is it supposed to mean something?"

"I don't know. It usually doesn't turn this hot unless…" Brenna looked around, suddenly aware that the pixies which had been trailing them were now gone and the green and gold leaves were no longer chiming. She licked her lips anxiously and inched closer to Roibhilin, who was still holding a hand to his nose.

"We need to run."

"I will certainly not run."

"It only burns like this when I'm in danger. Like when Treasach—"

"We are on *my* land. No one can hurt us here."

"But, Roibhilin—"

"You are being ridiculous."

Behind Roibhilin, a small head pulled away from a silvery tree trunk, and two large, black eyes glinted maliciously at Brenna. The creature was only two feet in length, its arms thin and long with thorns poking out all over the ash-colored body. The creature gave a gruesomely wide smile that nearly split its face in two, its eyes locked on hers. Brenna couldn't look away, and the key flared to life again, burning her through her clothes. Slapping a hand to her mouth, she took a step back as the strange beast peeled itself away from the middle of the tree, towering over Roibhilin as it raised claw-like hands to attack.

"What is the matter with you?"

"Look out!" With a cry, Brenna lunged at him, knocking them both sideways as the creature sprang forward. Narrowly missing them, it rolled along ground for a moment before springing back up. Where hair should have been was only a mass of twigs and spikes, and its oblong eyes narrowed in anger. Brenna felt nauseated just looking at the thing. It glared at Roibhilin who had righted himself and was drawing his sword.

"Give us the girl."

Roibhilin looked less than impressed by the creature's demand, and he pointed his weapon at it. "You are on my land, and you will leave it immediately."

It made a strange, breathless noise which Brenna assumed was a laugh and then it swayed on its spindly, twig-like legs. "Give us the girl, Roibhilin of *Coillearnach*."

The creature lunged at them again, and Roibhilin tugged Brenna to one side while cleaving the small creature neatly in half. It turned to ash before landing in a small heap on the floor, and Roibhilin examined his sword, seemingly unconcerned. Brenna stepped away from him, her heart racing and her legs feeling a little wobbly.

"What *was* that?!"

"A hawthorn pixie. Nasty things, but quite easy to get rid of, as you saw."

"Unless…" she began, trepidation creeping into her voice.

"Unless what?"

"Unless there are lots of them."

The ashen pixies appeared all around them, hanging in trees, clambering out of bushes, and gnashing sharp teeth. They were edging closer. For once, Roibhilin didn't look so sure of himself—and that was more than enough to scare Brenna.

"The girl!" They cried in voices like wind blowing through trees. "Give us the girl!"

"When I give the order, run for my home."

"But—"

Wielding his sword, Roibhilin struck out as three of the creatures sprang at him, and they immediately dissolved into gray ash. Four more were quickly descending from the trees above, and Roibhilin pushed Brenna toward the mansion.

"*Run!*"

She stumbled for a moment and then took off at a sprint, the hair on the back of her neck standing on end when she heard strange, windy howls rise out of their attackers. Glancing behind, she saw several of the creatures latch onto Roibhilin's back with their claws. Their thorny arms and legs tore into his clothes while he swung his sword at those in front of him. Skidding to a stop, she watched in horror as the creatures began to overpower him. They massed onto his form like a giant tumbleweed while their thorny bodies dug into his skin and caused black blood to ooze from the deep gashes they inflicted in his skin. Anger replaced fear as she picked up a rock from the ground and threw it, hitting one of the pixies square on the head. It squawked in surprise and crumpled to the ground. Several of the others glanced her way.

Taking the key from her neck, Brenna wrapped the chain around her wrist and held out the key. Her hands shook slightly, and she hoped that she looked braver than she felt.

"Is this what you want?"

With hungry eyes, the pixies clamored off of Roibhilin to edge toward her, their whispery voices hissing as they skittered closer. Brenna glanced at the house. She was only a few hundred feet away from it, and she was pretty sure that she was fast enough to outrun them.

"What are you doing?!" Roibhilin roared, hacking into several of the pixies that had lunged at him when he'd taken a step toward her. "Run!"

"No! I'm not going to let you die too!" Brenna glared over the creatures at Roibhilin, who looked stunned. "Find the girl for me, okay?"

"Of all the foolish—"

Whatever Roibhilin had started to say was cut short when three more pixies launched themselves at him. Brenna returned her attention to the horde of spiky creatures that had stopped several feet away, their grayish bodies forming a half circle around her.

"If you want it," she taunted the thorny creatures, "you'll have to catch me first!"

Spinning on her heel, she ran with everything she had in her. She could hear the flurry of leaves on the forest floor as the pixies took up the chase. She had just broken through the woods and onto the sandy path in front of the mansion when pain lanced up legs and sent her crashing to the ground. Two of the hawthorn pixies had grabbed onto her calves, their thorny arms tearing through her jeans and shredding her shirt as they scampered up her body and reached for the key dangling from her wrist.

Brenna pushed one off of her with her free hand, crying out when thorns tore the soft skin of her palm. She kicked her legs out as more of the pixies jumped on top, screaming when one bit into her shoulder with its needle-sharp teeth. Desperate, she flung off the pixie gnawing on her shoulder, taking a good chuck of her skin with it. She managed to throw another one off of her torso before four more joined the fray, clinging to her like burrs. Gripping the key in her hand, she drew it close to her chest as they tried to pry it from her, and tears streamed down her face as the creatures tore into her clothes and flesh. It wasn't long before Brenna's vision started to blur and her body became numb to the pain, though she was aware that the frenzied and flailing arms around her were attacking her body. Above her, the gray face of a pixie grinned as it grabbed her jaw painfully hard, cutting her chin and neck as it pulled her head close to its own.

"Today, Brenna of *Coillearnach*, you die. And then the world will be ours once more."

It laughed hollowly as it raised its clawed hands to deliver the final blow, and Brenna let the darkness that had been on edge of her vision take over. She only hoped Roibhilin would be able to grab the key before the hawthorn pixies did.

* * * *

"Are you sure this will work?"

"Of course! And see there, her color has come back. 'Tis good a sign as ever I've seen. Why don't you go and fetch some tea? And mind it's from her wo—"

"I know, I know. I'm not daft, woman."

Brenna groaned as the voices murmured above her head, and with great effort she managed to open her eyes as the sound of a shutting door thrummed in her ears. She winced as bright light greeted her weary vision.

"Ah!" exclaimed a soft female voice. "You're awake."

Groggily, Brenna tried to sit up against heavy silken sheets. The world tumbled in a lopsided manner, and a cool hand slipped behind her back to hold her upright.

"Easy there, love. Drink this."

A cup was pressed to her lips and Brenna swallowed reflexively. A thick syrup that tasted of some type of berry slid easily down her throat, and for the life of her she couldn't quite place the flavor. She felt clear headed almost immediately and took in her surroundings, surprised to find that she was resting in a huge, canopied bed filled with pillows and luxurious blankets. The room itself was large and airy, and a massive window to the right washed the space in soft, white light. Next to her, a woman was sitting in a chair, her blue eyes filled with concern and her brown hair falling in perfect waves down the length of her back. Brenna rubbed a hand over her eyes.

"Am I dead?"

"Dead?" The woman laughed and set the cup on an elaborately carved wooden table. "No love, you're not dead. But you're very lucky to be alive. If Master Roibhilin hadn't saved you when he did, well…there almost wasn't anything left to save as it was."

Brenna gulped and looked at her arms and hands. There wasn't a scratch or scar on her, and the heavy iron key rested warm and mellow against her chest. "What happened to me?"

"You don't remember?"

"I remember the pixies attacking, but I…I…Roibhilin saved me? Seriously?"

The woman laughed and leaned forward, taking Brenna's hand in her own cool, white ones. "'Tis true you were attacked, and you were very close to death, what with them nasty things shredding you to ribbons. But Master Roibhilin got to you in time with a few others, and here you are, safe and sound."

"'Others'?"

"Aye, a few of the guards. Lie back now—Master Roibhilin will become very cross if he finds you sitting up."

Brenna slowly lay back down, eyeing the woman as she adjusted the pillows so that she was propped up a bit more. "Thank you for helping me."

"Of course, love."

"My name is Brenna."

"I know." The woman smiled and brushed a hand on her forehead. "I'm Mahoney."

Brenna tried not to stare, but there was something odd about the woman. She was very pretty, perhaps in her late twenties, her pale skin almost translucent—it seemed tight, as if it had been pulled back. There was a smattering of freckles on her nose and cheeks, and while her large, gray eyes appeared as if they had seen a thousand lifetimes, they weren't bright like Roibhilin's or Nuala's. Brenna sat fully upright again, eliciting a tsking sound from her caretaker.

"You're...you're a human!"

"Well sure, what else would I be?"

"But I thought this was the fair—I mean, um...Roibhilin's land."

"It is." Mahoney laughed and sat back in her chair. "I was stolen by the Good Folk a very long time ago to be a caretaker for Master Roibhilin."

With her mouth agape and eyes wide, Brenna stared at Mahoney who, for some reason, seemed quite content to have been captured and whisked away for who knew how long.

"When were you taken?"

"In the year of Our Lord 1236." Mahoney laughed at Brenna's awed face. "From your expression, I imagine that quite a few years have passed."

"O-only a few," was her weak reply. "Wait...why did they steal you? I mean...didn't Nuala raise Roibhilin?"

A shadow of sadness flashed across the ancient gray eyes, and for a moment Mahoney's kindly smile faltered.

"It takes a lot out o' them, to give birth to one who isn't sickly. The women are very weak for a goodly amount of time, and so sometimes they steal humans to care for the wee ones. 'Tisn't all bad. Mistress Nuala was as kind as a queen, she was. She…" Her speech faltering, Mahoney turned her face to wipe her eyes.

Brenna felt badly for her and hunched her shoulders. "I'm sorry. I didn't mean to make you sad."

"Not a'tall, love. Her passing is still a bit of a shock to us all. But here now, I'm doing all the talking when you should be resting!"

Smiling faintly, Brenna lay back again then kicked uncomfortably at the blankets. It felt like her feet were swathed in something, and they were too hot. Throwing the blankets back, she was more than a little surprised to find that she was wearing a long, gray shift and, on her feet, her boots.

"Hey!" Swinging her legs off of the bed, Brenna stood and wrinkled her nose in confusion. "My boots are still on."

She took a few steps forward and felt her legs wobble. Gripping Mahoney's chair, Brenna smiled ruefully. Apparently, she wasn't as recovered as she'd thought. Squaring her shoulders, she took a few more shaky steps, carefully letting go of the chair. Mahoney trailed after her, wringing her hands worriedly.

"I was warned not to touch them. But please get yourself back to bed. Master Roibhilin would be quite vexed if he saw—"

"I thought I made it clear that she was to stay *in* bed."

Guiltily, Brenna looked up to see Roibhilin standing in an arched doorway, his eyes flashing with annoyance as he held a dainty silver tray laden with delicate cups and a teapot. The image of Roibhilin doing something so domestic was enough to cause her to laugh, and he clenched his jaw in response. Stiffly, he crossed the large room and set the tray to the side, ignoring Brenna's cries of protest when he picked her up and unceremoniously dumped her back onto the bed. Behind him, Mahoney hid a smile with her hand.

Brenna scowled. "I'm *fine*."

"*I* will decide when you are well. Tea, Mahoney."

Deftly, Mahoney went about pouring tea and then handed a cup to

Brenna. She eyed it suspiciously. Roibhilin glared down at her, the muscle in his jaw still twitching.

"Is there a *reason* you are refusing my hospitality, mortal?"

"I read that to eat or drink anything from your world would force me to stay here forever, or pine away and die from not wanting human food anymore."

"It is tea from your world—I saw to it. So was that remedy I gave you earlier, made from honey and elderberry."

"Oh."

The water was tepid, and Brenna grimaced as she gulped down the unpalatable tea in one swallow. Appearing a bit mollified, Roibhilin sat down in the chair Mahoney had occupied, his blue eyes piercing as he regarded Brenna in silence. She cleared her throat.

"Um… thank you, Roibhilin, for saving my life."

For several moments, he said nothing at all, and whatever he was thinking was impossible to interpret. Muttering something under his breath, he turned to his servant.

"Mahoney, leave us."

"Of course. And might I be so bold as to remind you, Master Roibhilin, that she is still quite weak. It will take a couple of hours for her to fully recover."

With those parting words of wisdom, Mahoney slipped out of the room. Brenna wished she had stayed. She turned her attention back to Roibhilin, drumming her fingers nervously on the silken sheets as she offered him a wan smile.

"Did I mention that I'm *really* grateful you saved my life?"

"You should be, you stupid, foolish girl!" Brenna winced as his voice rang out loudly in the room. Roibhilin leaned forward, his blue eyes darkening to an almost black color like she'd seen them do before. "Do you even *use* that brain in your head?!"

"Hey! I was trying to save your life!"

"It did not *need* saving." The chair scrapped against the floor as Roibhilin bounded up, his face reddening with his rising temper.

"Yes, it did!" Scrambling out of the bed, Brenna stood on unsteady legs. "You were going to die—I could see the blood. And I don't want you to get hurt because of me, okay? This is *my* responsibility, not yours, you arrogant, stubborn…" Brenna searched for the right word and came up with, "*jerk*!"

Roibhilin stared at her, slack jawed and eyes bright with both anger and disbelief. "You *dare* call me names?"

"If the shoe fits!" Brenna shot back before taking a shaky breath. "Look, I'm very grateful that you saved my life, but that's no excuse to yell at me for trying to do the right thing. Your mother wouldn't have wanted you to die, and I…I wouldn't want to see you dead, either."

They stood glaring at one another, Brenna's body trembling with fatigue. Slowly, Roibhilin sat back down, and Brenna slumped heavily onto the bed, feeling a bit light-headed.

"You are a very stubborn girl."

"Yeah, I get that a lot."

"And stupid."

"Gee, thanks."

"However, I begin to see why my mother might have chosen you. You are reckless and foolish…but you are brave, even when faced with something you do not understand. And you think on your feet."

Brenna's eyes widened. "Are you *apologizing* to me?" Pursing his lips, Roibhilin shifted uncomfortably in the chair and crossed his arms. Brenna grinned. "You *are*!"

"Tell me, mortal, where you got your scar."

"What scar?"

"The one on your back."

Brenna was thrown by the sudden change in topic and realized that there was no way he was ever going to actually say the word 'sorry'. It was the worst apology she'd ever received, but it was still better than nothing. Self-conscious, she put a hand to the middle of her back, grimacing when she felt the raised skin beneath her shift. She knew the scar well. It was an angry gash of pink that went from the left side of her back all the way down and to the indent of her waist.

"How do you know about it?"

"Mahoney saw it when she was changing you. You will explain it to me."

Feeling heat creep up her neck at Roibhilin's imperious tone, Brenna clutched at the key around her neck, counting to five to keep her temper in check.

"It was a long time ago, and I don't feel like talking about it."

"You will tell me."

"Why? So you can make fun of me or something?"

"No, because I wish to know."

Brenna realized she wasn't going to get out of explaining it—he would just keep pestering her. She supposed stubbornness was one of the things they had in common. Sighing, she gingerly leaned back against the pillows.

"I got it in Egypt. My parents and I were staying in Cairo, and I was walking in the markets when I saw this kid getting dragged into an ally by a few older guys. He couldn't have been more than eight, so I went to help him."

"You really are quite stupid."

Brenna shot him a dark look and he reclined in his chair, looking very sure of his statement.

"*Any*way," she muttered, "I went to help him. Two of the guys were beating up this poor kid, and when I yelled most of them ran off, but one of them stayed and tried to attack me. I sort of knew how to fight. I'd taken some self-defense classes, and I managed to punch him in the nose and daze him."

She could still remember the boy's terrified and bloodied face, tears filling his eyes and streaking his cheeks to form a sort of gruesome mask. She shivered.

"But I didn't hit hard enough, and the next thing I knew there was this pain…" Brenna touched her back again, wincing in recollection. "And then I blacked out. I woke up in a hospital, and the doctor was there talking to my parents. They said they were amazed I'd lived and that I was very lucky that the knife hadn't paralyzed me. They didn't do a very good job of sewing it up, though, so now I use this scar to remind me—"

"Never to do something so foolish as to get involved in someone else's affairs?"

"No!" She shot Roibhilin an irritated expression. "To remind me that in life, doing the right thing isn't always easy or safe, and sometimes it requires sacrifice. I may be reckless, Roibhilin, but just *living* is a risk." She clenched the bed sheets between her fists, blinking back tears. "You and Treasach keep asking me to give you the key and stay out of your business. But I think…I *know* there's a lot more going on here than either of us realize, and I'm pretty sure that whatever's going to happen in your world is probably going to affect mine, too. So, really, it *is* my business."

Brenna was unsure of many things, but she was certain that what she was doing was right. Crossing her arms, she jutted out her chin stubbornly, fixing Roibhilin with a steely-eyed stare.

"I'm willing to risk my life because Nuala lost hers defending me. If this kid is important enough that your mother died for her, then it's got to be worth the risk, don't you think?"

A knock on the door made both of them turn, Roibhilin looking more uncertain than she'd ever seen him. "Aye?" he called out.

"Master Roibhilin, the queen has asked for you to attend to her and wonders what is keeping you." Mahoney waited in the doorway, looking worriedly between them.

Roibhilin stood. "I will be there momentarily."

"Yes, sir." She shut the door quietly behind her, and Roibhilin began to pace the floor, clearly agitated. Brenna looked out the window and then frowned. The daylight had never changed, and she wondered what time it was.

"Roibhilin, how long was I out?"

"In your time? I believe fifteen hours."

"*What*? No!" Leaping from the bed, Brenna was halfway to the door in a blind panic before her knees buckled and Roibhilin caught her under the arms before she smashed her face into the stone floor.

"You are not yet strong enough to walk."

"But I have to get back home! Patrick must be so worried. Omigod…my mom is going to *kill* me! Roibhilin, take me back right now."

"No."

"I *have* to go home. Please!"

She must have looked more scared than she thought, for Roibhilin sighed and shouted for Mahoney. After a brief conversation, Mahoney rushed from the room and came back a few moments later with Brenna's clothes in her hands, looking for all the world as if they'd never been shredded to ribbons. While Roibhilin left to make plans—or so Brenna assumed—she hurriedly threw on her clothes. Mahoney kept an eye on her, smiling and shaking her head.

"What is it?"

"Nothing," she said with a laugh.

"Then why are you laughing?"

"Well..." Mahoney paused then grinned wider. "I have not seen Master Roibhilin this excited in a very long time."

"I'm sorry, did you say *excited*? Because he looked pretty annoyed to me."

Taking a brush that Mahoney offered, she ran it through her thick, knotted hair, wincing with each stroke as she attacked it viciously.

"Master Roibhilin is not always very good at expressing himself. I haven't seen him this emotional in a fair long time."

"Yeah? The only thing he ever expresses to me is annoyance. He's always angry at me."

"Are you finished yet, human?"

Rolling her eyes as Roibhilin's impatient voice yelled at her through the door, Brenna handed the brush back to Mahoney with an exasperated sigh. "See what I mean?"

"'Tis just his way, love."

"Well, his 'way' sucks."

The door opened then, and once more Roibhilin was dressed in his cape-like tunic. Before she could ask him about it, he ushered her through a long, twisting hall and then down a flight of stairs that landed them in what she assumed was the entryway of his home. A massive crystal chandelier floated above them, and little beams of light bounced off it onto the black-and-white checkered floor they were standing on. Brenna's legs were beginning to work a bit better, and Roibhilin guided her outside.

"Come, I have found a shortcut for you."

"A shortcut?"

"Do you feel well enough to run?"

"Um, not really."

"Very well." Before she could protest, he swung her up onto a white horse that had been waiting patiently outside the entrance steps. Ignoring her shout of surprise, Roibhilin easily jumped on behind her, taking up delicate silver reigns.

"For my sake, mortal, I hope you have a strong stomach."

With a flick of the reigns, the horse took off like a shot, and the force threw Brenna back against Roibhilin's chest. The world blurred together in bursts of white and green, and she gripped the voluminous folds of Roibhilin's green cloak for dear life. The horse was a smooth runner—she couldn't even hear its hooves strike the ground—but she still felt dizzy due to the speed at which they were flying.

"Where are we going?!"

"To your school."

"Are you kidding me? People will see you!"

"You forget, human, that people choose to see what they wish to see. They have long since lost the ability to perceive us."

Brenna could hear bitterness lace his words and she looked up at Roibhilin, but his expression was as enigmatic as ever. She wondered if perhaps he disliked humans because they no longer saw the fairie world. It was probably very hard, she decided, to be completely invisible to everyone.

"We are almost there."

Looking forward again, Brenna's eyes widened when she saw that the road ended at a large boulder…and the horse wasn't slowing down.

"Um, Roibhilin, there's a rock."

"Aye."

"Shouldn't we avoid hitting it?"

"What for? That is where we are going."

He urged the horse into an even faster gait, and the great beast lowered its head as it charged the boulder. For a moment, she was sure they were all going to be dashed against the rock's surface, but they passed through it as easily as if it had never been there. Before she could draw another breath, they were rushing through an earthen tunnel, roots and dirt falling into her hair as they raced through. The air stinging her cheeks was cold, and the smell of damp earth filled her senses. A light appeared on the horizon and rapidly expanded. The horse gathered itself before lunging upward, and she could feel the animal tucking its powerful legs beneath itself as it flew into the light.

It landed easily on a road and quickly slowed it break-neck speed to a walk. Brenna rubbed at her eyes, trying to adjust to the brightness. Blinking hard a few times, the world came back into focus and she felt her jaw go slack when she realized they were standing on the road that she and Deirdre had run down only a couple weeks ago. The forest was to their right, and Roibhilin stopped the horse at a clearly marked trail.

"It is noon, I believe. Is that sufficient enough?"

"It's going to have to be. Thank you."

He merely inclined his head and helped her slide off of the horse. She looked up at him, biting her lip.

"Roibhilin?"

"Aye?"

"Um…I know we didn't really get to talk, but I'll tell you all I know, which honestly isn't much. You remember that I told you your mother said I have to find the child by Samhain, right?"

Roibhilin nodded his head tightly.

"Well, when you saved me from Treasach, there were goblins with him looking for the little girl, too. And they were talking about killing her and…and something about getting to be in their 'proper place' again when they spilled her blood on the floor. Do you know what that means?"

"No." The horse pranced nervously when it heard shouting coming from the field across the forest, and Roibhilin stroked its neck, calming it down. "But it does not bode well. Samhain is in three days—that is not much time. And I must find a way to bring Treasach to light for his treason."

"So…you believe me?"

Roibhilin looked off into the distance, his expression unreadable as his fingers tightened on the reigns.

"I do." He gazed down, looking at her in such a strange way that it made the hair on the back of her neck stand on end. "I do not know why Treasach would do such things. Perhaps he is being coerced. He has great power, and there are many who would wish to see him harmed. It does not excuse his crimes, however." His expression turned grim. "I will come for you on the morrow; I must go to the queen now. She will already be displeased by my tardiness."

"I really am sorry about Treasach, Roibhilin. I wish it was someone else."

He nodded sharply and, with a slight tap of the reigns, the horse sprang forward, galloping down the small trail leading through the forest, not a single hoofprint marring the dirt road. Shaking her head and feeling a bit disoriented, Brenna made her way through the woods. She wondered how she was going to find the child in three days' time, or protect her for that matter. How could a human protect someone from malevolent fairies? Brenna stopped then smiled as a thought struck her. Kathleen Fergus would know.

Chapter Ten

Brenna's smile was short-lived as she drew closer to the other side of the forest, the sounds of people running and exercising reminding her that she didn't have her school clothes, let alone her gym uniform. She dodged behind a bush when a few girls jogged by and then poked her head out, scanning the field for anyone familiar. Frowning, she leaned forward slightly as she saw a group of boys playing football in the distance and tried to see if Patrick was among them.

"Brenna, is that you?"

"Gah!" Falling back onto her bottom, Brenna snapped her head up to see Deirdre staring down at her, a dark brow raised and her slender arms resting on her hips. "Deirdre!"

"Sure, who else would it be?" With a lopsided grin, she helped Brenna to her feet and then whistled when she got a look at the array of roots and dirt in her blonde hair. "Have you been in the woods all this time, then?"

"Um…define 'all this time'."

"I mean," said Deirdre as she glanced over her shoulder and lowered her voice, "since last night."

"How do you know about last—"

"Patrick told me. Wait." Deirdre forced a cheerful smile and waved to a cluster of girls that jogged by as she pretended to tie her shoe while Brenna ducked behind the bush again. After a few moments, Deirdre signaled for her to stand.

"What exactly did he tell you?"

"Nothing specific-like. Here—jog next to me and I'll try and get you to the lockers without being seen. I've a spare set of gym clothes for you, and we'll talk at lunch. PE's almost over, and aren't you lucky!"

"But—"

"C'mon!"

Grabbing Brenna's arm, Deirdre hauled her through the bush and onto the field, managing to get halfway around the track before Brenna begged her to slow down. Her lungs were on fire and her legs felt as wobbly as noodles. Deirdre frowned.

"Are you sure you're all right, Bren? You're a bit pale."

"I've had a long night."

"Sure, I can see that! Here now, we're almost there."

After a few more half-hearted attempts at jogging, Brenna made it into the locker rooms where Deirdre gave her the combination before heading back onto the field. The shorts were a bit small, as was the shirt, but after a bit of tugging and adjusting she was fully dressed. Never in all her life had she felt so exhausted or weak. Standing up, she took a few steps forward and winced as every muscle in her legs screamed in protest, reminding her that she'd overdone it on the field. Mahoney hadn't been kidding when she said it would take a few hours to feel normal again. Sitting back down on the nearest bench, she waited for the bell to mark the end of PE, using a brush she found in Deirdre's locker to get rid of most of the dirt and tangles in her hair. By the time her friend was ready to go, Brenna felt recovered enough to walk, albeit slowly.

"So," began Deirdre as she led the way to her house for lunch, "what were you doing all night that had Patrick going out of his mind with worry, then?"

"I, ummm…" she wracked her brain, trying to come up with a believable excuse.

"Brenna Morgan, you're not going to go and lie to me, are you? Because I can see you working one up right now." Deirdre narrowed her large, brown eyes and Brenna felt heat creep into her cheeks. They had stopped in front of the house, and the smaller girl seemed almost as formidable as Roibhilin with her militant stance.

"I don't *want* to lie to you. I just…" Brenna ran a hand through her hair. "I just can't tell you. It's kind of a secret."

"Are you saying that you can't trust me?"

"No! No. I just...can't. The less you know the safer you are."

A cold gust of wind blew between them, causing Brenna to shiver. Deirdre sighed, dropping her hands from her sides before opening the low, iron gate leading to the small garden in front of the house. Clouds were rapidly building in the sky, dark and heavy with the threat of another rainstorm.

"We'd best get in before it rains. Da's left us all some sandwiches."

Meekly, Brenna followed Deirdre into the house, blanching when she saw heaps of clothes piled on every available surface of the square living room. Dirty plates and cups peppered the tables or were placed haphazardly on the piles of clothing.

"What happened here?"

"My brothers," said Deirdre grimly. "I haven't had time to clean up after them and—Jesus! mum's picture!"

Hands shaking, Deirdre gently picked up a small picture frame from off the floor and carefully lifted a photo from the broken glass.

"Is it okay?"

"Yes." Deirdre hugged the photo to her chest. "It's the only one we have of her. Da put the rest away and won't tell us where they are."

"Did she die?"

"Yes. Well...no." Deirdre handed the picture to Brenna. The woman staring back at her looked like a slightly older version of Deirdre, though her features were a bit more delicate. Her lips were curved up in a smile, but it didn't quite reach her round, dark eyes which were busy staring off into the distance as if longing for something. She looked, Brenna noticed, very sad. Taking care to be gentle, she slipped an arm around her smaller friend's shoulders.

"What happened to her?"

"She drowned in the ocean five years ago. At least, that what da says. She went out in a boat to row 'round the harbor and this huge storm just flew in...we never saw anything like it. The waves were massive, and lightning struck four houses. It damaged half the boats in the harbor, as well. The thing only lasted fifteen minutes or so, but everything along the coast was an absolute wreck."

"Oh, my God. I'm so sorry, Deirdre."

Shaking her head, Deirdre took back the picture, tracing her mother's image with slender fingers. "But I don't think she died. I think she's still alive."

"How do you know?"

"I just...do. I would have felt it." She put a hand to heart. "We found her boat, you know, washed up a half mile away on a beach like it had been put there on purpose. It wasn't damaged at all, and the oars were tied to it."

Rain pelted against the window and roof in a sudden fury at the exact same moment that thunder boomed around them, causing both the girls to jump. Deirdre smiled and then carefully set the picture on the kitchen table.

"So you see, I know she's alive out there somewhere. Here." She handed Brenna a sandwich and poured them both some milk before sitting down at the kitchen table— the only clothes-free surface. Brenna stared through the window into the watery world outside. They sat in silence for several minutes, each lost in their own thoughts.

"I'm sure you're wanting to know what Patrick said last night."

Brenna tore her gaze from the window to look at Deirdre who was munching thoughtfully on her sandwich. "Well—"

"He didn't say much. Only to please call your mum and tell her that you were spending the night at my house. I have to say, Bren, my life has gotten fair exciting since you came here."

"Not as exciting as mine," muttered Brenna darkly.

"What?"

"Nothing." She gave an apologetic smile. "Thank you. I'm sorry you had to lie."

"Think nothing of it! We can't tell our parents everything, you know. It's against the rules or something. But sure, I wish you'd tell me what deep, dark secret thing you're doing. Maybe I could help."

The thought of Deirdre getting involved with the fairies made Brenna's stomach drop, and she shook her head emphatically. "You already are. Thank you for covering for me."

"Sure. Feel free to ask for help anytime—it's what friends are for."

They had just started cleaning their plates when they heard a loud knock at the front door. Brenna's heart leapt into her throat and then started again when Deirdre opened the door to reveal Patrick. A large, black umbrella kept the rain off of him, though his dark, windswept hair still looked slightly damp. Deirdre looked him up and down in surprise.

"What are you doing here?"

"I heard Brenna was with you."

"She is." Deirdre pointed to Brenna who stood in the doorway between the kitchen and the living room. "Safe and sound, as you can see. And she won't tell me a thing. Maybe you will?"

Patrick raised his brows and Deirdre laughed.

"It was worth asking, anyway. Come on then, you're letting in all the cold."

Closing the umbrella, Patrick stepped past the threshold, his hazel eyes locking onto Brenna. She felt her heart tighten a bit. She wasn't sure if it was because she was scared of what he was about to say or because it dawned on her that she thought he looked handsome. Maybe the concoction Mahoney had given her had something other than honey and berries in it. She shook herself and then hesitantly went into the living room, her hands clasped together behind her back.

"Um…hi, Patrick."

"Brenna." His expression was impossible to read, and Deirdre looked between the two of them. "Do you two want me to leave you alone, then?"

"No," Brenna blurted at the same moment Patrick said "yes."

"I think," said Deirdre as she picked up a big armful of clothes from the couch, "I'll just go and put these in wash. Carry on with whatever it is you two are going to do. I warn you though, Patrick, my da has a strict 'no snogging' policy in this house. And he'll know if there's been any."

"Snogging? What's that?" asked Brenna, confused.

"Nothing," muttered Patrick as he scowled at Deirdre's retreating back.

"Then why do you look so embarrassed?"

"I'm not embarrassed."

He cleared his throat and Brenna rolled her eyes. "Whatever you say."

Running a hand through his hair with an air of exasperation, Patrick marched across the living room, his voice low so that it wouldn't carry. "Why didn't you come back when you said you would?"

"I ran into some trouble."

"Trouble?" He frowned. "What sort of trouble?"

She debated telling him about the hawthorn pixies, but the memory of how angry he was when he'd learned that Roibhilin had kicked her into a creek was still fresh in her mind. Sighing, she tugged on a lock of her hair, knowing that she couldn't lie to him after all of his help.

"We were attacked."

"Attacked?!" His voice rose, and Brenna slapped a hand onto his mouth. He knocked it away, his tone quiet but furious.

"By who? Did Roib—"

"Roibhilin," she interjected defensively, "saved me, actually. It was hawthorn pixies that attacked us."

Patrick looked less than happy with that statement and crossed his arms in front of his chest. "They were after the key, then?"

"Yeah." She took the object in question out from under her shirt. "What I don't understand is why Treasach wouldn't just take it from me when he had the chance. Or Roibhilin, for that matter. I mean…they both had opportunities to just steal it, but all the do is ask—or threaten—me to give it to them."

"I don't know myself, or else I'd tell you. Did you find the girl?"

"No." Brenna sighed. "Roibhilin says he'll be able to find her if she's on his land…but we only have three days till Samhain, and then…" Her voice grew quiet.

"What?"

"Bad things will happen if we don't find her in time. I'm not sure what exactly, but I know it'll be really bad."

"Then we'd best find her as soon as possible."

"Sure, just let me get my magic wand and conjure her here." Brenna threw her hands up in the air, frustrated. "And even when I *do* find her, how am I supposed to protect her from things like Treasach and hawthorn pixies? I feel so stupid for not thinking about any of this sooner." She began to pace the floor, stopping short when she nearly bumped into Patrick. "Would your grandmother know of a way that I could protect her?"

"I don't know. But sure, you're welcome to ask."

"I'll do that." She glanced up at Patrick. "I'm really sorry that I worried you. You know I didn't mean to."

"Yeah, I know." He uncrossed his arms, looking tired, and Brenna noticed he had dark circles under his eyes.

"Were you up all night?"

"I managed an hour of sleep. Your mum wasn't very happy when I called her."

The thought of her mother getting angry—and at her—was a very scary thing. "How upset was she, exactly?"

"She shouted at me for a good while."

"Yikes."

"I wouldn't go home straight away, if you can help it."

"That's not really an option." Brenna groaned. "She's going to murder me. No—she's going to torture and *then* murder me. Then she's going to find a way to bring me back from the dead so she can kill me again."

"Talking about your mum, are you then?" Deirdre's chipper voice interrupted Brenna's rant, and she nodded her head miserably. "It's glad I am I'm not in your shoes."

"Gee, thanks for your concern."

"Anytime." She glanced at the clock and whistled. "We better shove off. School's going to start soon."

The rain had slowed to a heavy mist accompanied by a bone-chilling wind, and the thunder that had been booming overhead was already dying down and far away. Brenna shivered as the wind blew against them, and Patrick handed her his jacket. She managed a quick 'thank you' between clenched teeth. The key warmed her chest beneath her shirt, and she looked to the forest, expecting to see the little pixies floating around. None appeared, however, and Brenna put a hand to her chest, wondering why the object was acting up. Perhaps there was something there that she just couldn't see. She really hoped not.

After a brief walk through the forest and promising to stop by Patrick's house that night, the rest of the day sped by much too quickly for Brenna's liking. With a pounding heart, she waited outside of the school for her mother. The clouds were still low in the sky and occasionally let loose short downpours. It was during a reprieve from the rain that Rachel drove up to the school, and Brenna gulped when she saw the serious look in her eyes. Taking a deep breath, she walked over to the car and opened the door. For once her mom was silent, her green eyes dark and shuttered.

"Um…hi, mom."

"Hello, Brenna."

Her mother's voice came out flat and devoid of any emotion, and Brenna felt her stomach knot up. Without another word, they sped down the road to the cottage, the tension so thick that it was a wonder they could even breath. After skidding to a stop, her mother stomped out of the car and Brenna timidly followed her into the house, shutting the door gently before locking it. Her mother had stopped in front of the kitchen counter, her usually animated body still and ramrod straight. Save for the rain and the ticking clock on the fireplace mantel there was no other sound, and when mother spoke Brenna flinched at the hardness in her voice.

"Brenna Morgan, I want to know why you've been lying to me."

"I haven't—"

"*Don't*," she snapped as she whirled around to face her daughter, "you *dare* start this off with another lie."

"But I'm not—I haven't lied to you!"

"You expect me to believe that?"

"Yeah, I do!"

Her mother's temper flared to life, much to Brenna's relief. She could deal with her when she was yelling, but the quietness was something new, and it rattled her. "I haven't lied to you," she persisted.

"I find that very hard to believe. You've been acting odd ever since we came here." Her eyes narrowed. "Are you doing drugs?"

"What?! No!"

"Then what is it? Why am I getting calls in the middle of the night from Patrick saying that you're staying at Deirdre's when you had your phone and could've told me yourself, hm? And getting lost in the woods last week? Brenna, you have an excellent sense of direction. Did you think I wouldn't notice that? And your hair!"

Brenna instinctively grabbed a lock of her now shoulder-length hair, her guilt rising. "I…I…" She couldn't think anything good to say.

"'I' *what*, Brenna? Is school too stressful for you? Are you being bullied?" Her mother's green eyes were bright with unshed tears, and in a few steps she was around the counter and in front of Brenna, her slender hands grasping her shoulders tightly.

"What is going *on* with you?"

More than anything, Brenna wished she could tell her mom everything. But Rachel wasn't one to believe in the fantastic. Her father was the one who had always encouraged her to believe the strange and mysterious, to look for the magic in things. For all the creativity her mother possessed, she'd never had the need or inclination to believe in anything that she couldn't see. And if Brenna told her about Roibhilin and Nuala, she knew beyond a shadow of a doubt that her mom would ship her off to some remote island in South America. Rachel gave her shoulders a squeeze, snapping her daughter from her thoughts.

"Brenna, please." Her eyes were filled with hurt, and it broke Brenna's heart to know that she'd been the one to cause it.

"I...I can't tell you, mom. But please believe that I would if I could."

Closing her eyes, she released Brenna's shoulders as if she'd been burned, taking a step back. Tears welled in Brenna's eyes, and she followed after her mother who leaned heavily against the back of the couch.

"Mom, I'm not doing drugs. I'm not. I just..." She struggled to find the right words and found nothing but an empty blank in her head. She shrugged her shoulders helplessly. "You just have to trust me."

"Trust you? When you're God knows where doing who knows what in the middle of the night?"

"I was at Deirdre's."

The look her mother gave her was one of disbelief, and Brenna looked away, not able to hold her stare without feeling guilty. Rachel rubbed her eyes, looking tired. "Your dad's still in India for two more weeks. Maybe we should leave Ireland."

"No!"

"Brenna—"

"No. Please. *Please.* I...there's something I have to finish first. Just a few more days, mom. A few days, and then everything'll be okay again."

Rachel was silent as she rubbed her head. After a few moments, she looked up, eyeing Brenna with suspicion.

"Does Patrick know what you're doing?"

"Yes. He's helping me." That much she could admit, at least.

"And Deirdre?"

"She doesn't really know anything. At least, I don't think she does. Please mom, trust me. You *know* me. When have I ever done anything bad?"

Her mother's lips thinned into a grim line, her brows knit together in a deep frown. "Are you in some sort of trouble? I'm your mother. I should be able to help or make a phone call or something."

Brenna shook her head slowly. "This is something I have to do on my own."

Her heart beat wildly in her chest and her palms felt cold and sweaty as she waited for Rachel's response. Gradually, the older woman walked to the front of the couch. Brenna followed her warily. They sat in silence together, both clasping their hands in their laps. Rachel stared up at the ceiling while Brenna stared at her feet, unsure of what her mother was going to do or say next.

"Your father would tell me that you're almost grown up and to trust that you know what you're doing. That we raised you to be independent and to think for yourself."

"Mom—"

"But you're my little girl, Brenna. I'll *always* worry about you." She looked at her then, looking more puzzled than angry. "You've never lied to me. You've always been honest." She took a shaky breath before continuing, "So I can only assume that whatever it is you're doing right now is for a good reason."

"It is, mom. I swear."

"But can't you just tell me what it is?"

Brenna shook her head miserably and her mother rubbed her head, clearly getting a headache. "And you're sure you're not in trouble?"

"I'm not. A friend is, though."

"Do I know this friend?"

"No." Brenna clasped her hands together, keeping her eyes on her feet as her stomach started to unknot itself. Beside her, Rachel slumped her shoulders, looking worn out.

"I should just pack you off to India with your dad. Or at least ground you."

"But—"

"I'm not going to." Running a hand through her springy red hair, she gave a resigned sigh. "I'm probably making a terrible mistake or breaking some sort of parental law, but if you're helping a friend..." She took a deep breath, her green eyes filled with grim determination. "Then I believe you."

The tears that had been building up in Brenna's eyes slipped down her cheeks, and she flung her arms around her mother, holding onto her tightly. Rachel fiercely returned the embrace, and Brenna could feel her mother's tears on her neck.

"But no more lying to me, Brenna. If you have to go out at night, tell me."

"I will. I promise."

"Good."

After a few moments, they pulled away from each other, and both wiped at the tears on their cheeks. Brenna offered a watery smile. "Thank you, mom."

"I try to remember that you're almost grown up and that you have to make your own decisions without my input. You're so much like me. Stubborn, independent..." Rachel smiled, though a hint of sadness lingered at the corners of her upturned lips. "Your grandmother could never understand why I wanted to travel the world or why I was so tenacious. I suppose it's why I always encouraged your independence. I didn't want to stand in your way like my mother did with me. And anyway, you're much too strong-headed for anyone else to change your mind once you've decided something." She skimmed her fingers along her daughter's hair, sighing once more. "But did you *have* to cut your hair? Couldn't you have gotten your tongue pierced or a tattoo like a normal rebelling teenager?"

"It was an accident, really."

"What, you ran into a pair of marauding scissors?"

"Something like that." Brenna gave a small laugh, glad to see her mother's sense of humor return. There was a knock at the door, startling them both. Her mom wiped at her eyes, pinching her cheeks to get color in them before going to answer it. Patrick stood in the entryway, his truck running nosily behind him like a wheezing old man.

"I'm sorry to interrupt, Mrs. Morgan, but my gram is asking after Brenna."

With raised brows, her mother looked to Brenna who was already standing. "Does Kathleen know what's going on?"

"Um…sort of."

"I see." She turned back to Patrick, eyeing him from head to toe. "Patrick Fergus, if anything happens to my daughter, I will hold you personally responsible. Do you understand me?"

Patrick's cheeks took on a decidedly pink tinge under her mother's narrowed eyes, and for all of his height and athletic looks, he had the appearance of a chastised five year old. He nodded his head and Rachel pressed her lips together.

"Brenna, why don't you find something else to wear? And I would appreciate it if you came home tonight."

"I will."

"Good." She speared Patrick with a particularly scathing glare. "Eight o'clock, young man, and no later."

"Yes, ma'am."

After Brenna changed into warmer clothes and a jacket, the two scurried away to his truck. Patrick let out a loud breath as he threw the vehicle into drive. It whined for a moment before lurching forward down the muddy lane.

"Your mother is the scariest woman I've ever met."

"Tell me about it."

Patrick chuckled quietly, glancing her way. "Did you not get in trouble, then?"

"Kind of…but then it sort of worked out."

"You're fair close to your mum, aren't you?"

"Yeah. She's pretty much my best friend." Sighing, Brenna twined her hand through her hair. "I hate not being able to tell her any of this."

"Why don't you?"

"She wouldn't believe me. She's not exactly like your grandmother, you know?" She fidgeted in her seat for a moment, looking out the window at a rapidly darkening world. The ocean was flat and gray, mirroring the sky above it. Patrick turned into the lane leading to his home, and Brenna focused on him again. "Did I mention that I'm really, really thankful for your help?"

"I do seem to recall you've said it now and again. But it's nice to hear all the same."

The truck coughed and sputtered to a stop a few feet from the house, letting loose another loud *thunk* as he switched off the ignition. In front of them, the welcoming lights of his cottage flooded onto the green grass before them. She smiled across at Patrick, unbuckling her seat belt.

"I mean it. I don't know what I'd do without you. You're a great friend to do all of this and just…believe me."

"Sure."

Brenna rolled her eyes at his light, dismissive tone. "Whoa there, don't make it sound like it's such a big deal," she said sarcastically.

"'Tisn't."

"Well, it is to me." She wrinkled her nose in annoyance. "I mean, I'm sure you do nice stuff like this for people all the time, but—"

"I don't."

"Excuse me?"

"I don't go 'round doing nice things for everyone."

The look in his eyes caused Brenna's heart to flutter strangely, and she felt a little breathless under his suddenly intense gaze.

"Oh."

All of the air seemed to leave the truck. Somehow, something in the atmosphere had changed, and Brenna saw Patrick not just as she had known him but as someone altogether different. He leaned forward slightly, and her heart did another little flip. She wasn't sure what he was going to do, but she found with some surprise that she probably wouldn't mind it.

"Brenna, I—"

Whatever he had intended to say was interrupted by Kathleen knocking on his window. He quickly pulled back, and Brenna felt her cheeks grow warm in embarrassment as she tried to figure out what had just happened.

"Are you two going to be in their all night, then, or shall I let the tea get cold?" Kathleen smiled warmly at them, and Brenna quickly scampered out of the truck. The elderly woman took her arm and tucked it into her own thin one, a knowing look in her eyes.

"Brenna, I've heard whispers and chatters that you've had a run in with some goblins."

"How did—"

"Sure, you didn't think you were the only one the Good Folk spoke to, now did you?" She laughed lightly and led Brenna into the house where the smell of dried flowers and tea permeated the air. "Patrick, why don't you bring the tea 'round?"

Guiding Brenna to the couch, Kathleen made sure that she was comfortable before sitting down in the rocking chair across from her. "It seems there were some things that you've gone and left out." She glanced down at the shoes on Brenna's feet and made a clucking sound with her tongue. "Did I not say to use that shoe only in case of an emergency?"

"It *was* an emergency at the time, Mrs. Fergus. And it's kind of been one ever since. I wouldn't feel safe taking it off."

"I see. Ah, thank you, love." Kathleen accepted a mug from Patrick and waited until he'd handed a cup to Brenna and sat down himself before speaking again.

Turning her attention back to Brenna, she fixed her with a thoughtful gaze. "Then I'm afraid there isn't much I can do in way of helping you, child. For its well and sure I know the games of the Good Folk, and they don't take kindly to meddling."

Biting her lip, Brenna clutched the mug in her hands, the heat warming her cold fingers. "I don't want you to get in trouble, Mrs. Fergus. I just have a couple of questions."

"I'll answer you if I can."

"Thank you." Brenna tapped the ceramic with her fingernails as she carefully formulated her line of inquiry.

"I wanted to know how…if I had to protect myself from the Gentry, how would I go about doing it? I know iron works, but what if it's not enough?"

"Iron works on most, 'tis true," nodded Kathleen, "but if they're able to ignore it, I do have something that might help."

Setting her cup on the small, rickety table next to her chair, she stood up and walked over to the kitchen, carefully lifting something from a hook above the sink. Returning to the sitting room, Kathleen presented Brenna with what looked to be dried daisies linked together from stem to stem to form two delicate necklaces. Placing her mug on the floor, Brenna gently took them into her own hands.

"What are they?"

"Daisy chains. As pure and innocent as anything ever made. Keep them 'round your neck and no harm can come to you, not even from nasty things like goblins. But mind they don't break."

"Thank you." She fingered the dry, fragile flowers. "Will these really keep them from harming me? I mean…they just look so frail."

Kathleen chuckled and eased herself back into the rocking chair. "Sometimes the simplest things are the most powerful."

"Gram, Brenna wanted to know about Samhain."

"Why would she be wantin' to know about that?" Kathleens' voice was unexpectedly sharp and her gaze even sharper. For a moment, the room seemed to grow cold, and Brenna shivered despite her fleece jacket.

"There's something I have to find by Samhain, and I was told it was extremely important that I do so before then. Patrick told me that Samhain is just another word for Halloween."

"Did he, now?" Kathleen sat back in her chair. Picking up her cup of tea, she began rocking, lost in thought, her head tilted to the side as if she was listening to something only she could hear. Brenna glanced over to Patrick who simply shrugged his shoulders and took a gulp from his own mug.

"Samhain is a time when our world and those invisible are closest, when all manner of good and bad can come out on the roads. 'Tis then when celebrating and feasting occur among the Good Folk. People have forgotten how dangerous it is to be out on Samhain, even in this country. The Veil between our world and theirs becomes thin-like, and it's easy enough for them to be seen and touched even by those who don't believe."

A shiver ran along Brenna's arms as she thought of the hawthorn pixies with their windy voices and sharp bodies.

"I would warn against being out during the night, Brenna, especially with that shoe on your foot."

"I don't really have a choice."

"Then wear those daisies and stay off the roads, for on Samhain they'll be filled with all manner of travelers."

Patrick and Brenna exchanged uneasy glances, and she peered down into her cup where her reflection rippled in the dark water. Somewhere within the house, a clock chimed the hour of seven.

"Mrs. Fergus—"

"Kathleen."

"Kathleen. Do the Good Folk kill people?"

"Not generally, no. Steal children and pretty girls, yes. But they don't kill people...at least, not without good reason."

"Do they kill each other?"

With a clatter, Kathleen's cup descended hard upon the rickety table and the old woman paled. Brenna half stood but Patrick was already up, wrapping an arm around his grandmother's frail, stiff shoulders.

"Gram?"

Kathleen didn't speak; her eyes were fixed outside the window as she sat like a stone in her chair. Brenna watched helplessly as Patrick gently shook his grandmother, calling to her several times to no avail. After several minutes, Kathleen's body slumped as if being cut loose from a string, and she passed a trembling hand over her eyes as she spoke in a weary voice, "Do you have the key on you, child?"

How Kathleen knew about the key Brenna had no idea, and she wasn't about to ask her, either. Instead, she knelt gingerly in front of the elderly woman, nodding her head slowly. Kathleen gripped her hand.

"It's afraid I am for you, Brenna." She exhaled a shuddering breath. "Be sure to keep iron on you, and the daisy chains upon your neck. And have courage, for I see a darkness coming. A terrible darkness."

Brenna looked to Patrick then. He still had his arm around Kathleen's shoulders, and his own hazel eyes were as worried as she felt. "Gram's, I'll get you another cup of tea."

"No, Patrick, it's my whiskey I'm wanting. I'm cold."

Without so much as batting an eye, Patrick crossed to the kitchen and filled a clean mug with a good dose of the golden liquid. Handing it to Kathleen, he motioned for Brenna to follow him to the kitchen sink, keeping his voice low.

"I think I should take you home. Gram..." he began.

"I understand. Why don't I just call my mom to come pick me up?"

"Well..."

"You should take care of your grandmother, and I wouldn't want you to leave her alone."

The two glanced back over at Kathleen who was sitting in her rocking chair, looking haggard as she sipped from her mug and stared grimly out the window. Brenna bit her lip. "Will she be all right?"

"In time. She sees things sometimes...it takes a lot out of her, but this is the strongest I've seen in a while yet."

"Is it like that every time she talks to the Good Folk?"

"It's not the Gentry she's talking to when she's like this."

Brenna called her mother, informing her that Kathleen wasn't feeling well. Rachel came over in record time and spent the next half hour making sure Kathleen was truly comfortable before taking her daughter home. As they pulled up to the cottage, her mom frowned thoughtfully.

"I'm supposed to go to Tralee tomorrow, but I think I'll go and stay with Kathleen while you're in school. I hate to think she'd be all alone in that house."

"I'm sure she'd really appreciate that."

Not feeling particularly hungry, Brenna made herself a quick dinner of soup and a slice of bread before she trudged her way into her bedroom, unable to concentrate on the school work waiting there. Outside, the rain that had been pattering gently atop the ground gained speed and began to pummel viciously against the glass pane. With a sigh, Brenna closed her history book and crawled into bed. It groaned under her weight before settling down. Beneath her shirt, the key remained cool, and Brenna placed her hand over it as she stared at the daisy chains she'd placed on the tiny dresser next to her bed. How flowers could protect her from fairies she wasn't sure, but if Kathleen said they would, then she believed her.

Closing her eyes, she listened to the storm beat against the windows and hoped that it wouldn't be raining the next day. With Kathleen's warning of coming darkness, Brenna wished that for once the gray would just go away.

Chapter Eleven

Tapping her foot impatiently, Brenna checked her phone once more, frowning when she saw that it was almost eight and Roibhilin had yet to make an appearance. The day had dawned clear and bright with an abnormally blue sky and fair weather that made it feel more like spring than fall. She hadn't even needed her jacket when she'd left her house that morning. After her mother had dropped her off at school, Brenna had waited until she'd sped off toward Kathleen's before dashing to the edge of the small forest behind the school. The sun was making its trek across the sky, and students coming through the wooded footpath gave her odd looks as she parted bushes and glanced behind trees.

"C'mon, Roibhilin. Where are you?"

Save for the twittering of birds, nothing else answered her, nor did Roibhilin make some sort of annoyed comment from behind her. Narrowing her eyes, she gripped the chain with the warm key around her neck. Tiny sparks of light appeared then, flitting among the branches of the wavering trees like specks of dust. A smile flickered briefly across Brenna's lips as the little pixies made their way toward her, and she glanced around to make sure no one was near before calling out to them. A few zipped toward her face, laughing in their wind chime voices.

"Have you seen Roibhilin?"

"Have you seen Roibhilin?" The pixie asked back. The woods echoed with her question as they copied each other before bursting out into tinkling laughter. One landed on her shoulder, mimicking her annoyed facial expression. Brenna gently scooped the tiny, glowing being into her hand. It sat complacently, tilting its head as it examined her with oblong, black eyes.

"Please, little pixie, can you show me where Roibhilin is?"

It tilted its head in the other direction, and Brenna sighed. "You can't understand me, can you?"

"You want Roibhilin, Brenna of *Coillearnach*."

The matter-of-fact statement that drifted clearly from the little pixie's mouth startled Brenna so much that she took a step back, causing the little being to alight and hover above her hands.

"Yeah, that's right! I want Roibhilin." She knelt down so that her nose was level with the small creature. "Do you know where he is?"

"Where he is?" With the exception of the pixie in her hand, the others repeated her question.

"I know," said the pixie, its long, delicate arms and legs swaying loosely.

"I know," the others copied.

"Where is he?" Brenna asked again.

The pixie gave a little shudder and then shot up before banking to the left. Brenna realized she'd have to run, because it certainly wasn't waiting for her. Dropping her school bag, she dove into the forest, tripping several times on the damp, slightly marshy ground. The other pixies followed after her, laughing and diving into her hair and through the woods. Ahead of her, the one pixie slowed down for a moment, allowing her to catch up before darting off again, and Brenna had a hard time keeping her gaze trained on the being of light as it weaved through branches and leaves. It paused again to look over at her and then veered between two bushes, disappearing from sight.

"I'm really starting to hate bushes," muttered Brenna as she struggled through the waist-high branches and ferns. Her foot caught on a root and she flew forward, barely able to keep herself from falling face-first onto the ground as she crashed through the last of the plants. Taking a deep breath, she straightened and then frowned. All around her, the pixies had stopped, having formed a twinkling circle at the outskirts of a small clearing. Jagged rocks of a strange, blackish-gray color jutted up from the ground in a haphazard circle while springy, green grass lay soft and damp under her feet.

The pixie that had led her into the forest strayed into the circle, and

Brenna felt goose bumps rise on her arm as an electrical current rushed through her.

"Is this where Roibhilin is?"

"Go here." The pixie flew in a small loop, its delicate limbs graceful as they motioned at the ground. Brenna tugged on a strand of her hair, confused.

"But I *am* here."

"No," the pixie said, giving a little shake of its head. "Go *here*."

It darted toward the ground before backing away slowly, and Brenna took a step closer, following the tiny ball of light as it left the circular outcropping. A twig snapped somewhere behind her and the pixies disappeared as one, rushing up into the protection of the trees. Her heart racing, Brenna whirled around, body tensing as the memory of the goblins filled her head.

"Hello?" she called out nervously, hoping more than anything that it wasn't Treasach.

No one replied for a moment, but then a bush shuddered, revealing Patrick as he struggled into the clearing. Brenna nearly fell to her knees in relief, and she glared at him. "What are you doing here?"

"I saw your bag by the entrance of the woods and thought you might have gone and gotten into trouble again."

"Oh, no. I'm fine."

"Then what were you doing? School's nearly about to start."

"I was following some pixies."

Stepping out of the circle via the way she'd first come in, Brenna stomped through the bushes once again. Patrick followed, shaking his head.

"You shouldn't trust them. They're harmless most times, but they like to lose humans in the woods, you know."

"They seemed like they knew where they wanted to me to go."

They exited the woods together, and Brenna was surprised to see that for all the running she had done, she really hadn't gone that far. Picking up her bag, she headed back toward the school's entrance where Deirdre was waiting for them. Her thick, curling black hair had been pulled up into a high pony tail, causing her brown eyes to look even larger. Brenna smiled and waved to her.

"Morning, Deirdre! Did you wait long?"

"Not really, no. Good morning, Patrick."

"Morning."

"Say, that's a strange necklace you've on you. Where did you get it?"

Glancing down, Brenna saw she'd left the key free on top of her shirt. She quickly tucked it back in. "It's just something I found when I was going through the woods a few days ago."

"A key? Sure it looks fair old. D'you think it's a key to the fairie world?" Patrick and Brenna must have looked shocked, because Deirdre began to laugh. "I'm only jokin', you know. And here I thought you had a sense of humor, the pair of you!"

Brenna laughed uneasily but Patrick remained silent. Deirdre glanced between them before shrugging her shoulders, letting the subject drop. Smiling, she looped her arm through Brenna's. "Anyway, I'm glad I caught you before school started. I know it's a bit sudden, but my da's letting me have a Halloween party at home."

"With all of those clothes lying 'round? How would you fit people inside?" asked Patrick as the three made their way into the crowded halls.

"Here now, I cleaned it up, I'll have you know! So, will you come, then? It's this Friday, and da's going to cater and everything!"

They stopped at the bottom of the stairs, and Brenna and Patrick shared a furtive glance.

"I...don't know if I can go." At the crestfallen look on Deirdre's face, Brenna took her hand. "But I'll try."

Deirdre narrowed her eyes. "Does this have anything to do with why you've been out at night?"

"Yes."

"I see." Sighing, Deirdre gave Brenna a quick hug. "Well sure, if you can't make it I won't go and hold it against you. But I'd be fair pleased to have you there. And you know, so would Colin."

"Whose Colin?"

"Sure, he's in your classroom! He's been gone on you for a while."

"'Gone' on me?"

"It means," said Patrick with a slight snap to his voice, "that he likes you."

"But...but I don't even *know* him!"

Deirdre laughed up at Brenna, ignoring Patrick's glare.

"Well sure, you're always off day dreaming or some such to ever notice. Lots of the boys 'round here like you, Bren. I should know—they all come to me asking what sort of things you like. I told them if they were so keen on knowing, sure why don't they go and ask you themselves?!"

Above them the bell rang, and the students that had been huddled together dispersed in a flurry of rushing feet and echoed shouts. Brenna was forced up the stairs as Deidre called after her.

"Think on it and see if you can't come!"

"I will!"

Patrick's put-out face was the last thing Brenna saw before she was swept all the way upstairs. After narrowly avoiding getting slammed into a wall by a rowdy group of boys that shoved past, Brenna made it into her classroom. She had been assigned a seat close to a large, soaring window in the back of the room. It was easy to see how the building had once been a Gothic church with its arched windows and stone walls, but somehow it seemed fitting that it was now a school.

Brenna glanced down at her booted feet and saw that her repeated tromps through the woods were causing the green to show through the faded black dye. Feeling eyes on her, she looked up to see a boy with floppy brown hair and pale blue eyes rimmed with red sitting at a desk across from hers. He was staring at her outright. His cheeks took on a pinkish color, causing the numerous freckles on his face to stand out as his eyes met hers, and he hurriedly looked away. Brenna looked back down at her desk, trying hard not to smile. *That* had to be Colin.

Gazing out the window, she wrinkled her nose. Was she really that dense when it came to the opposite sex? She hadn't even realized that a boy who was in the same class liked her. And last night in the truck with Patrick...her cheeks felt hot and she put her hands to them, trying to rub away the blush. She had to admit that Patrick was cute, and nice, and...well. He couldn't be anything but a friend, because she was pretty sure that if he ever became anything more her heart would break when she had to leave the country. The teacher began class in Gaelic, interrupting her thoughts. Brenna sighed.

Irish Gaelic had proved to be much harder than she had anticipated, and reading it made things even more difficult. She had never been wonderful at languages, but somehow Irish seemed just about the hardest she'd ever attempted to learn. It was musical and beautiful, but she had no idea what people were saying when they spoke it. It didn't help that nothing sounded like it was spelled. She let her gaze flicker to the window again, and the teacher's voice faded away as her swirling thoughts took over once more. Outside, the sky was still blue and cloudless. Sunlight shown on the bright green grass and treetops beyond.

Taking out her key, she fingered it lightly before letting it dangle free in front of her. Her thoughts wandered to Roibhilin and where he was. She looked to the forest, expecting to see him glowering at her from down below. A twinge of disappointment tugged at her when all she saw were bushes and an empty forest. Roibhilin wasn't as terrible as she had first thought, and he'd saved her twice now, even if he wasn't very good at it. Despite his insults and quick temper, she'd found that he was kind of amusing and even a sort of friend. *Well*, thought Brenna as she wrinkled her nose, *maybe not a friend, but he has the potential to be*.

"Brenna, *cad é sin i mBéarla?*"

"Huh?" Lifting her head from her hands, Brenna cringed when several people giggled, though the teacher standing only a few feet from her desk didn't look amused. He shut the book in his hand with a loud *thud*.

"I asked," he explained in an extremely annoyed voice, "what does *leanbh* mean in English?"

"Oh." Brenna blushed. "It means 'little girl'."

She held her breath as the teacher studied her closely. Finally, he turned around and spouted off something else in Irish that Brenna found impossible to follow. After a few minutes when it was clear that he'd lost interest in her, she let her attention drift back to the window. She only had two days to find the little girl, three if she counted Halloween, but she really hoped it was before then. For the first time she found herself wondering what the little girl looked like. Maybe she had dark hair like Deirdre, or silvery tresses like Nuala. The thought of a tiny Nuala caused her to smile.

Something gently hit the side of her neck. Frowning, she looked down, shocked to see that the heavy key was no longer dangling in front of her. Puzzled, she followed the chain's path, and her heart stopped. Against the laws of physics, the key had pulled itself sideways and was pointing straight out the window, level with her eye. It stayed there for a moment longer before dropping again, and Brenna grabbed it. It was cool to the touch, as if it hadn't just defied gravity. Releasing the key, she stared at it, waiting for it to rise again. Save for the slight swaying of each breath she took, it remained motionless. A bell rang, breaking her concentration and signaling that class had ended.

"Brenna?"

Her head snapped up at the sound of an unfamiliar male voice. Colin was standing in front of her desk, his cheeks turning redder by the second. She gave him a warm smile; it looked like he was pretty shy.

"Hi. You're Colin, right?"

"Ye-yeah!" His voice became high-pitched and he cleared his throat, lowering his tone once more before continuing, "Em, so…so Deirdre told you about her party, then?"

"Yeah, but I don't know if I'm going."

"Oh. Right. Yeah, me too. I mean, I was thinking of shoving off to Killarney for the pubs or somethin'."

He leaned back against his desk and crossed his arms, but his foot slipped from under him and caused the desk to slide forward with a screech. Hastily, he put the table back, and it took biting the inside of her cheek for Brenna to not laugh. She really didn't want to hurt his feelings, and it looked as if it had taken a lot for him to talk to her. She smiled kindly at him.

"Well, I mean, I think Deirdre's party is going to be really fun. I'm just not sure if my mom will let me go."

"Oh." He looked so deflated that Brenna felt guilty.

"But you know, she might change her mind." The bell rang loud and piercing once more, signaling that the next class was about to start. "I hope you go. I'm sure we could talk more there."

His face grew redder, if that were possible, and he nodded his head so much it reminded her of the bobble head she'd seen on a taxi dashboard in India. Brenna smiled again as he snuck a glance at her as he walked away. With a small chuckle, she quickly gathered her things and headed to her next class. School quickly turned her attention away from the key, and she tapped her foot impatiently as she sat through her next class. By the time lunch arrived, Brenna barely waited for the bell to finish ringing before she jumped out of her seat and dashed out of the room, flying down the stairs in her haste to get outside to experiment with the key. She had just rushed around the side of the building when she slammed into something hard, nose-first.

"Jesus Brenna, are you all right?"

Rubbing her smarting nose, she looked up to see Patrick staring down at her, concern in his hazel eyes.

"I'm fine. Sorry, I'm kind of in a hurry."

"Sure, I can see that. Where are you off to, then?"

"They key floated."

"Come again?"

"Follow me and I'll explain."

Brenna walked impatiently toward the woods where they were less likely to be stopped or overheard, recounting what had happened to the key.

"But I don't know *why* it levitated. I didn't do anything special."

Removing the chain from her neck, Brenna sat down on the grass, resting her back against a tree. The key dangled there, swaying slightly in the breeze. Patrick leaned against the trunk, studying the iron object.

"Are you sure you didn't do anything? Maybe it was just reacting from moving your head too fast."

"Patrick, it was stick-straight and this high!" She lifted it up to her eye level, pointing it out and away from herself. "And it stayed that way for a while."

"Well…" Patrick frowned. "Do you think it went and reacted to something you said?"

"I didn't say anything—I was in class. I was just looking out the window and thinking about Nuala and the *leanbh*. I was trying to imagine what she looked…like…" she trailed off.

Realization hit her like a ton of bricks and she scrambled up to her feet, still holding the key away from her. Patrick straightened.

"That's it!"

"What's it?"

Brenna put a finger up to silence him and then took a deep breath, closing her eyes as she tried to picture the little girl in her mind. She frowned, thinking of how the child was probably locked in a tower or a house of some sort. For a moment, an image flashed across her inward vision, too fleeting to really make out.

"Jesus!"

Patrick's exclamation jolted her and she snapped her eyes open. The key had lifted again, pointing to her left as it strained to free itself from the chain. It gave one final tug before dropping, and Brenna let go of a breath she hadn't realized she'd been holding.

"I knew it!"

"Brenna, how did you do that?!"

"I thought of the *leanbh*. And…" She thought hard for a moment.

"And what?"

"I think this key is a compass." She looked at the key. "Find the *leanbh*."

For a few seconds, nothing happened, but then the key began to shake before shooting to the right again as Brenna kept her mind focused on thoughts of the little girl. When she stopped, it dropped. Elation, fear, and excitement rolled through her. With a whoop of joy, she threw her arms around Patrick in a tight hug.

"This is it! I did it! We can find her! That'll show Roibhilin. Oh!"

Brenna released her grip on her friend, missing the stunned look on his face as she looked into the forest.

"I have to find Roibhilin."

"Just go to the mound after school."

"No. I have to find him right now. He was supposed to be here earlier, anyway."

"Oh, is that a fact now?" Patrick's voice was filled with sarcasm along with a touch of anger, and Brenna smiled weakly.

"Did I forget to mention that?"

"You did." His eyes narrowed. "I thought I told you that you weren't to go with him alone. Look what happened last time you up and ran off."

"Well, that was an accident."

"I'm getting the feeling," said Patrick grimly, "that accidents are a common thing around you."

"Only since I came to Ireland." Brenna grinned gamely then sighed. "Look, Patrick, I *have* to go. Roibhilin sounded very certain that he'd meet me this morning, but he never showed. What if something happened to him? And anyway, I have to let him know that I can find the girl now. I'm wearing the leprechaun's shoe, so it shouldn't take too long." She placed the chain back around her neck. "I'll be careful—I promise."

Brenna was halfway through one of the bushes when Patrick grabbed her arm, and she turned her head, surprised to see his face inches from hers, hazel eyes an almost gray color. Her heart quickened.

"I won't stop you…you're too stubborn and I know better than to try and tell you to stay," he said in a gruff voice. "But don't go and do anything brave, Brenna."

"I'm not brave, Patrick."

"You are. And 'tis as bad as being foolish. Come back by dark or I'm coming after you."

"But—"

Her protest was cut short as his lips pressed against hers. Her eyes widened, and for a moment she was sure that time really did stop. His grip on her arm slackened and he stepped away, a small smile quirking his lips.

"Go, Brenna, before I change my mind and stop you."

"Uh…uhhh…yeah." She nodded her head slowly then shook it. "Um. I'll…yeah."

Her feet took off without her, and she was a several feet away before she came to her senses again. Stopping, she turned around, poking her head from around a tree to call out to Patrick's retreating form.

"Patrick, my mom—"

"I'll tell her you've gone."

"Thank you!" She bit her lip. "And just now—"

"When you come back," he said over his shoulder, "we'll talk it over."

Brenna grinned then bounded back into the woods, feeling light-headed and even a little silly. "C'mon Brenna, focus. Focus!"

As hard as it was, she managed to push thoughts of Patrick aside and keep her eyes peeled for the ring of bushes that the pixies had led her to earlier. After scouring the forest, she finally managed to find the strange rock circle. Moss and tiny white mushrooms grew in between the stones, and Brenna walked carefully into the grass clearing. The smell of wet earth filled her nostrils, stronger than she had remembered it. Gripping the key, she closed her eyes.

"Little pixies, are you here?"

"Are you here?"

The tinkling mimicry of her voice had her smiling in relief, and she opened her eyes. The pixies floated down from the treetops but once again stopped short of going inside the circle.

"Where is Roibhilin?"

"Where is Roibhilin?" Once more they copied her question as one of the glowing beings flitted over to her, and Brenna held her hand open to let it land on her palm.

"Can you take me to him?"

"We will take you, Brenna of *Coillearnach*."

"Brenna of *Coillearnach*."

The pixies around her echoed each other, their voices resounding through the woods. With a little hop, the pixie in her hand floated upward, hovering over her palm for a moment before flying a few feet in front of her.

"Here."

It made a little dipping motion toward the ground where a dark-green ring of grass just large enough to place both her feet had appeared, and Brenna took a deep breath before stepping inside of it. In a sudden flurry and a burst of light, the pixies swirled around her, causing the world to flip sideways before spinning around sickeningly fast, and she stumbled to her knees as she felt a rush of wind hit her chest. Brenna closed her eyes and gripped the grass, placing every ounce of her focus on not throwing up. She was sure she was being moved, but the ground beneath her remained solid. Her stomach suddenly dropped then, much like how it did when she was on a rollercoaster, and then the falling sensation stopped. Slowly, she opened her eyes then gaped in surprise.

She was crouched in a golden field. Slowly, she stood up and put a hand to her brow to shield her vision from the sun and better scan her surroundings. Tall grass waved in a warm, summer breeze, the tips of the blades just brushing her waist. Flowers bobbed in between the grass, their petals beautiful and a strange shade of red. She could hear a creek babbling in the distance, the faint sound akin to a harp. The pixies swirled around her lazily, looking tired as they landed on flowers or took to resting in her hair.

"Where are we?"

"Roibhilin." One of the pixies on a blade of grass answered weakly, its whispery voice sounding far away.

Frowning, she looked at the endless, rolling hills in front of her. There wasn't a tree in sight, and Brenna was sure that this wasn't Roibhilin's land. Another warm breeze swept across her face and caused the grass to turn different shades of gold as the long, slender blades bent down like an undulating sea. Everything smelled fresh and clean, and Brenna felt the hills call to her, urging her to run across their gentle slopes. Rubbing her eyes with the heel of her hands, she ignored the call. Instead, she placed her fists on her hips and wrinkled her nose. The pixies clearly thought that Roibhilin was here, and for all of their giggling they actually seemed to know what they were doing.

Turning around, she felt her mouth go slack in awe and her breath catch in her throat. A massive castle composed of white rock, soaring arches, and cascading waterfalls pouring around its walls towered regally in the distance. Beyond it stood a jagged, dark-blue mountain range, causing the castle with its spires and peaks to stand out in sharp relief. She carefully took a pixie from her shoulder, cupping her hands as a rush of warm wind tousled her hair, and she thought she could hear bagpipes and flutes.

"Is that where Roibhilin is?"

"Yes, my dear, it is."

Fear shot down her spine as the pixies took flight. Brenna closed her eyes, willing herself to remain calm before turning to face Treasach whose voice had answered her so sweetly. He was dressed in a fine, green tunic, though most of it was covered by the same green cape that Roibhilin often wore, and encircling his wavy, black hair was a golden band that glinted dully in the sunlight. She took a step back and he shook his head, his smile beautiful and deadly.

"Now now, Brenna, I wouldn't run." He held out his hand, his smile mocking. "If you would be so kind, child, as to give me the key."

"No." Brenna gripped it tightly, holding it to her chest. Treasach seemed unconcerned and she felt her temper flare. "If you want it so badly, why don't you just take it from me?" She tilted her chin stubbornly. "You know I can't fight you."

"'Tisn't honorable for a *Tuath de Danann* to take." He looked so affronted that Brenna almost believed him. Almost.

"You killed Nuala." She fumed angrily. "You don't have any honor."

He chuckled, clearly amused. "I am afraid, dear girl, that you've been lied to. *She* was a traitor."

"She was not!"

"I assure you, mortal, she was." Treasach's gaze swept past her and his smile deepened. "Ah, just in time."

Brenna glanced over shoulder, blanching when she saw a group of men on dark horses riding toward them at an alarming speed. Treasach sauntered up to her, and she gritted her teeth together as he took her chin between his fingers, his bright blue eyes cold.

"You see, Brenna Morgan, I do not need to make you give me the key. You will give it to me quite willingly. Those men coming toward us are the Riders of the Sidhe, and they do not take kindly to intruders upon the king and queen's land. Give me the key and I will not let them harm you."

Brenna jerked her head from his grasp, backing away slowly. Treasach chuckled and then raised his hands. Beneath her feet, Brenna could feel the ground rumbling as the horses drew nearer. There was no escaping now. She stood as tall as she could, hoping that she looked braver than she felt.

"Never. And you won't get the *leanbh*, either."

"Oh, but I will. I always get what I want. It's a shame you didn't agree to my bargain, for you're such a lovely thing. Guards! Here is the traitor you have been looking for."

Faster than she could blink, seven swords were pointed at her throat, their silver tips glinting. The men carrying them were both tall and beautiful, their faces chilling. How they had gotten off their horses so quickly or so silently was something that Brenna was sure she would never know.

"Kneel," commanded one of the guards in a quiet but hard voice.

She slowly sank to her knees, wincing when one of the blades nicked her skin. Treasach brushed past one of the guards with easy arrogance, kneeling down so that his face was level with hers. He looked vastly amused, and Brenna resisted the urge to spit in his face. Barely.

"Have you changed your mind now?"

She narrowed her eyes then smiled defiantly "You wish. Go ahead and let them kill me. Then you'll never get the key."

"If that is your wish." He stood then and spoke in a much louder voice. "Brenna Morgan of *Coillearnach*, you are hereby under arrest for treason to the crown."

"*Coillearnach?*" One of the guards spoke up, sounding surprised. There was a slight shift in the atmosphere, and Brenna noticed several of them exchanging glances, clearly uneasy. The guard spoke up again, examining her warily.

"Are you sure, Lord Treasach, that she is of the house of *Coillearnach?*"

"Yes, quite certain. I saw the mark myself."

"But sir," chimed in another guard, his sword lowering slightly from Brenna's neck, "the house of *Coillearnach* has never before—"

"Do you doubt me, Turlough?" Treasach's temper was showing but he quickly calmed himself, easing his face into a congenial mask once more. "Have you ever known me to be of poor vision?"

"No, my lord. But..." The guard called Turlough glanced down uncertainly at Brenna, and she realized that he appeared to be much younger than the men around him. His light-brown hair fell stick-straight to his shoulders, offsetting the intense green color of his eyes, and his skin was so pale that it was lighter than even Deirdre's. For some reason, he reminded her of Roibhilin. The thought of him caused Brenna's spirits to rise, and she looked pleadingly at Turlough.

"I only came for Roibhilin." She heard the men mutter amongst themselves at this announcement, and Turlough lowered his sword farther, eyeing her with some interest. "I came to see him, that's all. I'm not a traitor. I'm not even one of you!"

"But Brenna," said Treasach with a smile so smug that she felt any hope she'd had instantly plummet, "you are."

Stepping away, he folded his arms across his chest as one of the guards grabbed her arms and tied them behind her back.

"Please," cried Brenna, "I haven't done anything wrong! I just wanted to see Roibhilin. Find him and he'll tell you I'm not a traitor, or one of you, or anything!"

"Her voice is quite annoying, is it not?" Treasach put a hand to his head. "Will one of you silence her?"

"Please, you have to believe me!" Brenna gazed imploringly at Turlough, trying not to let her fear show. "I just wanted to see Roibhilin, that's all. Please go get him."

"By the moon and stars, must I do everything myself?"

He slapped a thick, black fabric over her mouth and tied it tightly behind her head. Treasach stood over her, a bag in his hands. He leaned in close, his breath hot on her ear as he spoke. "You will die, Brenna Morgan. And when you do, you can be sure that Roibhilin will have the best view."

His smile was the last thing she saw before he threw the bag over head and hoisted her onto a horse. She wondered fleetingly if this was the darkness Kathleen had seen coming. She wished she would have listened.

Chapter Twelve

After a ride that came to an end all too soon, Brenna found herself being shoved into a cold room with the hood still stuck over her head. Without a single word from either Treasach or a guard, they slammed the door shut. After a few muttered curses, she managed to loosen the rope around her wrists enough to slip out of them, and she pulled the hood from her head. The lighting was dim, and the smell of wet, chalky stone pierced her senses. She waited for her eyes to readjust to the new darkness before taking in what she could of her surroundings.

All around her, gray stone was piled unevenly and narrow windows placed high above let in slits of light which spilled onto the cold but relatively clean flagstone floor. Moss with tiny white flowers grew from the cervices of the damp walls, and a wooden door stood in front of her. She walked over to it cautiously. Unlike Roibhilin's door, this one was without carvings or knotwork, the wood worn and as unwelcoming as the room it guarded. She gave it a tug, unsurprised when the door didn't so much as creak.

"Great."

Her voice bounced off the cavernous ceiling, and she stamped her foot in frustration before trudging over to a stone in the back of the room that had been roughly carved into a chair. She sat down upon it heavily, trying to make sense of her situation. She could feel tears prick her eyes, but she blinked them back. Crying wasn't going to fix anything, and neither was panicking. Taking a deep breath, she distractedly shook a hand through her short hair. What was it Kathleen had said? *Keep your wits about you.*

"Saints preserve us, a girl!" came a voice.

"*Gah!*"

Brenna jerked back, bumping her head against the stone chair as something lunged at her from the shadows of the large room. A man dressed in tattered, brown rags was staring at her. His large, pale blue eyes were almost completely round, and a frizzy, red beard hid his lips until he smiled, showing crooked and uneven yellow teeth. Brenna slapped a hand both to her smarting head and her nose as a blast of putrid fumes erupted from his mouth.

"Are ye a wee lass, then?! Have they sent ye to be my bride at last? They've been promising me so long…" He poked at her arm and Brenna leapt out of the chair, flattening herself against the wall.

"I'm *not* your bride!"

"A shame, a shame." The man bemoaned sadly, folding in on himself as he curled up in the chair. "I was a great lord, you know. A lord of so many subjects and cattle. I would be a great husband to you. You would have all the land and milk you wanted."

"I don't want land."

Brenna skirted along the wall and inched her way back toward the door. The man began muttering to himself, and Brenna closed her eyes against the sight before banging her fist on the door.

"Is anyone out there?!" Nothing but silence greeted her and she pounded on the door again, a bit more desperately this time. "Please! Someone open the door!"

"'Tis a fine scrape you've gotten yourself into, Brenna Morgan. And here I always thought I was the luckless one."

Startled, Brenna turned to see the leprechaun sitting atop the chair. The muttering man had skittered away, hiding himself in the shadows on the other side of the room once more. The leprechaun chuckled, and even in the poor lighting his shocking orange hair and bright red coat stood out.

"How did you get in here?"

"Sure, there isn't a door in this world or the next that can keep me out." His black eyes twinkled merrily and he tapped his long, slender pipe against his lips. He looked around the room, clearly amused. *He probably thinks everything's amusing*, Brenna thought dourly.

"How did ye go and find your way to Midhir's court, then? 'Tis a hard place to find."

"The pixies took me."

"Pixies?" The leprechaun looked surprised, but then he laughed, clapping his hands in delight. "Those pesky troublemakers! They've gone and done ye disservice, lass! And here you are in a cold dungeon."

"Hey, I *asked* for their help. I was trying to find Roibhilin, and I wouldn't have found him without them."

"Do ye see Roibhilin here, then?"

"Well, I mean...*no*." She groaned and walked over to the stone wall, leaning against it while the leprechaun puffed on his pipe and looked at home sitting atop the chair.

"Brenna Morgan, you're a brave lass, but you don't do much by way of thinking a thing through."

"I know." She ran a hand through her hair as smoke from the glossy, wooden pipe between the leprechaun's lips swirled above her. "Can you get me out of here?"

"Well and sure I could have you out as quick as a wink, but you wouldn't be likin' me price. No lass, yer safer here than downstairs, I promise you."

Brenna sighed, her brief spike of hope quashed, and she slumped onto her knees. "Treasach said that Nuala was a traitor."

"She's as much a traitor as I am a horse," snorted the leprechaun. "Now, the past is the past, and 'tis the future ye need be thinkin' of. Why did they go and throw you in here?"

"Treasach said I was being arrested for treason to the crown."

"Treason?" For once, the leprechaun didn't sound amused and he stopped puffing his pipe. "That can't be. You're not of their court."

"I *tried* to tell them that! But Treasach said I was one of them."

"Well, well. 'Tis a fine web they've spun 'round you. Even I can't make heads or tales o' the matter."

"But I'm not one of them, am I?"

"Sure and how would I know that?" He narrowed his eyes. "If they're to try ye in their court...well. You're on Midhir's land. He's a fair sort as far as the *Tuath de Danann* are concerned."

"The Tooth...de Danann...what's that?"

"You mortals call them all manner of things like Good Folk, Gentry, Good Neighbors, The Others, or," and here the leprechaun's lips twisted into a grimace, "*fairies.* But for all of time they're the *Tuath de Danann*, right and proper. The Children of Danu. Or the Men of Dea, as they are sometimes known. Did ye not know that?"

"I might have read it somewhere," Brenna hedged, not wanting to admit that she knew almost nothing about them. She changed the topic quickly. "Midir is fair, huh? Will he believe me?"

"Perhaps." The leprechaun hopped from the chair, his well-made shoes clattering loudly on the pavers as he began to walk restlessly around the room. He put his pipe away after a few turns, tucking it into his red vest.

"When ye get to court, don't try to plead to the king. Look to Queen Etain—she will be easier to win over. And if you win her favor, you'll win the king's."

"But how am I supposed to convince them I didn't do whatever it is they think I've done?"

"Speak the truth, mortal."

Brenna threw her hands up in exasperation. "What if they don't believe me?"

"Then *make* them believe you."

Growling in frustration, Brenna tugged at her hair. Her eyes narrowed in suspicion. "Why are you helping me, anyway?"

He paused before he spoke taking out his pipe once more and puffing on it thoughtfully. "Duty."

"Duty? What kind of duty?"

"Who are you talking to in there?"

Whirling around, Brenna saw the large door open, revealing Turlough. His long, red cape swirled around him like an angry cloud, and the frown on his face was thunderous. Brenna glanced over to the leprechaun only to find that both he and his smoke had once again disappeared. She looked back to the guard who had crossed his arms over his chest in a gesture that reminded her too much of Roibhilin.

"I was talking to myself." She studied him, and then took a chance on her hunch. "You're a good friend of Roibhilin's, aren't you?"

He looked startled before his frown deepened, eyeing her cautiously.

"And how would you know that?"

"You stand like he does."

Turlough quickly unfolded his arms, and his cheeks took on a rosy color as he glared at her. "His mother fostered me."

"Fostered you?"

"She took me in to train under her before I became a Rider of the Sidhe." He cleared his throat then. "I should not be talking to you."

He turned to leave and Brenna dashed after him.

"Wait!" Desperate, she seized his cape. Faster than she could blink, she found herself dangling high on the wall, held up only by Turlough's forearm. She gasped for breath as his limb smashed tightly across her chest, his vivid green eyes glittering dangerously.

"I'm sorry! I didn't mean to. I only…" She glanced at the man in the corner who was watching them with wide eyes.

"I'm afraid he's going to kill me."

"Who?"

"That man."

Warily, Turlough spared a look over to the unkempt man and then slowly released Brenna. She took in gasps of air as she slid back down to the floor.

"He will not harm you."

"But he thinks I'm going to marry him."

Turlough's lips twitched into a smile, his anger subsiding. Brenna didn't see what was so funny about it.

"He thinks *everyone* who comes in here will marry him. He drank too much of our wine long ago and has never been quite right ever since. Her Majesty did not have the heart to cast him back into the human realm."

Glancing over her shoulder at the shaggy heap, she felt a pang of sympathy. Now wasn't the time to talk about a man who wanted to get married, though, and Brenna returned her attention to Turlough.

"Your name is 'Turlah', right?"

"Aye." His guard came up yet again, and Brenna knew that she had to tread carefully.

"Could you tell me…I don't know what I've done to be a traitor."

"And you think I would know?"

"Well, don't you?"

Turlough's lips thinned and, as he scrutinized her, he seemed to come to a decision. He strode over to the door, peering outside before closing it slightly, his voice low and grim. "You are to be tried for the murder of Nuala of *Coillearnach*."

Brenna's eyes widened and she took a step back. "I didn't kill her!"

Clearly not believing her, Turlough opened the door wide and stepped outside. Brenna's temper flared.

"I *didn't* kill her! Ask Roibhilin—he'll tell you!"

"Roibhilin is also being questioned."

"What?" Her heart sank and Turlough's free hand clenched into a fist. "I do not believe it of him. He is as my brother, and never would he…" He shook his head, distrust in his eyes once more. "You are easy to talk to."

Brenna blinked in surprise, her temper forgotten at the change of topic. "I…um. Thanks?"

"'Tisn't a compliment." He scowled, eyeing her up and down. "You remind me much of Aideen."

"Who?"

"Roibhilin did not speak to you of her?"

"The only thing Roibhilin and I talk about is—" Remembering who she was speaking to, Brenna pursed her lips. There was no point in trying to defend herself against someone who didn't like her, even if he was Roibhilin's friend. "Well, we've never talked about Aideen," she muttered. "Whoever that is."

"No, I suppose he would not have done," said Turlough almost to himself. "Here now, leave me alone, and do not cause a ruckus any longer."

With those parting words, he slammed the door. Brenna rolled her eyes before marching back to the stone chair to sit and think. In the shadows, the bearded man gazed at her longingly.

"Are you my bride?"

"*No!*"

The man sighed and rocked a little. "I would have made you a fine husband. I have land, you know."

"Ugh."

Rubbing her head, Brenna sighed. She was pretty sure that she was going to be as insane as the deranged man in the corner by the time they came to get her. Closing her eyes, she held the key in her hand and hoped that Roibhilin was faring better than herself.

* * * *

"Brenna Morgan of *Coillearnach*."

Startled out of a sleep she hadn't realized she'd fallen into, Brenna snapped to attention. The door had opened to admit two guards who were unfamiliar to her, and she almost wished it had been Turlough. At least he wouldn't have looked as intimidating as the stone-faced men before her.

"You've been summoned."

She slowly rose to her feet, wincing when her muscles protested at the movement. Falling asleep on a stone slab definitely hadn't made for a comfortable sleep. Combing her fingers carefully through her hair and rubbing the exhaustion from her eyes, she tried to keep herself from shaking. She had nothing to fear, she reminded herself. She hadn't done anything wrong. The men motioned for her to follow them and Brenna squared her shoulders, refusing to let them see how nervous she was.

The bearded man howled after her, and his animalistic cries sent shivers up her spine before they were silenced when the heavy wooden door was pushed shut. With one guard behind her and the other in front, they led her down a long, brightly lit hallway lined with enormous tapestries depicting moving animals. In the distance, she could hear music being played followed by muffled laughter and shouts. She rubbed her arms as goose bumps formed on them. Looking up, she saw that the rounded roof supported several crystal chandeliers, but how they were giving off light she wasn't sure.

Brenna was so busy staring up at them that she missed the first step down a long flight of stairs, and were it not for the quick tug from the guard behind her she would've probably broken every bone in her body. She smiled weakly up at him as he righted her.

"Thank you."

Her gratitude went unanswered. The farther they went down the spiraling white staircase the louder the music and the voices grew.

Brenna glanced up the stairs, surprised. She had always thought that dungeons were in the basements of castles, not at the top. The guards motioned for her to stop when they reached slender double doors sporting now-familiar carvings. Her heart hammering in her chest, Brenna tried hard not to flinch as the guard flung them open. She wasn't sure what she was expecting to see, but a massive room full of men and women in the throes of what looked to be a very festive ball was not one of them.

"King Midhir, we bring to you Brenna Morgan of the House of *Coillearnach*."

"Bring her forward," a beautiful, baritone voice called out from the other side of the room over the crowd's laughter. The airy music stopped instantly and the large assembly turned as one, quickly parting to form a clear path straight down the center of the room. Brenna's feet were rooted to the spot as the guard in front of her moved aside, revealing high vaulted ceilings speckled with dancing lights and wooden beams strung with thick garlands of flowers and greenery. She was pushed forward, and Brenna felt as though she were a five year old who had gotten caught crashing her parent's party. Finding it difficult to breath, she stepped into the room, an act which caused several of the court women to step back. Others eyed her with interest and many with distaste. Clenching her teeth together, Brenna held her head high and marched forward.

"You are *not* guilty of anything, Brenna," she told herself under her breath. "Nothing."

She tried to ignore the stares, but it was impossible not to stare back. The men and women were so beautiful that it was hard to disregard them completely. They were all easily a head taller than her, and most had their hair braided and woven with gold wire and precious stones. The women's vibrantly hued dresses were made of silks and gauze delicately embroidered with knot work. Their skin was pale and smooth, their lips and cheeks rosy and free of any imperfections. Brenna glanced self-consciously at her school uniform with its wrinkled, white shirt and baggy skirt. Heat crept up her cheeks as she ran a hand through her thick, blonde hair. She looked even more like a scarecrow than usual.

Trying not to draw too much attention, she discretely tried to straighten her skirt as best she could when she heard a low gasp. Startled, she stopped and then felt her stomach drop. Roibhilin was standing only a foot away from her with Turlough at his side at the front line of the crowd. Brenna opened her mouth to call to him, but he shook his head tightly, his lips set in a grim line. Through the silence, the baritone voice called out to her.

"Many welcomes to *Bri Leith*, Brenna Morgan."

The guards departed then, leaving her to stand before two of the most beautiful people she had ever seen. Atop a low platform, a man broad of shoulder with a head of wavy, golden hair sat in an ornate wooden chair. He looked to be no older than his early thirties, and his deep blue eyes were so bright that even at twenty feet away she could see them clearly. His lips weren't smiling, but they tilted up at the corners as if he were secretly amused at everything before him. Next to him on a delicate, silver chair sat a young woman so elegant and flawless that even the other women of the court couldn't compare to her. Her hair was the same color as her husband's and hung in thick braids that had been twisted in loops around her head. Her full lips were unnaturally red, and her green dress brought out the deep blue of her eyes.

The queen glanced at Brenna for a moment before letting her gaze slide away, clearly uninterested. Brenna took a step back in dismay; the queen was human. Her eyes didn't have the same intense coloring of her husband's and reminded her of Mahoney. Turning her attention back to the king, she did the only thing she could think of. She bowed.

"Thank you, Your Majesty."

"Will you not have food or drink? I am sure you must very hungry, and I would not have a guest go hungry or thirsty."

While Brenna tried to understand why he was being so nice to her, two fairies only half the height of herself stepped forward, golden trays laden with fruits and cheeses in their hands. The smell coming from the plates was more intoxicating than anything she'd ever experienced before, and she clasped her hands together to keep them from grabbing at the food. She didn't want to end up like the man in the dungeon. Slowly, she shook her head.

"Thank you…but I'm not hungry."

The king laughed, the sound musical and genuine as he leaned forward, his eyes sparkling with humor. Brenna felt a blush rise to her cheeks. She could see now why the women in folklore could be lured so easily into the fairie realm.

"You are a clever girl. A lesser man would have taken the food."

"Well, I'm not a man."

Several people in the crowd laughed. The queen who had until now seemed disinterested suddenly looked to Brenna with a measuring eye.

"And humor. 'Tis a good quality in so fair a maiden. Do you not think, Etain?"

Midhir turned to his wife. She was looking not at Brenna but at the key around her neck. Her gaze went to her husband and she smiled, though Brenna thought it looked sad for as much as it was beautiful.

"Yes. And she is so well spoken for a mortal of her time. Very respectful."

"Indeed." Midhir stood then, and Brenna realized that as tall as Roibhilin was, the king was quite a bit taller. "Since you are neither hungry nor thirsty, Brenna Morgan, then we must now deal with the task at hand." He beckoned her closer, and Brenna cautiously took a few steps forward. Feeling on edge, she rolled a few strands of her hair between her fingers.

"You are a servant of the House of *Coillearnach*, are you not?"

"I don't think I am. I'm just a human."

"If that is so, then we cannot charge you, for as a human you are not bound to our laws. But we have reason to believe that you are a servant of that house."

Midhir studied her for a moment then raised his hand. A young boy with delicate features quickly left the crowd to join the king who bent down to hand him a tiny, gold-hilted dagger. Turning, the boy walked up to Brenna, his dark hair curling above green eyes. Quickly, he took the slender knife and cut off three of her buttons before tearing off the upper left side of her shirt. As one, the crowd gasped and their musical voices began to chatter, clearly excited about whatever it was they were seeing. Brenna put a hand to her chest, trying to feel for whatever it was that had them all talking. She felt nothing but smooth skin and, try as she might, she couldn't see anything, either.

Turning around, she saw Roibhilin a few feet away staring at a spot a little below her collarbone in shock before rubbing his head in a sign of vexation she knew all too well. She frowned, then groaned. When Nuala had told her to run, she'd felt a burning sensation on her chest; clearly she had done something to her. Brenna supposed it made sense now why the pixies in the forest kept welcoming her 'home'. Embarrassed, she tried to pull up her sleeve to cover her exposed shoulder and chest as she turned to the king. His expression was unreadable, but the queen was sitting up from her reclined position, looking oddly hopeful. Raising his hand once more, Midhir silenced the crowd.

"It appears, Brenna Morgan, that you carry the mark of the house." He cast his blue eyes over to Roibhilin.

"Do you recognize this girl as a servant of your house?"

All eyes turned to him, and Brenna held her breath. His emotions were as hard to read as the king's.

"I did not place the mark upon her and so must assume that my mother did." He looked to Brenna, and despite his calm expression she could see a muscle twitch in his jaw. If she lived through this, she was pretty sure he was going to kill her. "I will recognize it and her loyalty to my house."

Heat blazed in Brenna's cheeks as she released her breath, and the king turned his attention back to her. "Human or not, child, you promised fealty to the House of *Coillearnach*, and as such you will be tried as one of us. The charge leveled at you is the murder of your lady, Nuala of *Coillearnach*. Is this true?"

"No." Brenna's hands fisted at her sides of their own accord. "I didn't kill her."

"Do not believe her my lord. She is quite expert at lying."

Treasach came forward from the crowd, his smile and posture all ease and grace.

"I'm not lying." She narrowed her eyes as he made a tsking sound and cast a sympathetic glance upon her.

"You see, my lord? Quite expert. I believe she might even have convinced herself."

The crowd murmured amongst themselves, and Brenna felt her blush grow warmer. "I'm not lying!" Her loud voice silenced the speculating masses and even the king looked surprised at her outburst.

Clearing her throat, she took a few steps sideways to get away from Treasach who had sashayed himself next to her. "I didn't kill Nuala. I was trying to help her."

"Help her?" Etain spoke now, and she was sitting forward again, her eyes filled with some sort of emotion that Brenna couldn't quite place, but it gave her hope. She looked to Queen Etain, remembering the leprechaun's words.

"Yes, Your Majesty. She asked for my help, and I promised I would give it." She lifted her chin stubbornly. "I keep my promises."

"I see." And Brenna thought that she *did* see. Etain stood gracefully, stepping forward to put a hand on her husband's arm.

"Perhaps we should hear what this mortal has to say."

"My Queen," laughed Treasach, "surely you would not listen to a liar."

"I will listen to whomever I choose, Treasach." The queen's blue eyes were hard and cold, and Brenna's lips curled into a satisfied smile when she saw him roll his shoulders uncomfortably.

"Very well." Taking his wife's hand in his, Midhir looked to Brenna. "How are we to trust that you are telling the truth?"

"I...I don't..." She bit her lip, looking at the beautiful, expectant faces around her. She could feel sweat bead on her forehead, and she tugged absentmindedly on her hair, at a loss for words. How *could* she make them all believe her?

"Do not fear us, Brenna." The queen's voice was soft, much as how a mother would talk to a frightened child, and she smiled encouragingly. Slowly, Brenna nodded her head and took a deep breath.

"I know I'm not one of you, and you've never met me before. But I swear that I didn't kill Nuala. And I know who did."

Beside her, Treasach snorted in derision. Glancing over her shoulder, she shot Roibhilin a questioning look, relieved when gave her the smallest of nods. It was all the encouragement she needed. Turning, she faced the king and queen once more.

"Treasach murdered her."

The room filled with an audible gasp as all eyes turned to Treasach who appeared unperturbed by her accusation.

"Is this true?" Midhir's voice cut through the excited murmuring, and quickly the assembly fell silent, held in rapture at the drama unfolding before them.

"Of course not, your Grace." Treasach laughed, and Midhir leveled his intense blue eyes at Brenna. They were no longer filled with amusement.

"These are heavy accusations you lay at the feet of one of my best men, Brenna Morgan."

"I know I don't have…I don't have proof, but he's the one who killed her. I was there."

"She is clearly seeking to place blame on someone." Treasach sent her a condescending glance. "Indeed, I am surprised she does not lay the murder on Roibhilin himself."

"I don't need to blame Roibhilin. *He* wasn't the one who ran Nuala through with a sword."

Somewhere in the crowd, a woman shrieked and promptly fainted. Brenna kept her hands fisted at her sides, the insides clammy from fear. Midhir looked between the two of them, clearly troubled, while Etain kept her gaze steadily on Brenna.

"My lord, how can you take her word when she has no proof? I ask that for insulting my name and murdering Her Majesty's most trusted friend, we banish this human to the Fomorians and let them do as they will with her."

She had no idea who or what the Fomorians were, but guessing from the horrified looks of those in the crowd, they were probably something nightmarishly awful.

"My love," said Midhir, turning to his wife, "what do you council?"

"Indeed, this is a hard and strange circumstance." Etain straightened her shoulders, looking beautiful and wise all at once. Brenna's breath caught in her throat, her heart hammering in her chest when she looked into those blue eyes. "But I would hear this human's case." She stared at Brenna with her strange, flat gaze. "After all, Nuala would not have marked this girl if she did not trust her."

"What nonsense!" cried Treasach. "You would listen to the word of a mortal—a *stranger*—over mine, your own advisor?"

"Wait, you're the king's advisor?!"

Treasach shot Brenna an annoyed look. Clearly, she wasn't the only one feeling under pressure. She could feel the bright eyes of the *Tuath de Danann* boring into her, and though she couldn't hear them talking she was sure every single one of them found her guilty. She glanced down and brushed her fingers against the iron key which had become a touch warmer than her own body heat. She didn't have any proof of her innocence save for the key. Glancing up again, she noticed the queen regarding her with great sadness. It wasn't a promising look.

Beside her, Treasach recovered some decorum and put a hand to his chest. "Have I not always given you the wisest of council, Midhir? Have I given you reason to ever doubt my word or my loyalty?"

"No, Treasach, you have not."

"Then heed my words now. This girl is a danger to us and all at court and should be removed to the Fomorians immediately."

"I am *not* a danger." Anger rose over her fear and Brenna turned to face Treasach, green eyes flashing.

"Of course you are! Look there, Your Majesty, at the iron around her neck. She wears it for protection so that she might harm you or Her Majesty, Etain."

"That's a lie!" Brenna clutched at the key. "Nuala gave me this key!"

Midhir had to shout more than once for silence as the court erupted into a chorus of shocked and angry voices, and Brenna snuck a peek over her shoulder. Roibhilin's face was set in an unreadable mask.

"Come closer, child." Midhir's voice was hard as it echoed off of the stone walls. With weak knees, Brenna made her way up to him, halting on the low, third step leading to the platform upon which the royals stood. He motioned for her to kneel, and reluctantly Brenna dropped to her knees. Bending low, Midhir reached his large hand out to touch the key, but his fingers trembled and shook violently as he tried to do so. Sweat beaded his forehead and, with a hiss, he drew his hand back, rubbing his now-red fingers.

"By the moon and stars, that is a strong spell." He studied both the key and Brenna intently before straightening. "It would do you credit to give this key to me, for none can take it unless you give it freely."

Brenna's mouth fell open in shock. *So that's why Treasach and Roibhilin keep asking me for the key instead of just taking it*, she thought with some wonder. There was a spell on it. Ever so slowly, she stood up and clutched the key as she shook her head.

"I can't."

"Why?" Brenna detected a bit of anger in the king's surprised voice, and she licked her lips nervously.

"I promised Nuala I would protect it."

"Why would she give you the key?" The queen posed this question, and Brenna noticed that while she appeared aloof, her hands were clasped together and shaking.

"To keep Treasach from getting his hands on it." Brenna looked between Midhir and Etain, feeling as though something in them had shifted. "He wanted it, but she wouldn't give it to him. That's why he killed her. She saved my life, Your Majesty. I'm only trying to keep my promise."

"What did you promise her?" Etain's voice was nothing but a whisper, and she gripped her husband's arm tightly. Midhir glanced worriedly at his wife, placing his hand over hers.

"I promised—"

Brenna hesitated. Nuala had wanted her to protect the child, but could she tell them that? She glanced around. Were there more enemies in here than just Treasach?

Treasach laughed into the rapidly stretching silence. "Do not listen to her words, Your Majesty." Brenna spun around to see him approaching the dais. Despite his easy manner, she could see a slightly wild look in his eyes. He stopped before the steps, and the golden circlet around his black hair gleamed coldly in the light. "She would tell you only more lies to save herself."

"I begin to think that you protest too much." Etain narrowed her eyes, forcing Treasach into silence. "Please Brenna, tell me what you promised Nuala."

Brenna tried to keep her excitement down, and it took everything she had not to smile when she heard Treasach make a flustered noise. *Speak the truth*, the leprechaun had said. Taking a deep breath, she spoke as clearly and as loudly as she could to make sure that everyone in the great hall heard her, knowing this was her only shot to get the truth out.

"Your Majesties, Nuala was already wounded when I found her. She gave me the key and made me promise to keep it safe. I promised her I would, and then…and then she saved my life when Treasach tried to kill me. To kill both of us."

"How dare you accuse me of such a horrendous act!"

"I'm not accusing you," Brenna cried, "I'm telling you what you *did*!"

"Treasach, is this true?"

Midhir's voice was hard and cold, and Brenna turned to see that despite his commanding tone, his eyes were filled with pain. The queen had sunk to the floor, looking ill. Peering over Treasach's head, Brenna saw Roibhilin edge away from the crowd and into the aisle, despair and anger warring in his eyes. She wished that she could have told Roibhilin what had happened earlier, but it was too late now.

"Of course not, my lord! I am insulted that you would deign to even question me!" Treasach was all wounded pride, but Brenna could see fear flash across his face.

"It *is* true, Your Majesty," she pressed. "He killed Nuala for the key. She refused to give it to him."

Midhir closed his eyes, rubbing his forehead. When he looked up, his grief was plain on his face and caused Brenna's heart to ache.

"Treasach, you have been my friend these long years."

"Yes, Your Majesty. Which is why you must—"

"But I have been blinded by you for too long, it seems."

From the outskirts of the crowd, seven men in deep green velvet tunics appeared as Midhir raised a fisted hand, and Treasach's calm manner deteriorated.

"Midhir—"

"Do not speak another word." Midhir's voice was unforgiving and Brenna looked to the queen who seemed to have recovered slightly and was standing once more.

"For the murder of Nuala, you are to be tried—"

"*No!*"

Faster than she could blink, Brenna found herself plucked from the steps and dragged back down to the clearing before the platform. Treasach had seized her upper arm in a crushing grip, his fingers digging into her skin, and she cried out in pain as she felt her bone snap. Panting and dizzy, she fell to her knees. The crowd around them roared in anger, and guards lining either side of the hall held them at bay.

The pain in her arm caused the world to spin in a topsy-turvy manner before it righted itself, and Brenna took several long breaths to keep herself from throwing up. Treasach still had his hand on her arm, and the heat coming off of it made the pain worse. The key blazed like fire against her chest, and a distant part of herself wondered if it would leave a mark on her skin. Grimly, she looked up to Treasach, a tight smile on her lips.

"I guess you're not getting the child now, huh?"

"Be silent, you wretched human!"

"Treasach, unhand her!" The king had tried to step forward but Etain had stopped him, clinging to his arm. Brenna glanced over at Roibhilin and Turlough, both with swords drawn, blocking the crowd from coming any closer. Determined, Brenna spoke again, struggling to make her voice loud enough for everyone to hear.

"Your Majesty, the reason Treasach murdered her, why he wants the key…what I promised to protect wasn't just the key. Nuala asked me to—"

"She says nothing but more lies, my lord!"

"I promised I'd find and protect the *leanbh*!"

No one moved or breathed. The tension in the room was so thick that Brenna felt as though she could choke on it. Her vision was a bit fuzzy, but she could see the queen put her hands to her mouth and sink to her knees, tears streaming down her face. The king had stopped at the last step, stunned.

"*Leanbh?*"

"Yes." Feeling nauseous, Brenna used her free hand to hold the key up from around her neck.

"I promised Nuala to keep the key safe and find the *leanbh*. Treasach wants the child. He…he was going to sacrifice her. I heard the goblins saying it—and they were taking his orders."

"Lies!" cried Treasach, tugging roughly on Brenna's broken arm. Gritting her teeth together, it took everything in her not to let the darkness on the edge of her vision expand. She wished she could give him a kick, or bite him, but the world was spinning too much for her to do anything.

"Nuala was a traitor! That child she was protecting will kill us all!" he exclaimed. Through bleary eyes, Brenna could see the king slowly approaching. Treasach released her arm, and the pain subsided slightly. If she breathed slowly, she could keep the world in focus, and with great effort she managed to stand up.

"The only person who is a traitor is you, Treasach." The king stopped when he was only a couple feet away from his advisor, and Brenna narrowed her eyes when she saw Treasach's hand move ever so slightly.

"My king, I only killed Nuala to protect you!"

The audience gasped at his admission, and Brenna was sure that she saw something shining at his side.

"Nuala was a great and powerful protector of my wife, and this mortal has clearly gone above her own means to keep her promise. Treasach, you have dishonored your name and your family. Guards!"

"No!" Treasach sprung forward, a slender dagger in his hand as he launched himself at Midhir. Time seemed to slow down as Brenna flung herself in front of the king. All she could hear were her feet thudding dully on the floor. She was dimly aware of a tearing sound followed by a strange, hot pain in her back before falling heavily against Midhir's solid form.

Sound came rushing back to her with a mighty roar, and high-pitched screaming and cries assaulted her overly sensitive hearing before an eerie silence descended upon the room. Panting, she inhaled an earthy scent that reminded her of Roibhilin, and she looked up to see the king staring down at her feet. Confused, she followed Midhir's gaze downward and then nearly gagged.

Treasach's wide eyes stared back at her as his head rolled past, his golden circlet ringing against the flagstones. Black blood pooled in odd, uneven puddles along the floor. Brenna was aware of women wailing and men shouting, but somehow the chaos seemed far away as she staggered back from Midhir, feeling too warm. Shaking her head, she turned around, dazed. Roibhilin stood only a foot away from her, his sword drenched in black blood, his chest heaving as if he'd run a marathon.

"Roibhilin? Did you…?"

Brenna winced as she felt something stinging her back, and she awkwardly pressed her good hand to it. She could feel something warm and slick, and she pulled her palm away. Nausea roiled through her as she saw red blood drenching her hand like paint, its metallic scent filling her senses as she felt her knees give out. Briefly, she wondered why she always seemed to get stabbed in the back. The king shouted something from behind her, but it sounded muffled. Brenna was aware that Turlough had taken hold of her shoulders while Roibhilin's sword clattered to the ground. She tried to keep her eyes open, but her surroundings were blurring together, and the darkness on the edge of her vision was rapidly growing. She thought she heard someone call her name, but the numbing darkness came and she welcomed it.

Chapter Thirteen

Brenna heard voices from the murky depths of her mind, some familiar and some not. Several times she opened heavy lids to see faces that she recognized only to have them slip away again into darkness, and she gratefully slid back to that oblivion where she didn't have to think or feel. It was a cold hand on her brow that finally roused her from her sleep. She opened her bleary eyes, smiling faintly when she saw Mahoney's pale face hovering above her own.

"Thanks be, you're awake. Here now, love, drink this."

Dutifully, she swallowed whatever it was she found pressed to her lips. It tasted of honey and filled her whole mouth with something that was almost too sweet to swallow.

"Drink it all now, love."

Brenna grimaced and swallowed a mouthful before sitting up and sputtering. Mahoney sat next to her, gray eyes filled with relief as she set down the cup.

"What was that?" Brenna frowned. Her voice sounded like a frog's, and she rubbed at her sore throat.

"If you're after asking me questions, you must be feeling better. You gave Roibhilin and Their Majesties quite a scare."

Smiling gently, Mahoney brushed her pale hand over her charge's forehead, pushing her hair from her face. Accepting a cup of water, Brenna looked around. Once more she was in a bed, but this one was constructed of white wood, and a billowing, white canopy floated around her in a gentle breeze. To her right, double windows that led to a large balcony had been opened, and a warm, summer breeze smelling of flowers and fresh air wafted through them. Brenna inhaled deeply, contentment pouring through her. Her body felt heavy, and even sitting up so that her pillows could be adjusted took quite a bit of effort.

"Mahoney, what *happened*?"

"You were hurt." Mahoney gave her a pointed look, her brows raised. "Again."

"No, I mean after Treasach." The memory of his head rolling on the floor had Brenna feeling more than a little queasy. Mahoney patted her hand and poured another cup of water.

"Roibhilin took his life. And you saved the king's. T'was a brave thing you did."

"I don't feel brave. My body just kind of moved on its own..."

"Sometimes our bodies know what to do before our heads. Brenna, there are many people who wish to speak to you, but Roibhilin instructed me to keep them away until you were well."

Taking a brush from a drawer beside the bed, Mahoney pulled it gently through her hair, and Brenna sighed before sitting up to touch her back. Her skin was smooth save for her old scar, and try as she might she could feel no sign of any wound that Treasach might have left. Looking to Mahoney, she narrowed her eyes.

"Am I in trouble?"

"No." The woman laughed and set down the brush. "You've become quite the hero, indeed. It's sorry for you, I am."

"Sorry? Why?"

"You can be well and sure they won't ignore you any longer. And a more single-minded lot of people I've never met." Mahoney smiled. "Would you like me to fetch Roibhilin?"

"Ummm...that depends." Brenna recalled the last time she'd seen him. "Is he mad at me?"

"Of course not, love. Here now, lean forward."

Whatever Mahoney had made her drink seemed to take effect and, feeling much more rejuvenated, Brenna did as she was instructed with little difficulty. With a few swipes of the brush, a couple of twists, and a slight tug, Mahoney swept her hair up onto her head.

"Can you stand?"

"I can try."

Brenna carefully swung her legs over the side of the bed, her splotchy green and black shoes still firmly on her feet and reminding her that she wasn't sure how much time had passed—she could only hope it wasn't too much. Mahoney took up a silken green robe that was resting at the foot of the large bed. Helping Brenna into it, she tugged the right side to the left before fastening it with three ties. Walking to the vanity across from the bed was made easier with the support of Mahoney's arm, and Brenna blinked in surprise at her reflection as she sat down in a small chair in front of the mirror. Whatever Mahoney had done to her hair had caused the thick mass to look beautifully waved, two large chunks hanging loosely in front of her face. With deft hands, Mahoney took the free hair and braided it before pinning it up, a pleased smile on her face.

"There. As pretty as any girl at court, you are. Prettier, I would say."

"By the stars above, move!"

Roibhilin's irate voice came clearly through the large wooden door on the far side of the room. It burst open to reveal not only him but a host of other faces Brenna didn't recognize. Their shouts were muffled as Roibhilin slammed the door closed, his deep blue eyes flashing with annoyance. Brenna quickly stood, and Mahoney curtsied before moving away to the chair she had previously occupied.

"Mahoney, I thought I had asked you to remove them! How can they expect her to recover when they all have their voices raised?"

"I am but one person, Master Roibhilin. And might I point out you've gone and raised your own voice, as well." Mahoney gave Roibhilin an arch look which caused him to roll his eyes before they landed on Brenna.

He jerked back in surprise and then straightened, frowning. "You shouldn't be out of bed."

"I wouldn't be if I didn't feel better." She tugged on the robe, not quite sure what to do with herself or what to say to him. Roibhilin must have sensed her discomfort, for he sat down on a bench in front of the bed, and Brenna sank back into her chair.

"I suppose," he said with a somewhat surly tone, "I should thank you."

"For what?"

"For saving our king's life." He shifted in his seat, clearly uncomfortable. "And for clearing my mother's name."

"Oh. Um. You're welcome." She smiled, raising her brows. "Have you ever thanked anyone before?"

"Of course I have," he snapped

Brenna promptly crossed her arms. "Really? Because you're not very good at it. Most people, you know, *smile* and sound sincere when they say it."

"I would not say it if I did not mean it, human."

Rolling her eyes, Brenna uncrossed her arms. It seemed that his annoyed 'thank you' was as good as it was going to get. Not that she was surprised, as she recalled his less than stellar 'sorry' from last time. Clearing her throat, she opted to change the subject.

"Roibhilin, what happened? I mean…with Treasach."

"I killed him." Sadness darted across his face and he rubbed his eyes tiredly.

"I'm sorry." Nodding his head tightly, Roibhilin acknowledged her words before sighing, his shoulders sagging a bit. Brenna thought he looked defeated. "What happened after that?"

"He wounded you badly—you were bleeding very heavily." He looked at her through slanted eyes. "Do you always have to do such foolish things?"

Brenna shrugged, an action which elicited a sound of disgust from Roibhilin. "What happened then?"

"After Treasach was…well. Several others in court appeared to have been supporting him and tried to attack, as well. Stupid of them. After they were disposed of, King Midhir took you to this room personally, and Queen Etain saw to your wounds herself." He held up a hand when she opened her mouth to speak. "You have been gone from the human world for twenty-four hours. It is currently twelve thirty above ground."

Brenna bit her lip. She hoped Patrick had spoken with her mother, otherwise she could foresee a two-year stint in a jail in Borneo. "Can I go home?"

"Not at present, I'm afraid."

The baritone voice startled both Roibhilin and Brenna, and the former quickly stood to bow as Midhir swept into the room, a green cape held by a golden clasp swirling around his shoulders. With his hands on his hips, the king looked between the two of them and then motioned for Roibhilin to sit down. Behind Midhir, two childlike beings appeared, their twig-thin arms and legs bowed dramatically as they silently set down a wooden chair near Brenna. The king stood before her after only four great strides, and he shook his head when she tried to rise.

"No, my child, it is I who kneel before you."

Looking impossibly elegant, Midhir swept down onto one knee and took her hand in his, placing it on his chest. Heat crept up Brenna's cheeks, and she felt her heart flutter in an odd rhythm.

"Brenna Morgan of *Coillearnach,* you have saved my life, and for that I am in your debt."

Tears welled in her eyes, and she found it hard to swallow as she saw the king's immense gratitude. "No. I'm only glad I could help. Nuala would have done the same, wouldn't she?"

Midhir searched her face as if seeing her anew, and when he smiled she thought she saw tears in his eyes. "She would have done so, yes." He looked to Roibhilin then and stood, releasing Brenna's hand.

"I am in your debt, as well. As they have done for so long, your house has once more protected us. And now," he turned his gaze back to Brenna, "I am afraid that we can no longer exchange pleasantries. Time has run short for us, and my wife needs words with you. Are you strong enough, Brenna Morgan?"

"To listen to someone talk? Sure."

The king chuckled and made a motion with his hand. Outside the hall, the crowd had departed, allowing Etain to enter the room, the scent of delicate flowers following after her. Her hair was no longer in braids, falling instead to the floor in a living mass of golden waves. Her blue eyes were large and luminous. Had Brenna not still been trying to recover her strength she would have stood out of respect. With a flutter of delicate, green sleeves, Etain kneeled before Brenna and took her hands into her own slender ones.

"Brenna Morgan, you have saved my husband's life and brought honor upon yourself." She looked to Midhir who placed a large hand on her slim shoulder. She closed her eyes briefly before looking back to Brenna, smiling sadly. "Nuala chose well when she picked you. And it is many questions that you have, I am sure. Did Nuala tell you of…of the child?"

"No, there wasn't really time. She only told me to find her and to keep her safe before Samhain."

"Of course. It is a wonder I did not see this before." Midhir's voice was hard as he looked out the window, his free hand clenched into a tight fist. The hair on the back of Brenna's neck rose as she felt a current of electricity jolt through the air, the tension in the room now suddenly and inexplicably thick. Etain gripped her hands harder, and Brenna turned her attention back to the queen. Her eyes were swimming in unshed tears before a few slipped down her rosy cheeks.

"That child, Brenna Morgan, is mine. No one was to know of her." She took a shuddering breath, squaring her shoulders. "You see, she is prophesied to be both the demise and the savior of my people. And of yours."

Brenna jerked her hands from the queen's, stunned. Had Treasach been right all along? Had Nuala been a traitor? She must have looked ill, for Mahoney rushed over and put a steadying hand on her shoulder.

"I…I don't understand. If she's supposed to kill us all, then why did you save her?"

"Just as she can destroy, so can she create. In the wrong hands, she would bring destruction upon our worlds. But in the right ones…" Etain clasped her hands together, her head bowed down in sorrow as her tears spilled and created dark stains on her green dress. "It was foretold that in this year my daughter would be at her most powerful—and her most vulnerable. Those who would wish harm on us have been looking for her. Nuala had vowed to keep her hidden until after Samhain passed, when my daughter would no longer be such a threat. Treasach discovered this. How, I know not. But it was he who told our enemy of my daughter and put her and our world in danger."

Brenna put a hand to the key looped around her neck where it rested warmly against her chest. Her own hands were cold, and she gripped the iron tightly. "So, if I can keep her safe until after Samhain, then nothing bad will happen?"

"Yes, but…" Etain frowned, looking to her husband before turning her confused face back toward Brenna. "But, my child, we cannot ask that of you. You have done much for us already, and it is too dangerous to let you do so. Give me the key and I will send someone else to find her."

"No."

"Mortal, do as Her Majesty says." Roibhilin glared at Brenna as he bit the words out. She narrowed her eyes, brushing Mahoney's hand from her shoulder.

"Brenna Morgan, no one is questioning your courage or honor. Your responsibilities are done, and we will send you back to the safety of your world." Midhir's voice was gentle, and Brenna could see that though he spoke to her his mind was somewhere else. With a slight struggle, she stood up on shaking legs and jutted her chin out stubbornly as she looked up at the king.

"No. Nuala entrusted me to find and protect the child, and that's exactly what I'm going to do. Besides," she crossed her arms before continuing, "my world isn't exactly safe, either, and if I can help, I'm going to. I know how to find your daughter now, and I know how to keep her safe."

"We could lock you up and find the girl ourselves."

Brenna simply rolled her eyes at Roibhilin's threat. "Really? I seem to recall that the key has to be *freely* given, and I don't feel like giving it to anyone right now."

"Brenna, you do not understand the risks involved." Etain had risen to her feet, and she wiped at her eyes.

"Sure I do. If I get caught, I die. But I won't. I know how to protect myself." Roibhilin gave a short but derisive laugh, and Brenna glared at him. "I do. But I need to go to my house to get what I need. I can find your daughter, Your Majesties, and keep her safe. I won't take no for an answer."

No one spoke for several seconds. Finally the king sighed, his shoulders sagging somewhat.

"Very well. Brenna Morgan of *Coillearnach*. Bring my daughter back to *Bri Leith* and do so as quickly as you are able. I will prepare my army." His voice was hard, and a feverish light had entered his eyes.

"My dear, do not be hasty. If Brenna can bring our child back to us, there would be no need to go to war."

"They have threatened my family and our people and turned some of our own against us. There must be recompense for that. Roibhilin, will you ride with me?"

Clearly surprised at this turn of events, Roibhilin's normally cool expression gave way to shock, and his body jerked slightly. "Your Majesty, I am not a Rider of Sidhe—"

"You have more than proven yourself worthy. Ride with me and mine."

Before he could reply, Etain placed a hand on her husband's arm. "Do you not think he would be better served protecting Brenna? He knows the woods and hills above better than any and would be much helped by the pixies."

The king rubbed his chin thoughtfully. "You council wisely, Etain." He looked to Roibhilin. "You are charged with the safety of Brenna Morgan and my daughter."

"Yes, my lord."

"Good. And one other, I think. Roibhilin, fetch Turlough. He is worth three good men alone."

"Do you not think we should send more?" Worriedly, Etain gripped Midhir's arm, and he took her hand, kissing the delicate fingers with such reverence that Brenna felt a blush creep up her cheeks as she looked away. Roibhilin had also averted his gaze, instead casting his blue eyes toward a far wall.

"If we send too many, those who would harm our daughter might suspect we know too much of their plans. And we must act quickly. Roibhilin, go you to Turlough."

Bowing deeply, Roibhilin did as he was commanded, but not before casting a withering glance at Brenna. Rolling her eyes once more, she slumped back in the chair, feeling weary but awake. Etain smiled kindly at her while Midhir began to pace.

"I must gather my men..." He looked to his queen. "War will happen, Etain, and well you know it."

"I do not like it, Midhir. There is a feel about this that is not right."

"Excuse me, but who exactly are you going to fight?" Brenna fingered the key as she spoke, and Midhir frowned.

"I know not. But I trust that when you return with my daughter our enemy will be close on you. And when they appear, I will make a swift end of them." Midhir bowed over Brenna's hand. "Excuse me, now. I have much to do and very little time in which to do it."

With a brief kiss to his wife, he left the room. Etain stared after him. Wrinkling her nose, Brenna crossed her arms. "Does he really like to fight?"

"He is angry. With me especially."

"Why?"

"He did not know of our child."

Brenna felt her jaw go slack, and she stared at the queen in wonder. "You didn't tell him?! Why?"

"For the very reason you see now. He will go to war, and I fear for his life. Whoever wants my daughter is powerful. Powerful enough to turn my husband's own advisor against him." Etain sunk wearily into the chair that had been brought in and put a hand to her head. "I had hoped to avoid war, to keep my child safe from cruelty. It was perhaps foolish."

Placing her hand on the arm of the chair, Brenna offered the queen a wan smile. "I don't think it was foolish. My mom would do anything to protect me, too." She tilted her head. "How did he not know that you were…um…pregnant? Isn't it kind of obvious?"

"I was not with him during my growing months. I stayed with friends, and he was busy with The Hunt."

"Oh." Brenna didn't know what 'the hunt' was, but guessing from Etain's tone of voice she imagined that it was probably something more than an afternoon of shooting ducks.

"Do you feel well enough to walk?"

"I think so." Brenna rose to her feet on much steadier legs, and Etain sent Mahoney for some clothes.

"I'm afraid I cannot give you the clothes you wore before, but please accept one of my own daughters' dresses."

"You have another daughter?"

"I have several. And sons, as well. Hold out your arms."

Etain laughed at Brenna's stunned expression and, with Mahoney's help, removed her robe before replacing it with a dark-green dress that fell to her ankles in shimmering folds. Brenna studied herself in the mirror and blanched. She looked so…different. Behind her, Etain smiled.

"You look very lovely. These clothes suit you well."

"I feel weird."

"Ah, yes." The queen tapped a finger thoughtfully to her lips. "Women of your time wear trousers now."

"Wait...you know about human fashion?"

"We see everything you mortals do." Etain laughed and placed a small red cape upon Brenna's shoulders, securing it with a golden knot work clasp. It only reached her waist, but it was as warm as any jacket she had. "However, we do not see a reason to copy your people. Our lands may share the same place, Brenna Morgan, but we are worlds apart. Ah. Roibhilin, Turlough, you have excellent timing."

Dressed in matching, dark-green tunics and leggings, the two young men stopped at the doorway, bowing low. Turlough's straight, brown hair was tied back, and his light-green eyes widened slightly when they landed on Brenna. She felt a blush heat her cheeks at his frank gaze and wished that she were wearing jeans and a t-shirt. Roibhilin frowned and crossed his arms.

"Your Majesty, how will she be able to run if she is in that dress?"

"She needs it only until she is home, and I trust that you and Turlough will make sure there is no need for her to run." At Etain's commanding tone, the two boys bowed. Etain took Brenna's hands in her own once more, looking more worried than her light tone implied. "Brenna Morgan, Nuala has entrusted my daughter's safe return to you. Do not fail me."

"I won't, Your Majesty."

With a slight nod, Etain released her hands and stepped away. "It is the dawning of Samhain now. Travel swiftly and have courage. Roibhilin, Turlough."

With a nod to their queen, the two ushered Brenna out of the room. The hallway they stepped into was long and narrow, and the echoes of their boots bounced off the white walls.

"We must take to the woods, and from there to *Coillearnach*." Roibhilin spoke only when they'd descended several flights of twisting stairs ending at a heavy door that Brenna assumed led outside.

"Are you taking me to that rock door again?"

"No, I will take you to the mound. It is closer. Come."

Biting her tongue so that she didn't yell at Roibhilin for commanding her, she trudged after him, blinking to adjust her eyes to the daylight outside. The wind blew gently across her face, and in the distance, she could see the rolling hills stretched before her in a mix of gold and green waves. The sky was so blue it almost seemed unreal, and she found that despite the fast pace at which they were walking she hardly felt out of breath. They marched in a strained silence for several minutes, and Brenna pursed her lips tightly in frustration. Giving way to a light jog to catch up with Roibhilin, she tapped him on the shoulder, trying to keep her annoyance out of her voice.

"Does it ever get dark here?"

"Yes." His voice terse, Roibhilin made a left, leading them away from the hills and toward towering, dark woods that she hadn't seen before.

"But it's been so long."

"For you, perhaps." Roibhilin's voice came out agitated and Brenna stopped, grunting when Turlough bumped into her from behind. With an air of suffering, Roibhilin turned to face her. "Is there a reason, human, that you have stopped?"

"Why yes, as a matter of fact, there is." In three long strides, Brenna stood only inches from Roibhilin, and she tilted her head back slightly to look him in the eye. "I would like to know why you're being so rude to me."

"I am doing no such thing."

"You are! I'm trying to be nice to you, I even *worried* about you when I heard that you were being questioned, and now here we are and you're just being...being..."

"Distant?" supplied Turlough helpfully. Roibhilin crossed his arms and glared at his friend while Brenna put her hands on her hips.

"Yeah! What did I ever do to you to make you hate me? I get that you don't like humans in general, but the least you could do is give *me* a chance."

"I do not hate you," muttered Roibhilin as he looked away from her.

"You could have fooled me! All you do is yell at me or ignore me. Friends don't do that!"

"Friends?"

"Well, I mean..." Brenna's temper faltered at his slightly surprised tone. He really did seem perplexed. "Aren't we...sort of? We've both saved each other's lives and, well, if you'd *let* me, I think we could be friends. I'd like to *try*, at least."

Before Roibhilin could answer, there was a great rumbling beneath their feet as a loud horn from the castle sounded, the deep notes causing small pebbles on the road to quiver and sending a shiver down Brenna's spine.

"What was that?!"

"The call to arms." Roibhilin's expression was grim. "We must hurry. It is already well past noon in your world, and we do not have much time."

Quickening their pace, they followed the slim footpath into the waiting dark forest behind the castle, the branches so thick and the leaves so tightly bunched together that not even a flicker of sunlight could find its way through. The air smelled of damp earth and rotting leaves, reminding Brenna more of a cave than the woods. Still feeling a bit out of sorts, she remained silent as they walked down the narrow and barely discernible path. She realized with some surprise that the trees around her really were black, the bark rough and cracked. White mushrooms of gigantic proportions glowed eerily from their perches on the thick trunks, and every once and a while she swore that she could see strange, stick-like creatures skittering up the bark.

"Roibhilin, is this forest safe?"

"Not entirely, no."

"Then why are going through it?"

"'Tis faster." He glanced back at her, a single brow raised condescendingly. "Why? Are you frightened?"

"No." Brenna jumped slightly when she heard a branch snap. "I just think it's a bad idea to go through a place where we might get attacked."

"There's nothing to concern yourself over," chuckled Turlough as he tapped a finger on the hilt of his sword. "We've never met a creature here we couldn't defeat."

"That's...not really reassuring."

Brenna grimaced as Turlough laughed. After several minutes of walking in the cold woods, Roibhilin made a right, sending them into a thicket of massive, green ferns. Large trees whose roots intertwined with each other above ground made their progress much trickier, causing the small road they'd been following to vanish. Roibhilin seemed unconcerned and kept up his pace while Brenna tripped several times on the hem of her dress and the smaller roots hidden by leaves and ferns. She had no idea how the female Gentry walked in these clothes, but she was sure that she could convince them to wear pants if given the chance.

"Roibhilin, how much longer until we—ow!"

With a cry, Brenna pulled out the key that had once again burned her skin, and fear swept over her as she looked with wide eyes to Roibhilin who had turned around at the sound of her voice. His expression registered nothing more than slight annoyance as he drew a sword.

"Turlough, we've company."

"Already?" Looking more pleased than worried, Turlough glanced about the silent woods. "I thought we would get at least halfway through here without incident."

"As did I." Roibhilin took a better grip on his sword. "Ready?"

"I am always ready."

"On my mark, then."

Without so much as an 'excuse me', Turlough swung Brenna into his arms, and they took off at a run faster than she ever thought possible. The dark trees blurred together while, in front of them, Roibhilin kept his sword raised. In the silence of the woods, she became aware of a familiar rushing sound and looked around for its source. Frowning, she narrowed her eyes to see better and then blanched. She could make out ash-colored blurs streaking past her in the trees beside them.

"Roibhilin, to your right!"

Her warning almost came too late as a hawthorn pixie sprung from out of the woods, its claw-like hands poised to strike. With a fast jab, Roibhilin's sword pierced the spindly body, causing it to disintegrate almost immediately. Behind her, Brenna could hear the hollow cries of the pixies and she looked up at Turlough.

"Do you hear them?"

"I do, but they will not be on us for long. Hold onto my neck, Brenna Morgan, and were I you, I would close my eyes."

"Why would I want to—whoa!"

In one single leap, Turlough's speed increased and Brenna threw her arms tightly around his neck, hoping that she wasn't strangling him. Cold air stung her eyes when she tried to open them, and she turned her head against the force of the wind. Through slightly teary eyes she could see the pixies quickly losing ground until they were nothing more but little gray blurs against the dark woods. Closing her eyes once more, she marveled at the fact that despite the speed at which Turlough was running she couldn't hear or feel his footsteps. She wasn't sure how much time had passed or how much ground they had covered, but she knew that it was long enough for her arms to fall asleep and the cold wind to numb her body.

"You can let go now, Brenna."

At Turlough's amused voice, she opened her eyes to see that they had stopped in the golden field of *Coillearnach*. A few deer stared at them from a distance, their large, soft ears perked up as they watched them intently. Pixies floated around them, and Brenna quickly let go of Turlough. Roibhilin had sheathed his sword and was already making his way through the waist-high grass toward the slender doors that marked the entrance to the mound. Without a word, he opened the door and ushered both Brenna and Turlough through. Walking up the long, winding stairs was much harder than walking down them, and all three were breathing a bit heavier by the time they reached the top.

"Wait here."

All around her was darkness, and the only thing she could make out was Roibhilin's voice. A rumbling began then, and the floor beneath them vibrated and shifted slightly. Brenna had to throw her arms up in front of her face when a blinding light suddenly appeared, and with Turlough following behind her, she made her way out. The air was cool and fresh, smelling of both earth and rain. It took several seconds for Brenna to adjust to the light. The grass beneath her feet was wet and slightly muddy while above her the sky was clear, though she could see the remnants of a storm on the horizon. She gave a small shiver as a cold wind blew and the earth underneath her shuddered, signaling the door's closure.

"Come," said Roibhilin, brushing past her. "We've not much time to both go to your home and find the child."

Brenna tromped after him, rubbing her arms when the wind blew through the thin fabric of the dress. She couldn't wait to get home and change into her pants and a warm sweater. As they trooped around the hill, Brenna shouted when Turlough suddenly grabbed her, his sword raised.

"What gives?!"

"There is a mortal above us. Do not move."

"'Tis help," Roibhilin said from his stance on the edge of mound. Brenna's brows rose and she shoved herself out of Turlough's arms.

"I'm sorry—you asked for *help*?"

"No." He took her hand, which surprised her into silence, and pulled her up the last bit of the hill. "I had little choice in the matter."

"Brenna, is that you?"

If Roibhilin doing a kind act on her behalf wasn't enough of a shock, seeing Patrick standing on the other side of the mound certainly was. With a smile, she ran to him, hugging him tightly before pulling away.

"Patrick! What are you *doing* here?"

"Sure, I came to help. I figured you'd need a ride home." He looked over her shoulder to the Gentry, and Brenna turned around to face Roibhilin.

"You seriously let him help you? I thought you hated humans."

"The boy would not leave the mound until I promised to allow him to help. I did not have the time to deal with him as I wished."

It took all she had not to retort that he was a "boy" too, and she had to take a deep breath to keep her temper in check. Instead, she turned to face Patrick again, and the memory of their kiss surfaced unexpectedly, bringing a blush to her cheeks.

Now isn't the time for that! Brenna admonished herself, quickly squashing the memory. *I have to find the* leanbh *first, and then I can sort out my feelings*. Tugging on a lock of her hair, she hoped her blush wasn't too obvious or that her thoughts weren't written all over her face.

"We have to find the girl, Patrick. But I need to get home first. Roibhilin, Turlough, do you need a ride?"

Roibhilin's face was once again a mask of indifference, though

Turlough looked surprised, glancing from Patrick and then to Roibhilin. She wasn't sure why, but she thought she saw something like worry or recognition flash in his light-green eyes when he stared at Patrick.

"We will make our own way. Turlough."

Whirling around, Roibhilin walked past his friend who followed after him, speaking rapidly in their own language as he cast looks over to Patrick before disappearing behind the mound.

"We should go, then."

"Right." Brenna gave herself a small shake. "What time is it?"

"A little after four." Shrugging out of his coat, Patrick placed it on Brenna's shoulders.

She smiled. "Do I look that cold?"

"You do. C'mon then, let's get you home."

Walking down the mound was harder in her dress, and with a growl of frustration she gathered as much of the fabric as she could in one fist to hold it up. Patrick walked in front of her, and if he laughed or smiled as she muttered under her breath she couldn't hear it. By the time they arrived at the parking lot, Brenna was feeling warmer and for once she was happy to see the rusted truck waiting for them. *It might be a death trap*, she thought as she opened the door to get in, *but at least its heater works*. Turning on the ignition, Patrick peeked over at Brenna, and her hand flew to her hair once more, her fingers tugging anxiously.

"So…I know that I said I was only going to be a gone a few hours, but—"

"I'm not mad."

"Oh."

"But sure, I'd like to know why you've got a dress on."

"It's a long story."

"We've plenty of road."

Brenna's lips quirked up in a smile. Somehow, Patrick always knew the right thing to say. "Well, I've got good news and bad news."

"Oh?"

"Treasach's dead. And um…well…the little girl I'm supposed to find could destroy the world."

"I think," said Patrick, gripping the steering wheel tightly, "you'd better start at the beginning."

Chapter Fourteen

By the time Brenna arrived at her house, she was convinced that Patrick had to be the calmest person on earth. She had spoken quickly, knowing that they didn't have much time until they got to her house. The memory of Treasach's head rolling along the floor still made her feel queasy, and Etain's sad eyes and defeated shoulders were a vivid image in her mind. Patrick had listened through it all, never interrupting save for asking a clarifying question here and there. It was a welcome improvement from Roibhilin's short temper and demanding voice.

Hesitantly, Brenna opened the door to her home, sighing in relief when she found the house empty. A note was on the table from her mother telling her she'd gone to the village pub to rub elbows with the locals. There wasn't a word about her absence or her ditching school. Blinking back tears, Brenna carefully folded the note back. Her mom was trusting her, and she felt awful about it. While Patrick took a seat on the couch, Brenna shook her head and ran to her room to change. She struggled out of the dress, shoved her legs into a welcome pair of jeans, and threw on a long-sleeve shirt. Brenna paused, holding the iron key in her hand.

When she stopped to think about it, she had relied on Patrick a lot lately. And every time he had helped—or demanded to help. It was easy to see now that he liked her—had liked her for a while. She shook her head, wondering how she could have been so blind to it. *Or maybe*, she thought somewhat uncomfortably, *I did it on purpose*. Brenna hurriedly pulled a thick sweater over her head before gently taking the three daisy chains from her desk and placing the delicate blossoms around her neck.

Patrick called out from the living room, sounding agitated.

"Brenna, you've company!"

"Huh?"

There was a sound of the clock making a strangled, chiming sound followed by a loud smash. Brenna dashed down the hall. In front of her, Patrick was holding onto a wingback chair and Roibhilin had a hand on Turlough who was still wielding his sword over the destroyed clock that had called the fireplace mantel its home. There was a deep gash was in the wall where it had once resided. Mouth agape, Brenna put her hands on her hips, scowling at Turlough.

"What did you do that for?!"

"It startled me."

"I would say it did a fair bit more than that," Patrick said dryly. Turlough shot him a glare, sheathing his sword as he did so.

"We've no time for this. Mortal, do you have what you have come for?"

Brenna nodded her head at Roibhilin's clearly unhappy tone, holding up the daisy chains as evidence. Turlough bent down to inspect them, though he didn't try to touch them.

"These are quite expertly made. There is much magic in them." He looked to Brenna. "Who gave these to you?"

"Kathleen, Patrick's grandmother."

"Kathleen Fergus?"

"Yeah." Brenna frowned. "How do you know her?"

"She is well known." Turlough straightened, clearly done talking. Why was it that the Gentry seemed to enjoy leaving everyone wanting to know more?

"Mortal, the key." Roibhilin pointed impatiently to the object in question, and Brenna smiled, saluting to him. He made an irritated noise in the back of his throat which made Brenna grin even larger.

"I'm on it."

Squaring her shoulders, she marched outside and removed the key from her neck before replacing it with the three daisy chains. Closing her eyes, she took a deep breath, pushing away the sounds and thoughts around her, concentrating instead on the child. *She must be scared*, Brenna thought somewhat guiltily, *and sad*. She probably didn't even know who her mother was. The key suddenly shot up, straining against Brenna's fingers, forcing her to open her eyes. It was pointing straight down the drive. As quickly as she could, she set off in that direction, keeping her mind focused on finding the child. When she reached the end of the road, the key dropped before shooting to the left.

"We should take my lorry. It's faster than walking, I'm thinking."

Patrick's voice was close and startled Brenna, causing the key to fall heavily against the chain as her concentration broke. Roibhilin and Turlough were also behind them, their gazes locked on the iron key dangling in Brenna's hand.

"Do you guys want to ride?"

As one, they straightened their shoulders, looking both insulted and disgusted at the same time. "We will follow behind you," said Roibhilin.

"If you say so."

Brenna dashed back to the truck, and after a few moments of spluttering and a terrible squelching sound, it came to life. Putting her seatbelt on, she rolled down the window, wrinkling her nose as she saw a black plume of smoke escape the exhaust pipe in back.

"Are you *sure* this truck isn't going to die in the middle of the road?"

"Of course not. She's as good as the day she was made."

Thinking of the child was easier this time, and she found that she didn't have to close her eyes to do it, as the key responded to her thoughts easily. Patrick drove the truck down the lane before turning left onto the main road. They rode in silence, and every once and while Patrick glanced into the rearview mirror, an action which Brenna took to mean that Roibhilin and Turlough were keeping up with them. They drove for several minutes as the key continued to point straight, and she wondered just how much farther they would have to go. They passed the keep that overlooked the mound of *Coillearnach* and had gone only a mile down from it when the key suddenly swung left, pointing to a patch of woods.

"Hold on." Patrick shifted gears and made a sharp left onto a narrow, muddy lane that ended at an open space that could hold at least a dozen cars. Spotting a familiar, crumbled wall partially backing a forest, Brenna gave a shout as Patrick parked the lorry.

"Hey, this's where we went last week!"

Hopping out of the truck, Brenna looked around. The key pointed straight in front of her into a thicket of bushes that fronted a dense patch of forest just as Roibhilin and Turlough appeared beside her. She had given up being surprised by the swiftness with which they could run.

"Okay. This's it."

Brenna's stomach knotted with both excitement and fear as she made her way into the forest, her breath shaky as she tried to keep calm. She walked slowly at first, but the key began to pull harder, and soon Brenna found herself running through the woods, dodging branches and leaping over low bushes and rocks. It was after a near miss of getting her head smacked by a large branch that the key began to shake and the chain itself began to grow hot. Gritting her teeth together, Brenna kept her grip on the necklace, nearly dropping it as she stumbled over a rock. Though she had long stopped concentrating on finding the child, the key continued to guide her, pulling her left, then right, with an urgency she could feel in her bones.

"Whoa!"

Letting loose a shout, Brenna grabbed onto a tree as the key nearly pulled her into a deep creek. Gripping the chain tightly in one hand, she frowned. The creek was familiar. And so were the tiny pixies dancing around her. This was where she'd last seen the goblins and Treasach, or at least somewhere close to it. She caught her breath while she looked down the stream and recognized the fallen tree further down the creek she'd crossed only last weekend. Behind her, she could hear Patrick struggling through the bushes.

"Patrick, I have to go across."

"Brenna, just wait a moment!"

She didn't have time to wait. Taking in one last, steadying breath, she ran along the rushing stream until she reached the makeshift bridge. It was slippery from the moss that had grown on it, and had the key not been pulling so hard she was sure that she would have fallen in. She had to jump the last bit of the log and landed on the damp leaves and muddy bank on the other side. Brenna shivered when water seeped through her leather boots and mud squelched up the sides. Pulling her foot from the sticky mud, she wondered how the leprechaun's shoe could possibly be holding up so well. The key led her up the incline and then flew to the right, directing her past holes that had been dug by the two goblins before forcing her under several low-hanging branches. All around her, golden leaves floated down from a tangled canopy riddled with weak shafts of dying autumn light.

"C'mon…where is she?"

As if responding to Brenna's words, the key gave a shudder and pivoted to the left with so much force that it flew from her hands. She rushed after it desperately only to find that it had lodged deeply into the bark of an ancient, gnarled tree. The thing looked half dead with most of its branches void of any leaves or pixies, and the roots had risen up from the ground in a strange, knotted pattern for several feet all around. The trunk itself was so wide that she was sure it would take at least three grown men with their arms stretched wide to encircle it. Picking her way through the maze of bumpy roots, she grasped the key with both hands and gave it a good tug, but it refused to budge. Brenna wrinkled her nose, letting go to take a step back and assess the situation. Why would it launch itself at a tree? Her eyes widened as a very disturbing thought crossed her mind.

"No *way* did they leave a kid in a tree!"

Heart in her throat, Brenna took a better grip of the key and tried to turn it to the left. It didn't move. Frowning, she turned it to the right and jumped when it easily rotated. There was a wooden *clunk*, and Brenna stumbled away from the trunk, her green eyes wide as the large tree groaned and shuddered. A deep gash appeared in the bark at the base of the tree, snaking up to create a jagged circle that looked unmistakably like a door. With the creaking of a thousand snapping branches, the door swung inward, revealing nothing but blackness.

She could hear Patrick calling for her in the distance, but she remained silent. Carefully, Brenna walked closer to the gaping circle. The top of the doorway came only to her chest, and she bit her lip. Maybe it was like Roibhilin's mound; if she went in, it would probably be cavernous and lead to some sort of field. *Well*, she thought as she got to her knees, *there's only one way I'm going to find out*. Bracing her hands on either side of the opening, Brenna inched her head into the darkness.

"Hello?" she called out in a somewhat strangled voice. "Is anyone there?"

Nothing but silence greeted her, and she let out a sigh. Maybe there was another way in and this was only a trick door. Turning her head, she nearly jumped out of her skin when she saw a pair of bright blue eyes staring at her from out the black mere inches from her face.

Flinging herself away from the tree with a shout, Brenna landed on her bottom, her heart pounding while the eyes continued to gaze at her from the interior of the hole. She put a hand to her chest and took in large gulps of air, trying to regain her wits.

"You must be the *leanbh*, right?"

Her words came out as nothing more than a hoarse whisper, and the eyes continued staring at her for several, terrifying seconds until, finally, a delicate and ghostly white foot stepped out from the darkness and onto the moss-covered roots surrounding the tree. A small body quickly followed after, and soon enough a tiny girl stood before Brenna, looking no older than four and clothed only by the long, golden hair tumbling wildly down to the ground at her feet. She had a delicate frame, and in the light her pale skin glowed almost as brilliantly as her hair. The little girl considered the newcomer intently before taking a hesitant step forward.

Elation rushed through Brenna's mind as she gawked back at the child. She hadn't been sure what she was expecting, but a beautiful child of light was certainly surprising. It seemed somehow wrong that this tiny, little girl could destroy the world—or that someone would want to kill her when she was clearly the most innocent-looking person she had ever seen. Nervous, Brenna tugged on a lock of her own, shoulder-length hair.

"I bet…I bet you're wondering what happened to Nuala, right?"

The child tilted her head, looking puzzled. Brenna wrinkled her nose.

"You don't understand me, do you?"

Other than tilting her head in the other direction, the little girl indicated nothing. Brenna sighed. She thought of using the tiny bit of Gaelic she knew, but she quickly ruled it out. For all she knew, the little girl hadn't even learned *that*.

"Okay, we'll have to try to talk another way." Brenna stood up slowly so as not to startle the girl, offering a warm smile as she pointed to herself.

"Brenna."

The child seemed to consider this and then pointed to herself. "Saoirse."

"'Seer-shaw'?" The name sounded so elegant when the little girl said it but came out clumsily and odd when Brenna tried to pronounce it. Saoirse giggled and Brenna smiled. "It's a pretty name."

A twig snapped, and faster than Brenna could blink the little girl had disappeared back into the tree once more. Scrambling up, she frowned, putting a finger to her lips when she saw Patrick pushing through the bushes.

"Shh!"

"Brenna, what—"

"Shh!" She pointed to the gaping hole in the tree and Patrick froze. Roibhilin and Turlough appeared behind him, and Brenna held up her hand, stopping them from coming any closer.

"Roibhilin, I found her. But I don't think she speaks English."

"I want Nuala."

Stunned, Brenna turned around. The little girl was standing once more in front of the tree, her tiny voice sweet and musical.

"Or she does." She was glad she didn't have to rely on Roibhilin for help with translating, and she smiled. Saoirse gazed at them all with distrust, and Brenna realized that the child was shaking with fear. Carefully, Brenna sunk to her knees, not wanting to look intimidating.

"Nuala is...Nuala is away. I'm here to take you to your mother. We all are."

The little girl looked at the three boys with a speculative air, and Brenna took off her white, cabled sweater, holding it out.

"This is for you."

"It is a present?"

"Yes, it'll keep you warm."

"I like presents." She stepped forward and took the sweater, putting it on. It was large and fell to her shins, and she allowed Brenna to roll up the long sleeves so that her small, white fingers peeked through. The little girl held up an arm, inspecting the woolen sweater.

"It is very large."

"Well, you're supposed to grow into it."

Turlough cut into their conversation, his voice tense. "Brenna, we haven't time to talk—I can sense something coming."

She nodded her head and rose. "Saoirse, we have to take you home now."

"Nuala said I musn't leave the tree. It is not safe."

The little girl backed away from them and put a hand to the tree trunk, looking ready to run back into it. Brenna bit her lip, trying to figure out how to get the child to comply. Behind her, Roibhilin made a sound that she recognized as his temper flaring before he said something in his strange language to Saoirse. It caused tears to well in her large, blue eyes and spill down her cheeks. Brenna looked over her shoulder, glaring.

"What did you say to her?!"

"That there are others on their way to kill her."

"You don't *say* that to a little girl!"

"She is not a little girl. She is a *Tuath de Danann*."

"I don't care! She's younger than you, and that makes her a child."

Turning her attention back to Saoirse, Brenna gave her a gentle smile. She didn't have much experience with kids, but it seemed like the girl was pretty smart.

"Don't worry, no one's going to hurt you. That's why I'm here. Nuala sent me because she's busy. Do you understand?"

Rubbing the large sleeve across her wet cheeks, the small child nodded her head and stepped away from the tree, sniffling.

"Good. Now, I'm going to pick you up, because we have to run very fast, okay?"

"Is home far?"

"It's a little far."

Brenna gently picked up Saoirse, surprised at how light she was. Turning around, she faced Roibhilin and Turlough who had drawn their swords and were looking not at her but in the direction they'd arrived. Brenna could hear strange sounds in the distance, and the bushes around them were shaking violently.

"It is too late." Turlough looked to Brenna, his light-green eyes as serious as the day she had first met him. "I will hold them off."

"Not by yourself." Roibhilin gripped his friend's arm, and Turlough smiled.

"We've fought in larger battles and won. Go. I will catch up when I am able."

Roibhilin's lips pressed in a grim line of displeasure before he nodded his head tightly. Above them, several birds cried as they flew away. From the shuddering bushes only a few hundred feet away emerged a mass of strange creatures that Brenna had never seen before. She could spot several hawthorn pixies and a few goblins, but the rest were a mash of small, human-like bodies overridden with plant life. They varied in size and color, but they all had similar large, black eyes that could be seen even at a distance, glittering with the promise of death. The little girl in her arms cried softly and buried her head in the crook of Brenna's neck.

Without wasting another moment, Roibhilin shoved Patrick forward.

"Run, the pair of you, and try to keep up with me."

Roibhilin took off at a fast pace and Brenna dashed after him, Patrick following close behind. Running with a child, Brenna soon realized, was hard. Saoirse was light, but her long hair continuously snagged on twigs and caused her to cry out and slow them down. After a few attempts, Brenna managed to grab the mass and bunch it up, though running with no hands still made for a slower escape. From behind, she could hear the clash of steel followed by screams, and she hoped for Roibhilin's sake that Turlough would able to keep his word and come out alive.

"Where are we going?!"

"To another entrance. Jump!"

Brenna had no idea why he would tell her to jump, but she complied and was very grateful that she did as she soared over a shallow stream littered with what appeared to be water sprites. Landing on the other side, she looked back briefly to see that Patrick was easily keeping up with them. *It's a good thing he's in football*, she though grimly. How long they ran Brenna had no idea, but the sunlight was quickly fading, and the thought of running through the woods on Halloween night with a bunch of creatures chasing them wasn't appealing. She hoped the entrance was close.

After several more minutes of running, she could feel her legs strain and her lungs burning from the cold air. She wasn't sure how much longer she'd be able to keep going at such a breakneck pace. Patrick had caught up to her and was now running at her side, his own breathing a bit labored.

"Is the entrance close, d'you think?"

"I don't know. I hope so, because I'm about ready to give up."

"If you can talk," snapped Roibhilin with annoyance, "then you can surely still run. We are almost there."

Brenna let out a tired grunt of before concentrating on her breathing. She listened to the rhythm of her steps, and the rest of the world faded away along with her thoughts as she put one foot in front of the other. She barely registered the fact that Roibhilin had disappeared through a rock and, with eyes closed, she dashed through, as well. The smell of damp earth filled her nostrils, and several clumps of wet dirt fell on her head. Small torches of light dimly illuminated their way along the tunnel. Roibhilin led them through a dizzying array of twists and turns before he finally slowed down, stopping when they reached a cavernous, round room. Seven doors encircled them, each one with different scenes etched into the wood. Breathing heavily, Brenna set down Saoirse and sidled up next to Roibhilin.

"Where are we?"

"It is one of the entrances into many places. The third door will lead you into the halls of *Coillearnach* keep."

"You mean the castle that overlooks your mound?"

"Aye." Roibhilin's voice was hard, and Brenna's eyes widened.

"So the stories are true."

"What stories?"

"The one about Aideen."

"Who told you that name?" Roibhilin's voice was so low and frightening that Saoirse began to cry, and even Patrick took a step back.

"I...I..."

"If you dare to utter her name ever again, it will be last thing you say. Go to *Coillearnach* mound and stay there until I come for you. You will be safe so long as you stay on the mound. I must help Turlough."

Brenna nodded her head stiffly as Roibhilin opened the third door on the right. Picking up the tiny girl, both Patrick and Brenna went through. She jumped slightly at the force with which Roibhilin slammed it shut behind them. Except for their own breathing, there wasn't a sound to be heard in the new tunnel. Getting a better grip on Saoirse, Brenna began to march forward. Once more, tiny lights lit the room only enough to cast strange shadows on the walls. Patrick let out a low whistle.

"Who's Aideen?"

"I think she was the human girl Roibhilin once loved."

"Loved?" Patrick snorted. "I doubt it."

"I didn't believe it either...but from what I've been able to piece together, I think he did love a human. Ow!"

Brenna had been so busy talking over her shoulder that she hadn't seen the end of the hall. She rubbed her head as she backed up. In front of her stood an old door made of heavy wooden slates covered with dust. It looked as if it hadn't been used in at least a couple hundred years.

"Here, let me."

Brenna stood back as Patrick gripped a large ring that hung in the middle of the door. After a few good tugs, the door began to inch its way open. Even in the dim lighting, Brenna could see a fine sheen of sweat on Patrick's brow as he dug in his heels and continued to strain against the door. It creaked and groaned, slowly opening, allowing in a thin beam of blue light to spill onto the floor. With a final pull, Patrick released the ring and held up his hand as he stepped through the half-opened threshold.

"Wait here for a moment and let me make sure the coast is clear."

Before Brenna could argue, Patrick was gone, and she contented herself with setting down Saoirse to rub her tired arms.

"Is he your love?" Saoirse's light voice echoed down the hall, creating an almost musical effect. Brenna thanked any and all the gods it was dim enough that the little girl couldn't see her blush.

"He's...ummm...not yet."

"Ah." Saoirse seemed to ponder this then leaned back to look into Brenna's eyes with her own bright blue ones. "He has not yet won your hand." She nodded her head solemnly, sagely, appearing more mature than her young age implied. "Nuala says it is very important that a man be strong and brave and fight many battles before he can win the heart of a woman."

"Aren't you a little young to be hearing stories like that?"

"I do not know." Saoirse titled her head, looking puzzled. "Am I young?"

"Uhhh..."

Brenna was saved from having to answer her question when Patrick popped his head in through the doorway and motioned for them to come through. Grateful, Brenna reminded Saoirse to be silent, and together the three made their way up a narrow but long set of stairs, pausing when they were nearly at the top. Patrick glanced up the last few stairs and then bent his head down, whispering so that his voice wouldn't carry.

"We're below the main floor. The curator hasn't left yet, so we'll need to be careful."

They waited for several seconds as they heard footsteps echoing above them and held their breath as the steps drew nearer, pressing themselves against the cold, stone wall. A flashlight barely missed spotting them as it swept past, and they heard the curator mutter a few short words to himself before moving on, whistling as he did so. After a couple of minutes, Patrick led them up the last few stairs and, as quietly as they could, they ran down the large hall. Following a few wrong turns, they eventually found their way into the courtyard. The sun was almost completely gone, and stars were twinkling in the purple and blue sky.

"Roibhilin told us to meet him at the mound."

Brenna glanced over at the bump in the distance where the full moon's light cast a strange, silver lining onto the grass. Saoirse squirmed a bit in her arms, and Brenna adjusted her grip.

"It's fair too dangerous to go through the woods, and we don't want the child—"

"My name is Saoirse."

"My apologies." Patrick bowed deeply over Saoirse's hand which delighted the child to the point of giggling. "We don't want *Saoirse* to come to any harm. We need to get to my lorry—it'll be safer. Wait here, and I'll beep my horn when I get close."

"But what about all of those weird fairie things looking for us?"

"Turlough and Roibhilin are probably keeping them busy. It's only half a mile down the road; I'll be back in no time. Stay to the shadows."

Nodding her head, Brenna set down Saoirse and stood by a crumbling wall as Patrick ran out of sight.

"He is very brave." Slipping her delicate hand into Brenna's, the little girl watched closely as Patrick disappeared.

"You can say that again."

"He is very brave."

Brenna slapped a hand over her mouth to keep from laughing too loudly, and Saoirse tilted her head in confusion.

"I have said something wrong?"

"No, no. Just…um. Nevermind." Smiling, Brenna followed Saoirse's gaze as she looked up at the full moon.

"Brenna?"

"Yes?"

"Nuala is dead."

"How did—I mean, of course she's not. She just had a problem and couldn't come get you herself."

"No." Saoirse's blue eyes narrowed slightly as she placed a hand to her stomach. "I felt it here."

Before she could stop them, tears filled Brenna's eyes and slid down her cheeks. Try as she might, she still couldn't believe the lengths Nuala had gone to in order to defend Saoirse, to keep her safe. Even now—weeks after her death—she had set in motion a way to help the little girl stay alive. Brenna wiped the tears from cheeks, wishing that she had done something more to try and save her.

"Do not cry, Brenna. She died bravely."

"How do you know?"

"Because she was always brave. She did not fear the dark like I do. Once, she fought off a great number of strange creatures and she did not even flinch."

It was disconcerting to hear such a young child speak so calmly and with such comprehension, and Brenna felt goose bumps rise along both her arms. Roibhilin was right. For all her appearances, she wasn't wholly a child. Licking her lips, she bent down so that their faces were level.

"You're very brave too, Saoirse. There aren't many children who would take living in a tree as well as you have. And now you're out in the human world even though it's dangerous."

"That is not brave. I am very frightened right now. If you are brave, you are not scared."

"That's not true at all! Bravery is doing something even when you *are* scared."

The child was silent for several moments, clearly contemplating something. "You are brave as well, then."

"Well…I guess so."

"You are," Saoirse said confidently. "But now we must both be very, very brave. Braver than anyone else."

"Oh?"

Nodding her head, Saoirse lifted a pale arm and pointed past Brenna's shoulder. Brenna slowly turned around, feeling her breath catch in her throat. Silvery moonlight lit the tops of the large trees that lined either side of the courtyard, and on their bowing branches perched a group of hawthorn pixies. Their black eyes glittered, and their wizened mouths opened to let forth their hollow, wind-like laughter. Brenna stood as more of the pixies appeared, their thin, ash-colored bodies clashing with the dark of the trees. Brenna could hear Patrick's horn blaring beyond them, and she closed her eyes briefly. There was really only one way to get past the pixies. Picking up Saoirse, she began walking toward a group that was now scurrying out of the branches to plop onto the ground and encircle the two girls. Her eyes wide, Saoirse looked upon the horde, her small body beginning to shake.

"Are you going to fight them?"

"No." Brenna held tight to the child, trying to keep the fear out of her voice. "I don't have any weapons."

"But we will die."

"Not tonight, kiddo. Hold on to me."

Saoirse wrapped her arms around Brenna. With as much calmness as she could muster, Brenna continued on her path toward the gates leading out of the courtyard. She heard the horn again and began to walk faster. A hawthorn pixie to her right launched itself at them, and Saoirse cried out. Then she gasped. The pixie hissed as it was thrown back, and it dropped to the floor before springing back up again, shaking its tumbleweed head. A few more of the pixies attacked, each one bouncing off a good foot or so before it could actually reach Brenna. Smiling, she began running, laughing as the clawing creatures continued to get pushed away.

"What magic is this?!" wheezed a pixie as it ran alongside her. Brenna grinned and looked down at it before holding up one of the daisy chains around her neck. The creature shuddered and then veered away from her, letting loose a windy scream as it did so. The pixies fell back and Brenna smiled. Who knew daisies could be so useful?

"Brenna!"

She could just make out Patrick's truck in the distance, and she lengthened her stride as she dashed toward it. "I'm here!"

Patrick had already opened the passenger door for them, and Brenna hopped into the truck, slamming the heavy metal door on her way in.

"Jesus, Brenna, what were those?!"

"Hawthorn pixies. We really need to go now."

"Sure, I can see that."

Patrick tore down the main road toward the mound while Brenna caught her breath. The truck rattled and creaked, and she mentally urged it not to fall apart just yet.

"Jesus!" he suddenly braked, and the force nearly caused Brenna to hit her head on the dashboard.

"Patrick, why did you st—oh my God."

The lorry's large headlights cast a flood of golden light on the black road before them and onto a horde of creatures blocking their way. Saoirse began to shake in her arms again, and Brenna put a hand on her head, holding her close.

"What do we do?" Brenna turned to gaze at Patrick who was gripping the steering wheel and looking more than a little pale.

"Well, there's only one thing we can do."

"What?"

"Run the lot of 'em over."

"Are you serious?!"

Patrick nodded his head and adjusted his grip on the steering wheel as he settled into his seat.

"But—"

"If you can think of another way out, sure I'd love to hear it."

"Um…"

"Right, through we go, then."

Brenna gripped the side of the door as Patrick changed gears and slammed down on the gas pedal. The truck coughed and then rapidly picked up speed, drawing them closer to the mob waiting for them. *If we make it out of this alive*, thought Brenna as she clung to Saoirse, *I'll never badmouth this truck again.*

Chapter Fifteen

As Patrick tore through the first few rows of creatures, the lorry coughed and wheezed, its wheels wobbling as it trod over the horde. Brenna pressed her hand against the ceiling to keep from hitting her head as the vehicle vibrated and bounced, wincing as several dismembered arms and legs flew past her window. The engine gave a mighty *bang* as Patrick shifted gears and slammed his foot down hard. Not wanting to end up like their cohorts, what remained of the horde sprang away from the truck as it came barreling toward them. Patrick laughed as the they broke free, still intact.

"I can't believe that worked!" Brenna exclaimed, peering into the review mirror to see that the horde was already being left far behind.

"Neither can I!"

"Wait…you mean you didn't know that would work?"

"It's called rushing. We use it in GAA all the time."

"I can't believe you!" Brenna slapped his shoulder and he laughed. "You're as bad as my mom."

"I'll take it as a compliment, then."

"Sure, you do that. Oh, no…"

With wide eyes, Brenna pointed out the window. The entrance to the mound was blocked by even more creatures than had been on the road, and Patrick grimaced.

"There's no way we can go through them. My truck won't even make it up the mound."

"I know." Brenna thought quickly. "Oh! I've got it!"

"What?"

"There's an entrance to the fairie realm in the woods by the school."

"Right. Hold on."

Patrick lay on the gas once more, and Brenna sank into the seat. In her arms, Saoirse's tense body began to relax, and Brenna stroked her tangled mass of thick, golden hair.

"Don't worry, we're going to get you home safe and sound really soon."

The little girl nodded her head but remained quiet, and Brenna couldn't blame her. If she had spent most of her life in a tree, she'd be pretty freaked out right about now, too. Glancing through the windshield, she sighed. The large moon above them cast a cold light over the road, and the ocean on Patrick's side glimmered with the glowing orb's reflection. Brenna allowed herself to relax for a few brief moments, watching the dark, rolling hills on her side of the truck blend into the black sky.

This was all going to be over soon. Saoirse would be with her parents again, and Brenna would be able to go back to life as normal. *Well*, she thought, resting her head on the passenger window, *as normal as it's ever going to be.* Patrick shifted beside her, and she glanced at him. He looked as though he wanted to say something.

"What is it?"

"Brenna, when you were being chased by the pixies earlier, I saw them bounce right off you. How did you do that?"

Straightening, she lifted her head from the window and pointed to the flowers looped around her neck. "The daisy chains your grandmother gave me."

"I'm glad they worked so well. But it was a fair large risk you took."

"So was rushing your truck into an army of evil monsters."

"Fair enough." Patrick chuckled. "Saoirse, are you—whoa!"

Patrick veered to the right and nearly hit the stone wall lining the road before straightening, and the truck made a horrible squealing sound as the back fishtailed.

"What happened?!"

"There was something in the road, and—"

Brenna started as something thudded onto the roof, denting the metal. Setting the child onto the floor, Brenna instructed Saoirse to cover her head and then twisted around. Another *thump* could be heard from the truck bed, followed by what sounded like nails on a chalkboard. With her hands covering her ears, Brenna turned around and barely kept another scream down as a hawthorn pixie hurled itself against the back window. Dozens more were crawling up the side of the car, and their thorny bodies left fine cuts in the metal as they began to mass together in the truck bed.

"Patrick—"

"I see them. Hang on."

He swerved sharply both left and right, and while a few of the pixies flew from the back, most had latched themselves onto the truck before starting to crawl forward again, scratching at the glass with their claw-like hands. Brenna heard more heavy pounding on the roof before a large fist broke through. Then Patrick slammed on the brakes. Most of the pixies careened into each other, letting loose angry cries as the thorns on their bodies caught hold of each other. Whatever was on the roof tumbled onto the front of their car, its rotund body leaving a decent-sized dent on the hood. Patrick and Brenna gasped when the creature lifted its head, its beady, black eyes dazed, large teeth poking out from behind fat lips. Patrick held a hand to his nose as the stench of rotting fish filled the cabin.

"What is—"

"It's a goblin."

As if it could hear them, the creature gave a gruesome smile and then smashed its fist into the window, creating a large, spiderweb crack in the middle of the windshield. Brenna jerked back as it raised its other meaty fist to strike the glass again.

"Floor it!"

Not needing to be told twice, Patrick slammed his foot on the gas, and the goblin clawed at the front of the truck with fat hands before it rolled off of the hood. Brenna smacked her head on the dented roof as the truck ran over its large body. More pixies had clambered onto the back, though, and thanks to the thorns on their bodies several were ripping gashes into the frame as they began to clamber along the side of the vehicle.

"Patrick, they wouldn't know how a car runs, right?"

"Sure, like I know."

Saoirse let out a cry and jumped into Brenna's lap, her body quivering.

"What's wron—gah!"

The face of a hawthorn pixie stared up at her from a hole in the floor of the truck, its claw-like hands ripping through more of the metal as it tried to get in.

"Get away from us!" Brenna tried to kick it with her foot only to find that just as the flowers had kept the pixies from hurting her, they weren't allowing *her* to attack *them*, either. Desperately, she looked around and discovered one of Patrick's school books that had fallen between the seat and the stick-shift.

"Sorry Patrick, I'll buy you a new one!"

"A new what?"

Grabbing the book, she smashed it into the creature's face. It hissed, and Brenna stomped her foot onto the hardback, forcing the pixie through the hole it had made. It disappeared with a windy cry, making a dull *bump* as the truck rolled over it. Shaking, Brenna gathered Saoirse into her arms.

"It's okay, it's gone."

"Uh, Brenna?"

"What?"

"We need to jump."

Brenna stared at Patrick, not sure she'd heard him correctly. "What does *that* mean?"

"It means," he said grimly as another pixie tore into the hood of the truck and pulled out a bunch of wires, "that we need to get *out* of the lorry before these things get *in*. Can you see if there are any more on the road behind us?"

"I can try." Brenna glanced behind them and gulped. Not only were the hawthorn pixies massing onto each other and tearing the back of the truck to pieces, but they were helping up the goblin that had managed to keep hold of the tailgate. She couldn't really see anything else beyond that. "I can't tell. But I don't think so."

"Grand. We're near Deirdre's."

"What does she have to do with—"

"When I give the go-ahead, jump."

"'Jump'? As in, out of the truck while it's moving at a million miles a minute?"

"I'll slow down."

"Patrick, that's a terrible idea!"

"Do you have a better one, then? The lorry won't last much longer!"

As if on cue, the truck released a strong shake, and dark smoke began to spew from the hood as another pixie dug its hand into the engine and pulled up an important-looking tube. Brenna blanched.

"Don't worry, Bren—it'll be fine. Just jump and roll when I say so." He paused, looking over at her. "You trust me, don't you?"

"Yeah."

Patrick grinned, and Brenna smiled back as he took her hand and gave it a quick squeeze.

"On the count of three, then. Get ready to open the door."

"Ready." Brenna gripped Saoirse with one arm and put her other hand on the door handle, holding her breath as she did so.

"One."

With a sharp turn of the wheel, Patrick aimed the smoking truck toward the cliff, setting the tires squealing before it straightened and began closing the gap between land and water.

"Two."

The back window shattered, spraying shards of glass as the pixies' hollow voices filled the night air. The engine suddenly caught fire, and Patrick gripped the wheel as it began to shake and rattle.

"*Three!*"

Flinging the door open, Brenna felt a moment's dizziness as she saw the ground rush beneath her. She could hear Patrick jump out and, with a deep breath, she hugged Saoirse close and dove out of the running vehicle. She winced as she rolled repeatedly over rocks and dirt before slowing to a stop on soft grass. Quickly, she released the little girl and staggered up to see the truck soar over the cliff, engine blazing, before plunging nose-first toward the ocean. The pixies and the lone goblin had already abandoned the truck, but they were too far away to grab hold of the cliff. With their bodies tangled together, the creatures fell out of sight, and Brenna turned away from the cliffs.

"Are you all right, the pair of you?!"

Patrick was several hundred feet away, and his voice echoed as he made his way toward them, holding onto his side with a bruised hand. Brenna staggered up, checking Saoirse. Luckily, other than a thin scrape on her cheek, the little girl was unharmed.

"Yeah, we're fine! Are you okay?"

"Sure. A few bumps to show for it. Let me have a look at you, then." Patrick was covered in dirt and grass stains, and she could see another bruise already forming on his jaw along with a large welt on his forehead. Dusting his hands on his jeans, he checked both Brenna and Saoirse for any breaks. He smiled. "I've a feeling you'll both live. We'll need to get that cut on your leg fixed up, though."

Glancing down, Brenna found a decent-sized cut on her calf. "It does sting a little." She took Saoirse's hand and walked over to the cliff where tread marks could be seen grooved into the grass. "I'm so sorry about your truck, Patrick."

"It was an old hunk of metal. I can replace it."

"It was a hunk of metal that saved our lives. And so did you." Wrapping her arms around his waist, Brenna gave Patrick a tight hug that he returned before pulling away and running a hand through his disheveled hair.

"Well, at least we'll fit in when go to Deirdre's."

"What do you mean?"

A slow smile spread over Patrick's lips as he tore one of his sleeves. "Sure, I'm thinking zombies would be a fair accurate description of how we look."

"What is a zombie?" Saoirse's tiny voice piped up and Brenna smiled, bending down to rub some of the muck off of her face.

"Trust me—you don't want to know."

* * * *

"*Bejeebus*, Brenna! What did you go and do, fall down a hill?!"

Deirdre had her hands on her hips as she stood in the doorway of her home, eyes wide as she took in their haggard appearances. Brenna smiled wryly and held up one of her ripped sleeves.

"I'm supposed to be a zombie."

"Sure, I can see that." Deirdre glanced at Patrick, one brow rising. "Are you a zombie too, then?"

"Well sure, what else would I be?"

"Oh, I don't know, a GAA player who lost the game?"

Patrick glared at Deirdre's overly sweet smile and Brenna glanced behind them to make sure that none of the pixies had followed. They had only needed to walk less than half a mile to Deirdre's house, but it had been the scariest five minutes of her life.

"And who's this, then?"

Deirdre bent down to inspect Saoirse who was peering into the living room crammed full of teenagers in costumes. Patrick gently pulled her away from the door, setting her next to Brenna.

"This is my cousin. I'm to mind her tonight," was all Patrick said, taking the child's hand in his own. Deirdre smiled at the little girl before straightening.

"I didn't know you had a cousin." Deirdre's pale skin was even more pronounced thanks to the black leotard she had on, and the large, black cat ears looked like an extension of her thick, curly hair. Behind her, a rigid cat tail quivered as she moved to one side.

"Well now, I'm glad you both made it, but sure it might not be the best place for your cousin."

"You're right. We can't stay long—we're to send my cousin back home soon." Patrick spoke with confidence, and Brenna was impressed. She could never bring herself to lie and look at someone while she did it.

Deirdre sighed and opened the door wide, ushering them inside. "I wish you could stay longer. Here now, Brenna, what happened to your leg?"

Glancing down at the long cut on her calf, she grimaced. Dried blood had mingled with dust to create a truly gruesome sight.

"I cut myself on a rock on the way over."

"You've got to be careful going out at night. Goblins and who knows what roam about, you know," she said teasingly. "I've a first aid kit in the kitchen. It won't take a moment."

Hesitantly, Brenna left Saoirse with Patrick as Deirdre led her through the throng of people jammed into the small living room. Several people called hellos to Brenna and she waved back, surprised that so many seemed to know her, especially since she didn't recognize most of them.

"Here, have a seat on the counter."

Clearing a bowl and some empty cans from the countertop, Deirdre went to a cabinet and retrieved a white box while Brenna carefully situated herself atop the kitchen counter.

"So," chirped Deirdre as she took out a cloth and ran it under the sink faucet, "are you and Patrick gone on each other, then?"

"What?"

"Are you dating?"

"Oh! Um…I…I…" Brenna's cheeks turned red and Deirdre laughed, wiping Brenna's leg gently with the damp cloth.

"Sure, 'tisn't a problem, Brenna. He's fancied you since the day he met you, I'm fair sure."

"Deirdre, I—"

"Don't worry, my feelings aren't hurt any. It's glad I am that you're happy. He's a good sort, and sure its grand *craic* that for all the girls going mad over him, it's the Yank that gets him in the end! There, all finished."

Brenna glanced down to see that her calf now sported a roll of gauze, and she slipped off the counter. "I suppose I really do look like a zombie now. I'm sorry to do this, Deirdre, but Patrick and I have to go."

"Sure, I understand. Wait here and I'll get him. Going out the back will be easier than trying to get through this lot."

Deirdre disappeared into the crowd and Brenna sighed. Several people poked into the kitchen for glasses and Brenna handed them cups, feeling uneasy. She couldn't quite shake the feeling that getting away from the horde of pixies and goblins had been too easy, and she found her gaze drawn to the dark world outside the sliding glass doors, expecting to see the malicious black eyes of hawthorn pixies staring back at her.

"Brenna?"

Nearly jumping out of her skin at the unfamiliar voice close to her ear, Brenna whirled around, a hand on her chest. Colin stared at her in surprise, his red-rimmed eyes looking more watery than normal. He wore a strange, shiny black leather jacket that fell to the floor, and he held a pair of sunglasses in his hands. His floppy brown hair had been swept back, causing him to appear years younger.

"Colin. Hi." Collecting herself, Brenna smiled. "You startled me."

"I'm sorry." Sliding his glasses onto the collar of his coat, he leaned against the counter, bumping his head on one of the cabinets. He straightened hastily. "It's a grand party, isn't it?"

"Yeah. It's really…noisy." Brenna glanced to her left to see if she could spot Deirdre, but she was nowhere to be seen in the sea of costumed teenagers.

"What are you then, Brenna?"

"Oh! I'm a zombie."

"Sure, you're the prettiest zombie here."

Brenna's search for Deirdre came to a screeching halt and her gaze snapped back to Colin, her green eyes wide. Clearly surprised himself, Colin's pale cheeks turned a mottled red and he tugged on the collar of his jacket. They stood in awkward silence for several moments before Brenna cleared her throat, trying to change the subject.

"Um, so, what're you supposed to be?"

"I'm Neo."

"Who's that?"

"Neo. You know, from *The Matrix*." He struck a pose then dropped his arms at Brenna's confused stare. "Haven't you ever heard of *The Matrix*?"

"Well, my family traveled a lot and we didn't really have time to watch movies or TV."

"But it's the greatest movie of all time! You should come see it with me some time. The cinema down the way plays it most Friday nights."

"Oh. Um…I'd love to, but—"

"Her Fridays are booked."

Patrick's deep voice interrupted her words as he strode up to them, and Brenna's cheeks flushed nearly as red as Colin's. Colin looked as though he might say something, but Patrick raised a brow. With a muffled 'bye', he scampered out of the kitchen as quickly as he could. Frowning, Brenna turned to Saoirse—who was standing beside Patrick—and took her hand.

"Patrick, you didn't have to be so rude."

"'Tis better than letting him think otherwise."

"But—"

"You'd think," said Deirdre loudly as she pushed her way into the kitchen, "that people would have the decency to move for the owner of the house! I see Patrick found you first, then. Grand!"

Opening the sliding door, Deidre ushered them into the backyard with a flashlight in hand. A path zigzagged across the yard full of fruit trees and vegetable beds, and Brenna realized she'd never actually noticed how lush or wide the backyard was. A small, wooden gate was nestled between a rock wall at the back of the garden, and Patrick stopped them there.

"Wait here a moment, the pair of you."

Without bothering to open it, Patrick swung a long leg over the low gate and disappeared around the corner. Deirdre gave a low whistle, putting a hand on Brenna's shoulder.

"Brenna Morgan, you had better come back alive."

"Excuse me?"

"You didn't think I noticed how torn up the pair of you are? And you've been looking over your shoulder like you're fair certain something's going to come out and murder you." Deirdre glanced at Saoirse who was now half hiding behind Brenna, her brown eyes almost black and very serious in the dim lighting. "And anyway, what're you doing running about with a little fairie? D'you know how dangerous that is?"."

Brenna's eyes widened. "H—how did...I mean..."

"Sure, you must think I'm daft! I know a fairie when I see one."

"You...you mean, you see them, too?"

"Sure." Deirdre flung the word out as easily as if she were talking about her favorite color, and Brenna felt the blood rush from her head, leaving her feeling slightly dizzy. Deirdre laughed.

"But why didn't you say anything?"

"And when was a good time to tell you, I ask? You don't just go 'round to people saying you see the Fair Folk, now do you?"

"I...no?"

"Right. And here I didn't want you thinking I was some sort of crazy person. Look here, Brenna, you're my friend, and I'll do all I can to help you, all right? Fairies and all."

Tears flooded Brenna's vision and slipped down her cheeks as she hugged Deirdre to her tightly. Her friend's slender arms encircled her, and Brenna held onto the smaller girl, trying not to sob out loud. Deirdre giggled, pulling away as she wiped a few tears from her own cheeks.

"Brenna, you really haven't had friends before, have you?"

Shaking her head, Brenna rubbed her eyes. "Deirdre, I'll explain everything when I come back. I promise."

"You had better! I'm dying to know what sort of scrape you've gone and gotten yourself into."

"Brenna, there's nothing following us—let's go."

Out of the darkness, she could hear Patrick's voice come from somewhere down the road, and she picked up Saoirse once more, opening the gate before she turned to face Deirdre. In the moonlight, all she could make out were her friend's pale face and arms, and her eyes seemed larger than normal in the strange light.

"Deirdre, I—"

"Go on then, Brenna. I'm fair certain you've got a busy night ahead of you. Mind you don't stay on the roads."

With tears still in her eyes, Brenna nodded her head before closing the gate and leaving her friend behind, making a left onto the narrow lane that led to the main road where Patrick was waiting for her and Saoirse.

"C'mon then, girls. It's already gone on seven."

Together they hurried down the road squeezed between the large trees that separated Deirdre's house from the school. The slight scuffing of their shoes was the only sound she could make out, and she felt a shiver go down her spine at the eerie silence. Brenna paused as they reached the dirt road that led through the woods, bending down to pick up Saoirse. In her arms once more, the child wrapped her arms a little tighter around Brenna's neck. In front of her, the towering trees glowed in the moonlight and felt more ominous than normal. Patrick glanced over at her.

"Are you all right?"

"Yeah, I'm just thinking."

He didn't ask any more questions, for which she was grateful. They made their way into the woods and had a quick debate. Deciding it was best not to take any chances, they veered away from the main path. Darkness enveloped them, and both Brenna and Patrick stumbled several times on soft pockets of earth and rocks hidden in the dense ferns and foliage as they made their way deeper into the strip of forest. Thin strands of moonlight filtered through the canopy above, casting small pinpoints of ghostly, blue light onto the floor below. Patrick put up a hand abruptly, stopping their progress.

"Do you remember where the entrance is?"

"No. The pixies took me to it last time." Brenna's breath came out in misty puffs as she spoke, and seeing it reminded her just how cold it was. She looked down to Saoirse who was peering around with interest.

"Are you cold, Saoirse?"

"No." She held up an arm, waving it. "Your present is keeping me very warm. It is not very pretty, though. It is not green."

Brenna smiled. Clearly, Saoirse's taste was similar to her mother's. Glancing about, she frowned. Nothing but tree branches and moonlight filled her vision, devoid of any pixies. She closed her eyes, willing them to appear as she wiggled her toes in the shoe that the leprechaun had made. She was still amazed that it had held up so well—unlike the boot she'd bought to match it—and reminded herself to seriously thank him the next time she saw him.

"Welcome, Brenna of *Coillearnach*."

The tiny, musical voice that whispered in her ear caused Brenna to jump and her eyes to snap open. Little flashes of light appeared all around her, landing on branches and flitting through the air like fireflies. Smiling, she opened her palm, and the pixie landed on her hand, its light radiating warmth.

"You're here!"

"You're here!" cried the other pixies around her, and Saoirse giggled. Several of the tiny beings flitted in and out of the child's tangled hair, mimicking her laughter and filling the woods with the happy sound.

"We have fought an entire army, and here we find you all having a good laugh. It is pleased I am to know how seriously you are taking your duties, Brenna Morgan."

Turlough's dry remark pierced the air, and Brenna turned to see him and Roibhilin standing only a few feet away, both looking less than amused. Their once unblemished clothing was now severely stained with black splotches, and for once Roibhilin's wavy, golden hair wasn't immaculately groomed. Turlough's own straight locks looked like they would take days to completely untangle, and both sported a hefty amount of cuts and scrapes that had Brenna wishing she'd brought a first aid kit. The pixies flocked to the two young men, and Roibhilin gently swatted them away.

"They were only mimicking Saoirse." Patrick crossed his arms as he spoke, and Brenna could actually see a muscle in his jaw pulse.

Saoirse, who had been busy cupping pixies in her hands by the dozens, quickly dropped them at the mention of her name and wrapped her arms around Brenna's neck. Through her tangled hair, she peered at Roibhilin and Turlough, her large, blue eye filled with curiosity. Brenna frowned, pushing some of the girl's hair away from her own face.

"Look, we *are* taking this seriously. You can't blame us if pixies make her laugh, right? And anyway, are you guys all right? I mean, besides being covered in gore."

Her question seemed to throw Roibhilin and Turlough, for they both lost their militant stances and Roibhilin's annoyed look softened somewhat. "We are fine." He glanced at the child. "I thought I had told you to wait on the mound. It was foolish to come to the woods."

"We would have, but we got chased by a whole bunch of hawthorn pixies and some nasty goblins."

"They were on my mound?"

There was such fury in his voice that Brenna could swear she saw icicles form in the air as he breathed. Roibhilin had made his way to her in three long strides, and she had to tilt her head back to look up at him. She took a healthy step backward.

"No, only around it. We couldn't get in, so Patrick and I had to go to Deirdre's."

"Who is Deirdre?" Turlough piped in, once more at Roibhilin's side, though his pale green eyes constantly flitted over to Patrick. Why he was so interested in him Brenna wasn't sure.

"She's my friend. You guys didn't happen to see anymore creatures on your way here, did you?"

"No. Why?" Roibhilin's face was a mask once more, and Brenna couldn't detect even a hint of interest or concern. She rolled her shoulders uncomfortably.

"I don't know. I just feel uneasy. It seemed almost too easy getting away from them, and now...they're not even chasing us anymore."

"Perhaps they have retreated." Turlough folded his arms, looking thoughtful. Brenna fingered the flowers still looped around her neck.

"Maybe. I mean, I did have on these daisy chains. Maybe they told the others and they know not to try and attack me anymore."

"*That* is unlikely." Roibhilin put his hand to his sword, curling his fingers around the hilt. "I am sure they will be looking to create a larger army with which to find us. We must get you back to *Bri Leith* as soon as possible."

"That shouldn't be a problem. Can't we use the entrance in these woods?"

"No." Turlough scanned the dark forest, clearly starting to feel uneasy himself. "His Majesty has blocked most entrances to his lands in preparation for the war. There is only one entrance that can be used right now, and it is miles away."

"You have fought many times?" Saoirse voice came out slightly wobbly as she interrupted the conversation, her eyes fixated on a particularly large, dark stain on Roibhilin's green tunic.

"Of course we have." Turlough seemed insulted by the question and then glanced at Patrick once more, a smirk snaking across his face. "More than that boy behind you ever has, is that not so, Roibhilin?"

"I doubt he has fought in all his life."

Patrick's hands fisted at his side and he took a step forward. "I'll have you know—"

He had started stalking toward the two, and Brenna stepped in between the boys, glaring at Turlough. "Is there a reason you're picking on Patrick?"

"Reason?" Turlough shrugged his shoulders. "His face annoys me."

"His *face* annoys you? Are you serious?"

"When have I ever been otherwise?"

Brenna's temper flared to life and she had to count to five. Now wasn't the time to be quarreling. She couldn't wait until she returned

Saoirse to her parents, though, and then she'd be more than happy to remind Turlough what good manners were. "If it's as dangerous as you say it is, then we shouldn't be standing here arguing, should we? I swear, you're almost as bad as Roibhilin."

"I would like to hear you say that again."

"You're as bad as—hey!"

Brenna balked as something slid against her feet, and she felt the hair on the back of her neck rise. Roots that had the uncanny appearance of skeletal fingers had protruded from the ground to clasp tightly around her ankles, and the ground beneath her began to shift. Brenna struggled to pull her feet from the roots as they rapidly pulled her down through sediment akin to quicksand.

"Patr—!"

Brenna's cry was cut short as a vine-like hand slapped across her mouth and she lost her balance, falling backward. She watched with horror as dozens of long, bony arms shot up above before closing about her and Saoirse. She struggled against the strong bindings. As one, Patrick, Roibhilin, and Turlough leapt forward to pull at the roots, but like a steel trap they refused to budge, quickly dragging her down through the ground. Dirt began to fill her nose as she watched both Roibhilin and Patrick reach for her, but it was too late. She attempted to scream, but the ground engulfed her, and Brenna closed her eyes as she felt the cold, black earth swallow her whole.

* * * *

It was with some surprise that Brenna realized she could breath, and she opened her eyes slowly. The hands had stopped pulling her down, though they hadn't released her. All around her was darkness, and while she could feel her hair dangling behind her, she had no idea where she was or why the earth was apparently hollow. She shouted as the arms suddenly tightened and then rotated her so that she was right-side up. The hand on her mouth slid away, and several others slithered away from around herself and Saoirse. With her heart hammering in her chest and her breath shaky, Brenna tried to keep her wits about her. Wherever they were, it couldn't possibly be beneath the ground. There was no smell, no sound, not even a faint wind or chill in the air.

"Are you hurt, Saoirse?" Brenna's voice came out muffled, her voice lacking any form of an echo.

"No." She couldn't see the little girls face, but Saoirse sounded much calmer than she should, and that worried her.

"Um, okay. That's good."

Brenna tried to kick her legs before giving a shout as the rest of the arms loosened around her, causing them to fall through the darkness. The drop was a short one, and light appeared almost instantly. Brenna grunted when her feet smacked onto solid ground, and her knees buckled under her. Saoirse had rolled away, and she stood up much faster than Brenna was able. Feeling disoriented and slightly nauseous, it took several seconds for her to get her bearings and stand back up, and she rubbed her head which was starting to throb. Saoirse cried out and launched herself onto Brenna's legs, hugging them tightly.

Wincing at the pain the pressure brought to her recent cut, Brenna took the small child's shaking body in her arms, coughing when Saoirse hugged her neck with a little too much force.

"It's okay. I've got you."

Peeling the girl's arms from her neck, Brenna shielded her eyes to look around and felt her stomach drop. They stood atop a large hill, and the sky was filled with billowing, gray clouds that slowly roiled above. Only a few small streams of weak light filtered through the clouds, landing on the barren, windswept world below. Stunted, black trees that twisted and bent dramatically sideways dotted the relatively flat land, and craggy rocks in the distance jutted out from hardpacked sand like broken teeth, some of them nearly as tall as buildings. A blast of cold wind whipped back Brenna's hair, and in it she could hear the cries of a thousand voices, each one howling with sadness and regret. Saoirse began to sob then, burying her head into Brenna's throat.

"I smell death." Her words were nothing but a whisper, but Brenna could feel the child's warm tears land on her neck.

"Don't worry, Saoirse. We're going to get out of here…wherever 'here' is."

Turning around, Brenna felt what little hope she had die. As far as the eye could see was desolate moorland dotted with clumps of heather and what looked to be broken shields beneath tattered banners of various sizes and colors fluttering in the moaning winds. Shivering, Brenna turned her gaze back in front of her. In the distance past the large, imposing semicircle of jagged rocks was a blackened mountain range. She narrowed her eyes, leaning forward slightly when she saw a strange bump at the base of the mountains. After staring hard for a solid minute, she finally recognized what she was staring at. A massive edifice had been carved from out of the mountain, dominating a ring of rocks before it. Its spires mirrored the twisted trees smattered across the plains, and light poured out of windows onto the gray sands below from various parts of the large structure.

"Brenna Morgan of *Coillearnach*, you are most welcome."

Where once there was only a hill now stood an entire troop of strange, wizened-looking creatures, their black eyes alight with hunger and excitement. Their hissing voices chorused together in a truly insidious way as they swiftly created a circle around Brenna and Saoirse. Leading the horde was, of all things, a black goat. Huge, white horns curled high above its head before curving back in corkscrew curls, and its golden eyes held more danger than its innocent form let on. Brenna felt the hairs on her arms stand up when she looked into its eyes, and she had the sinking feeling that she was staring at death. Holding Saoirse tightly to her chest, she licked her dry lips.

"W-who are you?"

"I am the *Puca*, of course." The goat spoke in a surprisingly cultured tone, and Brenna blanched. She had read about the Puca in her folklore book.

"*The* Pooka? You…you foretell people's deaths, right?"

"Among many other things, but that is neither here nor there. Take hold of my horns, Brenna Morgan, and I will take you from here."

"Why should I trust you?"

"Because, mortal, the journey will be long otherwise, and these stupid creatures before you will make it more unpleasant than I."

The horde cackled then, shrieking with unholy laughter as they raised their frail arms and stamped their thin legs in a joyous ruckus. The Puca shook its head in irritation, and the mob quickly fell silent. Brenna jutted out her chin, glaring at the creatures. She wasn't going to let them scare her—it clearly only made them happier, and she didn't want to please them any more than she had to.

"And if I choose not to go with you?"

"Bravery will not help you in this place, Brenna Morgan, though it is admirable. Grab my horns now, for if you tarry any longer you will displease my master. And that would be the most foolish thing you have done yet."

Looking around at the encircling creatures, Brenna realized there was little she'd be able to do in the way of resistance given her present situation. Even with her daisy chains protecting them, she had no idea how to get back to her world, and she wasn't sure how much longer the strands hanging around her neck would shield them.

"Don't worry, Saoirse—we're going to get out of here," she one again reassured the little girl in her arms.

Straightening her shoulders, she took hold of one of the large horns, shouting when the Puca flung her onto its back with a flick of his head. She barely had time to secure Saoirse in front of her when the horde around them cheered and the Puca took off at a run, streaking down the large hill so quickly that Brenna lost her breath for a moment as her stomach lodged in her throat. Ignoring the crowd trailing after them, the goat picked up speed once he hit flat land and quickly left the creatures behind without once breaking his stride. The jagged rocks that had seemed to be miles away were suddenly upon them, made all the more intimidating by the fact that they cast no shadow on the barren ground.

"It appears, Brenna Morgan, that you have more help than anticipated."

The goat slowed to a walk, and Brenna twisted to look over her shoulder. Roibhilin was running after them, far ahead of the horde, with his sword drawn.

"Roibhilin!"

"Do not bother asking for his aid." The Puca seemed unconcerned that Roibhilin was nearly upon them, instead passing through an opening between two rocks at a sedate pace. Turning around, he watched in amusement as Roibhilin came rushing at them, then gave a bray of laughter when he fell to the ground, the sword skittering away from him. Brenna slid off of the goat and tried to go to him, but the Puca stepped on her shoe, holding her in place. Furious, she narrowed her eyes at the goat, struggling to pull her foot from under its hoof.

"What did you do to him?!"

"I did nothing. These rocks are made of iron. He is a young boy, and nearly as foolish as you."

Brenna looked up at the large, black stones then back to Roibhilin. He lay crumpled on the ground, holding his head. Saoirse had gone limp atop the Puca, slumping onto his neck, and Brenna felt tears prick her eyes.

"Why don't they affect you?"

"Because I am not made of the same as your friend. Take hold once more, for we still have much traveling to do this Samhain night, and the child will die soon if you do not remove her from these rocks."

"Do not get back on that beast!" shouted Roibhilin as he staggered back up, his blue eyes glowing with anger. With trembling fingers and an ill feeling in her stomach, Brenna hesitated before reaching out to grasp the Puca's horn. She turned to face Roibhilin.

"I don't really have a choice."

"Of course you have a choice! Stop being so stupid and come here!"

Behind her, the Puca struck the ground with his hoof, and the clouds above them gave a low rumble. "Roibhilin of *Coillearnach*, go you to your home and fight valiantly with your comrades. Take my horn, girl. There is nothing for you to do but go forward."

Reluctantly, and despite Roibhilin's angry shouting, Brenna closed her fingers around the goat's horn and alighted onto its back once more.

"By the moon and stars, mortal, get *off*!"

"Roibhilin, stop telling me what to do!" For once, Roibhilin closed his mouth, and Brenna smiled despite the tears in her eyes. "Don't worry. Everything's going to be fine. King Midhir wanted to know who's against him anyway, right?"

"For the love of—"

"This is the only way. Tell Patrick I'll see him soon."

Roibhilin struggled to snatch his sword from the ground before looking back up at her. Brenna felt her heart tighten when she saw the fear and worry in his eyes. Gripping his sword, he sheathed it. Despite the distance, she could make out Roibhilin's words as clearly as if he were standing in front of her.

"I will come for you, Brenna."

She was so stunned to hear her name come from Roibhilin's lips that she nearly tumbled off of the *Puca* when it shot forward. As she gripped one horn with her free hand, she glanced over her shoulder to where Roibhilin's tall frame was rapidly disappearing. Despite his harsh words and insults, he *did* care. Tears stung her eyes and fell down her cheeks, but the wind quickly vanished them. Why was it that Roibhilin had to wait until the last possible minute to say something nice?

"Brenna?" Saoirse voice was trembling and weak, and Brenna almost didn't hear her. Leaning forward, she pressed her forehead to the little girl's pale one.

"Yes?"

"Roibhilin is very brave."

"Yeah...I guess he is."

"He will save us." Saoirse's voice was quiet but sure, and Brenna smiled in spite of not feeling very happy or hopeful. How could Roibhilin save them if he couldn't even get past the rocks?

"I think the only people who can save us right now are ourselves, Saoirse."

"Hold tightly now, Brenna Morgan."

The Puca's voice was audible even in the howling wind. Brenna secured her grip on the horn and strengthened her hold on Saoirse as the goat suddenly lengthened its stride and built up more speed, rushing over what looked to be a bog. Half-decayed bodies of fallen warriors floated in the thick, black muck, their lifeless eyes staring up at Brenna in between piles of discarded flags, armor, and swords. The stench of rot and damp earth was overwhelming, and had she not been afraid of falling off the Puca's back she would have put a hand over her nose. Leaning forward again, she spoke into the goat's ear, trying her best to breath as little of the fowl air as possible.

"Was there a battle here?"

"No."

"Then what's with all the bodies?"

The *Puca* remained silent for several moments before speaking. "They are the spoils of wars from long ago."

Brenna frowned, trying not to look back down at the emaciated faces of the fallen. "Why would someone want bodies as a reward for winning a war?"

"It was not the bodies that my master wanted."

Brenna wasn't sure she wanted to know what exactly his master did want, so she stopped asking questions. From the hill, the land had seemed flat and barren, but now that she was on the ground she realized the landscape varied greatly, transforming from bogs to desolate, rolling hills covered in heather and hedges of dry, spikey shrubs. As they drew closer to the large edifice with its twisted spires, a massive wall that had previously blended in with the architecture suddenly appeared, surrounding the structure that had been carved into the mountain. Slowing down to a walk, the Puca stopped only when his nose touched the stone wall. There seemed to be no way in, and Brenna craned her neck back to peer up at the barricade, wondering if there was a guard of some sort who would let them through. Goose bumps rose along her skin as dozens of large crows sitting atop the wall stared back at her, their glossy feathers ruffling in the wind and their black eyes glittering intelligently as they studied her.

Saoirse quivered with fear, her slender arms gripping Brenna's waist painfully hard. With his hoof, the goat struck the ground with three heavy blows that echoed off of the wall, causing a few of the crows to take flight, their cries filling the air like a death knell as they soared overhead.

A fissure slowly snaked its way up the wall, sending chips of black rock flying and allowing a bright light to shine through. The ground beneath them began to rumble and shake violently as the stone wall suddenly groaned and parted, revealing a bridge that crossed over a deep gorge and led straight to the keep. Without waiting for the wall to open completely, the Puca crossed the cobblestone bridge and stopped when they'd reached a towering, wooden door adorned with iron bands and bolts the size of Brenna's head. The goat struck the floor three times once more, and the large door opened with a high-pitched *creak*, revealing nothing but darkness. The Puca rose up on its hind legs then, forcing Brenna and Saoirse from its back. It shook its head, and she had to take several steps back to keep from getting hit by the large, spiraling horns.

"This is where our paths part." The Puca turned to leave, his hooves clattering against the floor.

"Wait!"

"What is it that you want, mortal?"

"I…I read that you can foretell people's deaths. If you can tell when people die, then you would know if I'll…"

The Puca's golden eyes pierced through Brenna, stopping her from finishing her sentence. It stared at her intently, and for as long as she lived she would never forget the feeling of absolute fear that washed over her in that moment. Despite his goat-like appearance, she realized that whatever the Puca truly was, it was something grotesque and horrifying. It blinked then and swung its head forward, resuming his walk across the bridge.

"All humans die in time, Brenna Morgan."

Without so much as a flick of its tail, the Puca disappeared in the middle of the walkway, leaving her to face the door alone as the last echoes of its hooves faded away. Squaring her shoulders, she picked up Saoirse and stepped through the door, shivering when a wet, bone-chilling breeze wafted through from the darkness beyond.

Chapter Sixteen

The door slammed closed with a dull *thud*, and Brenna jumped. She waited several moments for her eyes to adjust to the darkness with little success. The cold around her seeped into the very marrow of her bones, and she was sure she would never feel warm again.

"A thousand welcomes, Brenna Morgan of *Coillearnach*. I have been expecting you for quite some time."

It took everything in her not to bolt out the door as the hauntingly lovely voice spoke to her from somewhere in the darkness. Taking a few steps away, Brenna winced when her back made contact with one of the sharp, iron-pronged bolts embedded in the door.

"Please, come in."

Torches on the high, stone walls flared to life. Above Brenna, seven circular chandeliers made of gold brought light to her surroundings. Eyes wide, she took in the grand hall she found herself in. It was a massive room with soaring arches and black timber frames around which strange shadow creatures crawled about. There wasn't a window to be seen, and tapestries depicting men in bloody battles hung on several of the walls. The room was pulsing with creatures that scurried and skulked at the fringes of the grand room while to the far left side of the hall sat twelve elderly women with bowed heads at a large, golden table, each sharing the task of creating yarn and weaving it. Brenna squinted into the dim lighting, trying to get a better look at what the women were making. Saoirse trembled in her arms, hiding her head in the crook of Brenna's neck.

"Come closer, child, that I might see the brave mortal who has brought our salvation to my door."

At the end of the long hall was a dais with an ornate, golden throne. A woman both beautiful and terrifying sat upon it, her dark-red hair cascading to the floor in waves. Her dusky eyes were large in her pale face, and when she stood yards of deep purple silk fluttered around her. Two dogs the size of ponies stood guard on either side of the throne. Their slender but muscular bodies had blended in with the shadows until they stepped forward, and their eyes were trained hungrily on Brenna. With fear having seeped into every bone of her body, Brenna hesitantly made her way to the dais, and Saoirse began to weep silently, the warm tears dampening her collar bone. Brenna gave her a reassuring squeeze. The woman smiled at them as they approached, but the action didn't reach her eyes.

"There is no need to fear me, Brenna Morgan, for I will not harm you."

The thought that the person she would have to face was a woman hadn't crossed her mind, and despite her fear Brenna was more than a little surprised. She had always assumed Treasach was working for another man. Her shock must have been apparent, for the tall woman smiled.

"Was I not what you expected?"

"I…I…well, no." Brenna stopped, taking a deep breath. Now more than ever she had to be brave. And more than that, she had to be smart. Licking her lips, she looked up at the beautiful woman with the predatory eyes. "Who are you?"

She smiled, her teeth white against full, bloodred lips. Beside her, the two dogs pressed against their mistress' side, their heads reaching all the way to her hips. Sniffing the air in front of them, they gave a low growl, stopping only when the woman placed her delicate hands atop their heads.

"I am The Morrigan. You have traveled very far, my dear. Please, accept refreshment."

Swiftly, the tall woman raised her arm and a small, goblin-like creature appeared almost instantly. He clutched silver cup that was nearly as big as his body, and he teetered precariously before arriving at the dais. The queen gently lifted the chalice and took a sip before holding it out to Brenna who shook her head slowly. An emotion—dark and dangerous—flitted across The Morrigan's eyes and caused Brenna's heart to momentarily stop in terror.

"You refuse Her Majesty?" One of the women at the golden table had spoken up with a screeching voice like a violin that had been badly tuned. Brenna turned to face her—then wished she hadn't. The old woman sitting closest to her had paused in her knitting to stand up, sporting twelve horns that grew around her head like a gruesome crown. The other women who had been half-hidden in shadows also stopped working in order to rise, each one with different amounts of horns protruding from their heads. The one farthest away only had one horn sprouting from her forehead, but all of the women's claw-like hands and black eyes were almost as horrifying as their spikey anatomy. Brenna hastily looked back to the queen who stared at her with raised brows and a tight smile.

"I don't mean any disrespect to your kindness, Your Majesty. It's just that I had a very large dinner, and I'm not very hungry or thirsty."

"A large…" The Morrigan laughed and handed the cup back to the goblin before sinking down into her throne. The dogs retreated, once more disappearing into the shadows save for their eyes focused intently on Brenna.

"You are a very brave mortal. It seems that humanity has not wiped out all of its heroes as I had suspected. Tell me, Brenna Morgan, do you know why you are here?"

"Because something dragged me down here and your Puca brought me to your castle?"

"This is all true." Narrowing her eyes, The Morrigan turned her dark gaze to the twelve women who were all still standing.

"Sit, good women, and continue your work."

With a few mutterings, the twelve elderly women sat back down, though they cast furious glances at Brenna every so often. The queen leaned forward and her two dogs followed the motion, their black noses quivering.

"I am sorry that you were taken so suddenly, but time is rapidly becoming my enemy. I did not have the time to send for you in a more befitting manner. But I can see, mortal, that you have no notion as to who the child is."

"Of course I do. She's Queen Etain's daughter."

"Etain…it has been many years since that name has been uttered in these halls. If you know she is Etain's daughter, then surely you know how precious she is to me. To all of us."

"I…I don't know anything about that. I just know I have to get her home."

"You are a terrible liar, Brenna Morgan. I do not like being lied to." The two dogs took a step forward, the wiry hair on the scruff of their necks bristling, and Brenna hastily backed away several feet as The Morrigan stood, pointing to Saoirse. "That child is our salvation."

"But I thought—"

"You thought what?"

"I…I thought that if you killed her, she would destroy the world."

In her arms, Saoirse grew very still. Brenna wasn't sure if the little girl was even breathing. She could only imagine the fear she must be feeling with that piece of news, but now wasn't the time to skirt around truths. The queen laughed then, a soft and melodic sound.

"I do not wish to kill her."

"Oh."

"I wish to sacrifice her."

"That's the same thing!"

"Do *not*," said The Morrigan in a deadly soft voice, "raise your voice to me, human." Brenna clamped her mouth shut, and the queen quickly reverted to a more amiable tone. "Clearly, they have not told you the truth. I find that Midhir and his court rarely do. I am afraid, Brenna Morgan, that it is *they* who have deceived *you*. And they can be very persuasive."

Slowly, The Morrigan sat back in her throne. Brenna held Saoirse tightly, wishing more than anything that she could just walk out of the hall and take the little girl back to her mother.

"You see, through the child's sacrifice, we will be saved."

"What do you mean?"

"Have you never wondered why humans can no longer see us, or why our worlds are separated?"

"Um, not…really."

"It is because we were tricked and forced to go underground, far away from human eyes, away from our beloved country." The queen's fingers tightly gripped the sides of the golden throne, her eyes flashing dangerously. "With this child, we can once again take control of the lands so unjustly taken from us."

"But…but you guys go above ground all the time. That's how I saw Roibhilin and—"

"It is not the same." The Morrigan waved a dismissive hand. "Once, we were a mighty and powerful people who did not bow to your concepts of time. We ruled Erie, and its people knew nothing but bounty and the thrill of war. And now look at it." The Morrigan's eyes glittered with passion and fury, and her voice deepened as she continued, "Filthy, desecrated. The people have forgotten how to see, they disrespect the old ways and the magic that they once knew. They have torn us down to be nothing more than fairy-tales and fanciful, winged creatures no bigger than a babe. With this child's help, humans will see our might once more."

Smiling, the queen looked off into the distance, clearly seeing a future that Brenna could not. Blinking, The Morrigan turned her dark eyes back to her guests. The stare was unnerving, and there was something in their depths that caused a wave of dread to roil through Brenna. Huddling the child as close as she could, she stuck out her chin stubbornly.

"If you're so powerful, couldn't you just *make* people see all of you again?"

"It is not as simple as that. To break the bond on us, the child's blood must be sacrificed."

Her heart hammering in her chest, Brenna felt a cold sweat bead her brow as the towering woman rose from her chair once more, leaving the platform to stand on the cold, stone floor in front of her. Even with her feet flat on the ground, The Morrigan was at least a good foot and a half taller than Brenna.

"Though Midhir and Etain do not say it, they want their lands back. But they have grown complacent and forgetful of what mortals have done. The only difference between us, my child, is that I am willing to do what needs to be done."

Brenna bit her lip and looked down at Saoirse. The little girl was as cold and as still as a statue, and she wondered if perhaps she had fainted. The queen kneeled then, and with delicate fingers she brushed some of Brenna's tangled, blonde hair from her face, tucking it behind her ears. The Morrigan's skin was like ice as it brushed against her cheek, and Brenna shivered. Even with her gentle voice and touch, true warmth never appeared in her black eyes.

"You have tender feelings, human, but they betray you. The child must be sacrificed for the good of many."

"Will I truly destroy the world?" Saoirse spoke up with her tiny voice for the first time since entering the keep, and The Morrigan smiled as the girl looked up from Brenna's neck, her blue eyes wide and filled with unshed tears.

"No, my *leanbh*. You will help create it again."

"Don't listen to her." Brenna took a healthy step back from the kneeling queen, jerking her head away from the reaching fingers. "Saoirse, it's only if you're put in the wrong hands that you would destroy the world. Queen Morrigan is only trying to trick you."

The queen rose from her knees and took in a sharp breath, clearly trying to keep her temper in check. The dogs growled beside her. In two bounds, they were circling Brenna with their long, dark bodies, so close that she could feel their warm breath on her face and hear the scrape of their claws on the floor as their eyes locked onto Saoirse.

"Like Midhir and Etain, you do not think of the future. You only see what is in front of you, not what will be."

Brenna took a few more steps back, glancing over her shoulder. She was halfway to the main door—maybe she could make a break for it. But to where? She frowned. There was nowhere to run *to*. An idea popped into her mind then, and she felt a stirring of hope flare in her chest. Etain had said that Saoirse's power was only good until midnight. If she could stall for time, Saoirse would be useless to the queen, and with the help of the protective daisy chains around her neck they could make it out and find a way back to their world.

"What would you do if you sacrificed Saoirse?"

"I beg your pardon?"

"What would you do if you were able to go above ground again and be seen by all humans?"

Brenna could feel the beady eyes of the twelve horned women boring into the back of her head. She jumped when one of the large dogs brushed its tail against her leg as both trod back to their mistress's side. The Morrigan didn't seem to notice Brenna's nervousness as she glanced once more to the door or the fact that the women at the table had stopped working to listen.

"Why do you ask this of me, human?"

"Because I want to know."

"I see." The Morrigan smiled, and this time it was terrifying. "I would take back what was stolen from us."

"And then?"

"That is not your concern."

"Well, you're talking about taking over the world I live in, so I think it is."

The queen's eyes narrowed, her temper rising. "You are impudent, Brenna Morgan."

"Yeah, I get told that a lot."

The Morrigan seemed to get taller as she straightened her spine. Her two dogs began to growl in earnest, their mouths parting to reveal wickedly sharp teeth. Brenna locked her knees to keep from taking a step back, trying to calm herself with the reminder that they were safe as long as she was wearing the daisy chains.

"I will forgive you your remark, mortal, because I find your spirit admirable. But do not think to repeat the action. Now come—the time grows near and I am sorely running out of patience."

If what I've been witnessing is patience, thought Brenna grimly, *then I'd hate to see what the queen looks like when she runs out of it.* She took a small step back, trying to slowly edge her way to the door or at least get close enough so that she could possibly make it out if she ran.

"I don't see why you want to go above ground, Your Majesty, if everything is as bad as it seems."

"Your questions are tiresome, and I grow weary of your attempts to stall the inevitable. Give me the child and no harm will come to you this night."

"No."

"No?" The Morrigan smiled suddenly, and the dogs growled deeply enough that Brenna could feel the sound through the floor. She whirled around to run, getting only three steps in before the horned women blocked her path. One of them—the old woman with ten horns encircling her head—reached out to grab Saoirse. She hissed as smoke began to curl from between her fingers. Pulling her hand back, she glared at Brenna.

"What magic have you, lass?"

"Look about her neck!"

Several of them let loose mighty howls of anger at the sight of the daisy chains. Brenna winced as their screeching voices bounced off the walls, creating an ear-splitting chorus. Still shrieking, the women retreated as Brenna moved closer to them. With more confidence in every step, she began to make her way to the door, a grim smile on her lips as the horned women moved aside with cries and hisses.

"I will ask you one last time, Brenna Morgan. Give me the *leanbh*," The Morrigan called after her.

"No." Brenna never paused in her march, but she did look over her shoulder, green eyes flashing with anger as her determined voice rang out in the suddenly silent hall. Even the strange shadow creatures on the wooden beams and outskirts of the room had stopped moving. "I may not know much about all of you, but I do know that if you ever step foot on our side of the Veil, we'll all be doomed. You don't want your land back; you want to kill people, or enslave us. And I'm not going to let that happen. So you can just take your monster-dogs and your goblins and stay here!"

As fast as her long legs would carry her, Brenna made a mad dash for the door only to skid to an abrupt halt as one of the dogs blocked her path. It had moved so swiftly that she hadn't even seen it running alongside her. When she tried to step forward, it gnashed its teeth and bore down on her, forcing her back several feet. An overwhelmingly sweet scent caused Brenna to turn around, and she smothered a scream. The queen's face was only inches from her own, black stare burning with a fevered, wild anger.

"S-stay back!"

Brenna held up the daisy chains. Saoirse began to cry loudly. A laugh, deep and cruel, bubbled forth from the queen's throat, and with a malicious smile she reached out, touching the three delicate necklaces that hung from Brenna's neck.

"How very clever of you, mortal, to have such strong protection." The daisy chains quickly wilted and shriveled at The Morrigan's touch before falling to the floor in a flurry of gray ash, and Brenna shouted in dismay. "But I am afraid they cannot protect you from me. It is a shame you did not heed my command."

Saoirse screamed as The Morrigan grabbed hold of her frail shoulders, and her delicate arms clung tightly around Brenna.

"Let go of her!"

Brenna kept her arms around the child's waist and pulled back. She growled in frustration when she realized that no matter how much she tried she was no match for the otherworldly woman's strength. Her feet began to slide along the floor as The Morrigan dragged them closer to the dais, and Saoirse's tiny, beautiful face was streaked with tears as she looked up at Brenna. There was resolution in her gaze, and Brenna felt her mouth go dry.

"Brenna, let me go."

"No, you're going home!" Brenna gave another tug, gritting her teeth. "Just hold on!"

The little girl shook her head, and she offered Brenna tiny smile, though her chin quivered and her eyes pooled with more tears. "All will be well. I will be brave, like you."

Saoirse's arms loosened, as did her legs which had been bandied around Brenna's waist. Her soft, pink lips pressed a warm kiss to Brenna's cheek and then she was gone, plucked from Brenna's tiring grasp.

"*No!*"

The Morrigan shouted triumphantly as Brenna lost her balance and fell to her knees. The horned women behind her cackled and clapped their hands in jubilation. Scrambling up, Brenna tried to run at the queen only to be blocked by the two black hounds whose sharp teeth and warning growls kept her from going any farther. Saoirse sat perfectly still in the queen's arms, her face now surprisingly serene and bereft of any trace of her earlier fear.

"Saoirse!"

"Do not speak, human, lest I change my mind and kill you where you stand. Gentle women, have you finished your shroud?"

"Aye, the finest we have ever made, Your Majesty."

The woman with six horns flew past Brenna happily, a deep green blanket interwoven with golden knot work in her arms. The Morrigan smiled as she fingered the material presented to her.

"It is very lovely, indeed. You have truly outdone yourselves, women of *Sliabh-na-mban*. And now, my dear child, it is time for you to fulfill your destiny."

Taking the blanket from the arms of the six-horned woman, she laid it flat upon a pedestal that had been hastily brought in front of her by a small, gruesome parade of creatures that looked more like tree twigs than humans. She gently placed Saoirse upon the round tabletop and smiled down at the unmoving child.

"Do not fear your death, young one, for your life will bring honor and glory to our people."

Extending her right hand, The Morrigan accepted a small dagger that was placed in her hands by another of the horned women. The handle was white and clearly made from some sort of bone, and the blade was made of a strange metal, its black edges smooth and wickedly sharp. Smiling, the queen looked into Saoirse's emotionless face and trailed her fingers along the little girl's pale cheek.

"You will bring about a new world, my little one, and your bravery will be remembered by all of those in this room this night."

Behind Brenna, the horned women lifted and then slowly brought forward a three-footed cauldron nearly as tall and as wide as themselves, grunting and moaning under its weight before setting it down in front of the pedestal. The Morrigan pressed a hand to Saoirse's chest and pushed her down flat on the slab while Brenna desperately looked about for any sort of weapon she could find. She had to stop this. She had to do *something*. A large fireplace that had been hidden from view by the forms of the horned women crackled behind the golden table, and leaning next to it were several pokers.

Warily, she took a few steps backward. The hounds eyed her, their ears perked, but they remained unmoving. Walking as quickly as she could without drawing any more attention to herself, Brenna hurried over to the fireplace. She grabbed the closest poker she could find, smiling when she saw that the rod was made of iron. She wasn't sure if it would hurt The Morrigan the way it had Roibhilin, but she hoped it would affect her at least a little. She also took one of the wooden spindles from the table glowing dimly in the firelight, and the two dogs raised their noses, sniffing the air. The horned women began singing in the same strange language she'd heard Treasach and Nuala speak, but these words made Brenna's skin crawl.

The queen began to speak in the same language, and Brenna could feel the air in the room begin to thicken and pulsate with energy. Above her, she could hear strange fluttering sounds, and she had to smother a gasp when she looked up to see dozens upon dozens of large crows lining every available beam, their black heads all turned to The Morrigan. Taking in a shuddering breath, Brenna hid the iron poker behind her back and began to walk as close to the two great hounds as she could, stopping only when they issued a warning growl. She was only a couple of feet away, but their large heads blocked her view of the queen and Saoirse. She wasn't sure if her plan would work or if it would even do any good, but it was better than doing nothing.

Licking her lips, she twisted the spindle behind her back until she had a good grip on the end of it. With a flick of her wrist, she threw it as hard as she could behind her. The wooden object clattered against the golden table before hitting the floor. The dogs bounded after it, growling and snarling, causing the horned women to falter in their chanting. The queen paused in her strange language to glance over at Brenna, the dagger already making a steady descent toward Saoirse's heart. With a cry that came from deep within her chest, Brenna hurled the iron poker at The Morrigan with every ounce of strength that her fear and desperation conjured up. Everything slowed down—even her heart—as the poker soared through the air. Brenna had been aiming for the queen's head, but the rod missed its mark. Instead, it impaled itself through The Morrigan's arm, and black blood fell to the floor as the queen dropped the dagger.

Her enraged shriek was so loud that nearly everyone fell to the floor, covering their ears to block out the horrific sound. The crows that had been perched on the black beams above began cawing and flying madly about the room. Multitudes of strange and bizarre creatures rushed to their mistress's aid, and amidst the confusion Brenna ran to Saoirse, dragging the small child off of the table. Not daring to look back, Brenna ran for the door, her heart beating so quickly that she was sure it would burst. She was nearly to the entrance when something heavy and hard slammed into her back. She twisted so that she fell on her side, keeping Saoirse safe. She gasped for breath as a heavy blow slammed her shoulder into the ground. Dazed and breathless, Brenna blinked several times as the glowing eyes of a hound came into focus. Its heavy, large paws pressed her shoulder tightly against the cold floor. When she tried to kick out, the dog growled and bared its sharp teeth.

Behind the hound, the queen let loose an angry cry so fierce and primal it caused Brenna's body to shake uncontrollably.

"I will render your head from your body, you wretched whelp!"

The Morrigan advanced on her with heavy footsteps. Brenna tried as best she could to try and get out from under the dog, but despite her struggles the hound refused to budge. It growled low in its throat until the queen was upon them, and only then did it stand aside. Grabbing a fistful of Brenna's shirt, the queen lifted both girls from the floor with her good arm. Her other continued to spill blood onto the floor below, scenting the air around them with a metallic odor. The Morrigan's eyes glittered with rage and the promise of an excruciating death.

"You are as foolish as *Cúchulainn*, and like him I will make an end of you."

Before Brenna could try to figure out who on earth the queen was talking about, The Morrigan grabbed Saoirse's neck with her bad arm, causing more blood to gush from the gaping hole in a warm, pulsating wave. Brenna's stomach turned at the sight of it.

"Don't touch her!"

She tried to pry away the queen's cold fingers from the child's slender neck but to no avail. The Morrigan gave Brenna a hard shake, causing the room to spin sickeningly for a moment. Saoirse began to go limp in her arms, and Brenna kicked out at the queen, meeting nothing but air. Tears streams down her face and landed on Saoirse's tangled hair as she could feel the life going out of the child's body.

"Stop it! Please!"

The queen merely smiled and locked her eyes with Brenna's. "*Your life will be next.*"

The door behind them flew open with so much force that Brenna heard it shudder against the wall. Wailing and shrieking erupted from the twelve horned women. The Morrigan looked past Brenna to the doorway, her red lips parted in surprise. She saw true fear flash through those black eyes.

"By the moon and stars...*Gae Bulga.* But this cannot be!"

The queen released both Brenna and Saoirse, and Brenna cradled the girl close as she fell to her knees. She carefully laid her on the floor and, with trembling hands, brushed lank strands of hair from the child's unmoving face. She patted Saoirse's pale cheek, tears pricking her eyes when the girl made no response.

"No, no, *no*. Be alive! Please be alive. *Please!*"

Lowering her ear to Saoirse's chest, Brenna listened desperately for the sound of a heartbeat. Dimly, she was aware that light had flooded the halls and that the crows above her were flying around in a panic. Dark shadows and the hordes of creatures were skulking farther into the deep hall, and the twelve horned women continued to wail. Brenna closed her eyes, trying to block out the distractions as she pressed her ear harder against the child's chest. A heartbeat, slow and faint, could be heard. Brenna pulled her head back, gasping mad laughter as she gathered Saoirse into her arms. Looking up, she saw that the queen had retreated several feet away, her dogs pressed against her side, snarling and growling.

"Brenna, hurry!"

The commanding male voice bounced off the walls, and Brenna's mouth dropped open in surprise. It sounded familiar, like...like...

"Roibhilin?" she whispered in complete disbelief. Relief poured through her. How on earth had he managed to get past the iron mountains?! She had never been happier to hear his voice or the grating demand that it always seemed to carry. Scrambling up, Brenna turned around and then felt her stomach drop. Standing in the doorway with a strange, long stick in his hands wasn't Roibhilin but Patrick. His gaze landed on her and, with the light pouring in behind from him, he looked exactly like Brenna imagined the warriors of old Ireland must have looked. It took her a moment to find her voice again, and when she did it came out wobbly.

"P…Patrick?!"

"Sure, and who else would it be?"

Chapter Seventeen

"But...but *how*?!"

"Now isn't the time to be talking, Brenna. Hurry and get behind me."

Her surprise wore off quickly as she rushed to Patrick. He glared at The Morrigan like he wasn't afraid of her, the hounds, or the horned women. His hazel eyes looked almost golden in the light, and Brenna could see a muscle in his jaw pulsing. Whether it was out of fear or anger she wasn't sure.

"Foolish boy, you dare to enter my halls uninvited?"

"You took something that belongs to me; I'm thinking an invitation wasn't needed."

The queen straightened and narrowed her eyes speculatively as she let her gaze wander up and down Patrick's rigid form. A smile formed on her lips, and she took the sacrificial dagger from a pixie that had retrieved it from the floor. Still smiling, she fingered the dagger, ignoring the blood that continued to pour from the wound in her right arm. The sight of black blood pooling across the floor made Brenna feel queasy, and she was glad that Saoirse wasn't awake to see it.

"You are a brave young man to wield the *Gae Bulga*."

"Aye." Patrick tightened his grip on the weapon.

Now that she was closer, Brenna could see that the object in his hands was far from the wooden stick she had originally thought it was. The staff was nearly as tall as Patrick's six-foot frame and was a milky white color with a strange, bluish tinge. Brenna frowned. It almost looked like it was made of bone. Atop the staff was a hook that had been carved to a sharp point, like that of a harpoon. All around them, shadowy shapes edged closer, and above them the crows that had been so wildly panicked were once more edging the black rafters, their sharp eyes glued to Patrick.

"Tell me, Patrick Fergus, have you the courage to use it?"

Several bowlegged pixies covered in bark launched themselves at Patrick without warning. Faster than Brenna could inhale a breath, Patrick's right hand struck out, wielding a short sword with an iron blade. He slashed clean through several bodies at once, and the pixies that weren't killed fell back, writhing on the floor as they clutched at missing limbs and howled in agony. Brenna's mouth fell open and she stared up at Patrick.

"Since when do you know how to use a sword?!"

"Just now."

"How is that even—"

The Morrigan laughed then, sending the rest of the pixies away to retreat hastily to the great room's corners and dark nooks. With a truly terrifying smile, she looked pointedly to the staff.

"Are you afraid then, human, to use *Cúchulainn's* weapon?"

"It isn't the blood of these imps that it wants, Queen Morrigan, and I'm fair certain you know it."

"You use braver words than you should, boy." The Morrigan threw open her arms, her smile growing wider, her tone mocking. "Come at me, then! If you are half the warrior *Cúchulainn* was, then you will not hesitate to battle me."

"Who is 'Coo-Cullen'?" Brenna whispered to Patrick, irritated with not knowing who this apparently important person was.

"A famous warrior." He glanced down for a moment at Brenna in disbelief. "Haven't you read about him in those books of yours?"

"I don't remember. There were a lot of stories, and it's not like a memorized them." Brenna looked to The Morrigan who was watching them with a mix of fury and excitement. Why didn't she just attack? Holding Saoirse close, Brenna glanced over at the *Gae Bulga*. Whatever the weapon was, it was clearly something that the queen seemed nervous about; she hadn't even sent her dogs after them. Patrick nudged her with his elbow, keeping his gaze on the tall woman across the hall.

"Brenna, we've got to go. There's only fifteen minutes left until midnight, and my weapon can only be shot once at a time. I can't afford to use it right now." Patrick's voice was low and rapid as he spoke, and Brenna had to concentrate harder than usual to understand him completely.

"Okay…and just *where* are we going to run to?"

"Leave it to me and keep up."

"But—"

Not letting her finish her sentence, Patrick sheathed his sword and put a hand on Brenna's back, pushing her into a run out the door, staying close behind her as they rushed across the threshold. She could hear the queen give a roar of anger and then a flurry of wings as the crows that had been perching on the timbers rushed past them, their voices screeching nearly as loudly as those of the horned women. Brenna ducked her head as their glossy feathers brushed against her skin and their talons snagged in her hair. She threw an arm over her eyes briefly as she and Patrick escaped from the black keep into the cold outside world. They were nearly on the other side of the cobblestone bridge when the ground beneath their feet began to shake violently. Grasping the low wall of the bridge for support, their run slowed to an unsteady walk. Brenna threw a glance over her shoulder and felt her heart stop.

A seemingly never-ending row of strange and terrifying creatures stood on the other side of the gorge with long spears, swords, and bows at the ready. Interspersed among the humanoid creatures were Gentry whom Brenna could only assume had taken up arms with The Morrigan. Those with spears and shields beat them on the ground in a steady rhythm while the ones with swords, axes, and bows stomped their feet in unison. With their beady black eyes trained on Brenna and Patrick, the gruesome army parted to make way for the tall and terrifying Morrigan. Her long, purple dress was now hidden by a deep red cape that nearly matched her waving hair.

A cold wind that smelled strongly of damp earth howled through the gorge and carried with it the cries and screams of warriors in battle. Brenna's body began to shiver and Patrick shook his head as if trying to shake away the voices in the wind.

"C'mon Brenna, there's no reason to look back—its forward we're going." He smiled gamely down at her, and Brenna smiled back. As long as Patrick was here, everything would be fine.

"Ready?"

"As ready as I'll ever be."

"Right. On we go, then."

Together, the two sprinted through the opening in the black wall. Brenna's eyes widened when saw that the landscape had changed dramatically. The bog was no longer there, nor the rolling, desolate hills or grayish-brown skies. Instead, black clouds roiled like angry snakes as thunder boomed high above. A large forest of dark, twisted trees that all bent to the left was illuminated as lightning forked across the sky. Black boulders jutted out of the pebbly, uneven ground, and behind them Brenna could hear the army begin their chase.

"To the left!"

Brenna sailed over a low rock and then made a sharp left, following Patrick's tall frame as he darted into the foreboding woods. He was sometimes hard to see as he dodged between the twisted, leafless trees. The low-hanging branches proved to be sharp, scratching at their faces and arms as they ran, and Brenna kept Saoirse's face tucked into her chest. Behind them, the snapping and tearing of both bark and branches could be heard, and this time there were no pixies to hold the horde back. Brenna could feel her initial adrenaline rush beginning to wane, so she focused instead on her breathing, forcing herself to ignore the pain inflicted by the trees as she tried to avoid as many of the branches as she could. In front of her, Patrick led them through a series of twists and turns, and she wondered how on earth he knew where to go.

A horn could be heard from somewhere behind them, and the sound caused Brenna to discover a new burst of speed. They ran for what seemed like hours, the woods proving to be a never-ending maze. She wasn't sure when they would find whatever it was Patrick was looking for, but she was beginning to think that perhaps they were lost. It wouldn't be the first time.

"Patrick, how much longer?!"

For several moments, he didn't answer, but then his voice carried back to her, almost impossible to hear as the wind continued to howl around them. "We're almost there!"

She wasn't sure where 'there' was, but she certainly hoped it would show up soon. Just as her legs began to scream for rest, Patrick turned to the right and disappeared from view. Brenna followed after him, slowing down when the world around her shifted and blurred together like a still-wet painting that had water thrown on it. For a moment, it all melted together in shades of black and brown before suddenly snapping into focus to reveal a completely different forest.

"Brenna, where are you?!" Patrick's voice seemed far away, and Brenna made a quick circle, feeling dizzy and breathless.

"I'm here!"

Wherever 'here' was. No longer did the trees have low, twisting trunks, and the wind had suddenly ceased its howling. She had somehow entered into a small clearing surrounded by tall pines and slender, white trees, their branches reaching out to create a thin canopy. The scent of pine needles and crisp, clean air filled Brenna's nose as she took in a deep breath. Beneath her feet, the ground was soft and springy with bright green moss and tufts of grass. Tiny, white flowers dotted the ground, glowing in the moonlight that filtered down through the tree branches. The world was still and quiet. Saoirse stirred in her arms, groaning softly as she rubbed her eyes.

"Brenna?"

Hearing the tiny, lilting voice caught Brenna by surprise, and she looked down at the little girl with a wobbly smile, trying not to make known how worried she had been.

"I'm here."

Saoirse opened her large, luminous blue eyes and then smiled sleepily, her cheeks rapidly gaining a rosy color once more. "Where are we?" Blinking, she looked around. "Have we died, then?"

"No. We were saved."

"By Roibhilin?"

"Patrick, actually."

The little girl's eyes widened and she looked over to the boy in question as he quickly made his way back to them from the other side of the clearing.

"He is a warrior after all."

Saoirse smiled, and Brenna thought that she'd never seen anything more beautiful. On impulse, she hugged the little girl to her chest, trying to be gentle as she did so. Tears filled Brenna's eyes and fell onto the Saoirse's dirty, woolen sweater as she tried hard not to sob. It was only just now beginning to sink in how close to death they'd been and how foolish she was to think that she could've faced such a powerful enemy on her own. Saoirse wrapped her arms loosely around Brenna's neck, tiny hands stroking her hair.

"Brenna, is Saoirse all right?"

"Yeah, she's fine." She turned and looked up at Patrick, rubbing a hand over her eyes to wipe away her tears. "Where are we?"

"I'm not entirely sure."

"Do you know where to go from here?"

"I do, but I really couldn't tell you the name of place we are now. Wait." Holding up a hand, Patrick tilted his head as if listening for something and then frowned.

"What's wrong?"

"I thought I heard drums."

"Oh." Brenna frowned, straining her ears to hear. Nothing but silence greeted her. She bit her lip; she didn't like being in the open, even if it was a peaceful-looking place. "How much farther do we have to go before we get to Midhir's lands?"

"I'm not entirely sure...I don't think much farther. Roibhilin said this was a shortcut to *Bri Leith*."

"Roibhilin? When did you see him?"

"He was the one who sent me to you and gave me this." Patrick waved the *Gae Bulga* slightly and, in the silvery moonlight, the weapon looked even creepier than it had in The Morrigan's hall. "I'm not sure what scared me more. The fact that he asked me nicely for help or that he went and trusted me with such a deadly weapon."

Brenna couldn't really believe it herself. Roibhilin had said that he didn't hate her, though his actions often reflected the opposite. But for him to place his trust in Patrick...Brenna blinked back more tears. He really did care about her on some level, maybe even saw her as a friend.

"Brenna, when Roibhilin told me what had happened to you, I..." Patrick cleared his throat and he looked away, suddenly appearing young and no longer the strong, unflinching warrior who had defied the terrifying queen. "I was afraid I was too late when I saw...when you..." he trailed off.

"I would have been. You came just in time, Patrick. Thank you."

He nodded his head tightly, clenching the staff in his hands as he looked back at her. His eyes were hard to see in the dim light, but Brenna could make out the fear in them as he relived what he had seen. Patrick raised his free hand to cup her cheek, his head lowering toward hers and his eyes intense with an emotion she couldn't quite place. Her breath caught in her throat, and the same fluttery feeling that she had felt so long ago in his truck came back as his lips pressed against hers. The world and its problems disappeared. Her eyes had closed for only a moment when the sudden sound of drums assaulted her ears. They both jumped away from each other, looking in the direction from which the sound was emanating.

"They're coming!"

Saoirse pointed over Brenna's shoulder, her blue eyes wide with terror. *Whatever it is*, Brenna thought as she tried to catch her breath, *I definitely don't want to see it*. Without uttering another word they began to run Patrick leading the way over the mossy ground. They could hear the beating of deep drums all around them. Patrick followed a narrow path that Brenna hadn't noticed before, and it led them into the forest of pines. A gentle wind came from behind, bringing with it soft whispers that encouraged Brenna to run faster.

There was no longer a need to defend her face against branches, and while that made running easier she quickly found that the path leading them through the woods was overgrown with ferns and fallen tree trunks, hindering their quick escape. Brenna could hear the sound of armored feet not far off, and she cried out in surprise as an arrow shot past her and embedded itself into a tree several feet to her side. Her body was tired from holding Saoirse and running with little rest or water, but she forced her feet to fall one in front of the other, pushing through the pain in her legs. Saoirse remained silent as she stared over Brenna's shoulders, her hands fisted tightly in her protector's shoulder-length hair. Another arrow was loosed, whistling past Brenna to land only a foot in front of her, and she had to swerve to avoid tripping over the shaft that had lodged itself into the ground.

"Patrick, we can't stay on this trail!"

"I know!"

He veered to the right and Brenna followed after him. She found herself charging down a steep hill, and she lengthened her stride to take advantage of gravity's pull. She didn't have time to think or question herself or where she was stepping. As she leapt over a particularly large fallen tree, she wondered if the creatures behind her were still on their heels.

"Brenna, *stop*!"

Saoirse's voice was so commanding that Brenna skidded to a stop so swiftly that the slippery pine needles caused her to slide and fall. Looking back, she saw several goblins roll past her, unable to stop themselves as their large feet and round bodies forced them to trip and roll down the forested hill like giant cannonballs. Patrick, who was a good fifteen feet in front of her, had also stopped to watch them roll down the hill, giving a shout of laughter when the creatures smashed hard into the awaiting trees and stayed down. Brenna could hear shouting in the distance, and she half slid, half hopped down the mossy embankment toward Patrick.

"Will this still lead us to *Bri Leith*? We've gone off the path."

"I'm not sure. But it's our best chance, I'm thinking."

"Mortal!" The windy, hollow cry made Brenna turn around. She wished she hadn't. What looked to be hundreds of little creatures stared back at her with glittering, black eyes, and thanks to the bright light of the moon as it moved from behind a cloud, she could see every hideous detail. Behind them, a row of *Tuath de Danann* had notched their arrows, aiming at her. It was a chilling sight, and she took a step back.

"Give us the child, Brenna Morgan!"

"Never!"

The creatures let loose a horrendous cry that was so loud Saoirse slapped her hands to her ears as the woods echoed the howls. Without waiting to see what they would do next—and Brenna had a pretty good idea as to what that was—she and Patrick began running down the hill again. Behind them, she could hear the pounding of feet and jostling of weapons. Squinting her eyes, she could tell that the trees were nearing their end, and she could only hope that *Bri Leith* was waiting for them on the other side.

"Saoirse, hold on tight to me!"

The little girl wrapped her arms and legs more tightly around her body. With a final burst of energy, Brenna ran through the last of the trees, smiling when she made out the large castle in the distance. Her smile quickly fled when she realized that what stood between her and safety was an entire army of *Tuath de Danann*. They were beautiful and terrifying all at once. Their armor and swords gleamed in the moonlight and their faces were grim. Leading them from atop a beautiful, white horse was King Midhir. His sword was raised high, shining brightly in the moonlight. Brenna and Patrick skidded to a stop. They were at least several hundred yards away from the long line of soldiers, and she looked to Patrick, her chest heaving.

"What do we do?!"

"Run to the other side."

She shook her head, aghast. "But we'll die!"

"They're not going to kill *us*, Brenna. C'mon, then!"

"This is the stupidest idea ever."

Looking over her shoulder, Brenna groaned. The Morrigan's army was screaming and howling as they rushed down the hill, and she heard a large horn sound from somewhere in the back of Midhir's army. The men began to advance then, running so quickly that they were rushing past to clash with their enemy before Brenna and Patrick could take even a few steps. Saoirse screamed as a gleaming sword swung at them, and Brenna ducked, tripping over the foot of an already fallen solider.

All around her was chaos and the clashing of metal. Brenna could see Midhir on his horse calling to his men and cleaving several goblins in half with one swoop of his large sword before kicking his steed deeper into the fray. Panic began to build, and she looked around frantically for Patrick. He was nowhere to be seen, and she had to dodge several swords that swung her way as she searched. There was no clear exit or easy path out, and Brenna wished that she had a sword or some sort of weapon with which to defend herself. *Then again*, she thought as she dodged another sword, *it would be better if I actually knew how to* use *one*.

"Brenna!"

Turning to her right, she saw Roibhilin making his way toward her, the sword in his hand easily slicing through several courageous hawthorn pixies that had leapt at him. Brenna smiled, glad to see that he was alive.

"You stupid girl!" With another slash, he impaled a charging goblin. His voice was almost impossible to hear over the din of metal and battle cries. "You are not to be here!"

"Brenna, look out!"

Saoirse's warning came too late, and Brenna cried out as an arrow pierced her leg, ripping through flesh and bone. She felt her knees buckle, and she could only watch in horror as a large club swung down to slam into her head. The last thing she saw as she fell was Roibhilin running to her, and she huddled Saoirse close to her body before the darkness took over.

* * * *

The feeling of a thousand tiny hammers hitting her head roused Brenna from the darkness, and she had to close her eyes against light. She counted to ten and then opened her eyes slowly. The scent of smoke, grass, and the metallic tang of blood assaulted her nose. She groaned, putting a hand to her throbbing head. She had somehow ended up on her back, and lying across her stomach was Saoirse—motionless, her long, golden hair riddled with knots and bits of wood. Brenna tried to sit up, groaning when her ribs protested painfully and the world around her tilted sideways. Panting, she fell back down, wincing when the back of her head connected with the ground.

Rubbing a hand over her eyes, she grimaced again. When she moved her head once more the world didn't move with her, and she turned carefully to the left, feeling nauseous when she saw the lifeless eyes of a goblin staring at her from mere inches away, blood dripping from the corners of its fat lips and large, tusk-like teeth. Brenna closed her eyes and turned her head away again. Her whole body felt as if it weighed a million pounds. She reached out to feel for Saoirse's neck, giving a shocked laugh when she felt a strong pulse leap against her fingertips. At least something had gone right. She wasn't sure who had won, but from the strange, eerie silence she knew that the battle was over. The sound of cawing drew her attention, and she watched as black crows flew overhead, darker than the sky that was gray with predawn light.

Resting her hand on Saoirse's matted hair, she smiled. It was over. The *leanbh* was safe and Queen Morrigan would never step foot in the human world again. Brenna gave a tired, hoarse laugh. It almost sounded like the plot of a bad movie. To her right, the sound of something moving made her turn her head quickly. Too quickly. Groaning, she closed her eyes against a fresh wave of dizziness. Waiting for the spinning sensation to stop, Brenna opened her eyes and then felt her heart stop. The hem of a purple gown flooded her vision, and she watched helplessly as the material began to fold in on itself as Queen Morrigan stepped over her and bent down, her dark eyes lit with a fiery anger. Black blood had smeared across part of her face in a gruesome half-mask, and her red lips were pulled back in a truly vicious smile.

"Brenna Morgan, you are very hard to kill."

The queen took Brenna's chin between two of her cold fingers, and when she tried to turn her head away The Morrigan pinched her already bruised skin, stopping her. Her smile deepening, the queen drew her face close to Brenna's, black eyes pooling with a maniacal light that caused a cold sweat to form on Brenna's forehead.

"You will not die today, mortal, but I will make sure that you do." Releasing her chin, she stood. A crow with glossy wings and liquid black eyes landed on the tall woman's shoulder. She stroked its feathery head and then stepped away from Brenna's battered body. "When you die, you can be sure that it will be I who carries the sword, and *I* who will rip you asunder for what you have done this night."

The crow cawed mockingly, the sound suspiciously like that of laughter as The Morrigan wove her way through the bodies littering the field. The throbbing in Brenna's head that had subsided somewhat came back in full force, and she happily let the darkness swallow her again, glad to not have to think about The Morrigan's threat or the crow's cloying laughter.

* * * *

"Please, you must go."

"Not until she wakes up."

"You are as bad as Master Roibhilin. At least have something to drink."

"No, thank you."

Hushed tones dragged Brenna from her pleasant dreams; dreams of rolling hills that went on forever and a wind that smelled of honey. She had been in the middle of running through golden hills alongside three laughing women whose beauty outshone even Etain's. A girl, more beautiful than her friends, with shinning, orange hair called for her to hurry. Brenna attempted to run faster, but no matter how hard she tried she found herself rapidly falling behind. The orange-haired girl reached for her, and Brenna tried to grab hold of the slender hand, but it slipped away. Hesitantly, she opened her eyes and Mahoney's pale, familiar face stared back at her.

"Mahoney…what…?"

"There, I told you she would waken, did I not? Oh!"

With an indignant cry, Mahoney was pushed aside as Patrick took the offended woman's place at the side of Brenna's bed. A bed. Blinking sleepily, Brenna put a hand on the silken sheets as she looked around. The room was familiar and different at the same time. She looked over to Patrick who appeared to be as healthy and clean as if he'd never been in a battle or saved her from Queen Morrigan's dark hall.

"Patrick? Where am I?"

"You're in *Bri Leith*."

"So are you."

"I am." He smiled, exchanging the floor he'd been kneeling on for a chair next to the bed. Brenna frowned, sitting up slowly. The delicate, white canopy above her swayed when she moved, and she called to Mahoney who was already starting to walk out of the airy room.

"Mahoney?"

"Aye?"

"Where is Saoirse?"

"As to that, Brenna, you will have to see for yourself. I'll let Her Majesty know you've awoken."

Slipping out the room, Mahoney closed the door quietly behind her, leaving Brenna alone with Patrick. After several moments of strained silence, she cleared her throat. She could feel the shoe that the leprechaun had made for her on her foot, though it was lumpy and hard, as if it had been left under the sun for several days. It clearly wouldn't hold up much longer.

"Patrick?"

"Yes?"

"How many days have I been out? And how are you here? I mean, won't time—"

"It's only just gone on eight in the morning at home. I came here at dawn, so no one will miss me. Unlike a certain someone I know."

Brenna smiled as Patrick helped her sit up straighter by fluffing a few pillows. Her ribs no longer hurt, and when she moved her leg it was obvious that it'd been completely healed. She also felt less tired than the last time she had come to in a bed. Gratefully, she accepted a water bottle that he handed to her.

"What happened to you, Patrick? I'm so sorry I lost sight of you."

"It was a crowded field, and there's nothing to be sorry over. I was able to get out on the other side, and I would have gone back in for you but for the fact that Turlough wouldn't let me."

"Turlough?" Brenna paused in taking a drink, frowning. "Are you guys friends now?"

"Definitely not." Patrick grimaced. "But he said Roibhilin had already spotted you and would bring you out. I didn't see him go in, but since you're here, I have to assume he kept his word."

Taking another sip of water, she wondered if Patrick had any idea what'd really happened to her. Judging from his happy demeanor she suspected he didn't, which was fine with her. She listened as he told her of the beautiful halls of *Bri Leith*, and laughed when he expressed how surprised he was to see several familiar faces belonging to the women and men he had once met as a boy.

"Honest to God, Brenna, I thought I'd fair lost my mind. They hadn't changed a bit, and there I was nearly as tall as the rest of them. They seemed a fair bit more intimidating when I was a lad."

A knock at the door made both of them turn, and Brenna smiled as Queen Etain entered, her deep gold hair braided and twisted in an intricate knot work pattern. A circlet was banded around her head, and her deep blue eyes lighted with joy when they alighted on Brenna.

"I am so pleased that you are well! I did not believe you could have recovered so quickly, but I am very thankful you have."

The queen rushed to Brenna's side in a flurry of green silk and open arms. Patrick had moved aside when she'd entered and grinned as Brenna's wide eyes met his while the queen enveloped her with a suffocating hug. The scent of wildflowers and clean air whirled around the room, making Brenna feel as if she could bound from the bed and easily run a hundred miles. Etain pulled away after several long moments, cupping Brenna's face with gentle hands as she carefully inspected her face.

"You have saved us all, Brenna Morgan, and we owe you a huge debt. But first we must speak."

The queen looked to Patrick and then smiled sweetly, an act which caused him to blush. Brenna grinned; it seemed as though she wasn't the only one who had been charmed by Etain.

"Patrick Fergus, we are in your debt, as well, but I would ask that you let me speak with Brenna privately."

"Of course." Patrick bowed deeply from the waist and then left the room, winking at Brenna before he shut the door. Etain's deep blue eyes stayed on the door for several seconds before she turned to Brenna, a knowing look in their depths as her lips curled up in a discreet smile.

"He is a brave young man. Just the sort of warrior that once roamed Ireland. And, like the warriors of old, he seems to have given his heart to a beautiful young woman."

"Uh, I…um…" Brenna fumbled for something to say.

The queen laughed and sat down in the bedside chair, the simple action made somehow elegant. How that was accomplished Brenna had no idea, but she was sure that she'd never pull it off herself even if she spent years practicing.

"I will tease you on the matter no longer, and it is a grave bit of business we must speak of now."

"Of course, Your Majesty."

"Words cannot express the gratitude I have for your bravery and kindness, Brenna Morgan. You have saved not only my daughter but our world and the people in it. I saw the crows in the field after the battle and knew then that it was The Morrigan, that it was she who you faced when Roibhilin could not enter into her lands."

"Yes, Your Majesty."

Etain's eyes grew sad then, and she took Brenna's hands in her own. "You must tell me everything that has transpired and leave nothing out, for I would know all that has passed."

After another healthy drink of water, Brenna began her tale, starting from when she and Saoirse had been dragged down into the earth. She spoke of the Puca and the horned women that had helped The Morrigan, what the dark queen had planned to do with Etain's daughter, and what she had said to her on the battlefield. Slowly, Etain withdrew her hands from Brenna's and stood up, walking to the window and opening it. A cool breeze that smelled of apples and crisp air filled the room, and the queen's shoulders drooped briefly, as if she had just taken on the weight of the world.

"Your Majesty?"

"Yes, Brenna?" Her voice sounded sad, and Brenna bit her lip.

"The Morrigan said that…that you and your people had been tricked by humans and were forced to go underground. Is that true?"

"It is and it isn't." Etain straightened her shoulders, placing her hands on the windowsill. "What you call 'underground' is simply…a between for us. But it was centuries ago, and we are happy here in our own lands."

"She also said that you wanted the same thing she did—that you wanted to be above ground, too."

Turning, the queen offered a fleeting smile, though it didn't hide the sadness in her eyes. She slowly walked back to the bed and sat on the edge, folding her hands in her lap. "At one time we did. Midhir was frightfully angry…but he has since accepted our life. In truth, it is quite a bit better here than it is on your side."

"Really? I…I think it might have been kind of nice to be able to see you and Roibhilin without having to constantly worry about what time of day it was."

"There are ways around that." Laughing lightly, Etain patted her hand. "But no, we would not want to go back. Our reign there is past. The people of your time have no use for the magic we hold. The world you live in is too different, and the people have grown blind even with their achievements and new technology. There is much they still do not see—much they have forgotten or *refuse* to see."

Brenna sighed. She supposed that Etain was right. If her kind all reappeared on earth, she could only imagine what scientists would try to do to them or what sort of wars The Morrigan would unleash. The thought of all the destruction and chaos that could have been inflicted caused Brenna to shiver. Etain nodded her head gravely, appearing to have read her mind.

"Perhaps one day people will again see the magic that is always around them, but until then we are happy to be where we are."

"I still feel bad. If only—"

"If only the stars were closer, the ocean smaller." Etain gave a laugh. "We cannot dwell on what if, Brenna—no good comes of it. The Morrigan and several kingdoms chose to live in those words, and it has ruined their hearts and twisted their minds. And we must now deal with their actions."

She pulled Brenna out of the bed and embraced her warmly. Brenna wrapped her own arms around the queen, feeling safe and almost as if she was being hugged by her own mother.

Laughing again, Etain pulled away. "However, these are not your concerns but ours. For now, we must thank you, as is right and proper. And Saoirse has been eager to see you. She sat outside your door for quite a while before Patrick was able to convince her to rest."

After sending for Mahoney, Etain left the room while Brenna changed into a light-green dress that fell down to the floor in soft folds. The sleeves were long and bell-shaped, the edges covered with tiny pearls and knot work sewn with a dark thread all over the fine fabric. Brenna winced as Mahoney used a comb and then a brush to work out all of the tangles in her hair. Only when she had swept it up into some sort of braided affair did she allow Brenna to leave the room. Pausing at the door, Brenna turned to face the human woman.

"Thank you for everything." Rushing across the room, she hugged Mahoney who laughed in surprise and hugged her back. Taking a step back, she studied Brenna with her ancient, gray eyes. Her cold hands softly brushed along the length of her cheek.

"It is I who thank *you*, Brenna Morgan. You have brought life to Master Roibhilin again, and for that you will always have my gratitude. Go now—it is best not to keep them waiting."

With one last hug, Brenna left the room, looking both right and left down the white hall. Patrick was nowhere to be seen, but Turlough stood across from the door dressed head to toe in varying shades of green and brown. His shoulder-length hair had been brushed back, and his light green eyes widened as Brenna stepped out from her room.

"You look very lovely, Brenna."

"Um...thank you. You look pretty nice, yourself."

"I do, do I not?" He smiled then, and his serious expression gave way to a roguish grin. "'Tis the truth I am certain to meet several beautiful women tonight."

"So you didn't just dress up for me, then?"

Turlough laughed loudly, and Brenna had to admit that when he wasn't being hostile or locking her in towers he was a surprisingly likeable person. Well, a nice member of the Gentry. He extended his arm and she took it gratefully, knowing that she was going to trip at least a dozen times on the long fabric trailing past her feet. Turlough kept a steady stream of conversation going as he led her down the long, winding halls of Midhir's castle, and he stopped when they passed through an arch that opened into the main hall.

"Roibhilin, I had thought you would be inside already."

Brenna had been busy checking behind herself to make sure she hadn't torn her dress when Turlough made his statement, and her head instantly snapped up. Roibhilin stood only a few feet away from them, his wavy, golden hair framing his face and blue eyes. The tunic he wore was made of green velvet unlike Turlough's simple linen one, and about his feet were a pair of leather boots featuring delicate, golden thread sewn in detailed knot work.

"Turlough, I would have a word with Brenna."

"Of course."

When Turlough made no signs of leaving, Roibhilin's polite mask faded and he frowned. Brenna grinned. No matter how hard he tried, she was pretty sure his frown was a permanent resting expression.

"*Alone*, Turlough."

"Well, why did you not say so? Brenna, mind you do not tarry for too long; it would be impolite to keep Their Majesties waiting."

Giving Roibhilin a pointed look, Turlough ambled down the hall and slipped through a door at the end of it, his booted feet muffled by the red carpet running down the center. Brenna looked up expectantly at Roibhilin, and when he continued to simply stare back she rolled her eyes and put her hands on hips.

"Roibhilin, you're the one who wanted to speak with *me*."

"Aye, I was thinking." His tone was surly and his scowl deepened as he grabbed her hand and slapped something into it. Surprised, Brenna looked down. A simple, reddish-gold ring gleamed up at her, and she looked at Roibhilin again, eyes wide.

"What is *this* for?"

"'Tis a gift."

"Oh." Brenna glanced back down at the golden band. "Thank you."

"It is a very special ring."

"Oh, no."

"What?"

"You're…you're not *proposing* to me, are you?"

Roibhilin's jaw went slack, and he looked nearly as disgusted as she felt. He even took a step back for good measure. "By the moon and the stars…*no!*" He crossed his arms, glaring at her even as his cheeks turned a slight pink color, whether from embarrassment or anger she wasn't sure. "If you would keep your mouth silenced for longer than a minute, you would know that I give it to you in friendship."

"Friendship?" Brenna was nearly as shocked by that announcement as she was by the ring. "So…we're friends?"

"We have fought together and, as you have so forcibly pointed out, we have both saved each other's lives. There is not a better basis for friendship."

He spoke the words gruffly, but his stance and face had softened. Brenna felt tears prick her eyes. Blinking them back, she smiled and extended her hand. For a moment, Roibhilin looked as though he would refuse. Then, slowly, hesitantly, he took it. Brenna clasped his hand, shaking it firmly.

"Friends, then."

"Aye."

After she'd placed the ring on her right index finger, Brenna walked beside Roibhilin as they went down the hallway. Her smile was so large she was sure it'd be permanently stuck that way. The great doors opened, and horns sounded on either side, causing her to wince.

"Brenna Morgan of *Coillearnach*, you are most welcome in our halls."

Brenna looked around. Hundreds of beautiful men and women had all turned to look at her, every face radiant with joy. Lush, green garlands filled with all sorts of flowers hung on every available column and timber, and ethereal music from somewhere outside wafted into the grand hall. The crowd had parted after Midhir's baritone voice had rung out, and Roibhilin gave Brenna a small shove when she didn't move.

"Come forward, Brenna Morgan, so that we might thank you for your deeds, as befits a hero."

Straightening her shoulders, Brenna approached the king and queen sitting upon their thrones, trying hard not to feel embarrassed by the multitude of eyes watching her. They were flanked on both sides by several boys and girls of varying ages, all of whom looked very much like Etain and Midhir, and Brenna assumed that they were the other children that the queen had mentioned before. And there, sitting on a small, silver chair in between her parents, was Saoirse. Her golden hair had been brushed and fell well past her feet in a shimmering mass of gold. Her dress was made of red velvet, and her smile seemed to light up the whole room. Brenna stopped when she reached the dais and bowed low, not knowing what else to do.

"No, Brenna. It is we who bow to you."

Etain rose and curtsied deeply, her left hand fisted over her heart. As one, Midhir and his children followed suit, and their blue eyes disappeared momentarily as they dipped their heads low. Behind her, Brenna could hear rustling, and she spun around. Tears welled in her eyes as the courtiers sank to their knees and bowed their heads in deference. Unsure of what to do and feeling self-conscious, she turned back to Midhir and Etain who had risen from their lowered stances. With a smile that could have melted ice caps, Midhir placed a hand on one of Saoirse's tiny shoulders.

"Brenna, my daughter wishes to give you a present."

Wiping the tears from her cheeks, Brenna tried to reign in her feelings. For all that she had gone through, seeing Saoirse safe and loved made it worth it, and she glanced over at Roibhilin. He had come to stand to her right, his face an impassive mask. Saoirse beamed up happily at Brenna and waved to her before picking something up from behind her throne. A change seemed to come over the small girl then, and she squared her shoulders before she stepped forward, her deep blue eyes boring into Brenna as her smile disappeared.

"Brenna Morgan, you have honored Nuala's promise to protect me."

Though her voice was tiny, it rang clear in the airy halls. Brenna stood still, captivated as the child spoke, looking far wiser than she ever remembered seeing her.

"You have also shown courage even when there was great cause to give up hope. You chose to fight—to take up a stranger's fight—and you have a saved my family, my world, and myself. For that, I present you with this."

With a few fumbled steps thanks in part to her long dress, Saoirse walked over to Brenna. She carefully went down on one knee before extending the thick bundle. Brenna took the present from the child's delicate hands, surprised by how heavy it was. She smiled down at the girl who, in turn, stared up at her expectantly.

"Thank you, Saoirse."

"Open it!" The child's serious demeanor disappeared as jumped up, bouncing on her heels. Her enthusiasm was hard to resist, and Brenna grinned, complying with the girl's wishes. She unwrapped the bundle with care then felt her jaw drop. It was the cabled sweater that she had given Saoirse when she'd first met her.

"It's, um…" Words escaped her, and Saoirse giggled.

"It is the 'sweater' you gave me." She smiled shyly. "It gave me courage when Queen Morrigan took me from you. It made me feel like you were still holding onto me…that was why I knew it would be all right. Now it can remind you of me, even if we are far apart. I will always hold you in my heart."

Placing down the sweater, Brenna fell to her knees and gathered Saoirse into her arms, hugging her tightly. It probably wasn't proper to cry in front of hundreds of people or hug a princess right in the middle of a ceremony, but she didn't care. Saoirse's tiny arms wrapped around Brenna's neck in a fierce hug, and she pressed a kiss to her cheek.

"I will see you again, Brenna. I promise."

Stepping back, Saoirse was picked up by Etain while Midhir helped Brenna up to her feet and placed his large hands on her shoulders. He turned her to face the crowd.

"Today we celebrate the return of our daughter and the safety of not only our lands but that of the human world. Like the heroes before her, I welcome her into our court, for she has proven more than worthy to be among us. Let us all remember the bravery and courage of Brenna Morgan."

The crowd cheered in one ringing voice, and the music that had been gentle and unassuming turned loud and boisterous, signaling the start of what looked to be a very long party. With shouts of laughter and mirth, the men and women began to dance and sing. Brenna shook her head in wonder. Food and drink of every sort were being passed around, and courtiers cheered to Brenna's health. She was introduced to all of Midhir and Etain's children in such a flurry of voices and names that she was pretty sure she'd never remember any of them. The daughters gave her light hugs, and the sons bowed over her hand with such grace that Brenna was sure her blush would never leave her cheeks.

When they left to join the revelers, Saoirse ran after them only to be thwarted by Turlough; he picked her up before she could reach the boisterous crowd.

"You are to stay with your mother and father," he told her with a smile. "But perhaps they will dance with you." With a little shove toward Their Majesties direction, he made his way to Brenna.

"Would you care to dance?"

"She will not be dancing with you." Roibhilin glared at his friend, and Turlough's smile, which was already large, grew bigger.

"Oh? Has she already promised you a dance?"

"She must go. Queen Etain has informed me that her family waits for her return, and we have prolonged her departure long enough. Her shoe will wear out soon."

Turlough looked disheartened for only a moment, and then he bowed to Brenna, a mischievous twinkle in his eyes. "When next you come, Brenna Morgan, I will dance with you."

"It sounds like a plan."

"Come, Patrick is waiting for you."

Clearly annoyed with Turlough, Roibhilin's voice came out as a sharp command and Brenna followed after him as he wound his way through the mass of dancers. Turning around, Brenna took one last glance at the dais where Etain and Midhir stood smiling at her, their arms around each other as Saoirse tugged on her mother's dress, laughing about something. Brenna raised her hand in farewell before slipping out of the opened door, closing it softly behind her. Patrick was standing on the other end of the hall, and Brenna felt the strange, fluttery sensation in her stomach again as he smiled at her.

"Ah, I almost forgot." Roibhilin paused in their walk and turned to face her, pulling down the shoulder of her dress.

"Oi!" Patrick's incensed shout could easily be heard down the hall as he began marching toward them, a scowl on his face. Ignoring Patrick's angry, advancing tromp, Roibhilin placed his palm over Brenna's collarbone. She winced as a searing heat burned her skin. Pulling his hand away, he nodded his head, looking pleased. Brenna pressed her fingers to her skin, surprised to find it cool to the touch.

"You are no longer of my house, Brenna Morgan. You are your own person once more and no longer bound to our world."

"Thank—"

Without looking away from her, Roibhilin grabbed Patrick by his shirt as he descended upon them, lifting him clean off his feet. Roibhilin's blue eyes snapped with anger.

"I could break you in two for intruding on a private conversation, Patrick Fergus. It is fortunate for you, then, that I am in a pleasant mood."

Patrick's cheeks flushed red with anger, and he grunted when Roibhilin released him none too gently onto the floor. The two boys glared at each other, and Brenna rolled her eyes as she placed a hand on Patrick's shoulder.

"Can you give us just a minute, please?"

His hazel eyes narrowed on Roibhilin, but after a few tense seconds he nodded his head tightly. "I'll wait for you at the door, then."

Brenna smiled and then turned to Roibhilin, glaring. "You don't have to be so mean! I would be dead—and so would Saoirse—if he hadn't saved us." Crossing his arms at her incensed words, Roibhilin looked more stubborn than ever. Brenna threw her hands up in the air. "You're making this difficult, you know!"

"What?"

"I wanted to say thank you! And, well, I wanted to say…your mom would be very proud of you."

They stood in the hallway for several moments before Roibhilin slowly uncrossed his arms, his scowl lessening slightly as he regarded her with an uneasy look. Brenna offered him a smile.

"I didn't get to know Nuala for very long, but…I really do think she'd be proud of you."

When Roibhilin continued to say nothing, Brenna sighed. She glanced over to Patrick who shrugged his shoulders and motioned for her to hurry up.

"Which way is home?"

"Go to the field in which you first came. The pixies will be there to help you."

"Thank you, Roibhilin. For everything."

Turning to leave, Brenna halted when she felt Roibhilin grab her arm. Peering over her shoulder, she could see that his scowl had deepened. *Whatever he's about to say*, she thought, *he clearly doesn't like it.*

"About the ring."

"Yeah?"

"If there is ever a time you find yourself in danger, break it and I will come."

"So…it's a magic ring?"

"Aye."

Brenna peered down at the unassuming band on her finger before looking back to Roibhilin. He really had meant it when he'd said that they were friends. With a laugh, she spun fully around and hugged him. He stiffened considerably, not that it surprised her. Pulling away, she patted his shoulder, grinning. With a final wave, she hurried over to Patrick who was eyeing the fairie with distrust.

"What's that on your finger?"

"A ring."

"A *ring?*"

She smirked at Patrick's disgruntled exclamation and looped her arm through his as she pushed open the heavy, wooden door. The wind greeted them with all the scents of autumn, and the golden hills beckoned her invitingly. Brenna took in a deep breath.

"I'll tell you about it when we get home."

Chapter Eighteen

"Brenna Morgan, if you don't get out here *right now* I swear I'll find that baby picture of you naked in a sink and show it to Patrick!"

"You wouldn't dare!"

"Try me, young lady!"

Throwing her hair into a hasty ponytail, Brenna ran out of her room before skidding to a stop in the living room, frowning when she saw her mother lounging on the couch reading a magazine. Putting her hands on her hips, Brenna narrowed her eyes.

"I'm sorry, you threatened me with humiliation because you wanted me to watch you read a *magazine*?"

"Don't be silly." Rachel glanced up at Brenna and raised her brows before turning a page and pointing her finger in a vague direction. "*That* is why I threatened you with humiliation."

"What are you talking about? You're pointing at absolutely noth—"

"Brenna, did you get taller again? Please tell me you didn't."

Startled by the familiar, deep voice, Brenna spun around to see her father standing in the doorway, a bag resting beside him. His blond hair was tousled and his broad shoulders filled the doorway, blocking out a good portion of the morning light. If it weren't for his glasses and his love of Hawaiian shirts, he would have been the sort of person who belonged on the pages of a fashion magazine. Brenna grinned when he had to dip his head slightly to get through the doorway; she'd almost forgotten how tall he was.

"*Dad*! What are you doing here?!"

"Well, I thought I was coming home, but if this's the kind of reception I'm going to get—"

"I mean," laughed Brenna as she threw her herself into his arms, "what are you doing here *now*?! You weren't supposed to come for another week!"

"I thought sooner might be better. Your mother tells me that you've been doing some really strange things."

Brenna smiled sheepishly. "Only a little strange."

"I wouldn't expect anything less. This is Ireland, after all. Fairies and all that."

"Dad, I missed you." Brenna wrinkled her nose, pulling away from her father's embrace to look up at him. "But why are you wearing your Hawaiian shirt? It's freezing outside!"

"A little fresh air is always nice, and it's sunny. Besides, I'm a Norseman! This cold is nothing." He smiled and shut the door behind him. Dumping his bag near the refrigerator, he wrapped an arm around Brenna's shoulder and walked into the living room where Rachel was just sitting up from her horizontal position.

"Now what's this I hear about you having a boyfriend?"

"Uuuuhhh…"

"She'd *love* to tell you all about it, Richard," exclaimed her mother as she jumped up from her seat, "but I'm afraid she's running late. She's going on a date."

"A date?" Releasing Brenna, he frowned. "But I just got home."

"You'll have plenty of time to tell Brenna all about the evils of men and lock her in her room later. Brenna, wear a sweater. You don't have the strong, thick skin of your Viking father here." Her mother grinned, slipping her arm around her husband. Brenna smiled at the sight. At last, her world was complete. Grabbing her coat from where it was draped on a chair, she saluted her parents.

"Will do, mom. Dad, I'll see you tonight!"

"But—"

"Bye!"

With a wave, Brenna raced out of the door and into the November day. Large, dark clouds loomed over the ocean, promising rain or snow. It'd been nearly two weeks since she had come home from *Bri Leith*, and life had finally settled into a normal pattern. She'd borrowed clothes from Kathleen before she had headed home, not knowing if or how angry her mother would be. When she'd walked through the door, though, Rachel had simply asked if she was all right and then hugged her tightly for several minutes. They hadn't spoken of it since, but Brenna knew that her mother was keeping a sharper eye on her. Shaking her head, she turned left at the end of the driveway and headed down the road to Patrick's. Her life wasn't exactly what it used to be.

Even without the leprechaun's shoe she could still see pixies darting to and fro in the woods, and sometimes they beckoned to her to play with them, though she rarely had time to do so. Having a boyfriend and a best friend on top of her schoolwork was pretty time consuming—and infinitely less dangerous. A cold wind blew against her, and she quickly pulled on the sweater her mother had urged her to bring. It was the white one Saoirse had returned, and she smiled at the memory of the little girl. Brenna wasn't sure when she would see her again or if she would ever get to return to *Bri Leith*, but for now she was just happy to be alive and not chased by a horde of horrific creatures.

Brenna was halfway to Patrick's when she felt the hair on her arms stand on end. She stopped, frowning. Turning around slowly, heart hammering in her chest, she hoped that whatever was there was something she could defend herself against. Nothing but the winding ribbon of black road greeted her, and Brenna let out a breath she hadn't realized she'd been holding.

"Alert as always, I see, Brenna Morgan."

Nearly jumping out of her skin, Brenna whirled around. Sitting atop the low, gray wall to her left was the leprechaun, a pipe in his mouth and his red coat bright against the green grass behind him. He looked much more lively and jovial than normal, and for once his hands were still. Brenna put a hand to her chest.

"You scared me!"

"Sure, a mere little leprechaun? Ye've faced scarier things than me, lass!"

He jumped off of the wall and neatly over the ditch in front of it, landing right next to Brenna. Smoke curled from the glossy, wooden pipe in his mouth.

"Walk with me a wee way, Brenna Morgan."

"Do I have a choice?"

"None a'tall. It's pleased I am to see you finally catching on."

The leprechaun took off down the road, heading to Patrick's, for all Brenna knew. Despite his two-foot stature, she had a hard time keeping up with him. Brenna belatedly remembered reading that leprechauns were notoriously fast. Faster than a blink, even. Or so they said. She was quickly beginning to realize that not everything she'd read was true. Curious, she closed her eyes and then opened them, surprised to see that the small man was still there.

"I'm not after running away lass, so you can keep your eyes closed as long as you've got a mind to." Brenna's cheeks turned pink with embarrassment and the leprechaun laughed. "You're a strange girl, Brenna Morgan. 'Tis why I like you. I knew the moment I saw you that you were the perfect lass for the job."

"What job?"

"Why, helping Nuala, of course. I had me doubts when you first showed up, but I'm glad I listened to my first thought. I'm rarely wrong about people."

Stunned, Brenna stopped walking. The leprechaun walked several more yards before he realized that she was no longer by his side. Turning around, he smiled at her, his bushy brows raised and his beady, black eyes twinkling with mischief.

"Is there a reason you've stopped, lass?"

"*You* chose *me*?" Brenna shook her head, frowning. "It was all an accident! I went for a run and stumbled on Nuala…I hadn't even met you yet!"

"Just because you don't see us straight away, Brenna, doesn't mean we aren't there. Come on then, lass; we haven't much time. Use those long legs o' yours and keep up."

Still in shock, Brenna numbly trailed after the small fairie as he hummed to himself, apparently very pleased. She wondered if she was ever going to get a truly straight answer out of him, but really, did it matter? She glanced down at the leprechaun.

"Why did you have to choose someone?"

"An excellent question, Brenna Morgan. And I suppose you deserve an answer." He turned his face up at her and then sighed, appearing a little less impish as he stared off into the distance.

"Long ago, Nuala saved me from a rather sticky situation, and I was obliged to be indebted to her. But she was a soft-hearted thing and said she didn't want anything a'tall. I don't like being in a person's debt, you see, so I struck out to help in another way."

"So you knew about the key and Saoirse and...and everything?"

"I knew nothing about it!" The leprechaun removed the pipe from his mouth to shine it on his jacket and then took a long drag from the stem, expelling thick, white smoke that curled high in the air. "And anyway, I didn't know she'd gone and died. No...I had other plans for you, my dear girl."

Brenna was almost too afraid to ask what those plans had been. The small man looked at her before chuckling.

"Here now, I wasn't about to throw you in harm's way. T'was quite the opposite. Nuala loved Roibhilin more than she loved her woods, 'tis the truth, and after he went and got his tender heart broken by that human lass o' his—"

"You mean Aideen?"

"He told you about her, did he?"

"No. Actually, he told me never to mention her name."

"Aye, well, 'tis a sad story, though 'tisn't mine to tell." Taking another puff from his pipe, the leprechaun slowed down, and Brenna was finally able to catch her breath.

"Now then, don't go 'round interrupting a story, lass. 'Tis rude. As I was saying, Roibhilin's heart had been broken, and I determined that the best way to repay Nuala was to help the one she loved most. But for all his kind ways, Roibhilin is a stubborn lad and prone to sulking. He'd been in a terrible mood for quite a while, and it caused Nuala no end o' grief, so I decided to remedy the matter and fulfill my debt all in one go."

"What do you mean?"

"Sure, I was going to have Roibhilin find a new lass to love! You're the prettiest girl I've seen in a long while, and you're fair stubborn. Stubborn enough to get Roibhilin out of his nasty sulk."

Brenna stared at the small, elderly-looking fairie with wide eyes, disbelief written all over her face.

"So you...you were playing matchmaker?" The thought was so funny that Brenna laughed out loud, and when she thought of Roibhilin's scowling face she laughed even harder. The leprechaun shook his pipe at her, his black eyes glittering with humor.

"You laugh now, but he's gone and stopped hating mortals, hasn't he, then?"

Wiping her eyes, Brenna managed to reign in her laughter. "Well, he doesn't hate *me*. But we're only friends. And barely that."

"Aye, well, a start is a start. I fulfilled my part of the bargain, and I've even answered your questions." The leprechaun leapt atop the wall and smiled as he tucked his pipe into his breast pocket. "Now, Brenna Morgan, ye've been a good lass, and I notice you're no longer wearing my shoe. T'was one of the finest I've ever made."

"Yeah, I...it sort of got ruined after I came home."

"Sure, I expected as much. Here, then, a present for you. Never let it be said a leprechaun isn't a generous sort when we've a mind to be!"

He tossed something black at her, and Brenna caught the object reflexively, barely keeping upright as she dived for it. Righting herself, she opened her hands and then gasped. A black leather shoe polished to a dull shine stared back at her, and it looked much more modern than the green one she had first received.

"Be sure you don't go and ruin that one, as well, for I worked on it especially for you. And now I'm off, for my debt is paid and *Eanchinn-duine* is waiting for you."

"'Aayn-kin dinnah'? Who's that?"

"'Tis not the time for questions any longer, Brenna Morgan. Go now, and perhaps if time allows we will meet again."

"But—hey!"

Before Brenna could stop him, the leprechaun was gone from the wall faster than she could blink—which she had. Sighing, Brenna looked at the shoe, fingering the sturdy leather. And here she'd thought she was done with adventures. Holding the shoe in one hand, Brenna glanced up the road and did a double take.

Where once there'd been a gray road that wound around a corner was now a forked road, both paths shaded by trees. Atop a rock in between the roads was a strange-looking black bird, but she was standing too far away to really put her finger on what was so off about it. With the shoe clutched tightly in her hands and her shoulders straight, Brenna walked closer to the forked road. The bird was turned away from her, clearly interested in whatever was on the ground. She played with a lock of her hair as she studied each path. Both looked almost completely identical, though the one on the left ran alongside rolling, green hills in the distance while the one on the right lead through a forest.

"Many welcomes, Brenna Morgan. I have been expecting you."

The bird that'd been facing away suddenly turned around, and Brenna stifled a scream. The fact that a bird was talking to her in a raspy voice was a bit startling, but it was the head that had her heart thrumming a million miles a minute. Atop the bird's black body where a beak and beady eyes should've been was instead a human head with wild, dark hair. Sunken, black eyes stared at her from sallow skin. Brenna found it very difficult to breath.

"It is not many who find my home, and you are most welcome to it. You are here to be told where your fate lies, aye?"

"I...I couldn't say."

"Of course you could, but you won't." The human head made a sound that Brenna supposed was meant to be a laugh but came out instead as a gasping, wheezing sound, like wind whistling through reeds.

"You are cursed, Brenna Morgan. A strong curse, yes, placed on you by The Morrigan."

"No I...don't...think so..." she replied slowly.

"She will rip you asunder with her own sword...a terrible curse."

Brenna felt the blood drain from her face and she gripped the shoe tightly in her hand as she edged as close as she dared to the human-headed bird.

"I thought she was just threatening me."

"Mortal, you are not yet wise to the ways of the people of Danu. You have been cursed. And no one has ever survived The Morrigan's curses. Even Cúchulainn fell to it."

"So what do I do?"

"You must chose a path." The human head angled itself toward the pathways, and Brenna licked her lips nervously.

"But which one is the right one?"

"Whichever one feels true." His black eyes peered into hers, and he hopped on the stone impatiently. "I see all that is past, all that is present, and all that will be. Yet you alone have a future unclear to me, for your fate has been tainted, and you are now free to choose a new way. What path do you claim, Brenna Morgan? Right or left?"

"I...I...give me a moment."

Feeling helpless, she looked back and forth between the two roads. Neither looked particularly gloomy or scary, and for the life of her she couldn't decide which one felt right.

"Time is running out for you, human. Choose!"

Brenna looked again to the left road where golden hills shimmered in the morning light. They reminded her of *Bri Leith*. Brenna's hands fisted at her sides.

"I choose the left road."

"So it shall be. Your fate has been set, and already I see your way clearing."

The bird hopped off of the rock and took flight, soaring over Brenna's head. She ducked when it glided low over her.

"The left road for Brenna Morgan. An interesting path, a dangerous path. Remember my words well, human. This road cannot be traveled alone. Share the journey and perhaps you will escape The Morrigan's curse. Perhaps!"

With a final swoop, it flew high into the sky. Brenna tilted her head back to see where it went, wincing when the sun shone brightly in her eyes. Blinking away the purple spots in her vision, she was startled to find that when they had disappeared the *Eanchinn-duine* was nowhere to be found, nor the rolling hills or forest. Instead, the long, winding gray road she'd originally been walking on stood before her.

"Brenna?"

In the distance, Patrick was waving as he jogged toward her. Brenna waved back before turning her troubled gaze out to the ocean with its white-capped waves. She wasn't sure what the *Eanchinn-duine* had seen, but she wasn't going to let The Morrigan kill her. Brenna smiled grimly and narrowed her eyes at the churning, white-capped waters. She didn't put much stock in fate, and when the time came she would carve her way into the world on her own terms. Patrick caught up to her then, a closed umbrella in his hands.

"What's that for?"

"Gram said it would rain."

As if they'd heard him, the clouds that had once been far out on the ocean rumbled threateningly overhead. A few cold drops of water fell to the waiting earth below. Smiling, Patrick opened the umbrella, raising a brow when he looked down at Brenna's new shoe.

"What's that you've in your hand?"

"A present from a friend."

"A small friend who makes shoes?"

"Exactly."

Brenna smiled, huddling under the umbrella with Patrick as the rain began to pour down in earnest. The *Eanchinn-duine's* words echoed in her head, and she wrapped an arm around Patrick's waist.

"Patrick?"

"Hm?"

"I'm glad I'm sharing the road with you."

About the Author

Katie Masters spent her childhood living in apartments, a teepee atop a lonely mountain with no running water or electricity, and a boat. She was fed a healthy diet of stories invented by her father and her mother made sure to read her the 'real' versions of fairy tales, as well as obscure books from around the world. Katie talks as much as she reads and currently lives in Southern California with a cat that thinks it's a dog. She stays as far away from the sun as possible, enjoys reading books and manga, and updating her BookTube channel when she's not writing, traveling, researching, or procrastinating.

Website: https://keeri120.wixsite.com/katiemasters/
Facebook: https://www.facebook.com/writingontheedge/
Twitter: https://twitter.com/Katie_Masters29
BookTube Channel:
https://www.youtube.com/channel/UCQinbL0QvV66yd0kvdE6SSQ
E-mail: keeri120@yahoo.com

CPSIA information can be obtained
at www.ICGtesting.com
Printed in the USA
LVHW111519051119
636418LV00002B/224/P